Dancing With the Virgins

Also by Stephen Booth

Fiction

Black Dog
Blood on the Tongue
Blind to the Bones
One Last Breath
The Dead Place
Scared to Live
Dying to Sin
The Kill Call
Lost River
The Devil's Edge
Dead and Buried
Already Dead

Dancing With the Virgins

A Cooper & Fry Mystery

STEPHEN BOOTH

WITNESS
IMPULSE
An Imprint of HarperCollins*Publishers*

This is a work of fiction. Names, characters, places, and incidents are products of the author's imagination or are used fictitiously and are not to be construed as real. Any resemblance to actual events, locales, organizations, or persons, living or dead, is entirely coincidental.

This book was originally published in 2001 by Collins Crime, an Imprint of HarperCollins Publishers Ltd.

EPub Edition NOVEMBER 2013 ISBN: 9780062302014

Print Edition ISBN: 9780062350435

10 9

Ancient sites in Derbyshire like the Nine Virgins stone circle are constantly under threat from vandalism, quarrying, erosion and abuse. They are also sacred sites, and are still actively used as places of worship. Please treat them with respect.

Dancing With the Virgins

Chapter One

ON THE DAY the first woman died, Mark Roper had radio trouble. At the start of his shift, he had been patrolling in the valley, in the deep dead spot where the gritstone plateau blocked out the signal from the telephone interface point at Bradwell. The silence had been unnerving, even then. It had made him conscious of his isolation in the slowly dying landscape, and it had begun to undermine his confidence and stir up the old uncertainties. But Mark wasn't frightened then. It was only later he had been frightened.

Normally, this was his favourite time of year – these few weeks of hesitation before the start of winter. He liked to watch the hills changing colour day by day, and the Peak District villages emptying of visitors. But he could tell that today wasn't quite normal. There was a feeling about this particular Sunday that made him uncomfortable to be alone on Ringham Moor. There was something strained and uneasy in the way the trees stirred in the wind, in the way the dry bracken snapped underfoot and the birds fell silent in the middle of the afternoon.

As Mark climbed out of the dead spot, his horizon widened until he could see across to Hartington and the Staffordshire border. But even on his way back across the moor towards Partridge Cross, he could not raise his Area Ranger. Maybe the radio handset he had picked up from the briefing centre that morning was the one with the faulty battery connection. Little things like that could change your life forever.

'Peakland Partridge Three to Peakland Zulu. Owen?'

No matter how many times he tried, his call sign went unanswered.

Earlier in the year, they had been burning the heather on this part of Ringham Moor. An acrid charcoal smell still clung to the vegetation, and it mingled with the sweet, fruity scent of the living flowers as it rose from the ground under Mark's boots. In places, the stems had been left bare and white where the bark had been burned off completely. They showed up in the blackened carpet like tiny bones, like a thousand skeletal fingers poking from the earth.

Mark's father had helped the gamekeepers many times with the swaling, the annual burning of the heather to encourage the growth of fresh shoots for red grouse to feed on. Conditions for burning had to be just right – the heather dry, but the ground wet enough to prevent the fire spreading down into the peat. You could get so hot controlling the flames that you thought your skin would be burned to a cinder, and if you were standing in the wrong place when the wind blew, you could end up black from head to toe. Sometimes, Mark recalled, his father had smelled like Bonfire Night for days.

The scent of the burned heather brought the presence of his father back to him now. It was a sensation so powerful that the tall figure might have been striding alongside him, swinging his huge, reddened hands, talking of working dogs and trout flies, and promising that he would take Mark and his brother on a shoot one day. But he had never carried out his promise. And he hadn't walked with Mark again, not for a long time now.

The impression left as quickly as it had come, leaving Mark clutching desperately at a memory, reaching for an image that dissipated like a wisp of smoke in the wind.

Fumbling at the radio, he tried again. 'Peakland Zulu. Can you hear me, Owen? Owen?' But still there was nothing.

As he climbed to the plateau, the weight of Mark's rucksack gradually increased, chafing his skin through the fabric of his red fleece, pulling down his shoulders and pressing on the muscles in his back. Despite the chill, his neck was wet with sweat, and he shivered as he came over a rise and the wind grabbed at him. The shadows of clouds were moving across the landscape below him. Brief patches of sunlight revealed a field dotted with sheep, a narrow stretch of tarmac road, an oak spinney, or the roof of a distant farmhouse. Yet the sight of human habitation only heightened his sense of being alone.

It was the environment, not the welfare of people and property, that had led Mark to volunteer as a Peak Park

Ranger in the first place. Once, he had wanted to save the entire world, but in the end he had settled for helping to protect one little bit of it. He had not imagined that he would be called on to tolerate the actions of people who destroyed and defiled the environment, people who had no respect for nature and the lives of animals. It was the most difficult thing he had to learn. Maybe even Owen Fox would never be able to teach him that.

One thing Owen had taught Mark was the importance of good communication; he had told him to stay in touch, always. But this early November day had been the wrong time for Mark to choose for his first solo patrol. Entirely the wrong day to be on his own.

'This is Peakland Partridge Three. Owen? Owen? Where *are* you?'

And, of course, it had been the wrong day for Jenny Weston, too.

JENNY HAD BEEN riding a yellow six-gear Dawes Kokomo. It had one-inch tyres, and a wire basket bolted over the rear wheel. It was hired from the Peak Cycle centre at Partridge Cross on a three-hour ticket, and Jenny had already ridden nearly five miles to reach the plateau of Ringham Moor.

The moor was littered with prehistoric burial mounds, cairns and stone circles, some so small or so ruined and overgrown that they were barely visible in the heather and bracken. It was not as well used as the moors to the south and west, Stanton and Harthill, but its tracks were more accessible to a mountain bike, its open spaces more solitary, its face that bit closer to the sky.

Ringham had become one of Jenny's favourite places. There were many reasons that brought her back, needs and compulsions that had worn a track for her bike tyres right to the base of the Hammond Tower on Ringham Edge. She carried an impression in her mind of the view down into the valley from the tower – that steep plummet through the trees on to a litter of rocks at the bottom.

It had been a blustery day, with showers that blew across the hills in squalls, bludgeoning the birches and scattering dead leaves into the heather. There seemed to be little life on the moor. But at the bottom of the track, Jenny had passed a youth wearing a red woollen cap pulled low on his forehead, with large ears that stuck out like table-tennis bats. He had been walking very quickly towards the road, and had refused to raise his head to meet her eye as she passed. Jenny had pressed down harder on the pedals, seeking to gain distance from the youth, so that she over-exerted herself on the slope and had to stop further on, gasping from painful lungs as she looked back. The youth had gone, and there was no one else to be seen – only a fistful of jackdaws drifting against the face of one of the abandoned quarries, and a herd of cattle lying restlessly in a field on the slope below the Virgins.

Jenny had always believed she was safer on a bike. Two wheels and the extra speed gave her the confidence that she could get out of trouble, if she needed to. A woman on her own, in a place like Ringham Moor, ought to think about being careful.

To get to the top of the moor, Jenny had to dismount and wheel the Kokomo up the steepest part of the path. She knew she was almost there when she reached the twisted Heart Stone, twelve feet high, with iron hand and foot holds driven into its sides.

At the top, the sandy track was cycleable, as long as you avoided the exposed rocks in the middle. It crossed a plateau of dark heather and whinberry, with patches of rhododendron on the southern slopes. There were old quarries on two sides, and sharp crags and edges on the east and south, where the plateau fell away into the valleys.

The crossing of the main paths was marked by a wooden sign scrawled with the name of the Nine Virgins and a yellow arrow. Around the sign was an area worn by many feet. Someone living in the valley had a peacock; its long drawn-out shriek drifted across the moor before dying away in the wind.

By the time she reached the Virgins, Jenny could feel the perspiration standing out on her forehead. Her Lycra cycling shorts were tighter on her hips and buttocks than they should have been, and the skin of her legs was pink and blotched from the exertion and the chafing of the wind.

She didn't mind the wind, or the cold, or even the exertion. Up here on the moor they helped to blow away the thoughts that would sit in the corners of her mind all the rest of the week, dark and evil-eyed. Nowhere else could she do that; certainly nowhere in Sheffield, where the crowded streets and the traffic only fed her anxieties.

In early November, the weather kept most people off the moor. But she could see that someone was sitting against the trunk of a tree near the stone circle, playing a few notes on a flute, toying with a tune that was vaguely familiar. She couldn't see the musician clearly, but she had an impression of long, fair hair and a multi-coloured sweater.

Jenny turned the handlebars of the bike away from the Nine Virgins and headed towards a path that ran down through deep bracken. The path turned into a stream bed later in the winter, and the ground was scoured to its sandy bottom. Tree roots ran close to the surface, bursting through to form ragged steps in the steepest parts. Beech-nuts crunched underfoot and the bracken was head high. It pressed close around her, its brown, dead hands brushing against her legs and rattling on the spokes of her wheels.

Beyond the dip, the Hammond Tower stood at the top of the slope. It was prominent on the horizon, tall and built of grey stone, but serving no apparent purpose. A walled-up doorway faced a flight of roughly cut steps and a steep drop off Ringham Edge. Fallen leaves filled a wide hollow between the tower and the rock outcrops they called the Cat Stones.

Jenny sat for a while on a broken ledge at the base of the tower, staring at the view across the dale, waiting for her breathing to slow down, but feeling the chill begin to creep over her skin. She shouldn't stay long, or her muscles would stiffen.

Down in the valley, she could see the farm, with a field full of cows, a cluster of gritstone buildings and a bigger, newer shed with a dark green steel roof. A track ran past the farm, and she studied it carefully for figures walking by the gate and heading up towards the tower. But there was no one today.

As she stood up to retrieve her bike, she noticed a crevice in the stones of the tower which had been crammed with crumpled drinks cans and cigarette packets. Jenny shook her head in irritation, but did nothing about the litter. It was a job for the Rangers who patrolled the moor.

A few minutes later, she had reached the stone circle again. The Nine Virgins were only about four feet high, and they stood in a clearing of flattened and eroded grass between clumps of birch and oaks. Fifteen yards from the circle was a single stone on its own, an outlier – the stone that they called the Fiddler. According to the legend, nine village maidens had been caught dancing on the Sabbath and had been turned to stone for their sin. The fiddler who played for them had suffered the same fate. Now the single stone looked lonely and isolated, condemned for ever to stand outside the circle.

Jenny stopped the bike and wiped her palms on a tissue. The hills were already misting into grey over the banks of bracken, but the clouds broke and allowed a trickle of sun on to the moor. There was no sound but for the wind whispering across the heather. There was no one to be seen now; she was alone. And it was perfectly safe on a bike – as long as you didn't get a puncture.

'Oh, damn!'

She dismounted and struggled to turn her bike upside down to inspect the back tyre. Immediately she saw the glitter of a sliver of glass. It had slit a gaping wound in the rubber tread and gone straight through to puncture the inner tube. She pulled the glass free, flinching at the sharp edges, and listened to the last gasp of escaping air. The tyre looked peculiarly lifeless as it hung from the wheel, the soft grey skin of its collapsed tube protruding under the rim.

Jenny knew what a hassle it was to get the tyre off the back wheel, repair and replace it, and she was already reaching that state of tiredness where everything felt like a major task. But there was nothing else for it. Sighing, she flipped the quick-release lever and dropped the wheel on the ground. The forks of the bike pointed into the air in an undignified posture, like a dead animal on its back.

She was reminded of a photograph that had been taken at the height of the panic over mad cow disease. It had shown a slaughtered British Holstein cow, a huge animal with its stomach bloated, its vast udder shiny and leaking a dribble of milk, and its four stiff legs pointing ludicrously to the sky. The cow had been waiting its turn to be rolled into an incinerator. Its photograph had been on the front of leaflets that Jenny had helped to distribute, and she had seen it so many times that the details had stayed with her ever since, along with other images of things that had been done to animals.

Automatically, she patted the pouch she wore round her waist, to make sure it was still there. Soon, she would have to decide what to do with what it contained.

Jenny shivered. The weather had changed, and the evening would be cold. The feathery stems of cotton grass created patches of golden mist close to the ground. They hovered just above the heather, moving in the wind like live creatures stirring in their nests.

It was the noise of the wind in Jenny's ears that covered the soft sound of footsteps until the walker was only a few feet behind her.

IN HALF AN hour, Mark was due to go off duty. Owen had given him exact instructions for his first solo patrol – a pass across the face of Ringham and a descent into the valley on the far side, where the moor turned into farmland. There he was to take a look at the walls and stiles and signposts for recent damage, and have a scout around for the worst of the litter left by hikers.

On the way back, he should have a glance at the Nine Virgins to see that the ancient monument was no more scarred than usual; have a word, perhaps, with any campers foolhardy enough to have pitched their tents in the woods. Mark couldn't imagine why anybody would want to camp on the moor at any time of the year, let alone in November. But still they did it. And they were breaking the law when they did.

Near the top of the track he noticed a crumpled Coke can, dropped by some careless visitor. Muttering angrily, he picked it up and slipped it under the flap of his rucksack, where it joined a small pile of chocolate bar wrappers, aluminium ring-pulls and an empty Marlboro packet and some cigarette ends he had found near the Hammond Tower, to be disposed of later. Mark couldn't tolerate the attitude that made people think it was OK to scatter the environment with litter. They thought their own convenience was more important.

If he had his way, Mark would ban these people completely from the national park. He would put tollgates on all the entrance roads and issue passes for admission. It might come to it one day, too. The park couldn't cope with the constantly rising numbers.

There were tyre tracks in the sandy soil here. That meant there had been a mountain biker this way recently. Mark knew his by-laws; he had read the regulations carefully, and he knew what was allowed and what wasn't. The Peak District National Park Authority had prosecuted mountain bikers before.

He smiled in satisfaction, then immediately felt guilty. Owen said the main skills you needed as a Ranger were tact and diplomacy. Why get into an argument when you could achieve more with a friendly word of advice? Mark knew he had a lot to learn. Sometimes he couldn't find the right things to say to people who appalled him with their stupidity and their disregard for their own safety, the property of others – and, above all, for the environment and its wildlife. That was their greatest crime, these people who desecrated the moors. The last thing they deserved was diplomacy.

Though it was only two o'clock, it would be starting to go dark in a couple of hours' time. For a few days now, Mark had noticed that peculiar half-light, like full moonlight, that came at five o'clock in the afternoon, when all the colours seemed to change and glow for a few minutes before fading into the darkness. The turning back of the clocks at the end of British Summer Time always worried the Peak Park Rangers. Walkers were liable to miscalculate and still be on the hills when it went dark.

The afternoon was turning cold, but Mark didn't feel the chill. The red fleece jacket he wore proudly, with its silver Peak Park insignia, kept him warm. It was also a reassuring sight for the visitors a Ranger came across – those who were lost and bewildered, exhausted or injured, or simply inadequately dressed and too poorly equipped for walking the moors. The sight of the red jacket was like a friendly beacon. It meant a Ranger approaching.

JENNY WESTON HAD been in the act of smiling when she died. Her smile had stiffened and shattered, twisting into a grin of fear as the knife slipped under her ribs.

The blade was sharp, tungsten coated, and with a lethal tip. It slit the cotton of her T-shirt and sliced easily through her skin and a layer of subcutaneous fat as it thrust towards her heart. A small patch on the front of her T-shirt turned red and a single spurt of blood splashed on to the handlebars of the Kokomo.

As soon as the knife was withdrawn, the wound closed and ceased to bleed on the outside. Jenny looked down, astonished, and pressed her hand to the red patch. Inside her ribcage, her heart sac was already filling with leaking blood; the pressure of it squeezed her heart and constricted its movement. Then her left lung deflated and a gush of fluids filled the cavity. She began to feel light-headed; her hands and feet turned numb, and her legs lost the strength to hold her body upright.

She made no resistance as she was grasped under the armpits and dragged across the clearing, with her heels leaving trails in the sandy soil. As fresh blood failed to reach her brain and extremities, her skin turned a dirty white; her legs and belly looked like lumps of boiled fish as they were deliberately exposed to the light.

The blade of the knife left a red smear where it was wiped on the grass. From the handlebars of the bike, a small trickle of blood had run down on to the front wheel. It dripped slowly from spoke to spoke, already darkening and thickening in the air, until it was absorbed into the ground.

By the time her attacker had finished, or not long after, Jenny Weston was dead.

MARK KNEW IT happened sometimes, but it was such a pointless thing to do. Mindless and irresponsible. Now and then the Ranger briefings mentioned a bike that had not been returned to the hire centre. Hirers had to give proof of their identity and leave a name and address, as well as a £20 deposit, so it was hardly worth trying to get away with a mountain bike, considering how easily you would get caught. But sometimes there was one who took the bike away with them. Occasionally, they simply abandoned it on one of the tracks, in a car park, or up here on the moor, like this one. None of it ever made sense to Mark.

The sight of the Kokomo under the gorse bush angered him unreasonably. Its presence was like a violation – the evidence of selfish humanity intruding into his world, like children pawing his most precious possessions with grubby fingers. The bike had been treated as just so much rubbish.

Then Mark looked more closely. A streak of red had stained the canary yellow paintwork of the front stem and left rust-like spots on the spokes. He shivered with misgiving and fingered the radio in his pocket. Suddenly he wished he hadn't come out alone, after all. There was no reassuring presence alongside him, no Owen there to know exactly what to do.

With a shaking hand, Mark made a note of the colour, model and number of the bike, crumpling the pages of his notebook in his haste to get it out of his pocket. The act of writing made him feel better, more in control, as if the ink marks on the page had magically brought a familiar voice from the air: 'Observe, keep a note, report back.'

'Yes, Owen,' whispered Mark.

Feeling the sweat drying on his forehead and the back of his neck, he forced himself to walk past the bike to where the stones were clustered among the spindly birches. Somebody had lit a fire here recently, leaving scorched earth and a pile of white ash. People were always lighting fires near the Virgins, as if they thought the flames might melt their stony hearts. At the midsummer solstice, there were hundreds of folk up here at night, and they did a lot more than light fires.

Mark stopped abruptly as he looked into the circle. The sensations that came reminded him of the terrors of his puberty, the physical sickness and the guilt. He tried to concentrate on studying the ground, to look for evidence of bike tracks or footprints. He tried to think about casting around for telltale objects that might have been dropped by someone who had been in the area. I'm observing, he told himself. I must observe. Be professional and calm, and don't rush into anything.

But he couldn't keep up the pretence for long. His eyes just wouldn't focus on anything else. With shameful fascination, Mark found his attention drawn to the centre of the stone circle, where the white shape lay in such startling, rousing incongruity.

'Oh, Jesus.'

The body of the woman sprawled obscenely among the stones. Her half-naked torso had been flung on the rough grass, her arms and legs twisted in provocative gestures. Her right knee was lifted high, to the level of her waist, and her left leg was stretched taut, as if she might be about to spring into the air.

Mark could see every detail of the muscles in her legs, the tendons rigid under the skin at the top of her thigh, the faint crinkling of cellulite on her hips. Her pose was a caricature of life, a cruel parody of flamboyance and movement. Her hands were tilted at the wrist, her toes pointed downwards, and her head nodded to silent music. She was spread against the ground in a final arabesque, in a fatal pirouette, or the last fling of an abandoned tango.

Mark wondered whether to write it down. But it sounded too strange, and his hand wouldn't write any more, anyway. Instead, he repeated it to himself, over and over, in his head. A dead woman dancing. She looked like a dead woman, dancing.

Chapter Two

Fifteen miles to the north, in the town of Edendale, the battle had been going on for an hour and a quarter already. The police officers in the front line were battered and breathing hard, their faces swollen with exertion, and their hair stuck to their foreheads with sweat. One or two had their shirts ripped. Another had blood trickling from a cut on his eye.

Detective Constable Ben Cooper could see his colleague, Todd Weenink, deep in the thick of it. Weenink had two PCs from the Tactical Support Unit close on either side of him, and there were more men coming in from behind to assist them. They looked exhausted, their expressions grim, but determined. They were struggling against the odds, fighting a battle of containment that they were constantly in danger of losing.

The students were charging forward in a solid mass, forcing the police to give ground under the onslaught.

In the melee, close up, anything could be happening – a poke in the eye, a boot in the crutch, teeth sinking into an ear. The police had not been issued with riot shields or helmets today; there was no body armour, no snarling Alsatians or horses to keep the students at bay. There had been no authority given for the use of special weapons, no tear gas canisters held nervously in reserve.

In addition, the police had to face a ceaseless barrage of noise – chanted slogans, shouts of abuse and a constant stream of profanities from a hostile crowd.

Cooper pulled his hands out of his jeans pockets and turned his coat collar up to try to shut out the cacophony. If he could, he would have closed his eyes, too, to avoid seeing the slaughter, to stop himself from imagining the consequences if the police line collapsed. In another moment, the day could end in total humiliation for Derbyshire Constabulary E Division. And not a single arrest made so far.

'What are we going to do, Sarge?' he said.

Detective Sergeant Rennie was an old hand. He had seen it all before. He rubbed his jowls, pulled his anorak closer around his shoulders, and winced as a PC went down and was trampled underfoot.

'Conduct a survey,' he said. 'We'll send out a questionnaire.'

Cooper nodded. 'I suppose so. But it's a bit pathetic, isn't it?'

'We'll make sure there are lots of tick boxes to fill in.'

'Even so ...'

Rennie shrugged and sighed. 'It's all we can do, Ben. Otherwise, we just have to sit back and let it happen.'

The police formed a wall and turned to face their attackers again. Beyond the opposing lines, Cooper could see the main buildings of the High Peak College campus, set on the lower slopes of the hill. They looked down on Edendale like benign giants, the educational heights of the Eden Valley.

He began to search his pockets for a packet of mints to take the taste of nausea from his mouth. He had a lot of pockets – in his jeans, in his checked shirt, on the inside and the outside of his waxed jacket. But all he found was a scatter of cashpoint receipts, two empty shotgun cartridge cases and half a packet of dog biscuits.

Cooper knew there was more than just education that went on in those college buildings on the hill. He had been there himself, for long enough to collect the A-levels he needed to get into the police service. His fellow students had accused him of being single-minded, as if his determination made them guilty about their own pursuit of parties and casual sex. But there had been a demon driving Ben Cooper that his contemporaries would never have understood – a jealous God who would not have tolerated parties.

Dave Rennie sat back comfortably in his seat and unscrewed the top of a vacuum flask. He offered Cooper a plastic cup, which he refused as soon as he got a whiff of the metallic tang of the coffee. The sergeant's expression was serious, his forehead creased with anxiety, like a man with a great responsibility on his mind.

'You see, if they get rid of the kitchen and sack the canteen staff, that means they'll put vending machines in instead,' he said. 'And then what would happen? I mean, would anybody use them? There's no point in spending money on vending machines if they don't get used. It would look bad in the budgets, wasting money at a time like this.'

Cooper watched Todd Weenink duck his head and drive his shoulders forward to meet a wiry-haired youth who'd been tormenting him all afternoon. There was a thud as their skulls connected and a scuffing as their feet lashed out.

The crowd behind Cooper began yelling. Then the police back-pedalled. Officers fell and were trampled as they lay on the ground. But Weenink broke away and looked around, bemused. His eyes were dazed, as if he might have taken a knock on the head. Then he looked up and caught sight of a student running past him, and made an instinctive grab. The student's legs folded beneath him under the impact of Weenink's sixteen stone, and they both sprawled in the mud, exhausted and gasping.

Cooper smiled. Quite by chance, it had been the right student Weenink had flattened. The High Peak College wing-threequarter happened to be in possession of the ball, and had been racing for the touchline, within seconds of scoring the winning try of the match. Even while the two opposing players were struggling to get up again from the tackle, the referee blew the final whistle. The match had been saved: 12–10 to Edendale Police.

'Thank God for that,' said Cooper.

'Honour preserved, I suppose,' said Rennie, putting away his flask.

'I don't know about that, Sarge. But our lot always trash the bar if they lose.'

Cooper left the touchline and headed for the clubhouse. In his early days in E Division, they had tried to recruit him to the rugby team. They had thought he looked tall and fit enough to be an asset, but had accused him of lacking ruthlessness in the ruck. Now his job was to order the jugs of beer for the changing-room celebrations. Loyalty to your colleagues meant doing such things on a Sunday afternoon, even when you would rather be at home watching videos with your nieces.

After ten years, Cooper was able to look back on his days at High Peak College with some nostalgia. His life had possessed a definite purpose then. Succeeding in his exams had been his role in life, and joining the police his destiny. The feeling had stayed with him through his time as a uniformed constable on the beat; it had followed him as he moved into CID and began to learn a different way of policing. His progress had been watched every inch of the way, and mostly approved of. Mostly. The times when he had made mistakes or expressed doubts were still imprinted in his memory.

Then, two years ago, everything had changed. With the violent death of his father, Police Sergeant Joe Cooper, a prop had been knocked from under him, and a great weight had been lifted from his back. His guiding hand had been taken away, and his life had been given back to him. But it had already been too late for Ben Cooper. He had become what his father made him.

'So that's why we have to do this Vending Machine Usage Survey,' said Rennie, pronouncing the capital letters carefully as he walked at Cooper's shoulder. 'To get an idea of the possible take-up on the proposed new refreshment facilities. It's so that somebody in Admin at HQ can make an informed decision. A decision supported by constructive feedback from the customer base.'

Cooper could practically see the internal memo that Rennie was quoting from. The sergeant had coffee soaking into his moustache. He was wearing knitted woollen gloves, for Heaven's sake. He looked like somebody's granddad on an off-season outing to Blackpool.

Cooper was conscious that his own thirtieth birthday was approaching next year. It loomed in the distance like a summer storm cloud, making him feel his youth was nearly over before he had got used to being in his twenties. One day, he could be another Dave Rennie.

'I think Todd might have got a bit of concussion, Sarge.'

'He always looks like that,' said Rennie.

'He got a knock on the head.'

'Don't worry – Weenink doesn't let anybody mess with him. He always gets his revenge.'

Todd Weenink was different, of course. During the last couple of months Cooper had found himself thrown together with Weenink in the latest round of restructuring in the division. In these circumstances, the relationship became almost like a marriage. The issue of 'them and us' became focused on a single individual. But there were times when you needed another officer at your side.

Without the man or woman at your side, you could find yourself looking the wrong way at the wrong time. You had to have a person you could put your trust in. They supported you; and you supported them. Cooper knew it was a law written in invisible ink on the back of the warrant card they gave you when you were sworn in as a constable. It was sewn into your first uniform like an extra seam; it was the page that they always forgot to print in the Police Training Manual.

Only a couple of weeks earlier, Weenink had been the man at his side when they had raided a small-scale drugs factory in a converted warehouse on the outskirts of Edendale. One of the occupants had produced a pick-axe, but he had been too slow, and they had executed a takedown between them, with no one injured.

Cooper reassured himself by thinking of his date with Helen Milner later on. Within an hour, he would be out of the rugby club and away. He and Helen hadn't decided where they would go yet. Probably it would be a walk to get the noise out of his head, then a drink or two at the Light House before a meal somewhere. The Light House was where they had gone the very first time they had gone out together. It was hardly more than two months ago that they had met again at Helen's grandparents' house in the village of Moorhay and resumed a relationship that had started when they were schoolfriends. But their new beginning had not been without difficulties. Nothing ever was.

The clubhouse corridor smelled of sweat and mud and disinfectant, with a permanent underlying essence of embrocation. Dave Rennie helped Cooper carry the jugs of beer to the players in the visitors' changing room. Then the sergeant's pager began to bleep.

'Oh, God damn it. What now?'

Cooper watched Rennie go to the phone in the corridor. He looked back over his shoulder at the changing-room door, which swung open with the constant passing to and fro of players and supporters. Todd Weenink was out of the shower, towelling himself in the middle of a raucous mob, his naked bulk perfectly at home in a melee of pink male flesh and echoing laughter.

Weenink already had a beer in front of him. It was amazing that he could keep up the pace. He had arrived for the match only at the very last minute, when everyone else was changed and ready to go out on the pitch, thinking they were going to have to play a man short, and cursing him for letting them down. No doubt Weenink had been out on the booze the night before and had woken up in someone else's bed many miles away, with rugby the last thing on his mind.

Cooper shook his head at the intrusive thoughts that came to him – the contrast between Weenink's muscular, hairy nakedness and the picture he carried in his mind of the last colleague he had worked so closely with. Todd's open, up-front, relaxed maleness was a world away from Detective Constable Diane Fry. Former Detective Constable, he should say. Now Acting Detective Sergeant.

It was a subject Cooper didn't really want to think about. It brought with it painful memories, some of which he still didn't understand but suspected might be his own fault.

After a few minutes, he realized Dave Rennie hadn't come back into the bar. In the steamy atmosphere of the changing room, he couldn't see Todd either. He had to shout to make himself heard, even when close enough to tap one of the players on the shoulder.

'Have you seen Todd Weenink?'

'He's gone,' said the player. 'Control bleeped Dave Rennie, and Todd went off with him. They went off in a hurry, too. Todd hadn't even managed to put his trousers on.'

'You're joking.'

'No, mate. I saw him myself, with his arse hanging out. Should you be with them?'

Cooper stared bleakly at the player. 'I'm not on call. Control wouldn't have asked for me.'

'Right. You're the lucky one, then. You can have a few beers.'

'A few beers, yeah. What more could I ask for?'

Suddenly, Cooper's mood plummeted. He felt as if he had just been jilted by a lover. If there was a job on, he wanted to be there. He wanted to be part of the team. He wondered why loyalty had to be so painful. And when would he learn to give his loyalty in the right direction? He ought to have learned that lesson from Diane Fry – their brief relationship had certainly been difficult enough to drive it home. Cooper shuddered at a premonition. He thought it likely that she could inflict more pain on him yet, given the chance.

THE POLICE VEHICLES cluttering up the roadsides at the bottom of the main track on to Ringham Moor made Diane Fry frown in exasperation. The scene looked chaotic, as cars with beacons flashing arrived one after another in the gathering dusk and slewed across the narrow verge. A minibus carrying the Tactical Support Unit was unable to squeeze through the gap left by the parked cars until a uniformed sergeant yelled at someone to move. Figures in reflective yellow jackets were caught briefly in the headlights as they passed aimlessly backwards and forwards.

Fry itched to take control of the situation, to bring order and a bit of sense to officers so charged with excitement and adrenalin that they were causing more trouble than they were worth. But, in fact, she shouldn't even be here at all. She had thought she had got away from E Division, that her few weeks in Edendale had been a bad dream she could soon put behind her. But here she still was, answering the call. And before she knew what was happening, she had found herself out in the Peak District countryside again, where civilization seemed like a dim memory and the twenty-first century was reduced to the fantasy of a Victorian novelist.

She stood with Detective Inspector Paul Hitchens on the rocks overlooking the road. A fine drizzle was settling on their clothes and in their hair, and turning the gritstone slab under their feet a shade darker. With Hitchens at her side, Fry felt as though she had taken another step closer in her ambitions. She was already 'acting up' as a detective sergeant, with a transfer to a permanent DS's job in the offing when the imminent re-shuffle took place.

A move couldn't come too soon for Fry. At all costs, she must avoid the crazy distractions and misjudgements that had plagued her in a spell shortly after her arrival in E Division from West Midlands. The name of her biggest misjudgement was Ben Cooper.

The thought of him immediately sparked the surge of anger that always bubbled somewhere deep in her stomach, churning thick and corrosive like an acid that flowed in her small intestines. It happened every time; it only took the mention of Cooper's name, or even a burst of the wrong music. There were cassettes that she used to play often in her car which she had been forced to throw away – not just casually chucked on the back seat, but hurled into the nearest wheelie bin, with their spools of magnetic tape ripped out and shredded like the innards of a rat she had once seen killed and torn apart by a police Alsatian in a derelict warehouse back in Birmingham. If there had been an open fire in her flat, she would have burned the tapes; she would have happily watched their plastic cases crack and twist and bubble, as they melted into a greasy smear.

Fry wiped a sheen of drizzle from her face, where it was starting to make her cheeks feel damp and uncomfortable. No, she hadn't quite managed to erase Ben Cooper from her memory yet. But she was working on it.

'We've arranged for you to see Maggie Crew at six o'clock,' said DI Hitchens. 'You'd better get going, as soon as this lot are out of our way.'

'Was she willing to see me?'

'Willing isn't a word I'd use. She's bloody hard work.'

'She's uncooperative? But why?'

'You'll see. Form your own impressions of her, Diane, that's the best way. We want you to get to know her. Get under her skin. Be an irritant, if you like.'

Fry knew she was being presented with a chance to do something different, to escape the routine chores that the Ben Coopers of the world would be allocated during this enquiry.

'I'm looking forward to it,' she said.

Hitchens nodded in approval. 'When *are* they going to stop messing about down there?' he said.

DI Hitchens was dressed casually, in denims and trainers, and he looked like a man who should have been doing something else. His cheeks were dark and unshaven, and there were specks of white paint in his hair.

'We've got to keep the road open,' said the sergeant importantly as he passed below them.

'Yeah. You're doing a great job. We can see that.'

'Control reckons the cavalry's on the way, Inspector. They tracked down a couple of your lot at the rugby match.'

Fry knew exactly what that meant. The rugby match was where Ben Cooper would have been with his friend, Todd Weenink, and no doubt DS Dave Rennie, too.

Cooper wasn't a rugby-playing man himself. From her own experience, Fry reckoned he was more likely to be taking out the half-time oranges and cleaning the players' boots, generally getting in the way and making helpful suggestions. But he would have been at the match to support his colleagues. Oh yes, Ben Cooper was a great one for supporting his friends.

'Oh, and you'll be pleased to know our lads won too!' called the sergeant.

Fry blew through her teeth and jammed her hands into the pockets of her coat, squaring her shoulders like someone bracing herself for a fight. Rennie, Cooper, and Weenink. The dream team. Just what E Division needed to stamp on a spate of attacks on women.

At last it looked as though someone had located another place to park. Radios crackled, the sergeant shouted, and cars began to move off, flashing their headlights and spinning their wheels dramatically on the grass as they went. But as the patrols and vans made space, another car arrived. It was an unmarked Mondeo – a private car, not a police vehicle. The doors popped open and a warm fug seemed to ooze out into the evening chill. A voice was raised in complaint from the back seat.

'I can't *believe* we left those uniformed bastards with all the beer,' it said.

Fry recognized DC Weenink immediately. He was damp-haired and pink-faced, and his voice sounded petulant, like an overgrown child. She watched in disgust as he poked bare, muscular legs out of the car door and struggled to pull his trousers on over his jockey shorts.

Parts of his anatomy bulged dangerously from his underclothes, and the buttons of his shirt were unfastened over his hairy chest. Even from several yards away, Fry knew that his breath smelled of alcohol.

She watched DS Rennie get out of the driver's seat. But no Ben Cooper. Suddenly, Fry felt more cheerful. Her shoulders relaxed, her lips formed a contemptuous smile.

'Well, if that's the cavalry,' she said, 'my money's on the Indians.'

DI Hitchens laughed. Weenink heard the laugh, and he looked around for its source. He grinned up at Fry, with his zip still open, his hands pressed round his crotch, the position of them emphasizing rather than concealing the bulge in his shorts.

'Excuse me, Sergeant,' he said. 'Can you use me at all?'

Fry stared at him, but Weenink's grin only grew broader, until it became a smirk. She turned to stride away from the road. She had no time to waste on petty irritations – not when a woman's entire life had already been wasted up there on the moor. She had seen enough wasted lives, and her own had almost been one of them. But not any more.

BEN COOPER TOOK a swig from his bottle, conserving the beer carefully, anxious about drinking too much. He didn't want to become a solitary drinker, though the temptation was strong.

A few minutes ago, he had rung Control to find out what was happening. They said the body of a woman had been found on Ringham Moor, fifteen miles south of Edendale. A suspected murder. The control room operator didn't need to mention the other attack that had taken place not a mile away from the same spot six weeks before. In that case, the victim had survived – just about.

Now Cooper's mind was no longer with him as he sat in the sweaty rugby club bar. It was elsewhere, drifting across the moors towards a flutter of tape and the flashing lights, the sound of urgent voices, and the scents and the electric crackle in the air that never failed to give him a buzz of excitement. That sense of satisfaction from taking his place in the team was a thing that couldn't be explained to someone who had never experienced it.

Yet tomorrow morning, he knew he would be sitting in the monthly Crime Strategy Meeting for Edendale Section. He would be discussing the section's annual local objectives, the implementation of liaison policies and the measurement of performance. Occasionally, in these meetings, they talked about crime. But they hardly ever talked about the victims.

Cooper watched the rugby players reach the traditional highlight of the evening, when they began to pour pints of beer over each other's heads. The bare wooden floor of the bar was already awash and turning sticky underfoot. Some of the students looked irritated at the way their clubhouse was being taken over by the more boisterous and more aggressive celebratory style of the police. Soon it would reach the point when it might be better not to have to witness a colleague committing a breach of the peace.

It was time for Ben Cooper to leave. He needed to be awake and alert for the meeting in the morning, and he had a stack of burglaries to work on, as well as a serious assault on a bouncer at one of Edendale's night clubs. With officers seconded to the murder enquiry, no doubt there would be someone else's workload to take over as well. Besides, if he stayed any longer, he would drink too much. It was definitely time to go home.

But home was Bridge End Farm, in the shadow of Camphill. Though he was close to his brother Matt, Matt's young family were gradually making the house their own, until their video games and guinea pig cages left little room for Ben. So for a while he sat on in the bar, like an old man in the corner watching the youngsters enjoy themselves, and he thought about the body on Ringham Moor.

With a bit of luck, the police team would find some obvious leads and get an early closure. There would be initial witness statements that pointed with clunking obviousness to a boyfriend or a spurned lover. Sometimes it was as if the perpetrator carried a giant, fluorescent arrow round with him and the word 'guilty' in bright red letters that were visible five miles away in poor light. All the team would need to do then was make sure they collected the forensic evidence at the scene without either contaminating it, losing it or sticking the wrong label on it so that no one could say afterwards where it had been found. It was amazing what could happen to evidence between the first report of a crime and the day a case came to court.

Cooper fought his way to the bar, shouting to the barman to make himself heard above the din. It seemed as though no one else in here wanted to sit down – they were all up on their feet, shouting at each other. The police were singing triumphal songs, having a great time. The students were starting to look hostile.

The American beer Cooper was drinking came in a brown bottle, with a black label and a faint wisp of vapour from its open neck. It was cold, and he closed both his hands round it, drawing a strange comfort from its chill for a moment before he turned and carried it away from the bar. Instead of returning to his corner, he slipped out of the door into the cooler air outside.

For a while, he leaned against a rail near the changing rooms, gazing at the empty pitch, watching the starlings that had arrived in the dusk to pick over the divots in the turf, searching for worms exposed by the players' studs. He became distantly aware of a more aggressive note to the shouting in the bar behind him, but decided it wasn't his concern.

Cooper continued to believe it was nothing to do with him right up until the moment that a six-foot six-inch student lock forward put a hand like a meat plate on his shoulder.

Chapter Three

DIANE FRY HAD never seen Detective Chief Inspector Stewart Tailby quite so agitated. The DCI loomed over his group of officers like a head teacher with a class full of pupils in detention, and he was shouting at the Senior SOCO from the Scientific Support Unit. Tailby's strangely two-tone hair was trembling in the wind as he turned and paced around the crime scene.

'We've got to hit this area fast,' he said. 'We can't possibly seal it off – we'd need every man in E Division. We need to get what we can before the public get up here and trample over everything.'

'Well, we *could* do it in a rush, but it won't be very selective,' said the SOCO.

'Sod being selective,' said Tailby. 'Take everything. We'll worry about being selective later.'

A few yards away, DI Hitchens manoeuvred to keep his senior officer within distance. Other officers ebbed and flowed awkwardly around them, like extras in a badly staged Gilbert and Sullivan opera, who had just realized that nobody had told them what to do with their hands.

'The light's failing fast,' said Hitchens, gazing at the sky.

'Well, thanks for that,' snapped Tailby. 'I thought I was going blind.'

The DCI strode over to the side of the stone circle and looked down into the disused quarry beyond it. There was a barbed wire fence, but it was too low to keep anybody out. On the other side could be seen the last few yards of an access road, which ended on the lip of the quarry. Diane Fry stretched her neck to see what Tailby was looking at. Someone had been fly-tipping from the roadway. She could just make out tyre marks, and a heap of bulging black bin liners, some yellow plastic sheeting and a roll of carpet that had been heaved off the edge. The rubbish lay scattered on the slope like the debris of a plane crash.

'Find out where the entrance to that quarry is,' said Tailby. 'And somebody will have to go down there. We need to find the rest of the clothes. Top priority.'

Hitchens had to dodge as Tailby wheeled suddenly and strode back towards the stones, avoiding the lengths of blue tape twisted together between birch trees and metal stakes. In the centre of the circle, the pathologist, Mrs Van Doon, still crouched over the victim under makeshift lighting. Tailby's face contorted. He seemed to find something outrageous and obscene in the posture of the body.

'Where's that tent?' he called. 'Get the tent over her before we have an audience.'

He turned his back and walked on a few yards from the circle, where a single stone stood on its own. DI Hitchens trailed after him at a safe distance.

'There's an inscription carved on this stone,' announced Tailby, with the air of Moses coming down from the mountain.

'Yes. It looks like a name, sir.'

'We'll need a photographer over here. I want that name deciphering.'

'It's well away from the path,' said Hitchens. 'We think the assailant probably brought his victim from the other direction.'

'So?'

'The inscription has probably been there for years.'

'Do you *know* that? Are you familiar with these stones?'

'No, sir.'

'Ever seen them before in your life?'

'No, sir.'

Tailby turned. 'No point asking you, Fry, is there?'

Fry shrugged, but the DCI wasn't waiting for an answer. He looked around to see who else he could find. 'You lot, there! Anyone seen these stones before? They're a famous landmark, they tell me. A significant part of our ancient heritage. They're an attraction. Visitors flock to see them. What about you?'

The officers shook their heads. They were the sort of men who spent their free time in the pub or in front of the telly, doing a bit of DIY or visiting the garden centre. The ones with kids went to Alton Towers and Gulliver's

Kingdom. But this thing in front of them wasn't a theme park. There were no white-knuckle rides or ice-cream vans. Tailby turned back to Hitchens.

'OK, see? We know nothing about it. We're all as ignorant as a lot of monkeys. This stone circle might as well be a Tibetan yak compound, for all we know about the place.'

'Yes, but –'

'Just see that it's done,' snarled Tailby.

Then the DCI looked back to where Mrs Van Doon was working. Fry could see that more inscriptions had been scratched into the dirt in the centre of the circle, close to the body. The letters were big and bold, and they spelled out 'STRIDE'. Whoever had made these was less interested in leaving a long-term record of his presence, though. The drizzle was hardly touching the marks, but a couple of heavy showers would wash them clean away.

'What about those, then?' said Tailby. 'You're not going to tell me those have been there for years?'

'No,' admitted Hitchens. 'They've got to be more recent.'

'When did it rain in this area last? Properly, I mean?'

Tailby stared around him. The officers gathered nearby looked at each other, then up at the sky. Fry sympathized. They were detectives – they spent all their time buried in paperwork or making phone calls in windowless offices; occasionally they drove around in a car, shuttling from pub to crown court and back again. How were they supposed to know when it had rained?

It was well known that DI Hitchens had just bought a new house in Chesterfield. Tailby himself had a ranch-style bungalow in a desirable part of Dronfield. Most of the other officers lived miles away, down in the lower valleys and the dormitory villages. Some of them were from the suburbs of Derby. It could be blowing a blizzard up here on the moor, piling up six-foot drifts of virgin snow, and all these men would see was a faint bit of sleet in the condensation on their kitchen windows.

'Does it matter?' said Hitchens.

Tailby smiled like a fox with a rabbit. 'It matters, Inspector, because we can't say whether the inscriptions were written in the last twenty-four hours or the last two weeks.'

'I suppose so, sir.'

Teeth bared, Tailby glared round for another victim. There was a shuffling and looking away, a lot of thoughtful glances at the grey blanket of cloud.

'You useless set of pillocks! Doesn't *anyone* know? Then find me someone who does!'

MARK ROPER FINALLY opened his eyes as Owen Fox parked the Land Rover behind the Partridge Cross briefing centre. The cycle hire staff had closed up for the night, but there were still a few visitors' cars left outside. A couple were securing their bikes to a rack. It occurred to Mark Roper that one of the cars that still stood dark and unattended probably belonged to the woman whose body lay on the moor.

'Come on, Mark. Let's get you inside,' said Owen.

For a moment, Mark didn't move. Then, slowly, he unfolded his legs and got out. He felt stiff, like an old man with arthritis. His jacket was crumpled, there were grass stains on his knees and black marks on his hands. He couldn't think where the marks had come from, but his hands felt unpleasant and greasy, as if there was something on his skin that would take a long time to remove.

He swayed and supported himself on the side of the Land Rover. Owen moved nearer, not touching him but hovering anxiously.

'We have to wait while the police come to speak to you, Mark,' he said.

'I know.'

'Are you up to it?'

'I'm all right.'

Owen Fox was a large man, a little ungainly from carrying too much weight around his upper body. His curly hair and wiry beard were going grey, and his face was worn and creased, the sign of a man who spent his life outdoors, regardless of the weather. Mark wanted to draw reassurance from his presence, to lean on his comforting bulk, but an uncertainty held him back.

Owen finally took Mark by the arm. But the reassurance failed to come. The contact was safe and impersonal, Owen's fingers meeting only the fabric of the young Ranger's red fleece jacket. Mark shivered violently, as if his only source of warmth had suddenly been withdrawn.

'Let's get inside,' said Owen. 'It's cold out here. You look to me as though you need a hot drink. A cup of my tea will bring some colour back to your cheeks, won't it? Green, maybe – but at least it'll be colour.'

Mark smiled weakly. 'I'm fine.'

'You're probably suffering from shock. We ought to get a doctor to look at you.'

'No. I'll be all right, Owen.'

The briefing centre was empty, but warm. The blackboard on the far wall contained white chalk scrawl that gleamed in the sudden light. The words meant nothing to Mark now. In the corner, the assistant's desk was scattered with papers – reports and forms, the encroaching paperwork of the modern Peak Park Ranger. Soon, a computer would arrive, even here.

Mark needed no encouragement to collapse into a chair near the electric heater. Owen watched him, his face creased with concern, then turned to switch on the kettle.

'Plenty of sugar in your tea, for the shock.'

Sugar, and a reassuring voice, thought Mark. The things that people needed were simple, really – such as stability and their own part to play in life. But it was Owen he had learned to look to for stability. Now he had an inexplicable fear that it would be snatched from his life again.

'The things people leave on the moor,' said Owen. 'Litter and rubbish. You'd think they'd at least take their dead bodies home with them.'

This time Mark couldn't smile.

Owen looked at him. 'I did tell you to keep in touch, Mark,' he said.

'I tried, Owen. But I couldn't get an answer.'

Owen grimaced. 'Those radios.'

I mustn't make him feel guilty, thought Mark. Don't make him take this burden on himself as well as everything else. Mark was aware that there were things he didn't know about Owen, that in their relationship he only saw the surface of the older man. But there was one thing he did know. Owen needed no more burdens.

BEN COOPER JUMPED at the hand on his shoulder and tensed his body for trouble. He cursed himself for having allowed someone to find him on his own in a vulnerable position.

The hand felt like a great weight. The tall student was massively built, with a red, sweaty face and a squashed nose. He leaned down and spoke into Cooper's ear with a voice that growled like a boulder in a landslide. At first, Cooper had no idea what he was saying. He thought the noise in the bar must have damaged his hearing permanently. He shook his head. The student leaned closer, breathing beer fumes on his neck.

'You *are* Constable Cooper, aren't you?'

'Yes.'

'I said there's someone on the phone for you. Some daft bastard who wants to know when it rained last.'

TEN MINUTES LATER, Cooper slid into the passenger seat of a Ford Mondeo as it scattered gravel on the sports ground car park.

'It's a what, Todd?'

'A cyclist from Sheffield,' said Weenink. 'She was found in the middle of the stones on Ringham Moor.'

'You mean the Nine Virgins?'

'That's the place. You got it in one. I can see why the DCI loves you.'

'Everybody knows the Nine Virgins,' said Cooper.

'I wish you'd introduce me, then. I can't find even one virgin where I live.'

Cooper could detect the sweet smell of beer in the car. He wondered if Weenink was fit to drive. It would be ironic if they got stopped by a Traffic patrol. Todd could lose his job, if he was breathalysed.

'Is Mr Tailby in charge up there?'

'He's SIO until they manage to pull a superintendent in from somewhere,' said Weenink. 'He's not a happy man. He's got a wide-open scene, public access, SOCOs scattered over a space as big as four football pitches. Also, he has a temper on him as foul as my breath on a Saturday night. But we have to report to DI Hitchens. And let me tell you, we're bloody lucky Hitchens arrived.'

'Yeah?'

'Earlier on, it was DI Armstrong at the scene. The Wicked Witch of West Street.'

'Don't say that.'

'The Bitch of Buxton, then.'

'Shut up, Todd.'

Weenink stopped at the junction of the A6, and seemed to spend a long time waiting for distant traffic to pass on the main road. Finally, he pulled out behind a tanker carrying milk for Hartington Stilton.

'You don't understand, Ben,' he said. 'That Kim Armstrong, she's so scary. I'm frightened she'll put a spell on me and turn me into a eunuch.'

'Will you cut it out?'

'No, seriously, Ben. They reckon she cursed Ossie Clarke in Traffic one day, and his balls shrivelled up like cashew nuts. The doctors are baffled. He's been off sick for weeks.'

'Todd –'

'Well, he has, hasn't he? Eh?'

'Ossie Clarke is one of the bad-back brigade. He has a slipped disc.'

'That's the official line. Don't let it lull you into a false sense of security. Anyway, we're in luck. They couldn't spare Armstrong from this paedophile enquiry. Apparently it's warming up for some arrests. There was the little girl that was killed –'

'Yes, I know.'

'So Hitchens has had to come in off leave. And you know he's just moved into a new house with that red-headed nurse? So *he's* not happy, either. It's a barrel of laughs up there, all right. Couldn't wait to get away for a bit, myself.'

Weenink was taking the back road past the fluorspar works to avoid the bottleneck in Bakewell. He took the bends gently, as if he was just one more pensioner on a Sunday afternoon outing.

'Todd? Can't we go a bit faster?'

'Mmm, the roads are a bit slippery with all these leaves,' said Weenink. 'Can't be too careful.'

THE ATMOSPHERE ON the moor was gloomy. It made Ben Cooper feel almost guilty about the buzz of anticipation that had stayed with him even in the car with Todd Weenink. The entire stone circle had been taped off, and lights were being set up to illuminate a small tent in the centre. More tape created a pathway as far as a gorse bush a few yards away. The tape twisted and rattled in the wind with a noise like a crowd of football supporters half-heartedly encouraging their team.

'There was an inch or two of rain during Thursday night, but it had dried up by morning,' said Cooper.

Several faces turned to stare at him. Hitchens raised an eyebrow, but Tailby nodded.

'Well, the ground was fine for lifting the sugar beet that morning,' explained Cooper. He drew a finger through a hollow on the top of one of the stones. 'On the other hand, there hasn't been enough sun since then to dry the moisture out where it's sheltered from the wind.'

He became suddenly aware of the nature of the looks he was being given. 'It's what you asked me,' he said.

Hitchens shrugged. He was wearing an old rugby jersey over his jeans, and might once have played for the divisional XV until he became senior enough to be more at risk of injury from his own side than from the opposition.

'Could Stride be a name?' he asked.

'What kind of man would leave his name written in the dirt when he had committed a murder, anyway?' said Tailby. 'And these stones ...'

'The Nine Virgins,' said Cooper.

'What are they all about?'

'They're the remains of a Bronze Age burial chamber. But local people call them the Virgins because of the legends ...'

'How old?'

'Three and a half thousand years, give or take.'

'The last virgins in Derbyshire, then,' said Hitchens.

Cooper kept his mouth shut. He watched a SOCO scoop up a tiny patch of bloodstained earth where the body had lain, while he listened to the faint laughter drop hollowly into the wind and disappear with a scatter of dead leaves.

In a short while, no doubt, a detective superintendent would arrive from another division to take over as senior investigating officer. He would be grumbling about the continuing vacancy in E Division that meant he had to be dragged away from his own patch, where there would be several other major incidents to be dealt with as well.

But this was the second attack on a woman in a small area, and this victim was dead. Panic would be setting in at higher levels, and those being kicked by the chiefs would soon be kicking the dog.

Though he knew Ringham Moor well, Ben Cooper found the area around the Nine Virgins disturbed him in a way it had never done before. The atmosphere was all wrong. There was nothing dark and claustrophobic about this murder scene, unlike so many others he had come across. Very often a killing occurred within a close relationship, usually within the confines of a family, where emotions ran high and someone was finally driven to extremes. Here, though, the feeling he got was of space and timelessness, a place where everything ran to its natural sequence, just as it had done for thousands of years. Here, the slow dance of the seasons repeated itself endlessly on an almost empty stage as nature rolled from life to death and back to life again.

Cooper had learned to keep quiet about his thoughts at times. Most senior officers, like DCI Tailby, prided themselves on being practical, logical men. Tailby was from Nottingham, raised in suburban streets and comprehensive schools. He preferred to leave it to people like Ben Cooper to be imaginative – he seemed to regard it as some kind of local idiosyncrasy, a queer characteristic inherited from the distant Celtic ancestors of the Derbyshire hill folk.

Cooper watched his fellow officers. Some of them certainly looked as though they felt disorientated and isolated from the realities of the twenty-first century up here. As if to emphasize the point, the sound of a steam train starting up seemed to reach them from the valley below.

'There's the train,' said Cooper.

'What?' said Tailby.

'It's the Peak Rail line. They run restored steam engines on it. For the tourists, you know.'

A white plume hung across the lights in the bottom of the valley, drifting with the breeze back towards Matlock and vanishing into the darkness as the chug of the engine receded.

Tailby spun on his heel. 'Time to talk to the Rangers,' he said.

'We'll need to get proper lights set up here, you know,' said the Senior SOCO, 'if you really want photos of that inscription.'

'Believe me,' said Tailby, 'I want *everything*.'

Chapter Four

THE YOUNG RANGER looked vaguely familiar to Ben Cooper. But then, he knew lots of Ropers – one of them had been his Maths teacher at school, another ran the garage on Buxton Road; and he had once arrested a Roper for indecency. They were all certain to be related.

Mark was a tall young man, with wide shoulders that didn't quite fit the rest of his body. His muscles had some catching up to do, but he was wiry and fit. Cooper noticed he had a small streak of vomit staining the front of his red Peak Park Rangers jacket. Somebody at the Partridge Cross Ranger Centre had made him several cups of tea. The tea had done nothing for his pallor, but at least his kidneys were working at full capacity. He emerged from the loo just as the police arrived.

Mark sat down unsteadily when DCI Tailby introduced himself and opened the questioning.

'I was patrolling the moor,' said Mark. 'Ringham Moor. I was on the path from the east, going towards the Virgins.'

'That's the stone circle.'

'It's just one of the stone circles. But it's the one that everybody knows.'

'All right.'

'I was near the Virgins when I saw a bike.'

'Hold on. Before that, did you see anyone else on the moor?'

'Nobody at all. It was quiet.'

'Nobody? Think right back to when you first left the centre.'

Mark looked automatically towards the window. Cooper followed his gaze. A silver Land Rover with a thin red stripe was parked outside. Beyond the Ranger Service sign on its roof, the dark hump of the moor was still visible against a pale sky.

'There was a man working in a field on this side of the moor, mending gates. I've seen him before. There was no one else.'

'OK. Describe this bike,' said Tailby.

Now Mark seemed to regain a bit more confidence. He produced a small notebook from the pocket of his fleece and turned the pages. But he spoke without looking at his notes. The scene was still fresh enough in his mind.

'It was a yellow Dawes. I recognized it as one of the hire bikes. It had been chucked into the bottom of a gorse bush, in the middle of some birch trees. One of the wheels was off too. I thought somebody had hired it and had an accident and just left it. They do things like that.'

'Who do?'

'Well, you know – the visitors. Tourists. They just leave a bike somewhere and say it's been stolen or they've lost it or something. You wouldn't believe the lies some of them tell.'

'Did you touch the bike?'

'No.'

'You're quite sure about that, Mark?'

'Yeah. I just looked for the number. Because I thought it was one of the hire bikes. And it was, wasn't it?'

'Yes, it was.' Cooper could hear the gratification in the DCI's voice. The fact it was a hire bike had made it so much easier to identify the victim. She had been obliged to leave her full name and address and proof of identity at the cycle hire centre when she took the bike out earlier that afternoon. So they had already established that her name was Jenny Weston, that she was thirty years old and divorced. She worked as a customer service manager in a large insurance office in Sheffield, and had taken a week's holiday because she had several days' leave to get in before the end of the year. By now, her parents had already been contacted, and her father was on his way to identify the body formally. If only it were always so easy.

'Then I saw something lying in the middle of the Virgins,' said Mark. 'I went to have a look. Although –'

'Yes?'

'Well … I could already see what it was. I could tell, from a few yards away, from where I found the bike. It was a woman. And she was dead.'

Mark moved his hands restlessly, brushing the front of his fleece. Cooper thought at first that he was trying to rub off the vomit stain, but realized he was wrong. The young Ranger was stroking the badge stitched to the fabric, fondling as if it were the breast of a lover, tracing the silver letters and the stylized millstone symbol of the Peak Park.

'Did you notice anything about the body?' asked Tailby.

Mark hesitated. 'Only that she was, you know …' His hands made half-hearted gestures. 'Her clothes …'

'You mean her clothes had been interfered with?'

Mark nodded.

'And did you notice anything else nearby? Anything unusual or out of place?'

'No.'

'So how close did you get to the body, Mark?'

'I walked as far as the nearest stone. The flat one. I didn't have to go any closer.'

'You were quite sure she was dead?'

'Oh yes,' said Mark. 'Oh yes.'

Mark suddenly went a shade whiter. His hand went over his mouth, and he made a dash for the loo. A second later, the police officers heard the sound of vomiting.

DCI Tailby sat for a moment longer, as if still listening for elusive bits of information in the Ranger's retching.

'Cooper, find that Area Ranger,' he said. 'He knows the lie of the land round here, if anybody does. Tell him we need to arrange proper access to the moor. We need the owner of the land or whoever. And we need to get into that quarry, too. Get on to it.'

BEN COOPER FOUND the Area Ranger waiting by his silver Land Rover outside the briefing centre. Owen Fox was in his early fifties, with grey hair and a thick beard that was going the same way. He was a comfortable badger of a man, with an even more comfortable smell of wool and earth.

'Mr Fox?'

The Ranger turned, with a distracted air. Though Cooper was wearing his dark green waxed jacket over civilian clothes, he thought Owen would recognize him as a policeman. People always seemed able to tell. They said it was something to do with the look in your eyes.

'Can I help?'

'I'm Detective Constable Cooper. If you've got time, I'd like to call on your local knowledge.'

Cooper explained that he had been given the job of opening up access to the disused quarry and of securing the route for vehicles to get to the crime scene.

'We need to see Warren Leach then,' said Owen.

'And he is . . .?'

'Ringham Edge Farm. He owns most of the moor. The old quarry road runs across his land. We can go in the Land Rover, if you like.'

The farm was reached by a back road out of the village of Ringham Lees, an almost invisible turning by the corner of the Druid pub. A group of a dozen or so youngsters were hanging around in a bus shelter near the pub. When they saw the lights of the Land Rover coming, two teenage boys ran across the road directly in front of its bonnet and stood laughing and waving from the opposite pavement.

'Some of these young people,' said Owen. 'Their common sense has left home before them. And it didn't give a forwarding address.'

'We get a lot like them in Edendale,' said Cooper.

'I bet you do.'

The Ranger had four radio sets in the cab of the Land Rover. The wide-band set under the dashboard was constantly scanning the channels for the Ranger Service and other local organizations. Another set was for the Mountain Rescue team. Behind the seats, fixed to a wire grille, were two battery-operated handsets on permanent charge for when they were needed. Cooper saw that there was also a satellite positioning device in a leather case. But the best-used piece of equipment seemed to be the vacuum flask. It was battered, but no doubt a welcome sight on a freezing day on the moors.

'Some of this technology is all right,' said Owen. 'But we'll be completely computerized one day. I only hope it's after my time. I was brought up to think "online" meant your mum had just put the washing out.'

Cooper laughed. 'Did you say this Leach owns the moor?'

'Part of it. It's all privately owned, one way or another. The PDNPA doesn't own any land, you know. Being a national park doesn't mean what people think it means.'

'No, I know.'

'But Ringham Moor is one of those places where the landowners have an access agreement with the national park, so Rangers are involved a lot. Especially with the attention the Nine Virgins get. They seem to have a special significance at the summer solstice – a bit like Stonehenge, you know? There can be two hundred or so people gathered up there – illegally, I might add, under the access agreement; not to mention the by-laws covering ancient monuments.'

'But what do they get up to exactly?'

'Oh, you wouldn't believe it. Music, jugglers, camp fires. Children and dogs running round. It's a bit like a medieval fair. One year we had to call in a mountain rescue team to carry off a young lady who'd been dancing from stone to stone, but fell off and broke her leg. Every year I pray it will rain – it keeps things quiet for a change.'

'So much for the peace and quiet of the Peak District.'

'Peace and quiet? One of our biggest jobs is looking after the safety of visitors. None of them have any common sense. If we left the fences off the old mine shafts, half of them would throw themselves in, thinking it was a new visitor experience.'

Owen Fox had a direct gaze and a sly smile in his eyes when he made a joke, though his face hardly moved. It took a bit of careful listening to understand when he was joking.

'I wouldn't want to work anywhere else, though,' said Owen. 'I've even picked the exact stone where I want my ashes to be scattered.'

They passed a large field containing a herd of black and white cattle and approached Ringham Edge Farm down a steep, narrow lane constricted between stone walls. The farm buildings were built mostly of the dark local gritstone, and the house itself had small, deeply-set windows that must let in little light. An extra shadow was thrown on the house by a large modern shed some distance from the track. Close to the shed stood the burnt-out shell of what looked like a Mitsubishi pick-up, the paint stripped from its bodywork and the interior of the cab blackened. Many farmers had the habit of letting all sorts of junk accumulate around their farm buildings.

Owen glanced at Cooper. 'Would it be best if I talked to him?'

'Leach? Is he likely to be difficult?'

'He can be. He needs handling right. Sometimes you have to let people think they're getting their own way.'

'Even when they aren't?'

'Well. Sometimes. You do know, don't you …'

'What?'

'It was Warren Leach's wife Yvonne who found that other woman a few weeks ago.'

'Of course – Maggie Crew.'

'She got as far as one of the fields at Ringham Edge. Yvonne Leach came across her lying unconscious under a wall. Leach himself just reckoned it was a nuisance, I think. It kept him away from his work for a bit. But this old quarry road is mainly used as a footpath now. It's a public right of way, and it runs right through the farm. When you have strangers walking past your door all the time, you can soon get to see them as an irritation. Some visitors think farmers are there as a public service, for providing toilets and telephones, or for pulling their cars out of ditches with their tractors. I can't blame Warren – not really.'

When Owen Fox and Ben Cooper pulled up in the Land Rover, they found two boys in a brightly lit byre. They were fussing over a Jersey heifer calf with huge eyes and long black lashes. The animal stood patiently, twitching her damp nostrils with pleasure as she was brushed on each flank until her red coat gleamed. One of the boys reached out to stroke the calf's muzzle, and she responded with a rasp of a plump tongue across his hand which made the boy smile with pleasure. Behind them, a wooden board was decorated with red and blue rosettes with long ribbons.

'Is this the calf that won at Bakewell Show?' asked Owen.

The boys looked uncertain what to say. Maybe they had been told not to talk to strangers, thought Cooper. But the Ranger wasn't really a stranger, was he? He had been to the farm before; he knew Warren Leach. It was part of the Area Ranger's job to maintain good relations with the farmers and landowners on his patch.

'Yeah, this is her. She's called Doll,' said the older boy.

'You're Will, aren't you?' said Owen. 'I can't remember your brother's name.'

'He's Dougie.'

Owen walked slowly towards the calf, hushing her quietly as she shied away and rolled her eyes at him. The boys held on to the halter nervously. But the animal calmed down when Owen began to talk to her, stroking her nose, gently following the lie of her coat along the side of her muzzle. He rubbed her shoulder to feel the firmness of the muscle and ran his hand down her spine. The calf relaxed under his touch.

'She's a beauty, lads. In superb condition. She's a real credit to you.'

'Thanks,' said Will. Dougie appeared to be about to add something, but changed his mind.

Both boys seemed shy, but the younger one was particularly uncommunicative. Cooper wasn't used to silent children. There were several kids of Will and Dougie's age in his own family – nephews and nieces and second cousins. But none of them was so quiet. They were too noisy, if anything. These days, children were no longer seen and not heard. It was when you could neither see *nor* hear them that you began to worry, if you were a parent. That was when they were at risk.

But these two were different. They had a reticence about them, a watchfulness that bordered on hostility, as if they had learned to be afraid of visitors.

'Will you be showing her again next year?' asked Owen.

That seemed to have been the wrong thing to say. The boys' faces fell, and Dougie looked as though he might cry.

'Your dad will take you to the show, won't he?'

Will shook his head. Now Cooper started to feel uncomfortable. 'Where is your dad?' he said.

'Up at the workshop.' Will pointed to the back of the house. The two boys looked relieved when they walked away and followed the roadway to a yard, where a metallic clanging came from a shed. Owen stuck his head through the doorway.

'Warren? Good evening.'

Warren Leach looked up from a bench lit by a dim work-lamp. He was a man with almost no neck. His torso, thick and solid, without a single curve, erupted into bulging shoulders with trapezius muscles that almost reached the line of his jaw. He was wearing blue overalls, with a wide leather belt strapped round his waist.

'Oh, it's you,' he said gruffly. 'It never rains but it pours round here, does it? What do you want?'

'Well, it might have been a friendly social call,' said Owen.

Leach snorted. 'Oh aye. Did you come past the shippon?'

'We did.'

'I suppose you saw those lads of mine. Are they still messing with that bloody animal?'

'They look as though they're doing a grand job with her, Warren. She's in fine condition.'

'Oh aye. Fine. And so she should be. The animal gets spoiled rotten. She's fed better than any of us.'

The farmer was fiddling with a steel coupling pin from a trailer's towing bracket. The pin trailed a short length of chain, which he swung irritably between his fingers.

'What's up now then, Ranger?'

'Warren, the police need to get access for their vehicles up through here for a while.'

'Oh?'

'On account of the woman killed up there. You know about that.'

Leach shrugged. 'It's no business of mine.'

'It's your land, Warren,' said Fox patiently.

'Is it part of the access agreement then? Some tourist gets herself done in and I have to put up with this lot roaring backwards and forwards over my land like maniacs?' Leach jabbed a finger in Cooper's direction, effortlessly identifying him as what he was. 'Well, it must have been in the small print, Ranger, because I missed it.'

'Can you leave that top gate open for the police vehicles to get on to the moor, please?'

'Leave it open? Why? They can open and close a gate like anyone else, can't they? Or have coppers lost the use of their hands as well as their feet these days?'

'It doesn't do to make the police think you're being obstructive,' said Owen.

'They can think what the hell they like.'

Cooper stayed silent, ignoring the aggressive glare. He was well used to it from the yobbos of Edendale. The only surprise was to see it in a middle-aged Dales farmer. But it was best to let Owen Fox deal with it – it was a chance for him to use his Ranger diplomacy.

'I suppose I might just have a word with Yvonne then, before I go,' said Owen.

'What for? She's got nothing to say to you.'

'Just being polite.'

Leach grunted, and the chain tightened in his thick hands until the steel links squealed against each other.

'It'll mean I'll have to move the cows down to the next field,' he said.

'Well, that's no problem, is it?'

'No problem? The grass is nearly finished in there. My milk yields'll be gone to hell. They're down already with all this disturbance.'

'It'll only be for a day or two, Warren.'

'Would there be compensation, maybe? The police have got money. My money, from the Council Tax.'

'I can't imagine so. Think of it as a public service.'

Owen looked at Cooper, but Cooper just smiled.

'Balls to that,' said Leach.

'Come on, Warren.'

Leach tossed the coupling pin into his other hand, slapping it against his palm. On a plastic drum, he had a square leather-bound case with steel clasps. Cooper wondered what it was. Somehow it didn't look like a piece of farming equipment, more the sort of thing a doctor might carry his kit in for testing a patient's blood pressure.

'Only for a day or two, and that's it,' said Leach. 'Tell your police friends they'll have to get a move on. Let 'em work the same hours that I have to work to keep this farm going, instead of knocking off for tea every five minutes. I've seen it going on. I'm not stupid.'

'Thank you, sir,' said Cooper politely. But the farmer only glowered. 'When would be convenient for an officer to come and talk to you?'

'What?'

'We need to take a statement from you. You're well positioned here to be a witness.'

'A witness to what? I went through all this with that other bloody woman that ended up on my land. I never saw this one either.'

'Do you know who she was?'

'Of course not.'

'Then how do you know you didn't see her?' Cooper smiled. 'Somebody will probably call tomorrow to see you.'

The two men began to walk back towards the Ranger's Land Rover.

'I'll be back to see you soon, Warren,' said Owen.

'Don't bother, Ranger. As soon as I see that red jacket of yours, I'll be halfway to Bakewell.'

THEY ALMOST RAN right into Yvonne Leach in the gateway as they drove out of the yard. She was a small woman, with wide hips and strands of light brown hair tied loosely back from her face. Owen stopped the Land Rover, and the woman shied away, as nervous as a sheep, rolling her eyes at the vehicle. But she couldn't slip past quickly enough.

Owen wound down the window. 'Yvonne – all right?'

'Yes.'

'We've just had a word with Warren. I wanted to tell you not to worry about what happened up there. There are plenty of police about here. You'll be OK.'

'I'm not worried,' said Yvonne, though to Cooper's eye she looked as scared as any woman he had ever seen.

Warren Leach's angry bellow came from the yard. 'Hey, what do you think you're doing? Get in the house.' They looked round and saw him glaring at Yvonne. She took the chance of sliding along the side of the Land Rover and scuttling round the corner.

Owen drove on up the track. They had to open two gates to get any further, and the Ranger took it slowly to avoid alarming the cows.

'Marriage,' he said, after a minute.

'What about it?' said Cooper.

'The most bizarre thing ever invented, in my opinion. You must see what I mean, in your job. Couples tied together for no apparent reason, making each other's lives a misery. Isn't marriage one of the major factors in crime? Domestics, you call them. Aren't ninety per cent of murders committed by the spouse?'

'Something like that.'

'Well, I rest my case. Weddings ought to be banned, along with other blood sports.'

'I thought the police were cynical, but I don't think I've reached your stage, yet,' said Cooper.

Then Owen looked at Cooper sideways and waggled his eyebrows. 'I can see you're not married yourself. You don't have that harassed look. You weren't thinking about it, by any chance, were you?'

'Well ...' Cooper considered the answer for a moment. 'I suppose it's kind of the way I see my life going, some day.'

'Mmm. Well, close your eyes or look the other way, then.'

THE RANGER PULLED the Land Rover on to a flat area of bare earth under a stand of beech trees. They were about two hundred feet further up towards the moor, looking down on the farm buildings and the fields around them. Beyond the farm was the village of Ringham Lees, its lights just visible in the trees in the valley bottom; and further away in the darkness, almost hidden by a spur of hill, were the spires of the two churches in the bigger village of Cargreave.

'Tell your lot they can park here,' said Owen. 'The Virgins are just over the rise. That way to the right leads into Top Quarry. Just ask if you want anything else. They say I'm the man who knows these parts.'

Cooper found the cab of the Land Rover was comfortable and warm, full of things that had a practical use, yet without the slightest conscious attempt at imposing the driver's personality.

'Do you live locally, Owen?' he asked.

'I've got a house over there in Cargreave.'

'I take it you're not married either?'

'Me? You must be joking. I may not be Einstein, but I'm not that stupid.'

'A bad experience?'

'Other people's experiences are enough for me, mate. I've watched them all go the same way. Those young lads that you meet, full of enthusiasm and vitality, all their lives in front of them. And what happens? A wife and a mortgage. Before you know it, they're coming into work half-asleep because the new baby's kept them awake all night, and then they're moving house to make room for all the family. In the end, they have to get a new job that they hate, just so that they can pay for it all. It's like getting a life sentence without having the pleasure of committing the crime, the poor sods. Not for me. There's just me and the cats, since Mother died.'

'Was that recently?' asked Cooper. The loss of his own father was recent enough to make him curious about someone else's experience of the death of a parent.

'It was a year ago. She was very old, of course. And she never feared death, that was a consolation. I used to take her to church until she couldn't get there any more. But she could see the church tower from her bedroom, and that seemed to be enough at the end.'

'And your father?'

'Oh, he's been gone a long time.'

'Don't you find that losing a parent makes the one that's left seem very precious?' said Cooper.

Owen looked at him cautiously. 'Yes, you're right. Actually, I think I might have worked with *your* father a time or two.'

'Yes,' said Cooper. 'I'm sure you did.'

After a moment's silence, Owen chuckled into his beard. 'No, I'm on my own. I'm a happy bachelor. Young, free and single, that's me. Well … two out of three's not bad. Nobody's really free.'

Cooper nodded. But he wasn't thinking about Owen Fox. He was thinking of Yvonne Leach and the two boys he had seen at Ringham Edge Farm. It was one thing to live a life restricted by obligations, in the way that Owen described. But it was another thing altogether when it was fear that ruled your life.

And Cooper's instincts told him that what he had seen at the farm was exactly that. It might be superficially concealed from the outside world, but it was bubbling very close to the surface. The Leaches were people whose lives were ruled by fear.

Chapter Five

SINCE DIANE FRY had arrived, the woman had kept her face turned away towards the window. The light from the desk lamp fell only on her left side, outlining her profile, delineating a high cheekbone and a straight nose. It highlighted the gold in a strand of hair tucked behind her ear, and it threw unmerciful shadows on the fine lines etched into the skin of her neck.

The apartment she lived in was austere, with minimal modern furniture, scrupulously clean, and cold, harsh lighting that created stark lines between light and shade. It was as if the rooms had been designed so that someone moving around in their cool spaces could know precisely where the shadows fell, where details were distinct and where they were not. Fry pictured the woman rehearsing her positioning in these rooms like an actress walking about a stage, seeking the best angle, presenting her most favourable side to the audience. On the other hand, perhaps she moved through the shadows by instinct alone – the instinct of a wounded animal. Because there was no mirror in this room to examine the effect in. No mirror, but a pale patch on the wall where one had once hung.

Maggie Crew sat behind a desk, as if conducting a formal interview with a client. On the desk, there were only a few items – a telephone, an ashtray, a paper knife. Along the side wall were a couple of shelves of law books and journals and a stereo system, finished in matt black, with neat racks of CD cases, their titles too small for Fry to make out.

Behind Maggie was a big sash window looking out over the roofs of Matlock. It had a view down the Derwent Valley to the point where it narrowed into a high gorge, with a hill above it that had been hacked and blasted into pieces by quarrying. Heavy green drapes hung from a brass rail over the window, capable of shutting out the natural light entirely during the day. Apart from that, there was little ornamentation in the room. The furnishings spoke to Fry of pretension without showiness, a subtle statement of the owner's disregard for the comfort of her surroundings. According to the reports, Crew spent all her time in this apartment now, shut away from the world. It wasn't difficult to understand why. She had been an attractive woman once.

'My name is Diane Fry, Maggie.'

Maggie nodded. She wore a man's Calvin Klein cube-design watch, all minimalist straight lines. A pad of

A4 ruled paper lay near her hand, with a silver ballpoint pen. But she made no move to write down Fry's name.

'I've been asked to work with you for a while, Maggie. If that's all right with you, of course.'

'You know I've already agreed to this. Although I don't know what good it will do.'

'I want to go through with you again anything you can remember. Any little detail may help us.'

Where you might have expected Maggie Crew to have let her hair grow long to cover the disfigurement, it was cut short, trimmed clear of her forehead. The left side of her face was smooth and white, her cheeks like the skin of someone who had spent too long in the dark. Her hands, too, were pale, the backs of them flat and shapeless. Fry wondered if Maggie was a woman who struggled against gaining weight. But she was not fat now. Her cheekbones were visible in her face, her shoulders were prominent under the fabric of a black jacket. Fry herself liked to wear black. But on Maggie it seemed to be more than practicality or an attempt to make herself look slimmer; more, even, than a fashion statement. There was an emotion in the blackness, a dark outer show to match her feelings, to fit the atmosphere of the room. It was a sort of mourning.

'What happened to the last one?' said Maggie.

'We just thought a change of personnel might help. A new approach ...'

'A fresh face.' Maggie smiled. She had small, white teeth, but her upper lip drew back a fraction too far, exposing a strip of pink gum and removing the humour from her smile.

'So.' She stared at Fry, measuring her like a potential employee, a candidate for a domestic's job. 'Diane Fry. What is different about *you*, then?'

'There's nothing different about me. I'm just here to talk to you.'

'Do you know how many people have said that?'

'It's all in your file,' said Fry. 'I know your history.'

'Ah, yes. You've read my file. So you have the advantage of coming here knowing absolutely everything about me. How helpful that must be. Perhaps you think you know more about me than I do myself. Perhaps you think you know how my mind is working, exactly how you might manipulate my subconscious?'

'Nobody wants to manipulate you, Maggie.'

'Then what *do* you want? What is it you all want with me? Don't you know by now that I can't give it to you? Isn't *that* in my file?'

'If we keep trying –'

'You think you might be able to make me remember. Then what? My memories might be able to help *you*, yes. But what will they do to me? What if I don't want to remember? What if my subconscious has wiped out the memories?'

'Do you think that's the case?'

'The doctors say there is no physiological reason for the memory loss. There is no damage to my brain. They tell me it's probably shock; they call it trauma. They say it's a safety device, which shuts down memories that the brain doesn't want. Wipes them out.'

Fry watched her, trying to hide the scepticism in her face. She heard the words, and recognized some of the phrases from the medical reports. But she didn't believe that you could wipe out memories completely, no matter how unpleasant. They left their traces everywhere, in the overlooked corners of your mind, and in the sensations of your body – the touch of your skin against your clothes, the sudden devastating echo in a sound, or the malignant resonance of a smell. Memories were cancerous growths, secretive and spiteful; sometimes you didn't know they were there until it was too late. Diane Fry knew all about memories.

'This is just an introductory meeting,' she said. 'I'll come back to talk to you again tomorrow, Maggie. If that's all right with you.'

'If you must.'

'It's very important now.'

'Ah.' Maggie hesitated. 'Does that mean you have another victim?'

'Yes, Maggie. And it's vital we catch this man before he kills again.'

Maggie stared at Diane Fry out of her good eye, assessing her sharply, staring with the unblinking curiosity of someone who rarely saw a new visitor.

'Kills?'

'Yes, it's murder this time. This victim died.'

Fry watched for a reaction. The trembling in Maggie's hands and the draining of the colour from her face gave Fry a small measure of satisfaction.

'We also want to put you on a witness protection programme. You know what that means?'

'Of course. Remember I'm a lawyer.'

'We'll ask you to consider finding somewhere else to stay, if possible, Maggie, until we think it's safe. In the meantime, a technician will call to install alarms in your apartment. You'll be given a phone number you can call at any time.'

Maggie took a moment to recover her composure. 'Is all that necessary?'

'Maggie, we're looking for a killer now. And you're the only person who can identify him.'

'I won't go away. I'm staying here.'

'But the other precautions ...' said Fry.

'All right. But there's one condition.'

'Yes?'

'If you're going to visit me, do not feel sorry for me. I won't talk to anyone who shows even the slightest sign of feeling sorry for me. Do you understand?'

'Of course.'

Diane Fry was glad when Maggie Crew turned away. Since she had met Maggie at the door of her apartment, it had taken her several minutes to settle down, to recover from the initial shock. The sight of her had made Fry's stomach muscles clench with vicarious pain as she tried to control her expression. But this woman must be used to such reactions by now.

Maggie Crew's face would never be the same again. The knife had sliced her apart. No plastic surgery could ever completely hide the long, ragged scar that mutilated her cheekbone, splitting her face into two halves like a zip, its raised lips still red and angry, the flesh stretched painfully tight. No surgeon would ever entirely smooth out the ridges of shredded and bruised skin that puckered the corner of her right eye, pulling down her bottom lid to expose the pink veins, and twisting the whole side of her face into a leer.

But there was more even than that. There was the psychological damage that had been done to Maggie Crew. Even to Diane Fry the damage was obvious, though she had never met the woman before. Maggie was a partner in a firm of solicitors in Matlock. She was a successful professional woman, used to feeling self-confident and sure of her own worth. But now she had lost that confidence; her image of herself had been ravaged, slashed to pieces by the knife that had torn her face.

Fry knew that the attack on Maggie had happened six weeks ago. As far as they could ascertain, she had been attacked somewhere near the Cat Stones, the line of rocks below the Hammond Tower, not half a mile from where Jenny Weston's body had been found. Maggie had been the lucky one. She had managed to stagger halfway off the moor before she collapsed from shock and loss of blood in the shelter of a wall, where she had been found by a farmer's wife next morning. The doctors said Maggie had been lucky, in that the knife had narrowly missed removing an eye. Fry hoped that nobody had tried telling Maggie herself that she was lucky.

Now Maggie was recovering at home. And that meant she had been sitting here, in this sparse room, hiding from the light.

'I suppose I should be frightened,' said Maggie.

'We're just taking precautions. No need to be frightened.'

'It would make a change – a change from finding people are frightened of me. They don't know how to react, most of them. They don't know what to say. They don't want to talk about my face. Do you want to talk about it? About what my injury means to me.'

Fry shrugged. 'Not particularly.'

Maggie looked surprised. Disappointed?

'They say plastic surgery might help. But not yet. The injury is too recent.'

'Yes, it takes time.'

'Oh, the body heals itself to a certain extent, in time. The blood clots, the wounds close over, fresh skin grows. They can do wonders with surgery, they keep telling me. But it's never quite the same, is it? You can't rebuild the original tissue, and your body remembers the injury. You're always marked in some way.'

The file said that Maggie Crew had received the appropriate counselling. She had gone through all the consultations with a psychiatrist. She had been encouraged to write down her feelings, to talk to Victim Support. The police had treated her with kid gloves for a time. But at the end of the day, they weren't getting what they wanted. Maggie Crew knew far more than she had told them. She had seen her assailant and survived. He was the same man, they now suspected, who had killed Jenny Weston. It was at this moment, more than ever, that they needed the information locked in Maggie's head.

Fry wondered how secure the apartment was. It occupied part of the second floor of Derwent Court, a converted spa hotel, a relic of the town's Victorian past as a health resort. The building had stood derelict for years before an influx of county council office workers had boosted the demand for housing in Matlock. Now comfortably-off residents lived at the end of its marble corridors and stared all day at an expensive view over the Derwent Valley, counting the cable cars as they ferried tourists to the Heights of Abraham.

At least there was a concierge in the lobby downstairs. She would have to have a word with him before she left – he would be able to keep an extra careful eye out for visitors to Derwent Court.

She stared out of the window into the darkness. The quarry-blasted hillside stood out white and stark on the skyline to the south. No attempt had been made to repair or disguise the damage that had been done to the landscape by the mineral companies. The scars had been left as a symbolic reminder, a legacy of the past. And perhaps as a warning too. A warning of what might easily happen again one day – if no one did anything to prevent it.

'Yes, some things take time,' said Maggie. 'Other things take a miracle.'

BEN COOPER HAD already formed a clear idea in his mind of what Jenny Weston had been like. There had been no shortage of details there, for once. The entry in the log at the cycle hire centre had given them the basics. Not only that, but the cycle hire manager knew which car was hers. Once they had got access to it, they had found her handbag in the glove compartment, with her diary and all the information they could possibly want, written on the front page in her own hand. It listed not only the name, address and phone number of her next of kin, but also Jenny's date of birth, her National Insurance number, the numbers of her bank account and her mobile phone, the names of her doctor, dentist and vet, her religion, the address of her insurance company, her National Trust membership number, her height and weight, and her shoe size. And her blood group.

And then her father, Eric Weston, had lost no time arriving from his home at Alfreton as soon as they contacted him. Cooper had arrived back at Partridge Cross from Ringham Edge Farm just in time to sit in on the interview with DCI Tailby. Mr Weston had been all too willing to tell them about his daughter. He recited the details eagerly, as if he needed to remind himself, too, of who Jenny was. Of who she had been.

Jenny had been married at twenty-one. Her husband, Martin Stafford, had not been liked by her parents. Police officers heard that one often, of course. Very few parents thought the men their daughters chose were good enough. But in this case, Stafford had lasted about three and a half years before his violent nature became obvious. Jenny had stayed with him another two years before they had finally parted.

The story was a familiar one. A woman abused, yet reluctant to believe that there wasn't something worth preserving in her marriage; convinced, somehow, that her man did what he did because he loved her. It seemed incredible to Cooper that some women continued to expect far too much of marriage. Their beliefs died hard.

Mr Weston was deputy head teacher of one of the Eden Valley secondary schools. He had that rather weary and worn look that identified middle-aged teachers. His hair was mostly on the back of his head, curly and untidy, and not trimmed on his neck for a long time. He wore a grey suit, but there were shiny patches on the trousers and an indefinable scent that reminded Cooper of his own school days. Chalk and musty text books, school dinners and badly washed schoolboys.

It seemed that Mr Weston was inclined to blame Martin Stafford for Jenny's death. This was despite the fact that, as far as he was aware, the two of them hadn't seen each other for three years.

'It would be just like him to have got in touch again, and for Jenny to agree to meet him, without telling us,' he said.

'Do you know where Mr Stafford lives now?' asked Tailby.

'No, I don't. I think Jenny knew. But she never told us that, either.'

'Why?'

'She thought we would interfere. We were so worried about her. She never seemed to see sense where that man was concerned.'

'There are no children from the marriage?'

'No.'

'That's fortunate, I suppose?'

'I'm not sure about that,' said Mr Weston.

Jenny had met Stafford while she was a student at the University of Derby. He had been a journalist then, working at the city's *Evening Telegraph* – a senior reporter with a flair for off-beat features, or so he had said. According to Mr Weston, Stafford had cultivated a knowing, cynical image, had drunk too much and had cared about little except himself and his career.

'Jenny was studying to be a radiologist,' he said. 'She was already in the third year of her course, and doing really well. She could have had a good career ahead of her, if it hadn't been for Stafford. She met him in a pub in Derby, and he made a beeline for her. She was an attractive girl. And far too trusting.'

'What happened?'

'She became completely besotted with him. She wouldn't listen to us when we told her to put her studies first, that her own career was more important. In the end, she gave up her studies to marry Stafford when he asked her to. She said she wanted to start a family with him. We had to accept it.'

'But you said there were no children?'

'No children. Only divorce.'

Even the divorce had come only after a series of short-lived reconciliations which were, according to Jenny's father, simply Martin Stafford's demonstrations of his ability to manipulate their daughter. He had some inexplicable power over her, and he was reluctant to give it up. The situation dragged on for a long time, painfully and unsatisfactorily.

'When it was all over, Jenny managed to get a job with Global Assurance in Derby,' said Mr Weston. 'But then she had to move to their new call centre when it was built in Sheffield. We didn't like it. It meant she was away from us, away from her family. She went to live alone in that little terraced house off the Ecclesall Road. It was too far away. All she had with her was her blessed cat, not even a dog. Her mother was very upset. She worried about what might happen to her. We both did.'

'You were worried that Mr Stafford might try to get back in touch with her?'

'Yes, of course. And that we wouldn't know about it. Anything could have happened.'

'But it didn't.'

'Well … not so far as we know.'

Mr Weston tried to recall a quick succession of boyfriends after Jenny had moved to Sheffield. All of them, he was sure, were men who were completely wrong for her. To Ben Cooper, Jenny sounded as though she had gone through those men like a woman looking for something she would never find, a woman whose better judgement had been cast aside. For what? A kind of penance? At one point, there had been an abortion. Jenny had not told her father at the time. His wife had told him about it, much later.

'That was something I could never understand,' he said. He shook his head, and Cooper saw the glitter of tears in the teacher's eyes. 'I never will understand it. Jenny always wanted children.'

And Jenny had hated her job, too. She had been good at it, had been promoted to supervisor, with twenty-five girls working for her. She had responsibilities and a better salary; she was well regarded by her employers and liked by her colleagues. But she had hated it.

'She said it was a sweatshop. She really disliked that. She kept talking about the pressure, unattainable targets, the constant surveillance by managers to make sure you were always working, the tedium, the repetitiveness, the strain of being polite all the time to customers who didn't want to speak to you. Oh, and the posters round the walls. They all said: "Smile".'

Jenny had also been depressed by the rate of burn-out among her staff – even the best of them lasting little more than twelve months in the job. Many sacrificed themselves, as Jenny saw it, to marriage and to raising a family, purely as a means of escape.

'She didn't even manage to make any proper friends. She said animals were preferable to people. It might have helped a lot if she could have made friends. But Jenny said she barely had a chance to get to know any of her colleagues before they were gone. All the new recruits to these call centres now are youngsters, straight from school into their induction training, pulling on their telephone headsets and believing that's what work is all about. In my position, I see them leaving school, full of hope, and I know what will happen to them. We do our best with them, you know, but that's how a lot of them end up. Very sad.'

'Did Jenny talk of escaping from the job?' asked Tailby.

'Oh yes. All the time.'

Of course she had talked of escaping; everyone did. She talked of working with animals, of being a veterinary nurse or running a wildlife sanctuary. But there was nothing she was qualified to do, and nowhere else she could go. Now and then she thought about her lost career as a radiologist. And those were the worst times, said Eric Weston. It was knowing it was too late that depressed her the most.

'The one thing that Jenny really loved was the Peak District,' said Mr Weston. 'We used to bring her here as a child at weekends and in the summer holidays. Days out in Dovedale and at Castleton. When she went to university she joined a student walking club and they hiked over all the hills in the area. They did the whole of the Pennine Way one summer, staying at youth hostels. It was where she always came back to.'

Later, after her divorce, Jenny had again spent as much time as she could in the Peak District, walking, but often alone, since friends didn't seem to last long. She had tried pony trekking a few times, said Mr Weston. But recently she had taken to mountain biking. She had her own bike at home, but had preferred to hire a bike from Peak Cycle Hire or from one of the Derbyshire County Council hire centres. Often she rode the trails created from the old railway lines. But at times, when she felt the need, she would leave the trails and set off on to the moors.

'Yes, Ringham Moor was one of her favourite places,' said Mr Weston. 'We went there once as a family, many years ago. Jenny and John – that's her brother – and Susan and me, a happy family together.'

And Mr Weston added that he thought, perhaps, Jenny might have been trying to recapture happy memories, a happiness that had escaped her in other ways. He didn't know what had prompted her to take to the moors on that particular day. He didn't know why she had headed for Ringham. He had no more answers to give.

Ben Cooper had walked away from the interview dissatisfied. Jenny Weston had not been anyone out of the ordinary. She had achieved nothing exceptional, and nothing extraordinary had happened to her during her lifetime. Could she really just have been another woman who had made all the wrong choices? If so, Jenny had been making the wrong choices right up until the moment she died. And one of those choices had been fatal.

Chapter Six

THE KITCHEN WAS the room the Coopers used most at Bridge End Farm. It had that familiar lived-in look which was inevitable with six people in the house, two of them children. Though Ben Cooper still lived at the farm, he had begun to find himself spending less and less time in the company of his brother and his family. He wasn't sure why this was, when his mother was still upstairs and in need of his support.

Matt had already been driven indoors by the darkness that was steadily drawing in now. He sat at the kitchen table with *Farmers Weekly*, reading articles predicting more gloom for the farming industry. In the sitting room, Matt's wife Kate and their daughters were watching cartoons on the TV.

'We'll be visiting Dad's grave next week,' said Cooper. 'It's the anniversary.'

'As if I would forget,' said Matt.

Matt turned the page of his magazine, but he no longer seemed to be focusing on the words. 'Don't say anything to Mum,' he said. 'You know it only upsets her. Now she's stable, it would be nice if we could keep it like that for a while, rather than causing another episode like the last one. It's not fair on the girls.'

'We can't just say nothing,' said Cooper. 'She'd be devastated if she knew we'd been to the cemetery without her.'

'But if she really hasn't remembered? Do we risk starting her off again? She's been doing so well recently. It could set her back months, going over it all again, just because it's the anniversary. It would be a kindness to let her forget.'

'I don't think it's honest,' said Cooper.

'Some things are best not remembered. With luck, her memory will let her down.'

'So schizophrenia can be a blessing. That's nice to know.'

'I didn't mean that, and you know it.' Matt put down the *Farmers Weekly* wearily and rubbed his face. 'I'm sorry. It's just –' He shrugged. 'There's no end to it, is there?'

The brothers didn't need to say any more to each other. It had all been said before, many times.

Kate looked in from the sitting room, releasing a burst of cartoon noise as she opened the door. Matt picked up his magazine again. Cooper had a book on the shelf that he was halfway through reading – *Captain Corelli's*

Mandolin. He always seemed to be years behind what everybody else was talking about. There was so little time to read. And often, like now, he couldn't concentrate on what was in front of him.

'Matt, do you know a farmer called Warren Leach?'

'Leach? Leach ... Where does he farm?'

'Ringham Edge.'

Matt frowned over his pages. 'I've heard of him. I don't think I've ever met him to speak to. Dark-haired bloke, miserable sort?'

'That sounds like him.'

'What's he done?'

'Nothing that I know of. I just came across him on an enquiry.'

'Ringham Edge. Small dairy herd, is it? And a lot of marginal land?'

'Yes.'

Matt nodded and went back to his magazine. He turned a page, but found nothing he liked any better.

'You know, some of them are in deep trouble,' he said.

'Who?'

'Farmers like Leach at Ringham Edge. Small-scale livestock farmers, with no chance of diversification. But he's only one of many, of course.'

'Things looked pretty depressing up there, I must admit.'

'It's all pretty depressing. All of it.'

'Come on, Matt. It's not that bad.'

'Yes, it is. It's all gone to hell. I can't see the time when farming will ever be the same again. Not around here, anyway. All the small farmers are going out of business. It's too much for them. Far too much.'

'Have you heard anything specific about Leach?'

Matt shook his head firmly. 'I said I've seen him, that's all. I don't actually know him.'

'But I expect you might know people who do.'

'I expect I might,' said Matt.

'There could be rumours about him. Farmers talk to each other, don't they? Down at the mart.'

Matt's face set into stubborn lines. 'Are you asking me to find out things about this bloke Leach?'

'Just … I wondered if you might hear anything, you know. If you did …'

'Sorry, Ben.'

'What?'

'I mean, no, I won't do it. I don't much like being asked to be some sort of secret policeman. I don't like being asked to be a policeman at all, come to that. You're welcome to that job.'

Kate stood in the doorway. She frowned at Ben and shook her head, scenting an argument between the brothers. She said arguments upset the children. And she was right to be protective – there had been enough disruption in their young lives.

So Ben Cooper said nothing, just nursed his thoughts to himself. He and Matt had never talked about their father properly. Not ever, in the whole of their lives. And when he died, it was too late to start. Yet Cooper longed to know what his brother felt; he wanted to be able to tell him what his own feelings were, how much he had come to resent the memory of their father, and how much that resentment hurt because it was such a contradiction to the way he had viewed him when he was alive. He felt as though he was trampling a fallen idol.

But he suspected that their father still was an idol, of a kind, for Matt. And it was the police that Matt blamed for their father's death.

Matt could have found out about Warren Leach, if he wanted to. He was right, of course – there were many farmers in trouble. There were farms left standing empty all around the Peak District now. At first, they had been snapped up by wealthy incomers, people who boasted of having 'a country house with a big garden', and thought it was a huge joke. Worst of all were the people who played at farming, filling a paddock with rare breeds of sheep, a Vietnamese pot-bellied pig, a donkey and a goat. They drove the real farmers to apoplexy.

And already buyers were getting choosier. Some of the older, more run-down farms that were coming on the market stayed unsold for many months. New owners could no longer rely on selling the land that went with them to provide the capital for work on the house. Neighbouring farmers didn't want the land – they couldn't afford it. And if it was difficult land, the high hill land, it was useless to them anyway. All they could keep on it were a few sheep, which themselves were worth next to nothing.

Cooper went upstairs and looked in at his mother's bedroom. She was sleeping, and her face was peaceful. He could always tell from her face the state of her mind;

the turmoil in her brain was reflected in the contortions of her expression, even in her sleep.

Satisfied, he got washed and changed and went back down to the kitchen. The girls, Amy and Josie, had joined their parents at the table, and the room was full of noise and life. Cooper waved goodbye and walked down the passage to the back door.

For a moment, he stood and looked at the farm. The outline of the buildings became clear as his eyes adjusted to the darkness. He could hear the cattle moving quietly, one of the dogs snuffling in the yard, a pheasant cackling, startled by some predator perhaps. Beyond the barn, the dark bulk of the hill came slowly into focus, its crown bare against the sky, but its middle faintly ragged, where the tree line followed the contours of the valley.

Most of the fields down here at Bridge End were good, rich land. They had inherited the farm from their maternal grandfather, who had died at some vast age, still tottering about the place in his ancient shiny black suit and his army boots, with baling twine tied round his trouser bottoms. Officially, the farm had passed to their mother, and still belonged to her. But Matt had been the one to run it, right from the beginning, when he was barely a year or two out of agricultural college and working as a cowman on a big tenanted farm at Rowsley.

Their father, Joe Cooper, had never been interested in the farm. He had been happy to let Matt take charge, though occasionally rolling up his sleeves on his off-duty days to help stack bales of hay or round up the sheep. Joe had been a big, powerful man. It ought to have been Ben

Cooper's abiding memory of him – tall and strong, with heavily muscled forearms and his huge hands wielding a pitchfork, his shirt open at his neck instead of buttoned up with a service tie at his throat, maybe laughing and at ease with his sons. But that wasn't Ben's lasting memory. Nothing like it.

Cooper wondered what the future of the farm would be. So many farmers were getting out – going bankrupt or just clearing out of the industry while they could. Pastures had been left to grow weeds and bracken encroached rapidly on to the higher fields, until some farms were like sores on the Peak. It was the farmers, after all, who had looked after the landscape of the national park. Within a generation or two, their absence would change the appearance of the countryside altogether.

A family that lost their farm would join the drift away from the Peak District into the soulless housing estates of the big cities, signing on to the list of unemployed in Sheffield or Manchester while their old homes were taken over by affluent city dwellers, their farmland converted into golf courses or pony trekking centres. To Ben Cooper, it was a neglected tragedy, a kind of surreptitious ethnic cleansing that would never trouble the United Nations.

He felt a familiar object bump his foot by the door. This strangely shaped lump of stone had stood by the back door of the farmhouse for decades, maybe for centuries. It was roughly rounded, with a broader base and a hollow in the middle, with a hole hacked through the bottom.

Everyone had used the stone as a boot scraper or a container for loose screws, until Cooper had seen a photograph in a local history book of an identical object. It was described in the caption as an Iron Age quern, used for grinding corn. It was two thousand years old.

The quern still stood by the back door of Bridge End Farm, unaltered from the last day it had been used for grinding corn. It had been emptied of screws and cleaned up. No boots were scraped on it now. The quern had always stood where it was, as far as anybody knew, so there was no suggestion of moving it. It was preserved for posterity. But nobody used it any more.

BEFORE COOPER COULD get out of the house, Kate called to him from the passageway.

'Ben, Helen Milner rang earlier this evening. She sounded a bit upset. She said you were supposed to be meeting her. I told her you were probably working.'

Cooper winced. Helen would have turned up at the rugby club looking for him – they'd had a date tonight. They'd been going out together for only two months. He knew all too well how she would interpret the way he had stood her up.

'I meant to phone her, but I completely forgot.'

'That's what I thought,' said Kate. 'And Helen didn't sound too surprised, either.'

THERE WAS NO one waiting at home for Diane Fry when she pulled on to the drive at Grosvenor Avenue. The old house was converted into flats and bedsits, and her neighbours were mostly students that she rarely saw. They seem to spend most of their time in the pub.

Her room was cold, with a peculiar damp chill that seeped from the walls even in summer. She was already realizing what an uncomfortable, depressing experience a winter in Edendale was going to be. The three-bar electric fire barely chased the chill from the room. And it ate money from the meter at an alarming rate.

She wound down with a few stretching exercises, until her body tingled comfortably. She couldn't remember when she had eaten last, and there was no food in the flat. But fasting was good for the body. It made her stomach feel tight and her brain active. She had found that eating meals caused her digestive system to drain her energy. Fry examined herself in the mirror. There was no injury to be seen on her own face. But it didn't mean there was no scar. It meant only that it was the sort of scar that nobody else could see, that no one else could tell the way she was marked. That was how she was so much luckier than Maggie Crew. So lucky.

Like Maggie, unwilling to reveal her disfigurement to the gaze of a stranger, Fry knew the bitter taste of resentment against someone who knew your innermost secrets. She had felt like telling Maggie that she ought to get out and face people. But surely it was equally futile to try to avoid the person you resented.

'What an idiot,' she said, then mentally gave herself a reprimand for talking to herself. But she had meant it for Ben Cooper really, thinking of him buddying up so cosily with Todd Weenink. In the end, they were two of a kind. Besides, she thought, even Ben Cooper didn't know *all* her secrets.

FRY DROVE INTO Sheffield, gradually relaxing as the vast sprawl of houses and factories closed around her, shielding her from the dark hills she was leaving behind in Derbyshire. She had first travelled into the city when she needed to find a martial arts centre away from Edendale, where the *dojo* used by Ben Cooper had become a no-go zone. Seeing the city streets then had reminded her exactly why she had come to this area.

She went straight into the centre of the city, circled the ring road and parked in a multi-storey car park near one of the main shopping streets, The Moor. Then she walked back towards the transport interchange at the bottom of the hill and waited for the carriages of a Supertram to pass before crossing the road.

The old railway arches at this end of the city would disappear when modernization reached them. But for now, they were home to a small group of people. No, not a group – they were a series of individuals. They lay in sleeping bags, under filthy blankets and cardboard boxes, huddled close together, yet still in their own completely separate worlds, not speaking to each other or acknowledging anyone else at all. They had isolated themselves for their own protection. Fry knew that the human mind was capable of shutting out many things when necessary, even the close proximity of other people.

The canal passed under the railway line here. There was a lock full of scum-covered water, waiting to lift boats another ten feet towards the hills around the city. The spaces under the arches had once been used for workshops and storage areas. For years now they had been boarded up, but the boards had been ripped off the doorways, exposing deep, dank caverns it would be foolish to enter.

Fry waited by the lock gate. After a few minutes, a figure stepped out of the shadows at the back of the arch and came towards her. It was a woman, a few years younger than herself. Her eyes looked simultaneously beaten and defiant.

'I've not seen you around here before. What is it you want?'

Fry stared at her hard, but failed to see what she wanted to see. 'I'm just looking,' she said.

'Are you after sex? Drugs?'

'No.'

'You must be the cops, then.'

'I'm looking for this woman.'

Fry took the photograph from her wallet. It was old and worn, taken at least ten years ago. She knew it was futile hoping for an identification, but she had to keep trying. If you gave up trying, you gave up everything.

'Never seen her before.'

'You haven't looked properly.'

'Is she in trouble, then?' The woman looked at the photo, and pulled a face, curling her lip and wrinkling her nose. 'Nah. She's too clean, for a start. And what sort of hairstyle is that, I ask you?'

'She may not look like that any more,' said Fry.

'Eh?' She laughed. 'You're wasting your time then, aren't you, duck?'

The woman walked away. Just like all the others did. Fry wanted to get her into a wrist hold, lock the kwik-cuffs, take her back to the station and question her until she found out what she wanted to know. But she was out of her territory here, in the position of begging for information. And she was taking enough risks as it was. In fact, she was a damned idiot. What had stirred up her need to follow this quest? It was a need she had tried to suppress for a long time, so why should it surface now? But she knew why. It was another thing that was the fault of Ben Cooper.

Fry considered how out of place Cooper would be here, in the city. He was chained like a prisoner to the area he came from. He would be completely lost in these streets; but he was never lost on the moors. Ben Cooper smelled his way around like a sheepdog – she had seen him do it, and it drove her mad.

But even Cooper would be indoors by now, probably at home among his relatives at that farm on the road towards Hucklow. He would be comfortably settled in his nest, just like the cattle lying in their straw in the sheds she had seen there once.

For Diane Fry, indoors was always the safest place to be. No one would choose to be out on the hills at night.

AND NOW IT was totally dark on the moor – a world of multiple shades of black that formed imaginary shapes and half-seen movements on the edge of his vision. The dancers weren't afraid of the dark, and nor was he. He loved to go wandering at night above the quarry, his arms outstretched like a blind man, gently feeling his way through the darkness, caressing the skins of the thin birches, touching the leaves that appeared in front of his face, letting his feet whisper and sigh in the heather, navigating by the glint of a star on a fragment of quartz.

In the darkness, he was able to sense the world completely. Not just the little bit around him, but the entire breadth and stretch of it, the whole roll and curve of its body and the movement of its breath. He could feel the warmth of the earth underfoot and touch the great, empty reaches of the sky. With a still mind and total concentration on the rhythms of his body, he could lift himself off the ground and soar into the sky. He had learned to see the darkened landscape flying past below him, drawing away from him faster and faster, until he could see the whole of the valley down there, the whole of the Peak District, the whole of Derbyshire, with its towns and villages suddenly dwindling into insignificance among the black hills, and the long strings of streetlights turning as fragile as the strands of a cobweb.

It was all so tiny and unimportant down there. It was nothing but a film of human detritus on the face of the earth. All it would take was one last heave of the tectonic plates below the surface, and all those towns and villages would be gone for ever as the landscape rearranged itself, tucking away the evidence of civilization like a chambermaid tidying the bedclothes, like a housewife shaking out the sheets to toss away the dead skin and fluff, and straightening out the covers to hide the stains.

He liked to imagine this happening; he cherished the image like a comforting dream. It was not so long ago, after all, that the last volcano had splashed lava and red-hot ash over the valley of the Derwent, and the last glaciers had ground their way through the limestone to carve those scenic gorges. Five hundred thousand years or so? It was nothing in a couple of million. And man had been here only a few thousand of those years, electric light a hundred. Nature could shrug off the infestation of civilization with one gentle spasm, the irritated twitch of a shoulder to shake off a fly. Then new valleys and lakes would appear, and entirely different hills would rise up in between them. And the birches would begin the task of colonization all over again.

He had no doubt this would happen one day. But not in his lifetime. The time of the promised millennial cataclysms had long since passed, leaving just more of the same petty human pain and despair.

No, he didn't fear the darkness; he liked it. But tonight there were people on the moor, policemen and lights. They were in the middle of the stone circle, like the occupants of an alien spacecraft, turning the night into a fairground, destroying the silence with the thump of their generator and their bored, meaningless chatter.

He knew their lights would make the shadows in the trees seem even darker, so that he was invisible to their unpractised eyes. It allowed him to get closer, until he was near enough to hear the Virgins sighing and singing in the wind, near enough to catch the faint fragments of the Fiddler's tune, its notes tangling in the tops of the birches and dropping to the ground with the leaves as they died. There was no dance tonight, only a dirge. There was no hope in the music that he heard, no whispers of encouragement from the stones.

And he knew it wouldn't happen for him now. He had thought his own world could be changed, that his life could be stripped and made afresh, the evidence of his past tucked away, the stains hidden from sight. But he had seen her face. And now it was too late.

Chapter Seven

BEN COOPER RUBBED a hand across his eyes. There were too many bodies pressed close around him in the darkness. He could feel their heat, smell their sweat and their cotton shirts, hear their breathing and the scraping of their boots. But all he could see was a bright square and a few vague shapes, the outline of a head or shoulder here and there on the edge of the light.

Just before they vanished, the Virgins had seemed to move. They had shuffled right and left, faded in and out of focus, come closer and backed away, as if they had been caught for a moment in a celebratory dance. Then they had disappeared with a click and the whirr of a motor, flicking out of sight in a white glare, with tendrils of smoke left drifting in the beam.

Cooper shifted uneasily, frustrated by the inactivity. It was early in the morning, but his mind was already alert. In fact, his imagination was streaming ahead of the facts, and vivid images were flipping through his brain. Yesterday, he had stood on Ringham Moor himself. He had felt the bite of the wind up there, and listened to it hissing through the dying heather as the birch leaves crackled under his feet. And he had seen where all this started – with the stones.

One indistinct shape stood out from the others in the darkness. From the corner of his eye, a subtle change in the pattern of the shadows suggested a face had turned towards him for a second. Cooper felt the brief glance like a draught of air entering the room and stroking its fingers across his face. Suddenly, he felt self-conscious and conspicuous, afraid to move a muscle for fear of drawing attention to himself. He knew it was not in his interest to attract her attention. He wouldn't know what on earth to say to her if he did.

A voice came out of the darkness. 'Forty feet across, on a shallow, sandy floor. Drag marks nearly twenty feet into the centre. No signs of a struggle. However ...'

The next slide appeared on the screen, bizarre and meaningless until the projector pulled it into focus. To Cooper, it looked as if an aerial shot had been taken from high above the earth, where the hull of an ancient boat lay half-buried in a desert. There was a ragged elliptical shape, dark red and scattered with black flecks. It was set in a strange, grainy yellow landscape like deep sand that blurred the edges of the shape and rolled away towards distant orange hills that cast no shadows.

He might have been looking at some kind of Noah's Ark, stranded on a remote mountainside in Syria, the subject of endless arguments about its reality. The jagged black marks in the centre could have been the remains of a petrified wheelhouse, crumbled masts and decking, or rigging long since turned to dust. But there was no natural sunlight in this desert, only artificial colours.

Then a shadow moved in front of the screen, and a weary face was caught by the light of the projector.

'You can all see what this is. It needs no explanation from me. Death would have occurred within minutes.'

Cooper had to shake himself out of his daydream. The police officers around him became solid shapes again, reverting to the familiar faces of a Derbyshire CID team. On the screen, they were being shown an enhanced post-mortem image, a photograph taken on the mortuary slab. The red ellipse was the entry wound made by a sharp, single-bladed knife an inch below the bottom rib. A fatal stab wound to the heart. Those pale orange hills were human flesh – the slope of a woman's abdomen and the lower edge of her ribcage. The grains of sand were her pores and skin cells, enlarged beyond recognition, distorted by lighting that drained all remnants of humanity from the corpse.

This yellow desert was the body of Jenny Weston. And no one was arguing the reality of her death. It was much too late for that.

'And we found so many damn camp fires you'd think there had been a boy scout jamboree up there,' said DCI Tailby, as the slide changed to a view of Ringham Moor. Cooper saw few smiles, and heard no laughter. It was too early in the morning, the subject was too lacking in the potential for a quick joke. The DCI tried again. 'But the

SOCOs tell us these were no boy scouts. Not unless they give badges for sex, drugs and animal sacrifice in the scouts these days.'

The briefing had been called early, while it was still dark. Many of the officers looked tired and bleary-eyed. They had gone to bed late last night and hadn't got enough sleep. But they would wake up as the day went on, as the caffeine kicked in and they were forced to concentrate on their tasks.

The incident room at Edendale Divisional Headquarters was only half full. Ben Cooper had been expecting there would be hardly anywhere left to sit by the time he arrived, but he was surprised by the sparse attendance. Then he discovered that teams were already out at the scene, up on the moor waiting for first light to continue the careful sweep for delicate forensic traces that would vanish or be utterly contaminated at the first sign of heavy rain or the first set of feet to trample over the site.

Alongside Tailby sat the Divisional Commander, Colin Jepson. They had to call him Chief Superintendent Jepson now. Although the rank was supposed to have been abolished in the 1980s, Derbyshire Constabulary had restored the title for its divisional commanders, though without the salary level that went with it.

No detective superintendent had arrived yet, though Edendale was still without its own CID chief. For the time being, Tailby was being allowed to make the running. Cooper thought the DCI looked a little greyer at the temples than the day before, a little more stooped at the shoulders.

The slide show they had begun with was depressing enough. The photographer had captured a chill bleakness in his establishing shots of the moor, and an impressionistic arrangement of angles and perspective in his close-ups of the Virgins. The slides of the victim had silenced the room, except for an increased shuffling of boots on the floor. They showed in brutal clarity the curious position of the woman's limbs, the absence of clothing on the lower half of her body, the red stain on her T-shirt. After the unsettling realism, the autopsy shots had concluded on a note of fantasy. As usual, they seemed divorced from the actual death, too clinical, and reeking too much of antiseptic to be human.

The most interesting result from the postmortem was that there had been no sign of sexual assault on Jenny Weston. So why had some of the victim's clothes been removed? There were two main possibilities – either her killer had been interrupted, or the intention had been to mislead the police.

NOW, WITH THE lights on again, Tailby was forced to admit that all they knew so far about the circumstances of Jenny Weston's death was the situation they had found on Ringham Moor, and a bewildering array of items recovered by the SOCOs.

'These camp fires – are they recent, sir?' asked someone.

'Some are clearly quite old,' said Tailby. 'A couple of months anyway, dating from the summer, when there is most activity up there. But others are more recent, with ash still present – we would expect it to be washed away into the ground after a few spells of rainfall. But the Peak Park Rangers for that area tell us there are often people camping on Ringham Moor, even in September and October. Right through the middle of winter sometimes. Even in the snow.'

'We've got some right little Sir Edmund Hillarys, haven't we?'

It had to be Todd Weenink who couldn't resist. He looked as crumpled as the rest, perhaps even more so. He had almost certainly had more to drink the night before than the average man could take. Casual flippancy seemed to seep out of him like sweat from a ripe Stilton. Cooper watched Tailby's grey eyes warm as he glanced at Weenink, grateful for the response.

'Of course, there's no indication so far that anybody camping out on the moor is necessarily a suspect for the attack on our latest victim, or even a witness. However ...' Tailby pinned a photograph to a big cork board. 'By a stroke of luck, we also have this.'

The photo showed a patch of grey ash, with a few black sticks of charred wood poking through it. The ash looked as though it had been roughly brushed over. And there, to one side, was the partial imprint of the sole of a boot or shoe.

'It's early days, yet,' said the DCI. 'But we're hopeful of an identification on the footwear. There's sufficient impression from the sole to get a match, we think.'

'But was it made at the time, sir?'

'Ah.' Tailby pointed to a small, dark smudge on the photograph. 'This is a trace of the victim's blood. The significant thing about it is that the print was made on top of the blood stain while it was still fresh.'

He nodded with some degree of satisfaction. Early forensic evidence was exactly what everyone prayed for. A boot print that would connect its wearer to the scene at the time of the offence – what better could they ask for at such an early stage? Well, a suspect with footwear to compare the boot print to, that's what.

'Read the preliminary crime scene report,' said Tailby.

There was another shuffling of papers. Cooper looked down at his file. There was a computer-printed list of items retrieved from the area around the Virgins, but it was a long one, difficult to take in. The SOCOs had taken samples of vegetation, including heather, whinberry, gorse and three types of grass. They had taken sections of bark from the trunks of the birches where they had been cut by a knife or splashed with an unknown substance. They had brought in stones, half-bricks, bags of ash and cinders, sheets of corrugated iron, a small metal grille like a fire grate, a burnt corner of the *Sheffield Star* where half a dozen screwed-up pages had been used to help light a fire, a British Midland Airways refresher tissue wrapper, a whole pile of aluminium ring-pulls, several cigarette butts, a Findus crispy pancake packet, and a selection of used condoms.

The forensic team had covered a wide area – all of the clearing around the stones, right into the birches and as far as the fence around the edge of the quarry. The SOCOs must have balked at the view to the east, towards the edge of the plateau. Cooper could remember a sea of bracken – damp, endless acres of it, stretching to the Hammond Tower and beyond, flowing over the edge of the cliff, dense and almost impenetrable. Beyond the bracken was a low wire fence with wooden posts, then beyond it a precipitous drop. From there, an object would plummet a thousand feet into the trees that grew at acute angles on the lower edges of the slope into the dale.

Scrapings had been taken from a pool of white wax that had solidified in the hollow of a rotten tree, while digging in what at first appeared to be a rubbish hole turned up the bones of an animal. There were latent prints collected from the handlebars, saddle, front wheel and crossbar of the Dawes Kokomo Jenny Weston had been riding, and more samples of blood had been scraped from the frame of the bike.

'We think the names on the stones are just old graffiti. The inscription scraped on the ground is more recent. It looks like "STRIDE". If it means anything at all to anybody, speak up.'

Nobody spoke. They were looking at two more photographs on the board behind Tailby. There were two women, alive and smiling at the camera, though the one on the left looked guarded, maybe a little bit haughty, as if the photographer were taking a liberty getting her in the shot.

'Are we looking at the same assailant in both cases?' said Tailby. 'Someone who was practising, as it were, on the earlier victim, Maggie Crew? Are we looking at someone who has succeeded in perfecting his technique with Jenny Weston?'

It was a very strange idea of perfection. Ben Cooper looked to see whether the other officers were reacting the same way. But most of them showed no surprise at the irony of the thought. Then something made him glance towards the far side of the room. Leaning casually against a desk was Diane Fry. She'd had her fair hair cut even shorter, and it gave an angular look to her lean face. He was sure she had lost weight, too. She had been slim before, but now there was a suggestion of something taut and thinly-stretched.

'Don't let ideas like that distract you,' said Tailby. 'We are treating this incident as an entirely separate enquiry, until the evidence proves otherwise. At this stage, we're concentrating on collecting information. All right?'

His audience seemed to take this as a cue to start shuffling their papers again, looking for what information there already was. Cooper dragged his eyes away from Fry and did the same. At this stage, the information was pretty thin. Forensics results were awaited. Initial witness reports were sparse. True, they had details of Jenny Weston – who she was, where she lived, what she had done for a living. The minute details of her life were starting to emerge. But there was nothing to show what had made her go cycling on Ringham Moor on an early November afternoon, and why she had ended up dead among the Nine Virgins.

'Somebody must have seen Jenny before she was killed. Maybe, just maybe, somebody also saw her killer. So have we got any leads so far? Paul?'

DI Hitchens stood up, straightening his jacket, looking much smarter this morning in his dark grey suit.

'We're looking at the likelihood that the killer arrived at Ringham Moor by car,' he said. 'We've already visited the houses close to the parking places on the edges of the moor, and we've collected a list of vehicles that were noticed around the time of the incident. It goes without saying that the vast majority of those vehicles will be totally impossible to trace. We're lucky, though. If it had been the height of summer, it would be a lot worse.'

There were sighs and nods. It was a problem nobody in E Division needed telling about. The number of cars from out of the area greatly outnumbered the locally registered ones, especially in summer. Many of the Peak District's twenty-five million visitors a year drove through Edendale and its surrounding villages at some time. Most were just passing through and were no different from a million other tourist cars. Nobody took any notice of them individually – they were just an anonymous mass, a crawling stream of red and blue insects covering the roads and car parks like insects swarming in the August heat. They were a naturally occurring phenomenon, like greenfly.

Visitors and their cars brought their own kind of problems for crime management. The mention of them reminded Ben Cooper that, right now, he should have been in the Crime Strategy Meeting.

'We need to trace Jenny Weston's movements exactly, particularly in the last couple of hours before she died.

DCs Cooper and Weenink will start with the cycle hire centre at Partridge Cross this morning,' said Tailby.

Weenink sat just behind Cooper in the incident room. He had a seat against the wall, his shoulders almost making a dent in the plaster. He looked as though he wanted to put his feet up on the table, but was resisting the temptation. There were only five officers in the Edendale section CID now, a closer-knit grouping since the recent reorganization. Cooper hadn't known Weenink so well before. He had the sneaking feeling that there was no one in the division who envied him.

For a while, Cooper had been convinced that his fall from popularity had only one cause – the arrival in E Division of Diane Fry, on a transfer from West Midlands. She was ambitious; some might say ruthless. Her arrival had coincided with the moment things had started to go wrong for Cooper, when his hopes of promotion had been set back in favour of hers. Fry seemed not to have put a foot wrong so far. There were people who made all the right moves without trying; and there were others who followed their own instinct wherever it might take them, and ended up in the mire. Cooper blamed himself for being naive with Diane Fry. It took time to earn trust.

Probably his father would have been able to tell him that. His father had seen everything there was to be known about office politics and in-fighting inside the police service. He had managed to steer clear of all that; he had never fallen victim to backstabbing from his colleagues. It had been the street that had killed him, in the end.

'There are a number of names and addresses on the list for interview this morning,' said Hitchens. 'Colleagues, friends, neighbours. We expect the list to increase as the day goes on. There have been several boyfriends, according to the father. They all have to be traced. Fortunately, we have the victim's own address book from her house. And, of course, there is the ex-husband. We need to dig out the details of Jenny Weston's life. Narrow those names down. Give us something to go on.'

'Hey, Ben,' said Weenink when the meeting broke up. 'This tracing her route business – are they saying we've got to go by bike?'

'Of course not,' said Cooper.

'Thank God for that.'

'We'll walk.'

DI HITCHENS TOUCHED Diane Fry's arm and kept her back while the others left the incident room. DCI Tailby looked at them both thoughtfully. Fry knew she must have had his backing to get the move up to Acting Detective Sergeant, but she wasn't quite sure how to read him yet. She was more comfortable working with either Hitchens or DI Armstrong, both of whom she felt she understood.

'The ex-husband, Martin Stafford ...' said Tailby.

'Do we have an address?' asked Fry.

'No, but we should be able to track him down through his employment record. He was a journalist, at least while he was married to Jenny Weston. I've asked for somebody to visit his old employers in Derby to look at his personnel records. With luck, they should have a note of any reference they gave him when he moved on. He may be completely out of the area by now, of course. Journalists move around quite a bit.'

'What about a current boyfriend?'

'Nobody seems sure who the latest one was, Diane,' said Hitchens. 'There are one or two of the girls at the call centre that she talked to about boyfriends sometimes. But they were very vague. Obviously, we're going through the address book. But she used phone numbers, not addresses. Results might take a little time.'

'I see.'

'We do have this note.' Hitchens held up an evidence bag. 'One of the team found it in the back of her diary.'

'What is it?' said Tailby. 'A love letter?'

'Hardly a letter. It's only two lines. And there's no evidence love was involved either. The note reads: "Nine o'clock Friday at the cottage. Buy some fruit-flavoured ones."'

Tailby stared at him. Fry remembered that the DCI was a lay preacher at a United Reformed Church in Dronfield.

'We believe it's a reference to contraceptives, sir,' said Hitchens.

'Yes?'

'Condoms. We think it's a fair assumption that the note is from a boyfriend. There's no date, and it's unsigned. But it looks fairly recent. Otherwise, why would it still be in her diary?'

'Good point.' Tailby put down the reports and took off his glasses.

'I take it you are to remain as SIO, sir?' asked Hitchens.

'Detective Superintendent Prince is tied up with this case in Derby, the double shooting,' said Tailby. 'A drugs territory dispute. We're getting some stick about it down there, apparently.'

'Yes.'

'It means Mr Prince can only keep a watching brief on this case, I'm afraid. But he thinks we've got a good start.'

'Possibly,' said Hitchens. 'But there is speculation about the other attack.'

Tailby shook his head. 'They smell different to me. This Jenny Weston sounds like a woman who got involved with the wrong sort of chap. It's an old story. You'll see.'

Chapter Eight

The Partridge Cross cycle hire centre was in a converted railway station. Past it ran what had once been the Cromford & High Peak rail line, now the High Peak Trail, a smoothly tarmacked stretch of track perfect for walkers and cyclists.

There was still a morning mist lingering in places, and the old railway cuttings seemed to have drawn it down on to the trail. It gave a damp nip to the air that hit Ben Cooper and Todd Weenink as soon as they got out of the car. But there were already vehicles in the car park. Some had cycle racks on their tailgates and mountain bikes hoisted high in the air. A family with three small children were strapping on their safety helmets ready to hit the trail. There were no traces of Jenny Weston left here now.

The day's weather forecast from the Met Office was posted on a board outside the hire centre, next to a notice warning hirers that bikes had to be returned by 6 p.m. in the summer, or by dusk in the winter. At the other end of the building a counter concession was selling ice cream, sweets and canned drinks. In a compound, they saw at least one Dawes Kokomo among the tandems and trailer cycles. Before they went into the hire centre, they stopped and looked at the bikes.

'You wouldn't get me on one of these,' said Weenink, immediately sitting astride a tandem and looking like a cowboy trying to mount a donkey. 'Unless it was with the right bird on the back, of course. Preferably the local bike, up for a quick pedal in the woods.'

Across the car park was the Ranger centre, a two-storey converted barn. They had passed it on the way in, and Cooper had noticed Owen Fox's silver Land Rover parked in the yard.

They found Don Marsden, the cycle hire manager, leaning against a wooden counter, wiping his hands on a cloth. He had been tinkering with one of the hire bikes, checking the tightness of the forks on the wheels, testing the brakes and adjusting the saddle. Now he was waiting for his first customer of the morning, a blank page of the log book in front of him.

Marsden wore a red sweater like a Ranger, but with a different logo on the breast pocket. He didn't look like a cyclist himself – he had a heavy paunch pushing out the front of his sweater and a goatee beard covering part of his double chin. Behind the counter, the office he worked in was crowded. It contained everything from a microwave oven and a personal computer with drifting parabolic shapes filling its screen, to displays of maps and route guides. It was just gone nine thirty and the centre had been open only a few minutes. Marsden gave them a cheerful greeting, and his cheerfulness didn't falter even when he discovered they were police officers.

'I was told you'd be back,' he said, offering his hand.

'We've got your earlier statement,' said Cooper. 'We're just trying to establish the victim's exact movements yesterday.'

'Fair enough.' Don leaned on the counter with an expectant smile.

'Is this the woman you remember seeing?' Cooper produced a copy of the photograph provided by Eric Weston, a picture of Jenny at her cousin's wedding two years before. Jenny was dressed in a dove grey suit. Unlike the others in the wedding group, she was not wearing a hat, and her dark hair curled round her face, the strands of it echoing the curve of her smile. She looked as though she had been enjoying herself for once.

'Oh, yes. I don't need to see the photo either,' said Don. 'I remember her. Weston, that's right. She's here in the book. She took out a mountain bike at twelve forty-five. It was what she always had. She was a regular, you see.'

'A regular? How often did she come?'

'About once every two weeks in the summer. I think she probably went to some of the other hire centres on the weekends in between. Winter, it depended on the weather. But we're open every day of the year here, except Christmas Day.'

'So you knew who she was.'

'I recognized her, of course. And you get to know the names of the regulars, after a bit. You have to enter it in the book, see, and on the computer. They have to show me some ID and put a deposit down on the bike. Twenty quid, it is. She gave me cash. Do you know …?'

'Somebody else will sort that out, I expect,' said Cooper.

'Right. Only it's not something that's happened to me before, the customer dying before they can reclaim their deposit. It's not in the regulations.'

Weenink had been flicking through leaflets advertising the local attractions of Lathkill Dale and Carsington Water. Now he seemed to take notice for the first time of what Marsden was saying.

'Did she chat to you, then?' he asked. 'I mean, did she just come in, pay the money and take the bike, or did she pass the time of day a bit?'

'She didn't say much really,' admitted Don. 'She was pleasant, you know. But I wouldn't have said she was the chatty type. Not with me, anyway. Women on their own are a bit distant these days. They learn not to be too friendly.'

He sounded regretful. Cooper wondered what his prospects were as an interviewee when the reporters and TV crews arrived, as they surely would. It was lucky they had got to Don Marsden before the cameras. He had a feeling the story might get embellished along the way later on.

'So what else do you know about her?' suggested Weenink.

Don shook his head. 'Just where she came from. I've got her address, look. The Quadrant, Totley, Sheffield. I've been through it once or twice, I think. She normally showed me her driving licence for ID. We have to go through the procedure every time. Can't make exceptions. But as for knowing anything about her – not really. Except I don't think she was married.'

'Oh? What makes you say that?'

'Dunno really. Just the way she was. Friendly, yeah. But it was more like she seemed to be able to please herself what she did. I had the impression there probably wasn't a husband and kids at home waiting for her to get back. Do you know what I mean?'

Weenink simply stared at the cycle hire man. This was his principal interrogation technique, the intimidatory stare. He had perfected the art of silent disbelief.

'You're quite observant really, Don,' said Cooper.

'I think so. You see all sorts here, you know. You get to recognize the types.'

'It was a quarter to one when she came in, you said.'

'That's right. It's in the book.'

'You saw her arrive, did you?'

'Yeah. I was standing in the doorway there, as it happens. It was quiet, like now. Maybe not so quiet as this, but quiet anyway. I saw her car pull up. A Fiat, right? So I came back in, and I had a bike ready for her. I knew what she'd want.'

'Where did she park?' asked Weenink, though he knew exactly where the Fiat had been found.

'Just over there, the first bay on the left.'

'Were there any other cars here?'

'One or two. Three or four, maybe. I didn't really count them.'

'Anybody else that you knew? Any other regulars?'

'No. But the ones who hired bikes are in the book here. The other policemen took their names and addresses. Of course, there are some folk who bring their own bikes. They don't come in here at all unless they want a map or something, or they want to ask directions. Some walk or go jogging. Them I don't notice so much.'

Cooper turned the book round to look at it. The next bike hire recorded after Jenny Weston's entry was nearly half an hour later, when a tandem had been signed out to a couple called Sharman, from Matlock. Other hirers weren't his concern, for now. Checking them out was somebody else's job.

'Did Jenny Weston ever tell you where she was heading?' he asked.

'No,' said Don. 'But she usually set off eastwards, down the trail towards Ashbourne.'

'Is that what she did yesterday?'

'That's right. It's sensible for somebody on their own to tell me where they're going. In case they have an accident or something, you know. There are times when people get lost and are really late back with the bikes. You start to wonder whether something's happened to them. But there's not much you can do, if you've no idea where they've set off to.'

'Jenny's bike was overdue for being returned, wasn't it?'

'Yeah, it was. She had a three-hour ticket. It should have been back here by a quarter to four, by rights. You have to pay extra if you go over – two pounds more. Or you can lose your twenty quid altogether. We're supposed to close at dusk anyway.'

'Did you worry about the fact she wasn't back?'

'I thought it was unusual, that's all. There's plenty of folk late back. But it was odd for her. She'd never been late before, so I did wonder. But when it came time to close, I would have been reporting in. Head office would have made a decision whether to call you lot. But, of course, young Mark Roper found her before that, didn't he?'

Cooper pricked up his ears. 'How did you hear that?'

'Owen Fox told me. He came through from the Ranger centre when he heard. It's practically next door, see.'

'Do you work closely with the Rangers?'

'We help each other out a bit. I've known Owen Fox for years. Good bloke, Owen.'

Weenink had wandered past the wooden barrier and was examining the bikes stacked in the back of the building.

'Hey, look at this.' He had found a machine that looked like a wheelchair with a unicycle welded on to the front. It had no pedals, but there were two handles in front of the rider, attached to a gear wheel. Weenink squeezed himself into the seat and waggled the steering from side to side.

'They're hand-cranked,' said Don, watching him cautiously. 'For disabled people, you know.'

'Brilliant.'

Cooper felt Weenink was starting to become an embarrassment. It always happened when he got bored.

'Well, thanks for your time, Don.'

'No problem. As you can see, I've got no customers.'

'You might find it gets busier later on.'

'Doubt it. Not at this time of the year, on a Monday. And half-term isn't until next week.'

'No, you don't understand. Once people see the news about the murder, it'll be crowded down here.'

Don looked shocked. 'You're kidding, aren't you? Why should people want to come here?'

Cooper shrugged. 'I can't explain it. But they will.'

'Oh, they'll be running coach trips,' said Weenink, grinning from the doorway. 'Tours for Ghouls Limited.'

'Not to mention the newspapers and the TV cameras.'

'Blimey.' Don looked nervously out of the doorway at the bike compound. 'I didn't expect that,' he said. 'I didn't expect people would be like that. Perhaps I'd better ring the boss and ask if I can close up for the day.'

'Close? Why would you want to do that? You could be a TV star, mate,' said Weenink.

Don smiled uncertainly. As they walked away, he was watching the car park entrance. He still wasn't sure whether they were joking.

DIANE FRY ALWAYS forgot. It slipped her mind every time how hopeful the family of a victim were when they saw the police on their doorstep in the early stages of an enquiry. They had such confidence, so often misplaced. An early resolution was their main hope, an end to the nightmare. They believed the police were doing their best, but rarely was a detective able to bring them hope.

Mr Weston was in the front garden of his house in Alfreton, raking leaves with an absorbed expression. He looked up sharply when he heard the police car pull into the drive. But DI Hitchens simply shook his head, and Weston turned back to his driveway and attacked the leaves with his rake as if he wanted to stab them into the ground.

'Was there something else you wanted to ask?' he said, when they reached him.

'A few things, Mr Weston,' said Hitchens. 'I'm sorry.'

'Can't be helped, I suppose. It'll go on and on, won't it?'

The Westons' house was a large semi in a style that might have been called 1920s mock Tudor, with stucco above and brick below. The Tudor effect was achieved by a few stray bits of black wood, which supported nothing, inserted into the walls.

But the house was substantial and well cared for. The front door was of some oak-like wood, and through the bay window Fry caught a glimpse of a lounge with cast-iron wall lights in the shape of flaming torches, a wheel-shaped chandelier supporting electric candles and a log basket on a brick hearth.

'I've taken compassionate leave for a few days,' said Weston. 'I need to look after Susan. The head of my school has been very understanding.'

Fry became aware of Mrs Weston standing in the background, listening. She was pale and looked tired.

'Have you found Martin Stafford?' she asked.

'Not yet, Mrs Weston,' said Hitchens.

'So he's got away.'

'We'll locate him, eventually.'

'He always had a violent tendency.'

'We want to eliminate him from the enquiry, obviously.'

Mrs Weston stared at him as if she didn't understand what he was saying.

'Susan –' said her husband.

'I always said he was no good,' she said. 'I was always afraid it would come to this.'

'I don't think we know any more about Martin Stafford than we've told you already,' said Mr Weston. 'There might be something at the house in Totley, I suppose. I mean Jenny's house. He might have written to her or something.'

'Trying to creep back,' said his wife.

'We've already looked there,' said Hitchens. 'We found this –'

The Westons examined the photocopy that he showed them. It was a note rather than a letter – just a few lines about an arrangement to meet somewhere. But it was addressed to Jenny, and it was written in terms that suggested a close relationship.

Mrs Weston coloured faintly when she reached the line about fruit flavours. 'There's no name on it,' she said.

'No,' said Fry. 'That's why we're showing it to you. In case you recognize it.'

'You think it might be from Stafford?' asked Mr Weston. 'There's no date on it, either.'

'Unfortunately not.'

'I can't really remember what his writing was like. Susan?'

'No,' said Mrs Weston. 'I mean, I don't know. It could be.'

'Did he ever write to you? Might you have something that we could compare it to?'

The couple looked at each other. 'Have we still got that postcard?' said Mr Weston.

His wife went to a mahogany dresser and opened a drawer. It was one of those drawers that were always full of things that you never wanted. But Mrs Weston soon located a plastic wallet of the kind that usually contained holiday snaps.

'I don't know why we kept it,' she said. 'But you can see what sort of man he is.'

Fry studied the postcard. It showed a view on one side of a beach lined with tourist hotels.

'Hawaii,' she said. 'Very nice.' She turned the card over. It was addressed to the Westons and signed 'Martin (your former son-in-law)'. The rest of it seemed fairly innocuous – a few lines about how hot the weather was, how luxurious the hotel, how stimulating the nightlife. 'Spent nearly £2,000 already!', it said, as if it was a boast.

'I'm not sure what it tells me,' said Fry. 'This holiday was presumably after the divorce.'

'Not only after the divorce – paid for by the divorce,' said Mrs Weston. 'He spent his share of the proceedings from the sale of their house in Derby. He never seemed to want for money, I don't know why. While Jenny had to spend all of her share and borrow more to buy that little place in Totley, Stafford went on this holiday in Hawaii. The postcard was to rub it in. No other reason.'

'Apart from Martin Stafford, we'd also want to try to trace any boyfriends that Jenny had recently,' said Hitchens.

'We've been asked that before,' said Mr Weston. 'I gave you some names that we knew. We didn't know of anyone else. Not recently.'

'She didn't talk to us about things like that,' said Mrs Weston. 'Not since Stafford.'

'Not even then,' said her husband. 'We had to work it all out for ourselves, what was going on. She didn't want to say anything against him. Can you believe it?'

'She was loyal,' said Mrs Weston. 'I tried to teach her always to be loyal to her husband. No matter what.'

Mr Weston looked down at the teacups. His wife continued to stare straight ahead, past Fry's shoulder. It was an aggressive and challenging stare, but it wasn't directed at Fry at all. It was hitting the wall behind her and ricocheting with unerring accuracy into the back of the seat next to her, passing through Eric Weston's heart on the way.

'No matter what,' repeated Mrs Weston.

Diane Fry was always fascinated by those little secret means of communication that passed between couples without the need for explanation. You had to be very close to someone to be able to do it, very familiar with each other's thoughts.

'But she divorced him, in the end,' said Hitchens.

Mrs Weston nodded. 'Young women are less tolerant. They have higher expectations of what marriage should be like. They come to a point where they can't tolerate it any more. You can't blame them, I suppose. But it isn't something I could do. My generation was brought up differently. We always believed that we had to grin and bear it, to accept our lot in life. To accept life's burdens.'

Mr Weston was looking more and more uncomfortable in his seat. He rattled his teacup in its saucer and cleared his throat.

'Can we take this postcard?' asked Fry.

'The writing doesn't look anything like the note,' said Mrs Weston.

'No, it doesn't,' admitted Fry.

'Well, that's that, then.'

BACK IN THE car, Diane Fry called in for an update on the other lines of enquiry. The teams canvassing neighbours in Totley had found someone who remembered a man looking for Jenny two weeks' previously, asking for her by name. The man was described as being of medium height and ordinary. He had been quite respectably dressed, and had spoken in a local accent. Very useful.

A second neighbour, who lived nearly opposite Jenny's house in The Quadrant, recalled a strange car parked in the road one night. A man had been sitting in it, but he had driven off at about the time that Jenny had left her house.

A third witness reported a light-coloured van, possibly an old Ford Transit or something similar, which had passed slowly along the road twice. At the time, the neighbour had thought it might be gypsies – 'totters', he called them – looking for scrap, or anything they could steal.

Several neighbours recalled female visitors to Jenny's home, including a girl with dark dreadlocks who had attracted particular attention in The Quadrant for a while. Dreadlocks were rare in Totley.

All the fragments of information had been passed to the officers interviewing Jenny's colleagues at Global Assurance. But none of the colleagues could remember Jenny ever complaining of being harassed by a disgruntled boyfriend. If it had been her ex-husband trying to get back in touch, Jenny had not confided the fact to anyone. But the incident room staff would put the information into the HOLMES system. Correlations might be thrown up. Just one detail could send the whole enquiry in a new direction.

DI Hitchens had been on the mobile phone to the DCI back at Divisional Headquarters in West Street. When he finished the call, Hitchens turned to Fry and told her what they wanted her to do next.

'You've got to be joking,' she said. But he wasn't.

MARK ROPER RATTLED a fork against the plastic bowl. Three cats appeared from the shrubbery at the end of the garden – a grey one and two tabbies. They ran with their tails in the air and brushed themselves against Mark's legs until he put their bowls on the ground and they began to gnaw at their chunks of meat.

While they ate, Mark went to clean out the bedding for the rabbits and freshen the water in their cages. The rabbits stared at him through the mesh, twitching their noses as they sniffed his familiar smell. For a while, Mark sat on an upturned milk crate to watch the cats feed.

Normally, he would have been at work, but he had been told to take a day off. He couldn't understand what they expected him to do at home, except to sit and think, to relive the moment he had found the body of the murdered woman, and to wonder about the events that had led up to her death among the Nine Virgins. Mark would have much preferred to be with Owen, to be busy with jobs that would take his mind off things. But he hadn't wanted to argue, in case they thought his reaction was strange.

He could think of nothing worse than sitting in the house all day, as some people did. He soon became claustrophobic and restless, and angry at the untidiness – the dirty clothes draped over chairs, the empty beer cans and overflowing ashtrays left on the floor.

In any case, the house contained nothing of his father any more. His clothes had gone, and so had his books, his walking stick and his stuffed Tawny Owl. The man who lived with Mark's mother now had removed every remaining trace of her husband from the house. But he had never thought to bother with the garden. Here, Mark recognized every item that his father had collected over the years – every lump of wood, and every stone. This milk crate was one that his father had found by the roadside and had thought might be useful one day. Mark had helped his father make these rabbit cages; the frames still bore the marks made by a saw and a plane held in his father's hands. Their relationship still lived on in these little things. These, and the nightmares that Mark suffered now and then, when he would wake up in the night, calling for his dad like a child.

Mark sat on the crate for a while and thought about the woman on the moor; and then he thought about Owen Fox. He had started to get used to relying on Owen for an element of stability in his life. The fear that the stability might be taken from him once again made Mark swear abruptly, so that the cats were startled and scuttled away from their bowls. The rabbits lifted their ears and gazed at him with their strange pink eyes. Like Mark, they were suddenly terrified of the unknown things that might lie beyond their cages in the outside world.

Todd Weenink looked up towards the road at the sound of a car approaching the cycle hire centre. Ben Cooper saw his partner stiffen, and heard him start to curse, low but vehemently. Spurts of Weenink's breath were hitting the air, swirling ominously. Cooper could almost see the curses forming into dark, solid lumps in the mist.

'Don't look now, Ben, but the weather just got a few degrees colder round here,' said Weenink.

The car that splashed through the puddles and pulled up in front of the hire centre was a black Peugeot. When it stopped, the headlights were turned down to sidelights, but its doors remained closed and no one got out. It sat there with traces of steam rising from its bonnet and mingling with the mist. And with each tick of its cooling engine, Cooper felt his heart chill a little more.

Chapter Nine

It was only an hour or so after the morning news that the first visitors started to arrive on Ringham Moor. They parked up on all the roadside verges, filling the lay-bys and blocking the field gates. Within a few minutes, the first of them began to wander up the tracks that led on to the moor. They came in ones and twos mostly, but some had brought their children for a day out.

'Look at them,' said the uniformed sergeant in charge of containing the crime scene. 'Can't you hear the conversations over the cornflakes? "Nothing much on the telly today – why don't we all go and see where the lady got herself murdered?"'

These people had come wrapped up well, in their sweaters and anoraks and boots and hats. They brought their cameras, too, and their binoculars. They took photos of any policemen they saw, and of the crime scene tape rattling in the wind; they were excited by the sight of the small tent that the SOCOs had erected in the middle of the Nine Virgins, over the spot where Jenny Weston had lain.

Officers had been posted to block the main paths. But they were too easily visible across the moor, and soon they found that people were simply cutting across the vast expanses of heather to avoid them. They shouted themselves hoarse and got the bottoms of their trouser legs soaking wet trying to intercept the stragglers. The sergeant called in for reinforcements, but found there were no more officers available. As always, the division was short of resources.

'"Just do the best you can,"' he reported. 'That's what they always say. "Just do the best you can."'

One young PC found himself being followed around by two old ladies who bombarded him with questions. They pulled at his sleeve and patted his arm and demanded to know whether there was a lot of blood, and how big the murderer's knife had been, and whether the body was still inside the tent. The constable appealed to his sergeant to help him. But the sergeant was busy threatening to arrest a small, fat man in a fluorescent green bubble jacket who refused to move as he stared at the tent with feverish eyes and asked one question over and over again: 'She was naked, wasn't she? It said on the news she was naked.'

Finally, the officers were forced to retreat, reducing the size of the area they were trying to protect. They clustered round the clearing, abandoning the heather and birches to the intruders, like a garrison under siege.

'Haven't they got anything else to do?' complained the PC to the sergeant for the tenth time. 'Can't they go and pester the ducks in Bakewell or something?'

'There'll be more of them yet, Wragg. It's still early,' said the sergeant, watching the green jacket constantly circling the clearing like a bird of prey.

'Early for what?'

'Early for the real loonies.'

'What do you call this lot, then?'

The sergeant shrugged as PC Wragg shook off the grasping fingers of the old ladies. 'These are just your normal, everyday members of the public. Wait till the pubs open. Then you'll see a real circus.'

'Christ, why don't they leave us alone?'

'It's a bit of excitement for them, you see. Some of them probably think it's a film set. They think we're filming an episode of *Peak Practice* or something. In fact, I reckon those old dears have mistaken you for what's his name, the heart-throb doctor.'

'Let's hope the forensics lot are finished soon over at the quarry.'

'Shush. Don't let on. The gongoozlers'll be over that way too, if they hear you.'

'I think it's too late, Sarge.'

The old ladies had spotted a police Range Rover and the Scientific Support Unit's Maverick parking on the roadway above the abandoned quarry. The pair set off at a brisk pace, adjusting their hats and twirling their walking sticks. A family with three children and a Jack Russell terrier had settled down on the grass under the birch trees and had begun to unpack sandwiches and flasks. One of the children got out a kite and unfurled the line. Another threw a stick for the dog to chase.

The sergeant looked around for the little man in the green jacket, and saw him crouched in the heather, his hands compulsively pulling up clumps of whinberry. He looked like a wild dog, eager and alert, sniffing the air for carrion.

'I'm sure I know that one,' said the sergeant. 'I've seen him somewhere before.'

'He looks as though he shouldn't be out on his own,' said PC Wragg. 'I reckon there ought to be at least two male nurses with him, carrying a strait jacket and a bucket of tranquillizers.'

'Don't you believe it,' said the sergeant. 'I've a feeling he's a respectable member of society. A teacher or a lawyer, something like that. I can't quite place him, but it'll come.'

Wragg held up his hand like a traffic policeman as he saw more walkers approaching. 'I'm sorry, ladies. This is a crime scene. I'll have to ask you to walk another way, please.'

'Oh, but we always come this way.'

There were four women, all in early middle age, with their hair tied back and their faces flushed and healthy. They were in bright cagoules and striped leggings, like a gaggle of multi-coloured sheep. They had probably left their husbands at home washing their cars or playing golf.

'Not today, I'm afraid, ladies,' said Wragg firmly. 'Please take another route.'

'He's very polite,' said one woman.

'Have you the right to stop us walking along here?' asked another in a different tone. 'It's a public right of way, after all.'

'That's right – it's marked on the Ordnance Survey map.' The third one produced the map as evidence and pointed at it triumphantly.

'All the same …' said Wragg.

The women began to turn away. But the second one paused and glowered at Wragg.

'You'd be better off making it safe for people to go about their business rather than stopping us using public rights of way. Get the man who's attacking women, that's the best thing you can do.'

PC Wragg watched them go. 'It's not my fault,' he said to their retreating backs.

'You'll have to get used to that,' said his sergeant. 'As far as the public are concerned, it's *all* your fault.'

The man in the green bubble jacket was still manoeuvring for a closer approach, watching the officers until they were distracted by something else, then creeping a few inches nearer.

'So help me, I'm going to thump him if he gets in reach,' said PC Wragg. 'Just the sight of him makes my skin crawl.'

Of course, Ben Cooper realized that the black Peugeot was familiar. It was just that he hadn't expected to see it here. Maybe it was destined to follow him around for ever, like a kind of ghostly hearse, with a phantom undertaker at the wheel.

'It's Diane Fry,' he said.

Todd Weenink cursed some more. 'Oh great. First the Wicked Witch of West Street, DI Armstrong. Now the Frozen Bitch from the Black Country. God, we could do without this. Stand by for a laugh a minute.'

'I thought she was already gone,' said Cooper.

'Fry? I wish.'

They watched Fry get out of the Peugeot and look around the car park. To Cooper, she still seemed thin, despite a heavy woollen jacket with a hood against the cold. She had never looked healthy – too much in need of a few good meals, and with a strength that was all sinew and technique, rather than muscle. For a moment, he wondered how she spent her time now. No one else in Edendale had taken the trouble to befriend her since his own efforts had failed. Diane Fry carried something dark and immovable on her shoulder, something that had accompanied her from West Midlands when she transferred. Cooper felt a *frisson* of unease at the thought of what might happen to her eventually, if she was left entirely on her own.

Finally, Fry saw them and walked directly towards Weenink. She took him aside and spoke to him quietly for a minute. Cooper could see that Todd looked unhappy.

But then he walked to their car and drove away without a glance, his face set into a scowl.

Cooper stood quite still, like a child reluctant to draw attention to himself. He wanted to shove his hands in his pockets to keep them warm, but was worried about how it might be interpreted.

He found the officer safety techniques from the training manuals running through his mind – extracts from the sections on employing empathy. Don't excite the suspect by sudden movements, they said. Show a willingness to resolve the situation by co-operation. That was fine. But there was one problem here. The manuals always recommended maintaining a verbal exchange with the suspect for as long as possible, if you were going to maintain empathy.

Cooper watched her as she took her time reading the notices in the window of the cycle hire centre, as if she were totally fascinated by the weather forecast or the penalties for returning a bike after the deadline.

'What's going on?' he asked. 'What's wrong?'

'Wrong?' Fry's stare was capable of raising the temperature of his skin until he felt his face was glowing like a red traffic light. 'DC Weenink is required back at Division, that's all.'

'Why?' said Cooper. 'What's so important that they pull him off the job just like that?'

'Sorry,' she said. 'I can't tell you that.'

'Can't? Does that mean you do know why? Or haven't they told you either?'

'It's nothing to do with you, OK?'

Cooper opened his mouth, then realized it would be a waste of time trying to explain that Todd Weenink was his partner.

'Right. OK. So now what?'

'Well, we're following Jenny Weston's route, aren't we?'

'We?'

'Since I've deprived you of your friend, you'll have to put up with me. Sorry. Is it this way?'

She turned away from him towards the trail. Cooper felt as though she had reduced him to insignificance with a mere twitch of her narrow shoulder. He followed her, a step behind, staring at the back of her head, trying to figure out what exactly was going on in her mind.

He knew their relationship had got off on the wrong foot. He had tried to be friends with her when she was the new girl in E Division and no one else had bothered. It had gone wrong, of course. But there was something in Fry's manner, something about the way she held her body when she spoke to him, that told him it was more complicated than that. Things always were more complicated than they seemed.

THROUGHOUT THE DRIVE to Partridge Cross, Diane Fry had been preparing herself for dealing with Ben Cooper by repeating a mantra to herself. 'Just keep him at arm's length. Don't let him get under your skin.' She knew the best thing was to concentrate on the job in hand and discourage conversation. But it had still taken her a few moments to bring herself under proper control when she found herself facing him, alone and with nothing to distract her attention. And as usual she found herself unable to deter him from making his infuriating small talk.

'So has your transfer has been put back, then?' said Cooper. 'Did something go wrong?'

'There's been a delay, that's all. Some kind of administrative hold-up. You're stuck with me for a while longer.'

'That's good.'

She looked at Cooper suspiciously. But, as always, he seemed to be saying only what he meant.

'Let's get on with it,' she said. 'There's a lot to do.'

Fry studied the cycle hire centre. With its collection of colourful bikes and the mist still hanging against the embankment, the stone building looked like a picture from a children's story book. It typified the air of unreality about the area that she had yet to come to terms with. Back in Birmingham, they would have flattened this place long ago for a new motorway link road.

'So this is Partridge Cross,' she said. 'I thought they were kidding me about the name. It sounds like something out of *The Archers*.'

'It used to be a railway station on the High Peak line –'

'I think you can keep that sort of stuff for the tourists.' She waited for Cooper to take offence. But all he did was raise his eyebrows.

'Diane, I know something went wrong between us before, but it shouldn't stop us working together,' he said.

She hated it when he was tolerant and reasonable. She would have preferred him to show signs of resentment. She had got the promotion that everybody's favourite detective constable had thought was owed to him by right, and surely it was inevitable that he would resent her.

Fry sighed. 'Have we got a map or anything?' she said.

THEY KNEW THAT Jenny Weston had set off from Partridge Cross an hour and a quarter before her death. She had headed eastwards on the High Peak Trail, where the strip of black compacted gravel provided easy going. Beech and elder trees overhung the trail, with nettles and brambles dying back on the verges. Jenny would have passed under the A515 before she left the trail and crossed the route of the old Roman road to begin the ascent to Ringham Moor.

The mist began to break up as they climbed away from the hire centre. A jet liner went overhead towards East Midlands Airport, leaving a white streak in the sky. A farm dog barked half-heartedly in the distance. In between the noises, it was so unnaturally quiet that when a flock of pigeons passed overhead the noise of their wings sounded as loud as the jet.

But a few people were already starting to arrive on the trail. A woman with iron grey hair jogged by. She was wearing purple Lycra and a clashing yellow bum-bag, and she had two large, shaggy dogs panting to keep up with her. Cooper stopped her and ran through the questions on his list. Had she been this way yesterday afternoon? Did she remember seeing this cyclist? He showed her the snapshot of Jenny Weston provided by her father, and described her bike and clothing. If not, who else had she seen? The woman did her best, but couldn't help. She urged the dogs on as she crunched away again.

Walkers began to appear in pairs, and once there was a small group of half a dozen. They all said 'hello' to the detectives, even before they were asked to stop and answer questions.

'Is it obvious who we are?' asked Fry uneasily.

'No, it's just the thing to do, if you're walking out here. It's a sign of comradeship.'

Fry snorted. Then a lone man passed them, walking slowly, with his head down. He was wearing a worn anorak, and his hair was dark and greasy. Fry's eyes hardened and her shoulders tensed. The man glanced at them nervously as he passed.

'Morning,' he said.

Cooper started to go through the routine with him, but he claimed not to have been in the area before. He let the man go, but Fry stopped when he was a few yards past them.

'I didn't like the look of him,' she said. 'We ought to check him out properly.'

'Why? He's probably just a bird-watcher or something.'

There were views across open fields on either side and the low bankings you could easily walk over. But half a mile further on, the scenery changed. The trail entered a rocky gorge with sheer faces of crumbling limestone. The rock had been hacked into sharp angles by the crude blasting methods of the railway builders. The bramble-covered slopes above them would be impossible to scramble up, and there were lots of places to hide among the tumbled rocks and deep crevices.

They were still some distance from the point where Jenny Weston had tackled the climb on to Ringham Moor. Ahead, there would be police tape and officers posted to prevent them approaching too near to the crime scene.

'Aren't we chasing hares?' asked Cooper.

'We have to go through the routine.'

'We ought to be looking at Jenny's life. Not where she was, but why she was here.'

'It's procedure.'

Up ahead was a tunnel, a black shadow across the trail. The glimpse of light and greenery at the far end only emphasized the blackness they had to walk through to reach it. As they entered, the ground underfoot became softer and carved into ruts by bike tyres. In the middle, the walls and roof were panelled with curved planks and buttressed with iron. Water ran steadily down the wooden sides and dripped from the roof. They had to watch for the gleam and flicker of it in the weak light to avoid the splashes.

'You're dealing with the earlier victim, aren't you?' said Cooper.

'Yes, Maggie Crew.'

'If it's the same assailant, I suppose the main hope we've got is Crew herself. She's the only witness.'

'She's crucial,' said Fry. 'If we're ever going to get an identification, it will be from her.'

'Only potentially crucial, I suppose.'

'Why?'

'She can't remember anything. Isn't that right?'

'I don't think it's as simple as that,' said Fry.

The tunnel had been driven through the rock face at the centre of the gorge, where pink gneiss showed through the limestone. Ferns clung in patches, and a silver birch had tried to colonize a high ledge. The only sounds were the dripping and their own footsteps, until a hissing roar began behind them. They turned to see a racing cyclist, his head down, his face invisible behind an aerodynamic helmet and wraparound shades. He was well past before they could stop him.

The original chunks of dressed stone in the tunnel walls had been filled in here and there with bricks. The number of small stones that had fallen at each side of the path looked a bit ominous, as if the tunnel was slowly crumbling around them. Behind the boarding, a mass of stone that had rolled down from the limestone face was prevented only by the damp boards and rusted iron from closing the trail completely.

'What do you mean, it's not as simple as that?' asked Cooper.

'What I mean is that she does have the memories. The current thinking is that she's burying them, though. Her mind is suppressing them because they're too upsetting. There's a blank for several hours either side of the incident, caused by the trauma. But there might be certain triggers, certain circumstances in which the memories will surface. We need to find a trigger. It could just be a sound, a smell, the sight of something she recognizes. We don't know.'

'But how are we even going to hope for that – unless we can face her directly with her assailant? Isn't there another way, Diane?'

She shrugged. 'The counsellors tried to help, but she got too distressed. So we're not allowed to pressure her into seeing a psychiatrist to take it any further.'

Now it was starting to get busier, with families out for the afternoon. Cooper and Fry crossed the road and began the ascent to the moor. They stopped to look at the field where the farmworker, Victor McCauley, had been working when he saw Jenny on her bike just after half past one.

They emerged above the remains of the mist, and Cooper stared across the expanse of heather and whinberry that covered the plateau. He wasn't quite sure about this Diane Fry who talked about triggers and the current thinking. It sounded wrong. He wondered if she had been on a training course recently.

'Jenny ended up at the Nine Virgins, that way,' he said. 'But we don't know which route she took across the moor.'

'Whichever way she went, it took nearly three-quarters of an hour from when McCauley saw her.'

'Yes. So she probably took the long route. Towards the Cat Stones and the Hammond Tower. Then past the top of Ringham Edge Farm.'

'Let's go there, then.'

There was no escape from the wind once they started to walk across the moor. The uniformity and lack of distraction in the landscape meant there was no escape from your thoughts, either. Or from the presence of the person you were with.

As they approached the Cat Stones, the wind seemed to double in strength, battering at them from the rocky outcrops. Cooper shivered, and Fry pulled her collar up higher. There was no life on Ringham Moor, apart from the vegetation, itself already turning brown and brittle. The moor was empty right the way across to the outline of the tower, perched above the steep drop on its eastern edge.

'Maybe it's a test, Diane,' said Cooper, after a while.

'You what?'

'Putting you on to Maggie Crew. You've got the hardest job. Maybe they're just putting you through the wringer. They want to see whether you come out the other side.'

At first, he didn't think she was going to answer. Fry walked on a few more yards, her eyes fixed ahead, concentrating on where she was going, oblivious to the fascinations of the landscape around her.

'Which I will,' she said. 'I come through everything.'

Chapter Ten

BEN COOPER RECOGNIZED the look of a martyr when he saw one. And Yvonne Leach had that look – the defeated air of a woman worn down by many years of battling against the odds.

But it was more than that. She had an expression that Cooper had seen in the eyes of his own mother so many times. For some reason, there were women who slipped into the role of martyr as if it were their destiny. At one time, Cooper had found the tendency so frustrating in his mother that he had become angry with her, though she was not the person his anger should have been turned against. For years now, he had been drained of the anger. The sight of Mrs Leach brought it all back to him.

'Sorry to disturb you, Mrs Leach. Is your husband around at the moment?'

'No. I don't know where he is,' she said.

'Perhaps he's about the farm somewhere?'

'Perhaps he is.'

She had kept Cooper standing in the yard, advancing from her doorstep so that he had to retreat to a point where he couldn't see into the house. He noted her defensiveness without surprise. Many of these small hill farmers were used to making do on little money, especially when they had children to raise. But when things became too bad, it was often the women on whom the burden fell; the women were the first to suffer the internal fractures that could tear apart their families and their lives. They always tried to hide it. But there were inadvertent signs – little giveaways that you could learn to see, with practice.

'I noticed the Land Rover wasn't in the yard,' he said.

'Maybe he's gone out, then.'

'Do you know where, Mrs Leach?'

She shrugged. 'He doesn't always tell me where he's going. Why should he?'

Now Cooper registered the note of defiance, and assessed the woman more carefully. Although her clothes were old, they were clean and neatly pressed. Her hair, streaking to grey, had not seen a hairdresser for some time, but it was brushed and tied neatly back. Cooper realized she had even applied a touch of make-up this morning. Her lips showed two unsteady lines of red, her cheeks traces of powder.

'If you see your husband, please tell him we'd like to speak to him again,' he said.

Then Mrs Leach smiled. It was a strangely elated smile, escaping through lips that trembled slightly.

Cooper wondered whether she was on the verge of hysteria, a step away from being tipped over the edge. He wanted to stay for a while and talk to her, to tell her to seek medical advice before it was too late. He wanted to tell her that those were the saddest words in the language: 'too late'. But he couldn't do that. It wasn't his job.

'If I see him,' she said. 'Oh yes, I'll tell him if I see him.'

'And how are the boys?'

She looked surprised, almost unnerved, as if someone had just delivered bad news.

'What?'

'Will and Dougie, is that their names? I saw them the other day. A couple of grand lads.'

'Yes.' Mrs Leach took a handkerchief from her pocket and began to twist it as she watched Cooper's face suspiciously.

'They were tending to a fine-looking calf. They said her name was Doll.'

'They showed her at Bakewell.'

'And won a prize, too.'

'They were that pleased,' she said. Her voice rose suddenly on the last word, as if she had lost control of her pitch. She screwed up the handkerchief and began to dab at her lips.

'I'm sure you must be very proud of them.'

Mrs Leach nodded.

'I suppose they're at school just now,' said Cooper.

She made an indecipherable noise through the handkerchief that might have been agreement.

'How old are they?'

'Six and nine – no, ten.'

'Both still at the primary school in Cargreave, then,' he said.

She nodded again.

'I suppose Will is going to be off to secondary school next year. Do they go to Matlock or Bakewell from here?'

'I forget.'

Cooper looked back to where Diane Fry waited impatiently at the gate, eyeing the muck in the yard with distaste. It was only the mud left by the hooves of the cows as they passed through to the milking parlour from the wet fields. But it should have been cleaned up by now. Ringham Edge had the look of a well-maintained farm in other ways – the house and the buildings were in good condition, the tractor he could see in the shed was almost new. But there was the burnt-out pick-up standing abandoned by the shed, and the yard hadn't been washed clean of mud for days.

'Is everything all right, Mrs Leach? No problems?'

Yvonne Leach laughed, and then looked at him with astonishment. 'What *is* it you want?' she said.

'We're trying to trace the movements of the woman who was killed on the moor yesterday. We think she might have come this way.'

'Oh?' She ran her hand across her mouth again, and kept it there for a moment. To hide an inappropriate smile or some other expression; Cooper couldn't tell. The woman's eyes certainly weren't smiling. He began to describe Jenny Weston. He showed Mrs Leach the photo. She took it in her hand and looked at it for a long time.

When she handed it back, there was a smear of lipstick on the edge of the print.

'No, no,' she said. 'I never saw her.'

'Did you see anybody else come by this way? Yesterday afternoon?'

'People are always coming by. It's a right of way, the track there. We take no notice of them, as long as they don't bother us.'

'It must have been fairly quiet yesterday, I suppose. Not many walkers.'

'Yes. Quiet.'

'I just thought, if it was so quiet, you might have noticed somebody more.'

Yvonne Leach seemed to be losing interest, or was thinking about something else. 'There was the other one, too. A few weeks ago.'

'Yes. She was attacked near the Cat Stones, we think. Up by the tower somewhere.'

'It was me that found her, you know. That time.'

'Yes, of course.'

'She was in a terrible state. Who would do a thing like that?'

'I'm afraid we don't know.'

'Is it the same man this time?' she asked. And she covered her lips again. She used both hands this time, as if afraid her mouth was running out of control.

'I'm afraid we just don't know,' said Cooper.

He saw that she had rubbed at her mouth so much that the lipstick had been removed completely, except for a small smudge in one corner of her lip. He turned to walk away. But as he crossed the yard, Cooper looked back and saw Yvonne Leach fold her handkerchief and begin to dab anxiously at her mouth all over again.

It was obvious the woman was in trouble, but what could he do? When he spoke to Warren Leach next, he could mention his wife's condition, but he couldn't hold out much hope that the man would listen. He could talk to the Social Services, and say he was concerned about the welfare of the two boys in the household. But he knew his concerns would be a low priority for them – they were overwhelmed with more urgent calls on their time. They were so stretched that they could only respond when something had already happened, when things had gone too far. They acted when it was already too late.

But Ben Cooper understood that. It was what the police did, too.

DIANE FRY WAS relieved that Cooper was quiet for once. Privately, she had no doubt they were wasting their time. The leads would come from elsewhere than from wandering around the landscape. There had to be a link between Jenny Weston's death and the previous assault – it was no more than half a mile away that Maggie Crew had been attacked among the boulders of the Cat Stones. Maggie and Jenny had been two women alone, unsuspecting. One was unable to describe her assailant; the second was dead. The worst scenario was that the victims had been chosen at random. Stranger murders meant no witness trail, and no motivation. The lack of relationship between victim and killer presented the investigator with a hopeless task.

That was why they needed Maggie Crew. Some day, in some way, she would provide them with an identification. Her memories had to come back.

At the top of the farm track, they met up with DCs Toni Gardner and Danny Boyle, who had been working their way backwards from the stone circle, via the Hammond Tower. They shook their heads at each other. A waste of time, they said. Then they walked back towards the Nine Virgins, where the group of uniformed officers guarded the taped-off scene.

Fry looked at the stones in incomprehension. What was all the fuss about? She could think of lots of better places to come to at night, even if what you wanted to do was take off your clothes and light fires and smoke a bit of cannabis.

'Kind of small for Stonehenge, isn't it?' she said. But Cooper didn't rise to the bait.

One stone had a flat top, and she found it was big enough to sit on comfortably. But then she remembered some of the traces that the SOCOs had collected from the stones and it occurred to her the flat stone had probably been used for other things than just sitting on. She looked around for Cooper again.

'The Nine Virgins? You people round here really do have active imaginations, don't you?'

Still he didn't respond. After a moment, they headed southwards, to where there was a view down on to Ringham Lees village. Swathes of leaves lined the path, and tiny quartz crystals glittered in the sand like fragments of glass. The birches rattled their dry leaves, and a pair of jays darted at each other among the trees. They could see there were members of the public on the moor now, lots of them. A small, fat man in a green bubble jacket stood by the side of the path and waited for them to draw level. He looked at Fry eagerly.

'Where are her clothes?' he said.

'What?'

'Keep walking,' said Cooper, without looking round.

Fry wanted to question the little man, but she followed Cooper as he veered off and took a rabbit track across the heather. The rough stems of the plants grabbed at her ankles. At one spot there was an area a few square yards wide which had been burned off, leaving black, brittle stalks that crumbled underfoot and a layer of ash that was gradually being washed into the ground by the rain.

'Hold on, Ben.'

He stopped impatiently. 'He's just one of the local weirdos. You can spot them a mile off. Let the uniforms deal with him.'

'I can't believe people like that. They're sick.'

'Right. But he's probably already in a Care in the Community scheme, or something.'

'What the hell's that?'

'Care in the Community? Well, it's a bit difficult to explain –'

'No – that.'

Fry was pointing at a fungus clinging to the bark of an oak tree. It was like nothing she had ever seen before. It was pale and bulbous, like a human organ that had been bleached or left out in the rain. She put her hand to it gingerly. It was firm to the touch at first, but gave under the pressure of her fingers like a fresh bread roll. White, not wholemeal. The fungus was dry on top, but cold and clammy underneath, and it moved slightly under her fingers.

Then she noticed that there were lots more fungi on the ground, all different kinds. Some were dark and coiled like dog turds, but black and ragged at the edges, as if they had been half eaten. Other fungi were like stones, some like cups, some like human ears.

Fry stared at them with revulsion. How anybody could visit this moor for pleasure she could not imagine. There was nothing to recommend it to anyone, except to the weirdos and the ghouls attracted by death and the bizarre.

Ben Cooper set off again and managed to get ahead of Fry to reach the edge of the plateau, where it dropped away into the valley. He stood on the precipice and felt the wind catch his breath and freeze the lobes of his ears. He felt as though he could step off the edge and let the wind carry him away across the patchwork of fields and dry-stone walls.

From his vantage point, Cooper could see the people on the moor winding their way in ones and twos through the heather and bracken. Yet the place still had a feeling of solitude and isolation, somewhere you could just be yourself, free of expectations. He understood what Jenny Weston had seen in the moor.

'It's so cold and bleak,' said Fry, catching up with him. 'What's the name of that pub in Ringham where we can get lunch?'

'The Druid,' he said, brought suddenly to earth.

'God, those Victorians. Romantic minds, they had. Anything more than a few years old had to be connected with Ancient Britons and Druids, didn't it? In actual fact, most of these rocks were just dropped here by glaciers or something, and got worn into these shapes by the appalling weather you get up here.'

'Well, I suppose so.'

'You sound disappointed. A bit of a Victorian yourself, aren't you, Ben? A romantic at heart?'

'We can get down to the village by cutting through South Quarry.'

'Fine.'

After Fry had turned away to follow the path, Cooper shook his head in despair. It was such a small mistake for a woman like Jenny Weston to have made. Yet it had been the biggest mistake of her life. Why had she chosen to come up here at the beginning of November? It was one of the quietest times of the year, when even retired couples were putting away their walking boots, turning up the central heating and pulling the sofa closer to the TV to watch their holiday videos. And for some reason, Jenny had let the wrong person get close to her. There were so many mistakes. It seemed as though she had been heading directly on a course towards her own destruction.

A FEW MINUTES later, Cooper slid down the last few feet of the slope into South Quarry, as Fry struggled behind him.

'Hello. What's this?' he said.

Unlike Top Quarry, these abandoned workings had been left with a level, sandy bottom, clear of debris. The entrance was open to the road, and sometimes cars parked in the first part of the quarry. The face wasn't so high there, and it was possible to climb a narrow track up and get straight on to the moor. Visitors normally stopped short of taking their cars on to the steep roadway that dropped into the lower part of the quarry, afraid that they might never get back up again, or that their wheels might slip off the edge.

But on the rock-spattered floor in the deepest part of the quarry stood a van. Whoever had driven it here had managed to find a flat area where the wagons had once been loaded with stone. The angle of the quarry walls hid the spot completely from the road fifty yards away. Unless you were looking, you would never find it.

'It's an old VW Transporter,' said Cooper. 'Long wheelbase version. And over twenty years old, if you can believe the registration plates. But look at the state of the tyres. This thing hasn't moved in a good while.'

Fry pulled out her personal radio. 'I'll call in and get them to do a check on that number. It's probably stolen.'

Cooper walked round the van carefully. As well as the back doors, there was a side loading door on the near-side. But the windows at the back had been painted over, in the way that market traders did to screen their goods from prying eyes. Cooper reached the driver's door and peered into the cab. The seats were worn and split, and a large cobweb glistened across the corner between the sidelight and the dashboard. An old curtain hung behind the seats, concealing the interior.

'They're going to call back in a minute,' said Fry. 'Is it unlocked?'

'I haven't tried yet.'

Cooper took a tissue from his pocket and tried the handle of the driver's door. The metal was tarnished and beginning to rust through the chrome. The button depressed, but there was no click of the catch, and the door didn't move. He edged round the bonnet. The manufacturer's VW badge had gone from the grille. No surprise there – at one time, the badges had been prized by local kids as trophies, as the initials were said to stand for their favourite catch phrase 'Very Wicked'.

The passenger door was also locked. So was the side door. And so were the rear doors.

'If this van was abandoned here by a car thief, it was a very security-conscious thief,' he said.

'Perhaps it's not stolen at all, then. Maybe it was somebody who couldn't be bothered taking it to the scrapyard.'

Fry's radio crackled. While she listened, Cooper crouched to look underneath the van, noting a missing section of exhaust pipe and a dark patch on the ground that might have been oil. A cover was missing from one of the rear lights, and there were holes in the wheel arches caused by serious corrosion.

'It's registered to a Mr Calvin Lawrence of Stockport,' said Fry. 'But there's no report of it being stolen.'

'Well, it hasn't been on the road legally since October 1999,' said Cooper, peering at the licence disc just visible behind the windscreen. 'Not that it means anything necessarily.' Discs were colour coded so that the month of expiry could be detected from a distance. But this one was so faded its original colour could have been any selection from the rainbow.

'So the owner has abandoned it, then. This Calvin Lawrence presumably. Just another MoT failure, that's all. We'll get someone to remove it and report the owner for illegal tipping.'

'It's odd, though. Why come all the way from Stockport to leave it here? There must be any number of out-of-the-way places on the way between here and Stockport that you could abandon an old van, if you wanted to.'

'Not to mention scrapyards,' said Fry.

'Funny that people never seem to think of that, isn't it? As if the countryside is here just for them to use as a huge dump-it site.'

'We're not here to worry about the environment, Ben. Leave that to your friends with the red jackets.'

But Cooper was still frowning. 'And if you were going to do that, why leave the plates on? It doesn't make sense.'

'It isn't our concern. We'll pass it on to uniformed section.'

'The funniest thing, though ...' said Cooper, as if she hadn't spoken. 'Have you noticed? The funniest thing about this van ... is the smell.'

Fry sniffed, but shook her head. 'Why, what is it? Petrol?'

'No,' said Cooper.

'Well, what then?'

Cooper stared at the side door of the van, his head cocked on one side as though he was listening to the sounds of its suspension rusting, or its rubber seals slowly rotting in the damp air. He waited until he was absolutely sure of what his senses were telling him.

'Chicken curry,' he said.

Chapter Eleven

MARK ROPER HAD watched the police walk away from the farmhouse at Ringham Edge. They hadn't got into the house, no more than anybody ever did. At first, he had thought the woman with Detective Constable Cooper might have been a social worker. Yvonne Leach had looked nervous when she opened the door, but it had soon become clear they had no knowledge or power that she might be afraid of. They hadn't even glanced at the big shed behind the farmhouse, either.

For Mark, the choice was impossible. If he went to the police with his suspicions, it would be obvious where the information had come from. Obvious to Warren Leach, at least. It would be bad for farmers to get the idea that Rangers were spying on them, reporting them to the police, to social workers, or to the RSPCA over things that were none of the Rangers' business. That would do nothing for relationships with landowners, which Owen said were so important to the Peak District National Park. There was no point in antagonizing Leach any further, so Owen said.

The source of the information would be obvious to Owen, too. And that would be even worse.

Mark moved slightly as Yvonne Leach crossed the yard. He knew his outline was camouflaged by the trees behind him on the hillside, and his red jacket was below the level of the stone wall. Mrs Leach wouldn't see him, anyway. The woman was too absorbed in her own troubles to see what went on around her. Leach himself had gone out an hour before. There had been police parked up the hill under the beeches, but they had ignored the farmer. They had nothing on Warren Leach, then. Not yet. Mark would have to wait a bit longer.

He wondered what Owen would do in the same situation. Probably he would recommend patience. But how long could you be expected to wait? How long could Mark be patient?

CAUTIOUSLY, BEN COOPER put his ear to the cold metal. It felt damp and uncomfortable. Fry looked as though she was about to speak, but he hastily held up a hand to silence her. He could hear vague stirrings from inside the van; he could even feel a slight movement in the side panel as the springs of the suspension shifted.

He gestured to Fry, and they both walked away from the van until they were out of earshot.

'There's definitely somebody in there. What do we do?'

Fry had no hesitation. 'We get some back-up before we do anything. No heroics. Not even from you, understand?'

'Fair enough,' said Cooper, and held his hands up like a man pleading for a truce.

Fry called in, and they waited, watching the van. They knew there were officers not far away, up on the moor. They had no more than a few minutes to wait – but it could seem like a long time.

FINALLY, A UNIFORMED sergeant and two PCs in stab-proof vests, with their hands on their side-handled batons, walked up to the van. As Cooper and Fry watched, the sergeant banged on the side door.

'Police! Open up!'

The sergeant had a heavy fist and his pounding made a noise that must have reverberated deafeningly inside the van. There was a sudden scuffling and muffled cursing, a moment of silence, then a clunk as the latch on the side door went down. The door began to move, screeching as its runner stuck, then sliding slowly open. The officers near the van tensed and took a couple of steps backwards.

'What do you want, man? Oh, shit.'

When the door was open about a foot, a face appeared, masked by a straggly beard and a woollen hat. The face was low down towards the floor of the van, with a bare arm stretched up to the handle. The rest of his body was wrapped up in a sleeping bag. All that was visible was the head and one arm.

'Step out of the van, please,' said the sergeant.

'You what?'

'Step out of the van, please, sir. Let me see your hands as you come out.'

'I'm in fucking bed. What do you want?'

'We need to talk to you. Is there anyone else in there?'

The sergeant ducked his head through the door, well clear of possible contact with the figure on the floor, and quick enough to avoid the door being slammed on his head.

'Right. Let's have both of you out. Sharp, now.'

Standing behind the sergeant, Cooper breathed deeply. A whole miasma of smells had been released by the opening of the door – not just the aroma of the chicken curry that had been eaten recently, but a small army of scents that competed with it for attention. Some of the smells were dark and musty, others sharp and metallic. Cooper longed to get inside the van and absorb the sensations. But he stood waiting patiently while the sergeant urged the occupants out into the welcoming arms of his constables.

'Come on, come on. Let's have you, son.'

'Oh God, hang on then.'

The face disappeared for a few seconds, and there was a heaving as a body was hauled from a sleeping bag. The sergeant kept a hand causally on the door. Finally, a young man emerged, bundled in clothes and muttering. He sat on the step of the van until one of the PCs helped him up.

'And your girlfriend as well. Out here.'

A second figure came out of the gloom, a slight, narrow-shouldered figure, moving more slowly, like someone still half-asleep. No – more than half-asleep, an actual sleep walker, with eyes that were barely aware of what was around them, as if they were focused on a dream world that no one else could see. This one said nothing, merely peering from a mass of tangled blond hair at the watching faces with faintly inquisitive eyes. Not angry or nervous, thought Cooper. Not frightened or aggressive. Just slightly puzzled, as if she had noticed an unfamiliar noise or spotted an animal she didn't recognize. She was clutching a blanket to her chest with thin, pale hands.

Cooper left Fry's side and moved a step closer to the van and took another sniff. There was no scent of drugs that he recognized. If they had been smoking cannabis inside the van, it would be detectable to the nose. But that didn't mean they hadn't been taking something else. He looked at the sergeant, who nodded in agreement. It might be an excuse for searching the van, if they wanted it. They could get a dog down here and take the vehicle apart in no time.

'Are you the owner of this vehicle?' the sergeant asked the youth with the straggly beard.

'Yes, it's mine,' he said. 'And it's not nicked.'

'Right. Let's have your names.'

'We're not doing anything wrong.'

'Names. You first.' The sergeant pointed at the youth.

'Homer Simpson,' he said.

Cooper and Fry smiled. At first, the youth might actually have thought they were appreciating the joke. But advance information was very useful.

'Nice try, Calvin,' said Fry.

He looked surprised, then deflated.

'It *is* Calvin Lawrence, isn't it? Of Benson Street, Stockport?'

'Is it me you're after?'

'Depends what you've done.'

'I haven't done anything. How did you know my name?'

'Listen, if you want to be anonymous, try taking the plates off the van. It's still registered in your name. Bit of a giveaway, that.'

'Shit.'

'Not much of a mastermind, are you, Calvin?'

'They call me Cal,' he said.

'Is Benson Street, Stockport, still your home address?'

'No, that's my parents' house.'

'Can we have your current address, please?'

'Number One, Quarry Avenue, Stonesville.'

The sergeant wrote it down. 'Where's that?'

Cal sneered, and looked at the other officers, inviting them to share his disdain. 'It's here, man. I live here.'

'In the van?'

'You've got it.'

'You're giving that thing as your permanent residence?'

'It's as permanent as anything is.'

'That might be debatable. Do the owners of this property know you're here? Have you got permission for overnight parking?'

'Jesus, are you real?' said Cal. 'Or did I just fall into an old Benny Hill Show?'

'No? In that case, you might find your home is more temporary than you think, son.'

Cal folded his arms across the holes in his sweater. A mulish look came over his face. 'You'll have to drag us out of here, if you want to move us.'

'Well, we can arrange that, if necessary.'

The sergeant looked at the girl. She had said nothing yet. In fact, her attention seemed to have wandered. She gently pushed some of the hair from her eyes as she turned to watch the movement of some home-made wind chimes hanging in a birch tree on the edge of the quarry. Cooper realized that the chimes were providing a constant background tune that made the sergeant's voice sound curiously discordant and out of place, a meaningless animal growl against the harmonies of a distant choir. The sound of the chimes seemed to mean more to this dreamy young woman than the small army of police officers who had invaded her home.

'And your name, miss?' said the sergeant.

She seemed not to have heard him. Her gaze remained directed into space, oblivious to the turn in the conversation, unaware of the attention that was on her.

'You, miss. Can we have your name, please?'

Then she turned and smiled at him, a whimsical smile, not unfriendly or sullen. She pushed back her hair again and her fingers danced across her face, fluttering on her cheeks in a curious gesture. Then Cooper saw the faint fuzz of hair on the jawline and the top lip, the Adam's apple and wide forehead under the hair. Not 'miss' at all, but another male.

Cal butted in, moving slightly to impose himself between his friend and the policeman.

'You've got it wrong again. We call him Stride,' he said.

The sergeant had noticed his mistake, too. 'OK. But I'm talking to him, not you.'

'Just don't talk to him like that.'

The sergeant stared grimly at the second youth. 'Your name, please, sir.'

The silence continued. The young man's eyes began to drift back towards the floor of the quarry, but too slowly for the sergeant. He reached out a hand, ready to grab the youth's arm. Cal tensed angrily, and the two PCs stepped forward.

'It doesn't matter.'

The youth's voice was soft. His lips barely moved, so that his words were no more than a whisper. But they all heard it clearly. The sergeant's hand stopped short of touching him, uncertain of what he had been about to do. He looked like a man who found himself with a passing swan in the sights of his twelve-bore, with his finger already on the trigger.

'If we don't get some identity from you, we're going to take you down to the station for questioning,' he said.

'Oh, right, here comes the harassment,' said Cal. 'What made you wait so long? Take him down to the station. You are so full of shit. I mean, what does it matter what name his parents gave him? What does it matter where he comes from? It's who he is, that's all you need to know. All anyone needs. Jesus.'

'Religious gentleman, are you, sir? They tell me if you call Jesus's name often enough, the Virgin Mary gets annoyed and tells you he can't come out to play today.'

Finally, the one called Stride sighed and shook his head. 'It doesn't matter. Not really. It's only a name.'

'I'm afraid we'll have to insist, sir. Otherwise, you can come with us.'

They waited expectantly. Finally, Stride sat down in the doorway of the van and leaned into the interior. The police began to look uneasy again. He pulled a cardboard box towards him and rummaged around inside it, reaching right down to the bottom through heaps of paper and clothes. Some of the contents he pulled out and deposited on the step, examining each one carefully as he handled them.

Cal watched him, his expression a mixture of concern and affection. Stride looked up at him, and something passed between them when their eyes met. Cooper cocked his head, listening hard for the sound of the message they were communicating, but it was something he couldn't fathom, maybe something quite beyond his own experience.

Then Stride suddenly held out his hand with an object that glinted, sharp and metallic. The sergeant already had his baton half out of his service belt by the time Stride opened his hand and showed it to his friend.

'Hey, that's the can-opener we lost,' said Cal.

The sergeant looked embarrassed, then angry. Stride smiled at him. His fingers went to his face again. They flickered against his cheek, like a repeated word in sign language. Did it mean he was laughing?

Then he produced a small enamel biscuit tin, whipping it in front of them like a conjuror producing a rabbit. The tin was a startling royal blue, with Victorian-style portraits in round, gilt frames on the lid. He popped the lid open, and showed them that the tin was crammed with small items: photographs, letters, postcards, the stub of an airline ticket, a few metal badges, a gold pen, a roll of yellowed newspaper cuttings.

'That's me,' he said.

The sergeant replaced his baton and took a plastic card-holder from him. The edges were cracked and split, and one corner was turned over. Inside was a card headed with the initials NUS over a badly coloured photograph, taken against a curtain in harsh, glaring light.

'This is your Student Union card?' he said, comparing the face to Stride's.

'When I was at uni in Sheffield.'

'The hair's longer now, but I suppose it's you.'

'It's me.'

'Simon Bevington.' The sergeant wrote it down, and noted the membership number. 'This address. What is it? Is this where your parents live, like your friend? Digs? Or what?'

'A bedsit.'

'I see. When did you last live there?'

'Six months ago. A year. Who knows?'

'This union card is last year's. When did you leave university?'

'January.'

'And where do your parents live?'

'I've forgotten.'

'Come off it.'

'My life has nothing to do with them any more.'

'I wonder if they agree with that, sir,' said the sergeant. 'We can trace them, you know.'

'I wish you joy.'

The sergeant looked round at the two CID officers, and turned back to the young men. 'We'll need statements from you. Then we'll see whether we have to move you from here.'

'Jesus,' said Cal.

'A statement!' said Stride. 'Can it be any statement I like? How about: "Sergeant, I love you"?'

Cooper watched the young man carefully. It was difficult to tell whether his manner was an act or not. But he had just succeeded in attracting serious attention to himself. Because it was certainly his name that had recently been scratched into the ground in the middle of the Nine Virgins.

Cooper sighed. The smell of chicken curry was making him hungry. But he was going to miss his lunch at the pub in Ringham, after all.

Diane Fry called in to report their whereabouts to the incident room, but finished the call with a thoughtful look.

'What is it?' asked Cooper.

'The team in Totley have been following up on Jenny Weston's visitors. Do you remember a girl with dreadlocks being mentioned?'

'Sure. The neighbours seem to have noticed every move she made.'

'They're pretty sure now that this girl was more than just a visitor. It seems she was actually living with Jenny Weston at her house for a while.'

'Have they identified her?'

'She was introduced to one of Jenny's work colleagues as Ros Daniels. She was aged about 20, and believed to be from Cheshire.'

'They'll be keen to question her, then. She has to know what was going on in Jenny's life better than anyone does.'

'Oh, they *would* question her, if they could find her,' said Fry. 'But it seems Ros Daniels is missing.'

BACK ON THE moor, an excuse had finally been found to arrest the little man in the green bubble jacket. He had been discovered lying naked in the heather in the middle of one of the smaller stone circles. He had been dreaming blissfully, apparently oblivious to anyone passing, just as he was unaware of his skin turning blue and his genitals shrivelling to the size of a button mushroom. The police had made him get dressed and charged him with indecent exposure. And PC Wragg had smiled.

Chapter Twelve

In South Quarry later that afternoon, Cal and Stride were sitting on a convenient rock alongside their van. They had two mugs of tea and were rolling tobacco into Rizla papers with practised fingers. Stride's movements were languid as he stooped over the task, occasionally pushing the hair back from his eyes. He wore what looked like an old greatcoat from an Army surplus store and a pair of combat trousers, with his tin of tobacco balanced on one knee. He was entirely concentrated on rolling his cigarette, his delicate fingers prodding the tobacco neatly into place. Occasionally, he smiled to himself, as if at some private joke.

It seemed to Ben Cooper that the one called Cal was altogether more watchful. Though he didn't look up, he was certainly aware that he was being observed. His shoulders were tense, and he frowned as he licked the edge of his Rizla before pushing his tobacco tin away in one of the pockets of a camouflage jacket. A stud in his nose glittered briefly as he turned to watch Stride light up. The skin of Cal's scalp was visible through his dark stubble, hardly any longer than the stubble on his cheeks.

'What do you make of them?' asked DCI Tailby.

'Mostly harmless,' said DI Hitchens.

Cooper laughed, and Tailby looked at him sharply. 'Was that a joke?'

'*The Hitch-hiker's Guide to the Galaxy*, sir,' explained Cooper. 'It's how the guide describes the planet Earth. Just those two words: "mostly harmless".'

The DCI looked at him for a moment. His grey wings of hair lifted in the wind that buffeted the quarry edge, then settled back on his temples like roosting doves.

'Douglas Adams,' said DI Hitchens helpfully. 'I liked Marvin the Paranoid Android, myself.' The DCI had turned his stare on Hitchens instead. 'Not that I meant it as a joke, sir. I meant these two – I think they're mostly harmless. No police records.'

Cal and Stride sat without speaking, smoking their cigarettes, staring into space, apparently at peace with the world. Cooper recalled that there had been cigarette ends in the inventory of items recovered by the scenes of crime team near Jenny Weston's body. But they had been Marlboro, not handmade roll-ups.

Above the VW van, a birch had rooted itself on a precarious ledge in the quarry side. Its lower branches were hung with small metal objects, bits of tinfoil and sections of baked bean cans tinkling and clanging in the wind.

'And what's all that lot supposed to be?' asked Tailby. 'Some new way of doing the washing-up?'

'Tree art,' said Hitchens. 'Bevington has written some poems that are stuck to the chimes. They're meant to create an atmosphere of peace and harmony, he says. Do you want to go and have a closer look?'

'No, thanks. Too much harmony is bad for me.'

Tailby glared down at the van. To Cooper, it seemed that it was taking a great effort for Cal not to look up and stare back.

'Can we positively eliminate them as suspects?' asked Tailby.

'They have no apparent connection with the victim, and there's no motive that we know of. There is no witness evidence to tie them in any closer to the scene than this.'

'What about their shoes?'

'I got a quick look,' said Cooper. 'Calvin Lawrence is wearing trainers, and Bevington has a pair of Doc Martens. Neither would match the partial print we found.'

'They may have a pair of boots in the van. I know they don't look as though they have much, but even these two could own more than one pair of shoes.'

'We'd need a search warrant to look in the van. We don't have reasonable suspicion.'

Stride lay back on the rock, letting his coat fall open, resting his head back so that he was gazing at the sky. His hands were resting on his face near his eyes, but the fingers were still. The smoke from his roll-up drifted straight up for a few feet, then was caught in the wind and dispersed. Whatever he could see up there in the sky caused him to smile with some deep, inner pleasure. The smile was so sudden that it made the detectives look up as well. But there was nothing to be seen except clouds scudding high across the moor. The clouds were growing darker. There could be rain soon.

'If you think those wind chimes are strange, Cooper has something else to show us,' said Hitchens.

They walked round the quarry edge to a sheltered spot enclosed by two rocks. In a shallow basin in one of the rocks were what appeared at first to be a series of giant candles. They were made of wax, a foot tall, and they had been carefully sculpted, each into the same distinctive shape, with a long straight shaft, faintly ribbed with veins, and a swollen, rounded head like a cowl, with a small hole in the very tip. They were all sorts of colours – swirling blues and reds, butter yellow, subtle tints of brown and green, and a pure white one, with delicate streaks of gold in the veins of the shaft. They stood like soldiers on parade, pointing permanently skywards.

'That's disgusting,' said Tailby.

'They represent the phallus,' said Hitchens.

'I can see exactly what they represent,' said Tailby. 'And phallus wasn't the word that sprang to mind.'

'I think it probably takes quite some doing to get the shape just right, like that. I was thinking of a nomination for the Turner Prize.'

'And who is the Leonardo da Vinci we have to thank for this lot?'

'The one called Cal. He's quite proud of them. He calls this place the phallus farm.'

'They're obscene.'

'I doubt they're committing an offence,' said Cooper.

'I don't want to look at them. Let's go back.'

They walked back round the quarry to the path. Cooper noticed a group of women appear on the far side of the quarry. They were wearing cagoules and leggings, bright and chatty. They looked down at Cal and Stride for a while, then walked past the birch tree and studied the wind chimes.

'Where's Acting DS Fry?' asked Tailby. 'Wasn't she here earlier?'

'She has one of her sessions with Maggie Crew,' said Hitchens.

'Oh, yes.' The DCI drew the words out like a sigh. He didn't sound hopeful of Maggie Crew.

Tailby stood quietly for a minute, staring at the van and the two youths. 'I've got a press conference to do in half an hour,' he said. 'What am I going to tell the TV and the newspapers?'

'How about telling them to keep out of our bloody way?' suggested Hitchens.

'All right,' said Tailby. 'I've seen enough. Let's go.'

The group of women had moved on. They could be heard chatting again for a while. But they fell very silent when they reached the rock that contained the phallus farm.

At the West Street HQ, they had already been making structural alterations to the canteen. They had succeeded in making it both smaller and less welcoming at the same time. Perhaps it was a deliberate ploy to make the introduction of the vending machines seem like an improvement.

But E Division was lucky. Their neighbours in B Division had no canteen at all. A mobile sandwich service called at the front of the building every lunchtime. Beyond that, it was a question of a kettle, a jar of Nescafé and a packet of chocolate biscuits in the corner of every office. There could be no 'canteen culture' when there was no canteen. Problem solved.

Ben Cooper carried a cup of coffee to a table where some of his shift were already sitting, and he arrived in the middle of a conversation that immediately made him uneasy.

'She's a real hard bitch,' Todd Weenink was saying.

Opposite Weenink was Toni Gardner, a DC from another shift, who still had her straight blonde hair tied back into a ponytail in the fashion of the uniformed officers. She nodded in agreement. 'She's a toughie, all right.'

'Who are you talking about?' asked Cooper, though he felt he could have a good guess.

'That Diane Fry,' said Weenink.

'A snotty cow, she is, too,' said Gardner.

Cooper settled down on a spare chair, concentrating on not spilling his coffee so that he didn't have to meet anyone's eye.

'She's just trying too hard,' he said. 'She'll settle down after a bit.'

Weenink shook his head sadly. 'I don't know how you can be so tolerant. I know *I* wouldn't be, if it was me.'

Cooper looked at the officers round the table, and he wanted to tell them about the time that Diane Fry had reluctantly confided in him the secrets of her past, the dreadful history of her family, and the heroin-addict sister she hadn't seen since she was sixteen. But he knew it was impossible to share this knowledge with anyone else.

'I'd tell her where to stick her stripes,' said Gardner. She smiled at Todd Weenink, as if willing him to notice that she was agreeing with him. Cooper realized that there was more going on here. Todd had an attraction for some women that he never fully understood. He supposed it was a kind of overt masculinity, the sense of sexual challenge in his dark smirk and the way he held his body. Yet these things were not what women said they looked for in men. Not the women Ben Cooper talked to, anyway.

Gradually, the conversation veered to other topics – grumbles about supervisors, night shifts and salaries. Every man there could have run E Division better than the Divisional Commander. Under their guidance, the clear-up rate would double. But then there were the courts to deal with, of course. Not to mention the CPS. The Criminal Preservation Society, they called it – the body of lawyers given the responsibility of prosecuting the alleged offenders the police produced for them. There was a general shaking of heads.

'And we're chasing up white vans tomorrow,' said Weenink. 'I can't wait.'

Finally, the other officers drifted away and left Cooper and Weenink alone.

'Are you all right, Todd?'

'Sure. Why?'

'I just wondered what all that was about earlier on today. What did you get called back for?'

'Oh, just the usual sort of bollocks,' said Weenink dismissively. 'Somebody upstairs with their knickers in a twist.'

On the television screen in the corner of the room, DCI Tailby's face appeared. It was a clip from the coverage of the press conference. Tailby was trying to look serious and professional, but hopeful.

'Todd,' said Cooper, 'what do you know about Maggie Crew? The victim that Diane Fry is dealing with.'

'I know she can't remember much about the attack, that's all. But I can't say I'd want to remember much myself, really. It's tough on a woman, getting her face messed up like that.'

'Do you know if she's ever been married or anything?'

'No. She's a solicitor, all business suits and fancy briefs. Likes to be called "Ms", I expect.'

'Has she got children?'

'Kids? You're joking. I bet her womb has cobwebs.'

Cooper ran his mind back over the earlier conversation. He felt dissatisfied with the way it had ended.

'Look, you have to realize she's a bit of an outsider,' he said.

'Who?'

'Diane Fry. Being an outsider can be a difficult thing to deal with. It takes time.'

'You don't have to tell me about that,' said Weenink. 'I'm an outsider, too. And I always will be. Neither one thing nor the other, that's me.'

'You mean because you're Dutch?'

'Half-Dutch. My dad's from Rotterdam. He came over to work in the British shipyards back in the seventies. He ended up in Sheffield.'

'What shipyards?'

'Exactly. There are none left. That's why he ended up in Sheffield. He worked in a steel mill, until that closed too.'

'I bet you got the piss taken out of your name when you were a kid.'

Weenink scowled. 'Are you kidding? I cursed my dad as a bastard every day, just because he gave me that name. It's pronounced like "Vaining" but with a "k" on the end, I'd say. I'd tell them and tell them till I was blue in the face, but do you think they took any notice?'

'It was a joke,' said Cooper.

'What was?'

'Taking the piss. Like "wee", you know.'

Weenink flushed. 'It's pronounced like "Vaining" …'

'… but with a "k" on the end. Right.'

Cooper began to look around the canteen for an excuse to leave.

'Anyway,' said Weenink slowly, 'when I got bigger than the rest of them, they stopped doing it.' His face solidified into his notorious stare. 'Once I'd smashed the first one's teeth in, anyway.'

'SORRY, TIME'S UP for the public. Next item on the agenda – minutes of the last meeting.'

The chairman of Cargreave Parish Council wore a white cardigan and a tweed skirt, and she was so short-sighted that she barely seemed able to recognize her colleagues at the far end of the table. Councillor Mary Salt preferred to be known as 'chair', but some members of the council refused to be forced into ways that sounded a bit modern. They still called her 'chairman', ignoring her angry, myopic glare.

Owen Fox didn't belong to Councillor Salt's party. He was an Independent, so his voice carried no weight in the important decisions, like where to spend the parish's share of the Council Tax. But he and the chairman had known each other for many years.

The parish room was cold and echoey, with a creaky wooden floor and a small stage at one end that had been turned into a Chinese laundry for rehearsals of the village pantomime. From where he sat, Owen could see Councillor Salt's legs tucked under the table in her flesh-coloured tights. Her legs looked tight and shiny, like sausage skins. His fingers itched for a fork to prick them.

The council meeting started with fifteen minutes of public questions. Usually, there were only one or two familiar faces sitting at the back of the room, sometimes no one at all. But tonight the room was full, and more chairs had been brought in. These people wanted to ask what action was being taken to make the area safe. They wanted a senior police officer to be brought to the next meeting to answer questions, and the clerk was instructed to write to the Chief Constable. Then the chairman moved the agenda on. The public were allowed only fifteen minutes.

The real business of the meeting involved correspondence from the National Park Authority about a visitor questionnaire and a landscape enhancement grant scheme. The county council had replied to a letter about street lamps, and there was another discussion about installing a height barrier at the entrance to the village car park to stop gypsies getting their caravans on. The success of the Millennium tree-planting scheme was reported, and next year's well-dressing considered. Mobile library visits were changing to alternate Thursdays. The bowls club were having a quiz night. Soon, the dangers of walking on Ringham Moor were long forgotten. The public got only fifteen minutes, after all.

'Any other business?' asked the chairman finally.

Councillor Salt looked round the table. Nobody responded, and Owen checked his watch. Not a bad time. Some of the other councillors would head for the Dancing Badger for a ritual exchange of gossip, but for Owen it would be a chance to get back to the house. Socializing in the village had never held any attractions for Owen; even less so now.

'Meeting closed, then.'

Owen made a dash for the door, trying to get out into the street before any members of the public could corner him and ask about the attacks on Ringham Moor. He didn't have the answers they wanted, no more than anyone else did. Nobody knew who it was stalking the moor. And nobody knew when he would strike again.

But Owen had his own thoughts. It only needed someone to ask him the right question, and he would no longer be able to keep them to himself.

Chapter Thirteen

THE LAMP ON the desk was tilted at an angle that directed light into Diane Fry's eyes and made Maggie Crew's face more difficult to see in the shadows between the lamp and the window. There was little light left in the sky over Matlock as the evening drew in, and Fry felt a creeping sense of unease in the apartment. If she had been in Maggie's position herself, she would have felt no reassurance from the panic buttons and the extra vigilance the police had promised.

'You understand that I need to talk to you, Maggie,' she said.

'You can talk as much as you like. I've got plenty of time.'

Fry's reading of Maggie's file and her discussion with DI Armstrong had convinced her that she had to be persistent if she was to get anything out of this woman. Deep inside, Maggie Crew had valuable memories locked in – memories the police needed, memories that would help them to identify a man who had now become a killer.

'I want to talk to you about our new victim,' she said.

Maggie waited, playing with the lamp. No sign of interest. Fry tried again.

'The woman found dead on Ringham Moor.'

Maggie shrugged. Fry felt a spasm of irritation, but controlled it. The file said that Maggie Crew was frustrated and bitter over the failure of the police to find her attacker. She mustn't let personal reactions get in the way of doing the job.

'I know nothing about your new victim,' said Maggie. 'Nothing.'

'Let me help you, then. Her name is Jenny Weston. She's thirty years old. I mean she was, when she died. She won't ever be any older now.

'Jenny Weston was five foot six and half, and she weighed sixty kilos. That's nine and a half stone. She had been trying to lose weight recently, but wasn't very successful. She lived in a modernized terrace house in Totley, on the outskirts of Sheffield, and she worked as a section supervisor at an insurance call centre. She might not seem to have had much in common with you, but maybe you would have got on with her. Jenny liked cycling and classical music, Haydn and Strauss. I see you like Strauss, Maggie.'

She nodded towards the stereo. A CD of *Tales from the Vienna Woods* lay on the top, the one case out of place from the neat racks. It was a rare splash of colour in the dark corner.

The light dipped slightly. Maggie's outline began to come back into focus as Fry blinked and her eyes readjusted to the darkness.

'Somebody loaned it to me,' said Maggie. 'I haven't listened to it.'

'Jenny bought her clothes at Marks & Spencer and Next, where she had store cards. She banked with the NatWest, but transferred her credit card account to one that supported Greenpeace. She was a big animal lover. She was a member of lots of societies, including the RSPCA, and she helped out as a volunteer for the local Cats Protection League. She had her own cat called Nelson. Do you know why she called him that? Because when she took him in as a stray he had an infection that made him keep one eye closed. Have you ever had a cat, Maggie?'

Maggie maintained the stare. Fry had no idea whether she was getting through to her.

'We know a lot more about Jenny. We know she borrowed show business biographies and Maeve Binchy novels from her local library. She drove a blue Fiat Cinquecento, but she didn't wash it very often. On the back seat were her spare shoes, an orange and her mobile phone. When we rang the number, it played "The William Tell Overture".'

Maggie's eyes were expressionless and unblinking, though her hands fidgeted restlessly and her shoulders were tense.

'No,' she said. 'I don't listen to Rossini, either.'

Fry had all the details of Jenny's life at her fingertips. Yet they knew almost nothing about the young woman who had stayed with her in Totley several weeks ago. Ros Daniels had disappeared as mysteriously as she had come, as far as Jenny's neighbours were concerned. She had been seen walking up The Quadrant one day with a rucksack on her back, and she had knocked at Jenny's door. Her hair was described as being 'in tangles' by an old man who had passed her on his way to the post office and who had noticed her heavy boots and the rings in her nose. He was seventy-five years old and not well up on modern fashions, but he was quite an observant old man. He had given it as his opinion that she hadn't been wearing a bra, either.

But it was only from a colleague at the Global Assurance call centre that the police had learned the young woman's name. The colleague had visited Jenny's home, and had been introduced. The miracle was that she had remembered Ros's name at all.

'She was a girl, really. I'd say she was no more than twenty years old. A student type, you know? All dreadlocks and combat trousers she was, and sitting slumped on the floor like she'd not even been taught how to use a chair. Never had a job, you could tell. Never had to work in a call centre selling insurance, that's for sure.'

'Did she say much?'

'"Hi." That was what she said. And that was said a bit contemptuous, like. As if she'd weighed me up in a glance and thought I was too boring and respectable and hardly worth bothering with. It was a cheek, I thought. I mean, if I'm boring and respectable, then so was Jenny Weston. So what was she doing at Jenny's house, this Ros?'

'Did Jenny never explain who she was?'

'Never. I did to try to ask her next day. Discreetly, like. I asked where Ros was from, and Jenny said from Cheshire. But then she changed the subject straight away, almost as if she'd said too much, though she hadn't told me anything at all. She didn't want to talk about her, that was plain. Well, she could be a bit stand-offish when she wanted to, could Jenny. I can't imagine what she had to do with that girl.'

Fry watched Maggie's hands moving impatiently. The cat had brought no response. That was no surprise. It was obvious there had never been a pet to disturb the orderly surroundings of Maggie Crew's apartment.

'Jenny's next birthday would have been on the 11th of December,' she said. 'She was a Sagittarian. She was interested in horoscopes, too. She wore a chain with a silver star-sign symbol – the archer, half horse and half man. She had made an appointment with her dentist for next Tuesday, because she was worried about a loose filling. Jenny Weston was the sort of person who started buying her Christmas presents early. In fact, she had already bought a cashmere sweater for her mother, and a book on Peak District aircraft wrecks for her father, who used to be in the RAF. She had even bought a toy mouse with a bell on it, for the cat.'

Maggie sighed. 'Why are you telling me all this? I don't want to know any of it.'

'Jenny had taken a week's holiday from work. It seems she loved the Peak District. But you do, too. Don't you, Maggie?'

'I used to,' she said. 'Something changed my view.'

'Well, Jenny must have loved it right up to her last breath. She never learned that disillusionment. She never had the chance.'

'So?'

'She was a member of the National Trust, too. We found lots of photographs she took at National Trust properties. That was another hobby of hers – photography. It seems her favourite place to visit was probably Hammond Hall. You know Hammond Hall well, don't you, Maggie?'

'It says so in my file, I suppose,' she said.

'You're a volunteer guide there, aren't you?'

'I used to be.'

'You might have met Jenny Weston, then. You might have shown her round some time, explained the history of the Tudor wall-hangings to her, or directed her to the ladies' toilets perhaps.'

'I never really notice the visitors, you know. They're just an anonymous mass. I forget them all as soon as they've gone. Unless they ask particularly interesting questions.'

'Jenny might have done that. She was interested in history.'

'Lots of people are.'

The volunteers co-ordinator at Hammond Hall had been interviewed after the assault on Maggie Crew. She had described Maggie as very knowledgeable. A bit cool and austere, perhaps, but some visitors preferred her as a guide because of the depth of her knowledge.

'Jenny may even have dealt with your car insurance,' said Fry, 'or the insurance on your house.'

'I don't think so.'

'How do you know? I haven't said what company she worked for.'

Maggie regarded Fry steadily from the side of her eye. 'This is getting tiresome. What exactly is it you want from me?'

'I want you to help us find the man who killed Jenny Weston.'

'And why should I do that?'

She shifted in her seat as she asked the question. Fry prayed she wouldn't turn towards her completely. She had got so far that she didn't want her nerve to fail now. She didn't want her face to show the reaction that made her stomach clench and her fingers tighten into tense fists.

'Because we think he's the same man who did that to your face, Maggie,' she said.

A minimum number of objects were lined up in an orderly line on the desk; no more than a paperweight, an ashtray, a telephone – and a wicked-looking letter opener shaped like a dagger, with a sharp blade and imitation rubies set into its handle. The letter opener was the only item of any ostentation in the room, and it stood out like a beacon, the light from the lamp reflecting in its red stones. In a moment of thought, Maggie toyed with its handle, turning it so that the tip pointed towards Fry, then spinning it away again to line up neatly with the paperweight in a satisfying geometric pattern.

'So tell me one more thing,' said Maggie. 'How was this woman killed?'

'She was stabbed to death.'

Maggie took her hand away from the letter opener quickly, and picked up her pen instead.

'It's a waste of time, you know. I can't remember any more than I have already.'

'I don't believe memories are gone forever, do you? They'll come back, Maggie. But they'll come back when you're least expecting them. You'll find they surprise you in ordinary things. It will be a face you see on TV that reminds you of someone. An item of clothing that you wore on the day. A glimpse of your own reflection in a window at night.'

Maggie's mouth tightened, and the lines round her good eye flattened out in anger.

'They *will* come back, Maggie,' said Fry. 'Better to let them come to the surface when you can deal with them than to allow them to ambush you when you least expect them. Believe me on this.'

Maggie stared at her. Gradually, her mouth relaxed. 'Are you talking from experience?'

Fry barely managed a nod. Ridiculously, the simple question had done exactly what she had been warning Maggie against. The burst of recollection was so strong and so physical that she was quite unprepared for it. She had to look away now, and be damned to her determination to look the woman in the eye. She stared at the drapes over the window, counting the brass rings on the curtain rail while she breathed slowly and steadily, counting to three as she inhaled, holding for another count of three, exhaling and counting; holding again.

It only took a few seconds before she was fully under control. She knew there was little outward sign. Most people noticed nothing, certainly her male colleagues. But Maggie was watching her fixedly, in absolute silence. When Fry met her stare again, something had changed. There was an indefinable difference in the atmosphere, as if somebody had just turned on the central heating, and a hint of warmth was beginning to creep into the cold walls.

'Would you like some coffee?' said Maggie.

Fry caught a glimpse into a kitchen as Maggie opened the door at the far end of the room. While she waited, Fry looked through her notes, checking the items she had marked for raising in conversation. One thing she hadn't mentioned yet was Maggie's family. The closest surviving relative was a sister, who lived somewhere in the west of Ireland.

She watched Maggie pour the coffee from a cafetiere. She wore no jewellery of any kind on her hands – no rings, no bracelet. There was no make-up on her face, either, though it might have helped to hide the scars. She wore no lipstick. Her only adornment consisted of two tiny gold studs in her ears, like miniature crosses.

'Last time you were interviewed,' said Fry, 'you weren't in a steady relationship, according to the notes. Is that still the case?'

'Yes.' Maggie smiled, without humour. 'They do put *everything* in my file, don't they? Yes, it makes life difficult when it comes to forming relationships. Nobody wants to have to look at a face that would frighten the horses.'

'Of course, a long-term relationship isn't to be taken for granted these days. Not everybody wants commitment. I suppose it depends whether you want children or not, and how you want them to grow up.'

'I've never wanted children anyway,' said Maggie. 'Some people think that's very strange for a woman.' She laughed, but it was a nervous laugh, at the thought of a disconcerting prospect. 'Well, perhaps I'll change. Perhaps I'll wake up one day and discover I have a maternal instinct after all. What do you think? We're all victims of our hormones, aren't we?'

Maggie put down the cafetiere. She picked up the pen that had lain by her hand all through the interview. She scrawled some notes on her pad, filling the empty lines for the first time. Fry leaned forward slightly to try to see what she was writing. But she could see that it was some kind of shorthand. Maggie wrote for a couple of minutes, concentrating as if Fry had suddenly ceased to be present. Then she threw down her pen.

'When will you come to see me again?' she asked.

'Wednesday,' said Fry promptly.

'Make it in the morning. Nine o'clock. My mind is fresher then.'

'OK.'

Fry looked at the big sash window and the remnants of the autumn sun forming red streaks and dark shadows on the roofs of Matlock. The sun was setting somewhere behind her. The light must be falling on the front of the building, because it certainly wasn't reaching the room where they sat. In the morning, it would be different. In the morning, Maggie's mind might be fresher. But the light would also be in the south-east, shining on this window. Lighting up Maggie's face.

WILL AND DOUGIE Leach were sitting quietly in the kitchen at Ringham Edge Farm. Their father had brought the portable television set into the kitchen, and they were watching the news, eyes fixed on the face of the newsreader as he spoke about interest rates, trade wars, and disasters in distant parts of the world.

It was well past the boys' normal bedtime. Their mother would never have let them stay up so late. She would have hurried them off to bed with warnings about being up early for school in the morning. But their father didn't seem to care. He forgot about them as long as they were quiet and didn't get in his way. And Will and Dougie had learned how to be quiet.

Warren Leach was crouched over the old oak desk in the front room of the farmhouse – the room he called an office. He had a desk lamp with a dim forty-watt bulb held over a scatter of papers. The boys had no real idea what the papers were, except that they were bad news. Every night he got the papers out and looked at them again. But no matter how many times he looked, they only ever seemed to make him more unhappy.

The news finished and some incomprehensible comedy programme started, with a lot of swearing. The boys shifted uncomfortably, knowing their mother would have been angry to see them watching the programme. But without her to tell them what to do, the boys sat on, their eyes growing tired, reluctant to move or make a noise in case they were noticed.

Finally, when little Dougie was already asleep with his head on the arm of the chair, Will heard the front door bang. Their father had gone out.

Will got up to switch off the television. He shook his brother awake, and together they crept up the stairs to their bedrooms. Their beds were unmade, the sheets tangled and uncomfortable. But both of them were so tired that they didn't notice.

But Will didn't go to sleep straight away. For a while, he lay staring at the ceiling and wondering where it was that his father went. He prayed that he hadn't gone near the shippon, that his father would leave Doll alone. Although people didn't come at night any more, Will knew there was nothing good about what his father was doing.

Will had lived all his life on the farm. He knew its patterns and routines, he understood the rhythms of its activities. And there was one thing that he knew perfectly well. There was nothing that could possibly need doing around the farm at this time of night.

Chapter Fourteen

'ALL RIGHT, WHAT's the latest weirdo count?'

To Ben Cooper, Chief Superintendent Jepson looked as though he didn't really want to know the answer. It was a question that risked spoiling the Tuesday morning meeting almost before it had started. Cooper tried hard to fade into the background of the incident room. He and Todd Weenink would be following up the line of enquiry about a white van reported in the Ringham Edge area, which one witness claimed to have seen before, and which might therefore be local. That was all the excitement he needed for this morning.

Cooper saw DCI Tailby hesitate at the Chief Super's question and look sideways at DI Hitchens. But Hitchens looked very cheerful for such an early hour, and he had the answers ready.

'Well, the uniforms on duty up there say they had trouble turning away a bunch of characters in black coats,' he said. 'Apparently they were carrying so much metalwork on their bodies they wouldn't have got through airport security without the help of a surgeon.'

'What did they want?'

'They said blood had been spilled on the Virgins, and that meant the power would manifest some time in the next twenty-four hours, so they had to be there to receive it.'

'Bollocks,' said Jepson.

'They were pretty insistent. In the end, they only retreated as far as the pub in Ringham. The inspector is worried that when they come back they'll be tanked up and more aggressive. Fortunately, I think we've managed to keep them out of the way of the other lot so far.'

'What other lot?'

'The other lot who say they have to perform a cleansing ritual dedicated to the Great Goddess, so as to dispel the influence of evil from the stone circle, which is a sacred place. Some of the bobbies were all for letting them go ahead with that one.'

'You what?'

'Well, they're all women, and it seems they have to perform this ritual naked.'

Jepson put his head in his hands and groaned.

'It's called "sky-clad",' said Hitchens.

'What is?'

'Having no clothes on. You're clad in nothing but the sky, so that you're much closer to nature and the Great Goddess.'

'Hitchens, are you enjoying this?'

'No, sir. I'm just reporting the information that the uniformed section gathered. They spent quite a while talking to this lot, I think. We might have some converts in E Division. They'll be wanting to form an Edendale chapter of the Order of the Golden Moon.'

'Haven't we had any plain old psychics and mediums, then?'

'You're kidding. Twelve at the last count. We've also had a dowser offering to locate the knife using nothing but a bent twig; an animal linguist who wants to interrogate the squirrels, because she thinks they could have been eyewitnesses, and a UFO expert who has proof that the victim was abducted by aliens for unspecified experiments which went wrong. Oh, and some preservation experts from that government department, English Heritage.'

'English Heritage? What the hell do they want?'

'They demand the right to inspect the stone circle for damage. They say it's a priceless piece of our cultural history.'

Jepson frowned. 'I've heard that phrase before. Is it from a book or something?'

'Could be,' said Hitchens. 'It seems to be *us* that English Heritage suspect of damaging the stones, by the way.'

'They're nuts. Get rid of them.'

'They're not half as bad as the press. That lot are all over us like a nasty disease.'

'Was that their chopper over the moor yesterday?'

'Sure. And it was also one of their blokes we pulled down from the top of a tree with his long lens. He'd already been up there a day or so, in camouflage gear. He slept tied to a branch. He said he learned how to do it at an eco-warriors' protest camp in Berkshire.'

'That's a neat trick,' said Jepson, half-admiringly.

'I don't know about neat. Twenty-four hours is a long time. You should have seen the state of the grass at the bottom of the tree. That's how we located him. Even our bobbies know human shit when they see it.'

Jepson pulled a face. Then he looked suspiciously at Tailby, who had been listening silently.

'What have you got to say, Stewart?'

'It's a pretty depressing story, I'm afraid.' Tailby sounded resigned. 'The sixteen fires we found remnants of, they were all set during the last three months. Some of the people who made them built them properly. Others … well, others were lucky not to have set fire to the whole moor. There are the animal bones we found buried nearby, too. First indications suggest a medium-sized dog.'

Cooper remembered seeing the slides of the animal bones. It hadn't been immediately obvious what they were. They were just slivers of something pale caught in the dark fibrous peat, like those burnt stems of heather, crumbling and white. Then the slide had suddenly come into focus, and the shapes of the white splinters came together in a vaguely familiar shape. He had thought of the farmyard at home, of rats caught by the sheep-dogs, and the discarded evidence of foxes hunting in the fields. But this wasn't quite the same. This was something much bigger, something with a heavier and wider skull than a rat.

'Do those two gypsies go in for animal sacrifices?' asked Jepson.

'The youths in the van? They're not exactly gypsies,' said Hitchens.

'Whatever they are.'

'They're just travellers, sir,' said Cooper.

'Travellers, my arse. They're not going anywhere. What makes them travellers?'

'They're classed as having no settled home, sir. A Volkswagen van doesn't count as a home under the law, even if it's broken down.'

'So what do they live on down there, Cooper? Nuts and berries, or what?'

'Our information is that Calvin Lawrence catches the bus into Bakewell once a week to collect his benefit money.'

'Ah. So he's a Social Security scrounger. What about the other one?'

'Simon Bevington isn't even registered for benefits,' said Cooper. 'He seems to stay in the vicinity of the quarry or on the moor. He doesn't claim anything. I suppose they must share what little they've got.'

'Oh, love and peace, hallelujah,' said Jepson.

'It must be enough for both of them – they hardly have an extravagant lifestyle. But they're not gypsies.'

'They could be circus trapeze artists, for all I care, Cooper. Have we asked them about animal sacrifices?'

'No, sir.'

'Then ask them. And find this Martin Stafford and the girl, Ros Daniels. We ought to be able to find at least one of them, shouldn't we? Is there anything else? And don't make it anything too exciting. I've had enough for today.'

'Well,' said Hitchens, as if suddenly noticing an important item that everyone had forgotten, 'there *is* the phallus farm.'

'*What* kind of farm?' said Jepson.

'Well, I don't mean Warren Leach's kind of farm. There are no EU subsidies for this particular crop ...'

WARREN LEACH WAS waiting for the milk tanker. It was one of the few routines that still held his day together. Bringing the cows in, milking, waiting for the tanker. The morning's yield was taken for Hartington Stilton, the local cheese made at the dairy in Dovedale. It was something most farmers were proud of, that their milk was going for Stilton. It was like still being part of the traditional dairy industry of the dales, not an anonymous unit of production for some huge commercial organization. Leach had once been proud of it himself, and had boasted about the quality of his milk. Now he found he couldn't care less. He would have been just as happy to pour the stuff down the drain or into the nearest ditch.

The lad who normally came to help him had not turned up yesterday or today, so Leach had done everything himself. Gary was one of the Dawsons, from over the moor at Pilhough. The Dawsons weren't up to much, but at least they were farming folk. But there had been a blazing row on Sunday afternoon, when Leach had lost his temper and sworn at the lad and accused him of being idle. Gary had threatened he would never come again, and it looked as though he never would.

In a way, Leach preferred it; he preferred to be left on his own, to have so much to do that it left no time for thinking. Yet it only lasted for a while, only until after the tanker had gone and the rest of the jobs held no urgency. Then, when there were no cows bellowing for attention, no tanker driver sounding his horn in the lane, when his sons had gone off to school in Cargreave on the bus – then he found the rest of the day stretched before him endlessly.

But this morning a car had arrived. He had been expecting the tanker turning in from the road, but the sound of the engine was wrong. The big diesel always made the glass in the windows of the farmhouse vibrate, and the layer of dust on the window ledge dance and slide before it settled into a new pattern. There had been plenty of police vehicles going by the farm for the past two days, of course – but they went straight up the lane, past the front of the shippon. They didn't turn into the yard like this car did.

Leach's chest grew tight with apprehension. He had known it would only be a matter of time before the men he feared arrived.

The farmer looked at his hands, astonished at the dirt ingrained in his fingers, as if he hadn't washed for days. How long had his hands been like that? He glanced at the steel cabinet where his shotgun was locked, and waited for the familiar surge of aggression to come, for the righteous anger to drive strength and heat into his limbs. He was the sort of man who ought to be able to see a bailiff off, no problem. But something was wrong. Somehow the adrenalin failed to flow, the flush of testosterone never came. He felt weak and helpless; he was alone and cornered, yet with no fight left in him. It was the feeling that he had always dreaded would come to him in the end.

Leach laughed quietly as he listened for the men to enter the gate. 'You've had it, Warren. What use are you now?' He thought of not answering the door, of hiding in another room until the strangers went away. It was what a woman might do, or a child. Was he reduced to that?

Unable to face the answer, he stood paralysed when the knock came at the door. A second knock followed, more impatient. Then Leach moved, without a thought in his head about what he would say. What did bailiffs do in these circumstances? Obviously, the men hadn't come alone in a car to take away his furniture. Maybe they had come to deliver a court notice. Maybe they had just come to check what he had that was worth selling. Good luck to them, then. There was precious little.

But they weren't bailiffs, after all, just the police again. The first face he saw he recognized immediately, and it reminded him that there were vitally important things he ought to have done, but hadn't. He had watched the police cars and vans go backwards and forwards across his land, cursing each one as they went, yet desperate to know what they were doing up on the moor, to hear what they had found out about the woman who had died. He longed for someone to tell him what was going on. Yet now these policemen had arrived, he didn't know what to do, except to tell them he had nothing to say.

'Detective Constable Cooper and Detective Constable Weenink, Mr Leach. We just need a few words, that's all. We won't keep you from your work long. We know how busy you farmers always are.'

The one who spoke tried a smile. Leach refused to be impressed. 'Cut the crap. I see enough of it round here.'

'If that's the way you want it.'

Leach looked at the other one, the big one in the leather jacket, and felt a small measure of his old confidence starting to return. 'What have they sent you two for? Ranger scared to come here any more, is he? Thought he needed to send in the heavy mob? You won't get anything out of me, anyway.'

'We're collecting information about vehicles seen in this area on Sunday,' said Weenink, staring at the farmer.

'Are you now? But they've asked me about this before.'

'We're following up a report on a van that was noticed leaving your farm entrance between two and three o'clock that day. Was that your van?'

'Does it look as though I've got a van? A Land Rover, but that's knackered. Otherwise it's a tractor or the back of a cow if I want to get about.'

'Does that mean I can put you down as "does not own a van"?'

'If you like.'

'The witness said it was a white van, but not very clean. Probably a Ford Transit.'

'Lots of those about.'

'Do you recall seeing this van?' asked Cooper. 'Did it belong to a visitor to the farm?'

'I don't get many visitors here.'

'But that afternoon you did, didn't you?'

'Not that I remember.'

'Could it have been a sales rep? An agricultural engineer? Something like that?'

'Can't afford to speak to either of 'em at the moment.'

'A parcel delivery?'

'You're joking.'

'Do you know *anybody* with a van of that description?'

'Listen, let me help you out. It would likely have been some bugger who'd got lost and decided to use my land to turn round on. Or maybe he'd stopped to have his sandwiches with his van blocking my gateway. That's happened before, too. Police'll never do anything about it, obviously. Too bloody busy, aren't you?'

'I'm sure if you phoned the station, they would send somebody out when they had a car available.'

Leach began to cough. He was wishing the policemen would go away; his lungs were responding as if he had an allergic reaction. He was too tired to argue with them. Besides, they didn't look as though they would put up with absolutely anything, the way the Ranger did.

'Do you get joyriders up here?' said Cooper. 'It's a quiet spot. They like to abandon vehicles somewhere and set fire to them.'

Leach followed the detective's gaze. He was looking at the scorched shell of the pick-up on the hard-standing near the big shed.

'A bit of an accident,' said Leach. 'I'll get a few spares off it when I get round to it.'

'This white van …' said Weenink.

Leach shrugged. 'I'd like to help, but –'

'What about your two sons?' asked Cooper.

'What about them?'

'Were they at home on Sunday? They might have seen the van. Can we speak to them?'

'They're at school.'

'Someone could call back later.'

'I don't know about that.'

'And your wife?' said Cooper. 'Was she here at the time?'

'My wife?' Leach finally spat out the irritation that had been troubling his lungs, narrowly missing Cooper's boots. 'You're wasting your time, mister. You can forget all about her.'

LATER IN THE morning, Diane Fry and DI Hitchens walked into the DCI's office. Tailby looked at them with a faint hope. 'Is there something?' he said.

'A couple of things on the parents. The Westons,' said Hitchens.

'Oh?'

'Number one, they had a burglary last year, at a weekend cottage they've got at Ashford-in-the-Water.'

'A weekend cottage? That's nice, on a teacher's salary.'

'Apparently, the Westons are planning on retiring to this cottage in a year or two. Presumably Mr Weston is taking early retirement. He's a deputy head, by the way.'

'A good pension, I suppose.'

Fry thought the DCI was starting to sound wistful. His own retirement date was a few years away yet, but he could make it come closer if he wanted to. She wondered how much the cottage had cost the Westons. She imagined honeysuckle growing by the front door and roses in the garden, a couple of loungers by a small pond with a few Koi carp. She tried to imagine Tailby living in such a cottage. But Eric Weston had a Mrs Weston to retire to his cottage with. It made a difference.

'A burglary, eh?'

'And we detected it, too,' said Hitchens. 'Who needs Home Office grants?'

Tailby grunted, unamused. The previous year, word had gone round that there was government cash available for special initiatives targeting residential burglaries. Divisions were invited to come up with their own projects – but there were criteria to be met. There had to be a target area with a high enough level of burglaries. E Division had failed to get the cash, because no matter how they juggled the geography or the time periods, the figures just wouldn't stack up.

'This was more than a burglary, actually. The place was trashed. It was a real mess – you should see the photos.'

'There's nothing new in that.'

'I talked to the investigating officer yesterday, anyway,' said Hitchens. 'At least he's still in the division. Usually you find they've long since moved on somewhere else, or they've packed it in and joined that firm of enquiry agents that set up in town a couple of years back.'

'What's the other thing?' asked the DCI.

'Well, Mr Weston had a little bit of trouble last year. There was an enquiry after a fatal accident to a child on a school trip he was leading.'

'OK. We might as well ask him about it, I suppose.'

'More than that, sir.'

'Why?'

Hitchens tapped the file. 'It all came out when we made the arrest for the burglary. This convicted offender, name of Wayne Sugden – it turned out he was the uncle of the child that died. It was no secret that the family blamed Mr Weston for the accident, because it was all over the papers. He got death threats, too, but we could never prove where they came from. It seems the Sugdens are a pretty close clan in Edendale. You're not safe if you harm one of their number.'

'So the burglary could have been revenge on Weston?' said Tailby. 'Is it significant?'

'There's one good reason it might be,' said Hitchens. 'This Wayne Sugden. He got sent down for twelve months, protesting his innocence all the way to Derby nick. But the trouble is – they let him out two weeks ago.'

BEN COOPER WAS back in the CID room when Diane Fry returned from her meeting. She saw him, but she started tidying files and brushing biscuit crumbs from an unoccupied desk.

'So, Diane, how have you been getting on with Maggie Crew?' he said.

He didn't think there was anything about his tone of voice that could have made Fry look sharply at him in the way that she did now.

'What's your interest in Maggie Crew?'

'Just asking.'

'She's not one of your underdogs, you know.'

'What do you mean?'

'I heard you at the briefing this morning. You couldn't help putting your oar in about those two travellers in the quarry, could you? You're turning into quite the little rebel, with this habit of sticking up for people against all odds.'

'That's not the intention.'

Cooper turned to one side and picked up some papers from his desk, dropping his eyes from contact with hers. He heard her sigh with exasperation and bang a chair on the floor. He let a few moments of silence develop before he spoke again.

'I've heard you're going to be working with DI Armstrong,' he said. 'When your promotion is confirmed.'

Fry didn't answer straight away. He looked up to see her frowning at him. 'She's doing some very good work,' she said.

'Yes, I know.'

'You don't sound too sure about that, Ben,' she said. 'What problem have you got with Kim Armstrong?'

'No problem, really.'

Cooper eyed the files on his desk. The work had been piling up since the murder enquiry started. There were so many things for him to follow up, when he had time. He was startled when he found that Fry had moved suddenly nearer to him and was staring into his face. He found her closeness intimidating.

'Come on, out with it,' she said. 'What are you suggesting about DI Armstrong?'

'Well, she's got her own agenda, of course. Everybody says that.'

'That's a load of crap, and you know it. Kim Armstrong is a capable woman doing a good job. She's in charge of a major enquiry, and she cares about what she's doing. There was a little girl that was killed …'

Fry ground to a halt. Cooper realized that he was smiling at her. The expression on his face must look ridiculous and derisive, but it was a natural response that had sprung from deep inside him at seeing Fry suddenly passionate in her defence of someone. He nodded at her, though the gesture barely seemed adequate.

She backed off, baffled. She picked up a waste-paper bin from the floor and put it on the empty desk, then began clearing out drawers. Cooper watched her hurl the leftover possessions of the previous occupant into the bin without looking at them.

'OK, Diane,' he said. 'You were telling me about this little girl who was killed. What happened to her?'

Fry pulled out a 1999 calendar with pictures of naked women draped over bright red sports cars. With a grimace, she tore it in half and thrust it into the bin.

'Nobody really knows,' she said. 'Nobody knows what awful things might have happened to her before she died.'

Chapter Fifteen

OWEN FOX FELT his fingers start to tingle. He thought about finding his gloves in his jacket pocket to protect himself from the cold. But he knew it wasn't just the cold that he could feel.

There were things that had passed through his hands during the past few years that didn't bear to be thought about. Most days, he could clear the memories from his head. He got out on the tops of the hills and let the wind blow them out of the corners of his mind. But somehow his hands still felt the memories of their own accord; his fingers still touched the blood and the slack limbs and the cold cheeks. It was as if he was forever holding a dead body, as if he carried that child with him every day, and always would.

Could the hands remember better than the brain? Sometimes it took only the touch of some object, normally familiar – the feel of the sleeve of a well-worn leather jacket, the bulge of fruit in a plastic carrier bag, a sudden spurt of warm vegetable soup from a bowl. And a thing so mundane could bring back an instant recollection that would set him trembling and unable to breathe, his throat twisted and knotted with anguish.

Sometimes a smell or a sound could do the same thing – just the familiar chemical reek of petrol on the forecourt of a filling station, or the tick of a cooling engine. But it was the feel of things that he couldn't escape; his sense of touch tormented him until he wanted to cut off his hands.

Owen followed the deep crease that ran across his palm from just below the index finger to the outer edge of his hand. He was fascinated by the way the line broke and diverged, forked into two and was crossed by other lines. In palmistry, it was supposed to be the life line, wasn't it? Or was that the other line, the one that ran across the base of his thumb? It didn't matter, anyway – both lines ended in a web of tiny creases like a smudge of gauze; there was no sudden stop, just a fading out in a tangle of vagueness and uncertainties.

He forced himself to pull his gaze away. He worried that staring too hard at his hands might make the shape of the child reappear, bright and unforgettable in her torn blue dress; still heavy and limp in his arms. Best to think of something else. Maybe there was something he ought to be doing to help Mark, to make it easier for him to get over the shock.

Mustn't feel guilty about Mark, thought Owen. He'll get over it, because he's only a young lad. Mustn't take on that burden as well as everything else. No more burdens. Let others take the guilt.

MARK ROPER WAS moving cautiously across the slopes of dying heather, placing his boots on the bare surface of the rabbit tracks to avoid the snap of dead stems. The spring of the peat underfoot felt like a welcoming response from the earth to his presence, the clutch of brittle foliage at his trousers like the touch of a friend. He had already been waiting for an hour. But none of the men Mark had been watching had seen him as he stood above them in the birches up the hill. Mark had left his red jacket at home today, and he had long since learned the art of being inconspicuous. He had also been prepared to wait as long as necessary for the policemen to leave.

He knew the two men were detectives, because he recognized one of them from Sunday, when they had questioned him. It was the one called Cooper. Mark had seen him again, with a woman, when he had talked to Yvonne Leach. This detective was young, and you could tell he was local. He was the one who lacked the hard-eyed aggressiveness that Mark had seen in the other policemen. In fact, he could almost have been a Ranger. This detective, Cooper, was also the one who had made Mark think of what his own brother would have looked like by now – if he had still been alive.

Finally, the two policemen had driven away down the track from Ringham Edge Farm. Perhaps they were heading back to the cycle hire centre, where the car park was full of police vehicles this morning and the first visitors of the day were getting an unpleasant surprise as they unloaded their mountain bikes and strapped on their cycling helmets.

Just over the shoulder of Ringham Moor were the Nine Virgins. And up there, Mark knew there would be more police, keeping the public away from the stone circle, like priests guarding an altar from the profane.

A hundred yards along the slope of the hill, Owen Fox was working on the boundary wall. There was still a lot to be done on the wall, and the Area Ranger would probably work on right through the day until the light started to go.

As Mark watched, Owen pulled on his gloves and picked up the new Pennine walling hammer he had bought only a few weeks before. It was a three-pound hammer with a sharp cutting edge fixed at a right angle to the shaft – a tool designed to slice the corners off the stones, so that only blunt edges protruded from the wall, leaving it solid and safe. Sometimes, Mark wished he could ask Owen to use his hammer and shape the rest of the world like that – with no sharp edges that could pierce the skin of his emotions or rip the protective veneer from his memories.

Owen had a small rucksack on the ground, with his radio aerial protruding from the top. Nearby, his stones were laid out in the order he would need them, leaving a clear work area. The ground was already levelled and the foundation stones blocked together. Now the building stones had to be laid, and co-ordination of hand and eye would be needed to know exactly which stone to choose to plug a gap.

Silently, Mark continued to make progress, until he was standing only a few yards from the wall. For a while, he watched Owen's hands as he worked. He was shaping the stones, carving them into new forms, until he had made them fit tightly together. When the wall was finished, it would be impossible to move a single stone by hand. Surely a man who could create with such care would never think of destroying anything?

Owen hefted another stone and swung the cutting edge of his hammer, slicing the gritstone into yellow shards that left a dusting of powder on his gloves.

'Owen?'

The Ranger looked up, surprised. His hammer was poised in the air, its edge catching the light, a little bit of golden stone dust trickling down the shaft on to his red fleece. Mark was shocked by the look that he had caught on Owen's face. He saw the Ranger start to compose his expression into an air of normality as he mentally rehearsed the lines he would use for a tourist. And then Owen saw who had startled him.

'What are you doing here, Mark?' he said. 'You should be at home.'

'So should you. It's your day off.'

Owen shrugged. 'There are things to do. This wall won't wait. The boundaries have to be maintained, whatever else goes on. No one will do the job but me. Certainly not Warren Leach.'

The wall formed a boundary where the top fields of Ringham Edge Farm met the woods. Mark had already helped Owen to replace a stile which had collapsed with use over the years. Its original builders had used flat gritstone slabs instead of wooden steps, and the structure hadn't done too badly – it had survived for the best part of two hundred years. But the weight of walkers' boots had proved too much, loosening the slabs until they shifted out of balance and became dangerous.

Now Owen had worked up the hill to a stretch of wall that had fallen. Walkers had been crossing here, too – the ones too lazy to walk a few yards to the stile. It was a double wall, but the topping stones had been dislodged one by one, and the weather had got into the centre, washing through the filling until the sides bulged and slipped.

Mark and Owen stood together among the scattered stones for a minute or two. Despite his proximity to Owen, there still seemed to be too much distance between them for Mark's satisfaction. The greeting he had received was not the one he had expected. It was not the reason he had waited in the trees until the policemen had gone. For Mark, the unfamiliar gulf between them felt like that yawning gap in the wall, waiting to be bridged by a careful hand.

'Did you talk to the police yesterday, Owen?' he said.

'Yes, they're talking to everybody.'

'What did you talk about?'

Owen laughed. 'You'd be surprised.'

He picked up a stone, knocked off some dirt, and held it up to the light to study it, like a diamond dealer examining the facets of a newly polished gem. Mark liked to watch Owen at work. He thought Owen was a completely different man when he was out on the hills. He never seemed at home in the briefing centre, sitting in front of the little electric heater, hunched at the assistant's desk scattered with paperwork.

'What was it they wanted to know, Owen?' Mark insisted.

Owen had been Mark's friend and mentor throughout his assessment and training as a Ranger and during his first few weeks in the job itself. Mark had become accustomed to the comforting presence of the bearded man in the red jacket; he had glowed with pride as people greeted Owen like an old friend, laughed at all his jokes and bombarded him with questions on every subject – questions he never failed to respond to with courtesy, even when he plainly didn't know the answer.

'It was just questions,' said Owen. 'They want to make use of my local knowledge. Don't they all?'

'The time of the next bus to Buxton, then? Or the nearest all-night chemist's.'

Owen smiled at Mark's tentative joke, a reference to a shared memory of an encounter with two elderly women on a remote track by a reservoir on the heights of the Dark Peak. It was enough to provide the surge of reassurance Mark needed, enough to ease the chill he had felt when he had first seen the expression on Owen's face.

'I wondered if the police might want to interview me again,' said Mark.

'You've told them everything, haven't you?'

'I think so.'

But Mark knew he hadn't, not everything. The policemen hadn't been as easy to talk to as he might have hoped.

There were some things you just couldn't say when they were writing down every word. There were things that sounded too stupid and strange. For a start, he didn't know how to describe to the police the way that the woman had looked to him as she lay among the stones. The way that she had seemed to dance.

'Anyway,' said Owen as he handed Mark a topping stone, 'it's all over with now. You can forget about it. Get on with the job. Why would they want to start bothering you again?'

Mark started stacking the stones to one side, lining them up on the grass, ready to be replaced when Owen had rebuilt the lower part of the wall.

'I don't know,' said Mark. 'I've never … well, I've never been involved in anything like this before.'

'I know, lad. Pass me the line.'

Owen took off his thick cotton work gloves and ran two lines between wooden pins along the damaged section of wall to mark out its alignment.

'But the police aren't so bad. They're just doing their job, like you and me.'

Owen's voice was slow and steady. Calming. It didn't really matter what he was saying, because Mark found it reassuring just to listen to the sound. He had never heard Owen raise his voice. There had often been occasions when he might have done – when a mountain biker or a motorcyclist openly defied his friendly warnings that they were breaking the law and risking prosecution; when ill-equipped hikers ignored both his advice and common sense and put their own and others' lives at risk; when a farmer, now and then, chose to be downright pig-headed. Farmers like Warren Leach at Ringham Edge, maybe. But Owen never got angry.

'So there's nothing to worry about. You tell them what you found, Mark, and that's all they need to know. As long as it's simple for them, they won't bother you any more. And if they do, just send them to see me, eh? I'll give them a flea in their ear.'

Owen smiled, showing his teeth through his grey beard, his eyes crinkling at the corners. Like most Rangers, he never wore a hat, and his hair was permanently windblown and untidy, curling into his ears.

'Owen,' said Mark.

'Yes?'

'Where were you?'

Owen smacked his gloves together to remove traces of mud and grit. 'When, Mark?'

'On Sunday afternoon. You know …'

Mark watched Owen's puzzled smile carefully. This time Owen smiled without showing his teeth. His eyes narrowed, but the crinkles were absent.

'You had a problem with the radio, Mark.'

'I just thought that maybe you weren't there …'

'But I wouldn't let you down like that, Mark. Now, would I?'

Mark looked past the wall and down at the farm buildings of Ringham Edge. They were gathered defensively round a crew yard like a medieval settlement, their gritstone walls turned outwards to the rest of the world. The biggest shed was much newer than the rest of the farm.

Its green corrugated steel roof was damp from the drizzle earlier in the day, and it gleamed now in the weak sun.

Mark thought for a moment of the woman on Ringham Moor. Her death had at least been sudden; she had been given no time to consider, no time to reflect on what she had done with her life, for good or evil.

Owen had told Mark there were times when it was best to back off, to avoid confrontation, to let something go. He said that a soft word was better than an angry reaction, that a cool head was better than that hot surge of blind rage that was inevitably followed by the realization that you had made a terrible mistake.

Mark passed another stone. It was furred dark green with lichen, so he knew it had come from the north face of the wall. When a wall had been built by Owen, it was solid and reliable, the absolute symbol of stability.

Mark decided he would have to ask Owen again tomorrow about why he hadn't been able to get hold of him on the radio. And maybe he would ask the day after, too. Just to hear a little bit more reassurance.

THE WESTONS SAT together, their faces no longer hopeful. They were losing faith in the investigation, disappointed by their first real contact with the police, dismayed by the realization of their fallibility. And they had noticed that at first they had been talking to a detective chief inspector, then an inspector; now it was a mere acting detective sergeant. The word 'acting' seemed to be the biggest insult of all.

'Don't take it the wrong way,' said Eric Weston. 'We're sure you're doing your best.'

'There are a lot of people working on this enquiry,' said Diane Fry patiently. 'There are lots of leads to be followed up. This is just one of them.'

'We understand. Really.'

Mrs Weston had set out teacups on a glass-topped table. She served the tea as a well-rehearsed routine, performed without any hint of welcome. In the same way, she had apologized for the condition of the lounge, explaining that they weren't bothering to decorate in view of their move, before long, to the retirement cottage at Ashford. New people always redecorated when they bought a house, she said. So why bother? It would only be wasted expense.

The log basket on the hearth was filled with paper and small sticks, ready to light a fire. A storage heater under the bay window was enough to take the chill off the room. But the decor looked perfectly presentable to Fry. Anything that wasn't stained by mould or hung with cobwebs looked fine to her. Back at the flat, anything that didn't have a layer of dust was meant for sitting on.

'I believe you've already been asked about a young woman called Ros Daniels.'

'We have,' said Mr Weston. 'We've never heard of her. When they told us she'd been staying with Jenny, we thought she was probably one of the girls she worked with, who had nowhere to stay. Jenny would have put her up for a while. She was like that.'

'But Ros Daniels never worked at Global Assurance, as far as we can tell.'

'So we're told. Jenny must have met her somewhere else.'

'Any idea where that might have been?'

'Sorry, no.'

'The only other people she ever talked about were the ones in the animal welfare groups,' said Mrs Weston. 'You could try them.'

'We will.' Fry stared at her cooling tea. 'I also want to ask you whether your daughter had mentioned being bothered by anybody. Did she complain about anyone hanging round outside her house or following her? Did she refer to any unwanted or nuisance phone calls?'

'I don't know what you mean.'

'Like a stalker?' said Mrs Weston. 'You mean like a stalker?'

'That sort of thing.'

'She never said anything,' said Mr Weston.

'There was the phone call,' said his wife.

'Oh?'

Mr Weston had retreated further into his armchair and was watching the two women helplessly, as if he was no part of what was going on.

'Jenny mentioned she had been phoned up,' said Mrs Weston. 'She didn't say it was a nuisance call, exactly. She just thought there was something strange about it. But she never took it any further, as far as I know. It just happened to be on her mind when I was speaking to her.'

'Who made this phone call?'

Mrs Weston stared at her. 'The police, of course. They said it was to check up on home security. But they asked some funny questions, and she didn't think it was quite right.'

'Did Jenny give you the name of the officer who phoned?'

'No.'

'A man or a woman?'

'A man, I think. Yes, definitely.'

'He didn't give any identification?'

'I've no idea,' said Mrs Weston irritably. She looked at her husband again, and back at Fry. 'You mean he might not have been from the police at all?' she said.

'I'm afraid that's possible.'

The couple shook their heads in unison. 'Jenny was always too trusting,' said Mrs Weston. 'It took her a long time to learn the truth about people. All those terrible men. She was better off with just herself and the cat, if truth be told.'

'Could this phone call have been in connection with the burglary at your cottage in Ashford?' asked Fry.

'Oh, the burglary,' said Eric Weston. 'Why do you want to talk about that?'

'We're following up everything we can, sir.'

'I suppose so.'

'You've not seen any sign of Wayne Sugden since then? Your daughter didn't mention him getting in contact?'

'But that man is in prison, isn't he?'

'Not any more, sir.'

'What?' Weston seemed roused to emotion at last.

'Do we take it you didn't know that?' asked Fry.

'Nobody told us that. Shouldn't somebody have told us?'

'It isn't usual,' she said. 'Unless there is a particular risk to the victims. In a rape case, for example, or an offence against a child. It can be quite a trauma running into a perpetrator unexpectedly in the street when you thought he was behind bars.'

'But not in this case.'

'It would have been thought unlikely that Sugden would return to burgle the same house.'

'But not impossible that he might return and track down our daughter to take his revenge, presumably.'

'Well …'

'Because that's why you're asking, isn't it? You must be thinking that it could have been him that killed Jenny.'

'It isn't as simple as that, sir,' said Fry.

'No?'

'There are certain aspects to the burglary which interest us, that's all. Am I right in thinking you were away at the time?'

'Yes, in Cyprus,' said Weston. 'We go there when we can during the school holidays.'

'And how long were you away on this occasion?'

'A month. I had to be back to prepare for the new term then. There's a lot of work to do before we start, you know. People don't realize that.'

'So you weren't using the cottage in Ashford at the time of the burglary.'

'No. We'd asked one of the neighbours to call in occasionally to check on things: water the plants, that sort of thing. They deliver free papers and all sorts of junk mail and just leave it sticking out of the letter box, you know. It's a complete giveaway that the place is unoccupied.'

Fry studied the log basket in the hearth. She felt the Westons staring at her, trying to divine the direction of her questions.

'And who reported the burglary?'

'The people next door. They heard glass breaking. Later, they noticed the window was broken. That's how he got in.'

'Yes, I see.'

'He made a terrible mess of the cottage, you know. He took a video recorder, a bit of cash and some jewellery, that's all. But it was the damage that was the worst thing. He broke chairs, he smashed pictures, threw Tabasco sauce on the walls and the carpet. Susan wouldn't use the cottage again until we had it redecorated and changed all the locks.'

'There were no fingerprints,' said Fry.

'He must have worn gloves. Even young children know to do that these days, don't they? But he was identified by someone who saw him near the cottage. And they said there were some fibres on his jacket from one of our armchairs. The evidence seemed conclusive.'

'I'm afraid we have to take another look at the question of motive. The Sugden family has reason to feel very bitter towards you.'

'Ah,' said Weston. 'You know about my bit of trouble. But it's not as if it will be in the police records, is it? My name was cleared completely. Still, some people find it difficult to forget.'

'Tell me what happened.'

Mr Weston shrugged apologetically. 'There was an accident, that's all. A boy was badly injured.'

'This was on a field trip?'

'Yes. We had taken a party to Losehill Hall. You know the National Park study centre near Castleton?'

Fry didn't know it, but she nodded, unwilling to admit the gaps in her local knowledge.

'There was a bit of a fuss about it at the time. Some hysterical reactions. There was a full enquiry by the education department. The police were involved for a while, but of course there were never any charges.'

'I see. You were in charge of the party?'

'Yes, indeed. But there was found to be no negligence on my part. It was an accident, pure and simple. Nobody could have predicted it. The boy slipped away from the party. I had warned them all personally about the danger, and we had the right number of adults supervising the group. All the children had been told to stay on the path. But some of them don't listen to what you tell them. Some of them have never been taught proper discipline.'

'That's down to the parents, I suppose.'

Weston smiled faintly. 'Try telling that to Gavin Ferrigan's family. They were most abusive. Aggressive even. We had some very unpleasant scenes, I can tell you. I was forced to take legal advice to protect my position. I couldn't have my integrity being called into doubt in that way; it was undermining my authority as deputy head.'

'You say the boy was badly hurt?'

'He suffered serious head injuries. I did my best. I pulled him out of the water, tried to keep him warm until the air ambulance arrived. But he'd hit his head on some rocks in the stream. Five days later, they decided to turn off his life-support machine.'

'But it blew over in the end, as far as you were concerned?'

'Eventually. There was a lot of talk – ridiculous, unfounded allegations. It was very embarrassing for a while. It made me feel ashamed, although I knew I had done nothing wrong. Everyone made me feel it was my fault. Everyone.'

'And Gavin Ferrigan's mother is Wayne Sugden's sister.'

'Apparently. The father, Ferrigan, was already in prison then for drug dealing. But the rest of the family turned up in force for the inquest. It was most unpleasant.' Weston shuddered at the memory. 'I kept being forced to justify myself. But I had nothing to apologize for, did I? I did everything right. I did my best for him.'

A FEW MINUTES later, Eric Weston followed Fry into the hallway to show her out. He hesitated at the foot of the stairs near the heavy oak door, looking back over his shoulder where his wife could be heard piling crockery in the kitchen.

'The accident to Gavin Ferrigan ...' he said. 'You have to understand it was a very difficult experience for me.'

'Yes, I'm sure it was.'

'It's just that ... some people never forget. Some people like to make you go on feeling ashamed for ever.'

The clattering in the kitchen had stopped, and Mr Weston suddenly seemed to notice the silence.

'Well, goodbye, then,' he said. 'Sorry we couldn't help any more. Anything we can do, of course.'

He ushered Fry outside and stood on the step with the door half-closed behind him.

'The Ferrigan thing – do you really think it's relevant to ... you know?'

'We can't say at the moment.'

'It would be very bad if it was,' said Weston. 'Very bad.'

He had stepped back inside the house before Fry had reached the gate. Fry heard Mrs Weston's voice raised querulously, and a subdued murmur in return, followed by the slamming of something against a hard surface.

She went back to her car and looked at her map. She wanted the quickest way out and back on to the hills.

Unlike Ben Cooper, Fry felt no desire to defend the underdogs – not when they were people like Eric Weston. But she was angry and embarrassed to find that Weston's words had awakened a deep echo in her own mind. She was appalled that a couple of sentences he had uttered had matched so exactly her own feelings, from a period in her life that was not so very long ago.

'It made me feel ashamed, although I knew I had done nothing wrong,' he had said. *'Everyone made me feel it was my fault. Everyone.'*

Chapter Sixteen

'WHITE VANS AND more white vans,' said Chief Superintendent Jepson, waving a handful of report forms. 'Do you *know* how many white vans there are? How many within two days' drive of here? Millions?'

'Quite a few thousand, certainly,' said DCI Tailby.

'Do you propose to check out every one? Are you going to send my officers out on a van-spotting tour of the country? Perhaps you could give them those little *I-Spy* books and tell them not to come back until they've ticked off one with a rusty wheel arch?'

'We could ask local forces to do that for us, of course.'

'Oh, of course. My colleagues in ACPO will love me. They'll call me the White Van Man for the rest of my career.'

'That would be rather unkind.'

DCI Tailby had been reviewing the information for the Divisional Commander. There was plenty of it – an entire flood of it, rapidly filling up the megabytes on the computer. None of it pinned down any known persons actually in the vicinity of the Nine Virgins at the same time as Jenny Weston, with the exception of the Ranger, Mark Roper. The nearest locations of individuals identified were those of the farmworker, Victor McCauley, the two young men living in the quarry, and the Leach family, who had been going about their business at Ringham Edge.

DI Hitchens had brought a map of Ringham Moor, with the locations marked by the incident room staff. The trouble was, there were too many paths winding their way across the moor. There could be other individuals that hadn't been seen. The white van wasn't much, but it was a start.

'And what about Europe?' said Jepson. 'Two days' drive? Do you realize this van of yours could be in any city in half the countries of the European Union by now? Are you planning some day-trips? Are you intending to besmirch my good name with Europol? I suppose they'll start calling me Monsieur la Camionnette Blanche.'

'We don't think it's a French make,' said Hitchens. 'More likely a Ford Transit.'

Chief Superintendent Jepson sighed melodramatically. 'If I start getting postcards from CID officers from all over the French Riviera, I'll want to know why.'

'I don't think any of that will be necessary, sir,' said Tailby.

'If we don't make any progress soon, it will be, Stewart. Does this Martin Stafford sound like somebody who'd drive a white Transit van, Hitchens?'

'No, sir. But who knows?'

'Who indeed? Correct me if I'm wrong, but aren't we the people who are supposed to find out things like that?'

'We're busy tracing Stafford right now.'

'I'm also interested in the witness who said this van she saw was local. How does she know it was local?'

'She thinks she's seen it before, sir. She remembers that it was dirty, and has a rusted wheel arch. She notices things like that, she says. When pressed, she said she associates it with animals.'

'We're following it up, anyway,' said Hitchens. 'Checking out farmers, and so on. As it happens, it's market day today in Edendale. Lots of vehicles in town. All we need is a bit of luck.'

'We do deserve it,' said Tailby.

Jepson nodded. 'And the witness saw this van in the entrance to Ringham Edge Farm. Visiting Warren Leach, then?'

'Could have been,' said Hitchens. 'But, as Mr Leach himself says, the driver could have been using the roadway for some other purpose. Bear in mind there's access to the moor there. It's the same access that we've been using ourselves for the last two days.'

'Obliterating any tyre tracks in the process, naturally,' said Jepson.

'Well, maybe.'

'Yes, we always like to wipe out a fair bit of forensic evidence right at the start, don't we? We're well known for it. One of our more outstanding talents, you might say.'

'I think you're exaggerating there, sir,' said Tailby.

'Am I?' said Jepson. 'I don't think so. Has it ever occurred to you there might be a case for keeping police officers *away* from a crime scene completely when a body is found? We might actually get better results that way.'

'It's a thought, sir,' said Hitchens. 'We could suggest it as a special project group for the Operational Planning Department.'

'I'll think about it. It was also Leach's wife who found the earlier victim, Crew, wasn't it?'

'That's correct.'

'We mustn't overlook any correlations that the computer throws up, Stewart.'

'We're not doing that, sir. I'm keeping Leach in mind until we can eliminate him.'

'What about boyfriends of the victim?'

'All accounted for, except for the one who wrote the note. All the others deny writing it, and their handwriting doesn't match.'

'And Stafford's writing doesn't seem to match, either.'

'I've sent the samples to a handwriting expert. But at first glance, they're quite unalike.'

'So, a mystery boyfriend, then. I suppose that's what you would call a start, is it?'

'A mystery boyfriend who drives a white van?' said Hitchens.

'A mystery boyfriend who drives a white Transit van with a rusty wheel arch, who has something to do with animals and who possesses a sharp knife and a pair of boots that match our partial print. That would be ideal, I suppose,' said Jepson. 'Is that all you want for Christmas?'

'If it's Santa asking, I'd wish for Maggie Crew's memories to come back as well,' said Tailby.

'Ah, yes. How's Fry been getting on with her?'

'It's slow going, by all accounts. Crew is completely closed in on herself. Putting Fry on her was a bit of a last resort. But we can't treat her with kid gloves for ever, not if women are going to start dying on us.'

'Are you sure Fry's the right person?' said Jepson. 'Where's Ben Cooper today?'

'Cooper's on the white van team,' said Hitchens.

'I can't help feeling somebody else might have been better than Fry. Cooper does at least try to understand people. He has a bit more empathy.'

'Well,' said Hitchens, 'we've done empathy.'

'And what about Sugden?' asked Jepson. 'It would be helpful to appear to be questioning a suspect. Politically helpful, I mean.'

'We're bringing him in now.'

'Good. And the woman from Cheshire – Ros Daniels?'

'Not a trace of her. It'll take a damn sight more than empathy to find *her*, I'm afraid.'

WAYNE SUGDEN HADN'T wanted to come to the station to be interviewed. It was understandable. He had been out of prison only two weeks, and the cells in the detention suite at Edendale carried bad memories for him. But in the end, they had just put him in an interview room, where Diane Fry and DI Hitchens found him bubbling with fear and anger.

'You can't leave people alone, can you? Once you've got a downer on a bloke, that's it. Am I going to get this for the rest of my life? I'd be better off back inside.'

'Let's just calm down, Mr Sugden,' said Hitchens. 'We only want a chat.'

'Oh, yeah? I know your chats. I'm saying nothing. Not a word. Fetch me a solicitor.'

Sugden could just about qualify as a match for the description given by Jenny's neighbour. He was about five foot eight, a little overweight from his spell of prison food and lack of exercise, with pale eyes and hair the colour of Dettol. His accent was certainly local. Maybe he could even dress respectably sometimes – when he finally put those jeans and the stained black sweatshirt in the wash.

'I know my rights,' he said. 'It's on the card. Here, you haven't shown me the card. I can make a complaint, you know.'

Fry couldn't raise any sympathy for Sugden. Maybe if she had just been released from prison herself, the last person she would have wanted to see was a policeman, and the last place she would have wanted to be was Edendale police station. But then, she would have thought of that in the first place before she got herself sent down for burglary.

'We're trying to eliminate as many people as possible from a current enquiry, Mr Sugden,' she said. 'We just want to ask you a few simple questions.'

'You weren't selling stolen video recorders, by any chance?'

'Hey,' said Sugden, 'I think that's a "no comment".'

'We'd really like to eliminate you from our enquiries, Mr Sugden.'

'Well, it wasn't like that. Right? And anyway …'

'Yes?'

'I was never there.'

Chapter Seventeen

THE OLD CATTLE market was close to Edendale railway station. The overgrown tracks that ran alongside the market were where the cattle waggons had once been unloaded, in the days when animals were moved by train. These days, they came in by trailer and by huge cattle transporters that brought half of Edendale town centre to a halt on market days as they attempted to negotiate the narrow corners.

The days of Pilkington & Son, Livestock Auctioneers, were numbered anyway. And not just because of their inconvenient location or the lengthening list of European Union regulations that became ever more difficult to comply with. The number of cattle markets was dwindling fast, even in rural counties like Derbyshire. And three years ago, the futuristic white sails of a new agricultural business centre that the farmers called 'Nine Nipples' had appeared fifteen miles away at Bakewell, part of a £12 million regeneration project. It had a vast parking area, modern penning, three sale rings, meeting rooms, an IT centre and conference facilities. Since it opened, Pilkington & Son had merely been counting the days.

As a result, a bare minimum of maintenance had been done on the buildings in Edendale during the past ten years. There were gaps in the roof and missing sections of corrugated iron in the walls, rusty gates falling off their hinges, and pens whose steel bars had been bent out of shape by vandals. At night, youths rode their motorbikes through the aisles like rodeo cowboys. On the street side, the windows were full of jagged holes where the panes had been used for target practice.

Outside, the open-air pens were surrounded by parked Land Rovers, muddy livestock trailers and transporters slewed on to the pavements. Ben Cooper and Todd Weenink had difficulty finding a space for their car, and ended up parking across the front bumper of a wagon owned by a haulier from Lincolnshire.

The main building held cattle, and two smaller ones across the road were for pigs and sheep. Many of the sheep pens were empty, but there were some Derbyshire Gritstone ewes crammed together between wooden hurdles. A man was trying to drive a group of piglets up a strawed ramp into a lorry with nothing but a wooden board and a mouthful of curses. Once in the lorry, the pigs clattered and squealed hysterically, before emerging back down the ramp as the man dodged and screamed, rapidly losing his temper.

A patrol car was blocking one of the side roads, with its hazard lights on and the stripes on its rear glowing bright red. A uniformed officer ran back to speak to them.

'It's bloody chaos here,' he said. 'No wonder Traffic have hysterics every time it's market day.'

'Where's the van?' said Cooper.

'Over there.' He pointed to one of the cobbled areas crammed with vehicles of all kinds. 'It's right at the back, so I'd say it won't be leaving for a while.'

'Have you got the details?'

'This is the registration.' The officer passed him a page from his notebook. 'It's registered to a Mr Keith Teasdale. An Edendale address, as you can see.'

'Thanks a lot.'

'We've been told to hang around for a bit, in case you need us.'

'OK. But don't make yourselves too obvious. Hide your baboon's bum, for a start.'

'We'll try. There's just nowhere to park. The town centre bobby is here, too, by the way. They expect to see him on market day, so he's no problem.'

Cooper and Weenink wound their way through the parked vehicles. They passed a fifty-foot-long transporter that already had two decks of calves loaded. A lorry that had been washed and scrubbed inside drove off with dirty water pouring out under the hinges of the tailgate. A farmer was trying to negotiate a cattle trailer into a space that was obviously too small.

When they found the Transit van, it was blocked in at the back of the parking area, with its bonnet against the wall and no way of reversing out past the trailer behind it.

'I suppose it *was* white once,' said Cooper, drawing his finger through the grime on the back doors.

Weenink had walked round the front, squeezing his bulk between the van and the wing mirror of a Daihatsu Fourtrak next to it.

'Has it got a rusty wheel arch?' asked Cooper.

'Two of them. Also a rusty passenger door and rusty sills all the way along this side. And look at all this crap hanging out of the side door.'

Cooper peered along the van. Strands of yellow straw stuck out from under the bottom of the side-loading door like a badly trimmed fringe of hair.

'It reminds me of a particularly hairy blonde I knew once,' said Weenink. 'She was a real goer. But stripped down to her knickers, she looked like Wurzel Gummidge.'

'Let's go and find Mr Keith Teasdale,' said Cooper.

A police constable and an RSPCA inspector stood chatting by the door, their uniforms almost identical but for the policeman's helmet. The RSPCA man looked like a farmer himself and nodded amicably at the customers walking past. Above their heads were posters advertising fertilizers and animal feeds.

Inside the building, market workers were channelling cattle through a complicated network of steel pens towards the sale ring. As Cooper and Weenink entered, a group of bullocks turned on each other and engaged in a shoving match in the passageway. Side by side, two of the animals completely filled the passage, and their flanks were squeezed against the five-foot high steel bars of the pens on either side. Yipping and shouting, the attendants flicked their backs with sticks until they went in the right direction. Then steel gates were shut along the passageways with a series of loud clangs.

At the back was the sale ring itself, surrounded by tiers of wooden benches like a miniature amphitheatre. Rows of farmers lined the benches, while others pressed against the steel tubular sides of the ring, their boots resting on a wooden platform like men propping up the bar at their local pub. Above them, the low girders supporting the roof of the mart were covered with roosting starlings.

In the ring were four men, booted and overalled, with sticks in their hands to keep the beasts moving through. The exits and entrances were just wide enough for men to squeeze through, but too narrow for animals desperate to escape from the claustrophobic confines of the ring and the circles of watching, predatory eyes.

Cooper stopped to examine the next lot coming in. They were store cattle, down from the hill farms, destined to go to arable land in the east for fattening and breeding. Some were spattered with mud and faeces; others had rear hooves that had grown into long, curved toes like Persian slippers, and they hobbled as they moved.

Some of the beasts went to press their faces against the steel sides of the ring to gaze back towards the holding pens until the men drove them away, making them parade for the buyers to see the way they moved. Then the animals would panic and skid on their own excrement on a concrete surface perfunctorily scattered with sawdust. The larger cattle made the men slip behind wooden barriers in front of the auctioneer's podium to escape injury.

As Cooper watched, one animal refused to be directed to the exit gate, and it ended up in the ring with the next beast. They circled and barged each other in confusion as the men set about them.

'Jesus, Ben, I think I'm going off beef all of a sudden,' said Weenink.

Cooper saw one or two farmers he recognized. Bridge End Farm was his brother's business, but he had been to enough auctions and farm sales with Matt to be familiar with some of the names and faces. There were a few who seemed to turn up wherever farmers got together. These events were their social life, as well as their livelihood.

The first farmer shook his head when asked about Keith Teasdale. The second did the same. Cooper continued to work his way through the crowd, followed by Weenink. The auctioneer was Abel Pilkington himself, and his voice never stopped. He rattled out his litany: 'Forty, forty, forty. Five. Forty-five, forty-five. Fifty where? Fifty, fifty, fifty. Am I missing anyone?' It became a continuous, semi-audible stream of figures, amplified and distorted by the microphone. It was impossible to see anyone bidding, but Pilkington had each beast sold in a matter of seconds and the next one on its way in.

'Aye, that's Teasdale over there,' said an old farmer at last. 'He's working in the ring, see.'

The man at the entrance gate to the sale ring looked either tired or bored. There were bags under his eyes and he moved with less energy than the others, though he was younger than some. He was a dark, thin man with heavy black stubble and a Mexican-style moustache and a shifty look in his eye. His entire skill lay in the timing of the opening of the gate. He barely used his stick unless an animal threatened to pin him against the side of the ring.

Cooper was beginning to feel light-headed with claustrophobia and the intensity of the noise. Most of the audience seemed to be shouting and chattering constantly to each other all around the ring, ignoring the auctioneer, while weighing up the animals from the corners of their eyes. There was a continuous bellowing of animals waiting to be driven into the ring or marshalled back into their pens. Gates clanged and cattle transporters started up outside. At times, the auctioneer could barely be heard above the din.

The sun came out and shone through the Perspex roof. The heat in the ring rose several degrees as it hit the dirty floor and sweaty bodies.

'How do we get him out of there?' said Weenink. 'I'm not going in that ring. Not without body armour and a riot shield.'

Cooper tapped one of the attendants on the shoulder and showed him his warrant card.

'We need to speak to Keith Teasdale. Tell him we'll see him in the car park, where his van is.'

They stood and watched as the man exchanged a few words with Teasdale. The bullocks in the ring circled, sniffing at the hands of the spectators. Even three feet away, Cooper could feel the blast of the breath from the animals' nostrils. One lumbered too close to the buyers, and they stood back, pulling their arms in to avoid getting them trapped against the steel bars. One bullock released a stream of green diarrhoea that hit the concrete and splashed an old farmer's trousers. He seemed not to notice.

Teasdale looked up at the detectives when the other man pointed. His face was expressionless, but he nodded briefly. Cooper and Weenink were glad to get out into the open air. While they waited, they read the signs on the outside wall of the office, which advertised farm sales. Farmers seemed to be selling off everything – their stock, their equipment, their land, their homes.

Back at the ring, the next lots were going in. Two-week-old calves that could barely walk were being sold for the price of a couple of pints of beer.

DCI TAILBY TURNED over the interview reports from the officers who had dragged themselves round a series of pubs in the back streets of Edendale. He suspected there would be some expense claims following the reports soon.

'So it looks as though Sugden's alibis will stand up,' he said.

'I'm afraid so,' said DI Hitchens.

'Typical. Motive, but no opportunity.'

'A bit like fish and no chips.'

'If you say so, Paul.'

'Do you want the latest news on Martin Stafford?' asked Hitchens.

'Fire away.' When Hitchens and Fry had entered his office, Tailby had been sneaking a crafty smoke of his pipe, to ease the ache in his head from staring at the computer screen. He waved his hand at the cloud of smoke to see the DI better.

'We've been following a bit of a long trail,' said Hitchens. 'Diane has the details.'

'Martin Stafford left Jenny Weston four years ago,' said Fry. 'And while the divorce was going on, he left his job too. He moved from the *Derby Evening Telegraph* to the *Leicester Mercury*. But he was there only eighteen months, then had a spell on a small weekly in Cheshire. I tracked one of the reporters down there. She said he drank too much, had affairs in office hours, boasted about his talents as a journalist but never bothered to put them to use. He generally seemed to give the impression he was too good for the place.'

'I can't say I'm warming to him yet. I don't suppose he lasted any longer at the Cheshire paper?'

'Less,' said Fry. 'Twelve months. He had a couple of blazing rows with the editor, then announced one day that he was going freelance.'

'Damn. End of employment trail, then.'

'His last employers have an address in Macclesfield, so I asked Cheshire to chase him up. But there's a Punjabi family living there now. Mail still arrives for Stafford, but they just throw it away.'

'What about the electoral register?'

'He's still registered at the Macclesfield address. The register is taken in October, of course.'

'Is that it, then?'

'Not quite, sir. I reckoned if he had been trying to set himself up as a freelancer, he ought to have tried some of the bigger papers in the region for work. So I checked with a few, just in case any of them had him on their books. The Features Editor at the *Sheffield Star* was very helpful and dug out a proposal letter from Martin Stafford from a few months back. The address was a flat in Congleton. That's as fresh as we'll get. And it's not too far away.'

'Phone number?'

'Got it, but we haven't tried it yet,' said Fry.

'You think he's still there?'

DI Hitchens took over. 'I think if he's getting no work as a freelance, he'll either have moved to another area, found some other kind of job entirely, or ended up on the dole. My money's on the second or third. Because he hasn't gone far from the district at any time, has he?'

Tailby looked pleased. 'I think you're probably right. Have we been in touch with Cheshire again?'

'I asked them to keep a discreet eye on the flat and see if anybody answering Stafford's description was around,' said Hitchens. 'We faxed them his picture from Jenny's wedding photo.'

'And?'

Hitchens smiled. He looked particularly satisfied with himself, as if he were the first man to bring good news all year. 'Stafford arrived home fifteen minutes ago,' he said.

The DCI regarded him with a mixture of emotions flickering across his face. Fry could see that Hitchens really got under his skin sometimes. But it was undoubtedly good news.

'How long will it take you to get to Congleton?' asked Tailby.

'Not long. If we drive fast.'

'Drive fast then.'

KEITH TEASDALE SMELLED as though he had spent all his life in close contact with cattle. But in the market car park, it was Ben Cooper and Todd Weenink who were out of place, with their alien smell of clean cars and offices.

'What's wrong with the van, then?' said Teasdale. 'It's got its MoT, look. It's taxed and insured. What's the problem?'

Cooper explained what they wanted to know, and watched to see whether Teasdale relaxed. But he remained defensive.

'Can't I drive where I want to? Without some nosey old biddy reporting me?'

Teasdale had brought his stick with him. He tapped it on the side of the Transit as he spoke, loosening some flakes of rust that dropped off the wheel arch.

'I'm sure we could find something wrong with it, if we looked,' said Weenink.

'We need some help, that's all,' said Cooper. 'If you were in the area, we need to eliminate you. If it wasn't you, we keep looking. It's quite simple.'

Teasdale looked at his boots and scratched the heavy black stubble on his cheeks. The gesture was intended to suggest that he was thinking.

'I get around a lot,' he said. 'I do little jobs for people. Farmers mostly.'

'What sort of jobs?'

'Anything I can get. There's only a couple of days' work here. The rest of the time I do a bit of fencing or ratting. That sort of stuff.'

'Ratting?' said Weenink.

'I clear rats out of barns and grain sheds.'

'You use terriers, I suppose?' said Cooper.

'That's right. Lot of rats around this time of year. They start looking for somewhere warm and dry to live when the fields are harvested and the weather turns colder.'

'Is Warren Leach at Ringham Edge Farm one of your customers?'

'I know Leach.'

'Were you there on Sunday?'

'I was up that way.' Teasdale hesitated. 'I was thinking of calling in at Ringham Edge, but I didn't.'

'Why not?'

'I ran into the lad who worked for him. Gary Dawson. Gary used to help Warren Leach with the milking and stuff, but he said he'd just walked out on him. He said Warren was in a terrible temper all the time these days. So I decided not to go up to Ringham Edge. He can be an awkward bugger at the best of times, Warren. In a temper, he's nasty. I can do without that.'

'And what about Totley? Do you know it?' asked Cooper.

'I know it.'

'Not many farmers up there. Not much ratting to do.'

'I do all sorts of jobs.'

Weenink was peering through the back windows of the van. They were painted over, but some of the paint had flaked off on the inside, and there were a few small gaps where the glass was clear.

'What's the going rate for scrap metal then, these days?' he asked.

'Hey,' said Teasdale, whose attention had been on Cooper. 'What are you doing there?'

'Scrap, eh?' said Cooper. 'The lady at Totley was right, then.'

'It's legal,' said Teasdale sullenly.

Cooper nodded. 'It depends how you go about it,' he said. And Teasdale scowled at him.

'Are you sure you weren't at Ringham Edge Farm?' asked Weenink.

'It would be helpful all round if we could eliminate you,' said Cooper.

Teasdale kicked the nearest tyre of his van. A few lumps of mud fell out of the tread. 'All right. Gary Dawson told me it'd be a waste of time, but I went up there anyway. I need the money I get from jobs like that. They pay me next to nothing here, and it won't last forever. You have to take the work where you can find it.'

'That's a bit more like it,' said Cooper. 'Now we know where we are. What time was this?'

'About half past two, maybe.'

'And were you at the farm long?'

'Five minutes. Just long enough for Leach to give me a mouthful of abuse. I wasn't standing for that, so I cleared off. I know things are bad up there, but there's no excuse for that, is there?'

IT WAS GETTING dark by the time Martin Stafford was brought into Divisional Headquarters at West Street. Stafford hadn't seemed surprised to see the police outside the door of his flat in Congleton. In fact, he had made a point of taking a careful note of their names and numbers from their warrant cards, as if they had brought *him* information that would be useful.

Diane Fry sat alongside DCI Tailby in the interview room. Stafford was dark and good-looking, his hair well brushed back and falling slightly over his ears. He had eyes that laughed all the time, and what was sometimes called a boyish grin. He was the sort of man that some women fell for without considering the consequences. He was the sort of man that some fathers would forbid their daughters to marry. The grin made Fry want to punch him.

'Yes, of course I heard about it. I saw it on the TV,' said Stafford.

'But you never thought to come forward, sir?'

'Not really.'

Tailby waited, letting Stafford fill in the gaps rather than leaping in with the questions. Fry suspected that the DCI was already feeling disappointed. Stafford had come too willingly and looked too relaxed.

'We hadn't had any contact with each other for three years,' said Stafford. 'I'm sorry she's dead, but – well, it may sound a bit hard, but she was nothing to do with me. Not any more.'

'Would you say there was a certain amount of animosity in your parting, Mr Stafford?'

'I'm a journalist, Chief Inspector.'

'So?'

'I don't use words like animosity. They don't fit in a headline.'

'I see.'

'Besides, most newspaper readers wouldn't understand what it meant. I'd be more likely to say spite. Yes, as far as Jenny was concerned, I might say spiteful. Still, I *am* sorry she's dead. Really.'

'When you say you hadn't been in contact, do you mean that you hadn't met for three years?'

Stafford smiled slightly. 'I mean we hadn't spoken at all.'

'No telephone calls?'

'No.'

'What about letters? Did you write to her?'

'We did all our corresponding through solicitors,' said Stafford. 'It seemed to help to filter out the venom.'

'You mean the spite.'

'Exactly.'

'But you did send a postcard to your ex-wife's parents.'

'Oh, that. They showed you that, did they?' Stafford laughed, as if amused at the prank of a child who didn't know any better. 'It was just a joke. I'm amazed they kept it. They could hardly have wanted a memento of me.'

'Was there some spite on the part of Mr and Mrs Weston as well, then?'

'Chief Inspector, in this case I would go along with animosity.'

Fry studied the leather jacket Stafford wore. It had been an expensive jacket once. It had probably taken a long time for it to get so decrepit. Or should that be scruffy?

'How's the freelance journalism business these days?' she asked.

'Tough,' admitted Stafford. 'Very competitive, you know. But I'm keeping my head above water.'

'Can't afford a smart car, then, I suppose?'

'I drive an Escort. It isn't exactly brand new.'

'When were you last in Totley?'

'Where?'

'Totley.'

'That's Sheffield, isn't it? I think I've passed through it from time to time on the way into the city. It's the sort of place that you do just pass through, if I remember rightly. Not the sort of place you'd stop. Unless you live there, of course. Is there a reason for that question?'

'Do you know where your ex-wife lived after the house you shared was sold?' asked Tailby.

'Well, I didn't,' said Stafford slowly. 'But might I make an intelligent guess that it was Totley?'

'Her neighbours have reported a man trying to find her.'

'It wasn't me.'

'The afternoon of Wednesday 22nd of October ...'

Stafford produced a diary. 'I have detailed records of my movements right here, Chief Inspector. I thought you'd never ask.'

'We'll take the details from you when you give a statement.'

'Fine.'

'Is the name Ros Daniels familiar to you?' asked Fry.

Martin Stafford shrugged. 'I have such a lot of old girlfriends, you know. It's difficult to remember all their names.'

'About twenty years old, hair in dreadlocks and a couple of rings in her nose.'

'Hardly, dear.'

'She was known to your ex-wife.'

Stafford shook his head. 'Jenny was mixing in different circles from when we were married, then. I've no idea who the person you're describing could be.'

'Very well,' said Tailby. 'That'll do for now.'

'I *am* sorry, you know,' said Stafford. 'But she was nothing to do with me any more.'

WHEN STAFFORD HAD gone, DCI Tailby seemed to want to sit for a while. Fry stayed with him, wondering if he wanted to discuss the interview, or whether he was content with his own thoughts.

'Did you believe him, sir?' she said.

Tailby looked at her in surprise. 'Of course,' he said. 'It rings true. He believes that Jenny Weston was nothing to do with him.'

'It seems as though she's nothing to do with anybody, really,' said Fry. And as soon as she had said it, the irony of the sentence lodged in a corner of her chest. It was as if the words hadn't been her own at all, but had been said by someone else about *her*. She was aware that her life had become completely solitary, apart from the unavoidable professional contact with her colleagues, who had soon learned not to enquire about her private life. She was nothing to do with anybody, really.

'Not quite true,' said Tailby, watching Fry curiously. 'There's one person out there that she has a whole lot to do with. Though maybe she never knew it.'

Chapter Eighteen

IN THE END, Wednesday morning looked set to be overcast. Diane Fry had come through the Forestry Commission plantations and down past Flash Dam. She was already slightly late, but she sat in her car at the top of Sydnope Hill for a while and looked down on Matlock. She was watching the clouds come closer. They were rolling in from the east, their shadows chasing across the slopes of the hills and into the town.

Fry had worked out where the roof of Derwent Court was, deep among the other roofs. At the moment, its tiles were glittering as the clear November sun fell on the remains of an overnight frost. She was due at Maggie's at nine. But by the time the clouds had closed in enough for her satisfaction, it was nearly five past. Fry started the car. Maggie would be annoyed that she was late, but that was tough. She didn't want any distractions today. It was difficult enough as it was.

From here, she could see how damaged the landscape was to the east. Huge sections had been gouged and blasted from the side of Masson Hill, on the opposite side of the town. Bare terraces of exposed rock had been left by the quarrying, flat and unnatural in the slope of the hill. She checked the sky again for clouds. It was safe. There would be no sun on Maggie's window now.

'So you did come back,' said Maggie a few minutes later. 'I imagined I might have escaped your attentions. I thought you might have forgotten me.'

'Never, Maggie.'

'Oh? You remember me for my sparkling personality, do you? My intellect? My savage wit?'

Fry noticed that Maggie had rearranged the lamps in the room. The lighting was softer, less uncompromising, perhaps designed to put her visitor at ease and make her more welcome. A new chair had been placed in front of the desk – this one was upholstered in green satin on the seat and back, and when Fry sat in it she found it remarkably comfortable.

The cafetiere stood ready on the desk with cream and sugar in a ceramic jug and bowl. By such signs, Fry knew she was making progress. But it was a fragile intimacy; it could be broken in a second, by the ringing of a phone or the scrape of a chair leg.

'I thought we were getting along fine before,' she said.

'Did you?' Maggie fiddled with the lamp, tilting the shade so that the shadows played backwards and forwards across her face. Fry found the effect disconcerting, as Maggie's good eye came first into the light, startling and white, then vanished again into the shadows of her face.

With the Weston enquiry going nowhere, it seemed to Diane Fry that her interviews with Maggie Crew were a kind of Eastern Front, the one place where the breakthrough might come, if there was going to be one. Maggie was their only real witness. She could identify her assailant. However she did it, Fry would have to drag those memories out kicking and screaming. So she sat here alone with this woman, struggling to get through to her, digging for her memories like a miner hitting rock.

'Have you thought about what we said last time?' asked Fry.

But Maggie responded with another question.

'Do you know how many visitors I get?'

'No.'

'Do you know what it's like sitting here wondering whether anybody will come?'

'I'm sorry.'

Maggie slammed back the arm of the lamp as far as it would go, throwing the full glare of the bulb into Fry's face.

'That's the one thing I told you I wouldn't tolerate. Do not feel sorry for me. Understand?'

Fry had to bite back the natural response, reminding herself that this was a woman who was in a psychologically delicate balance. She needed careful handling, not an all-out row. Not the accusation of self-pity and hypocrisy that had sprung to her lips.

'Let's start again, shall we?'

'Be my guest.'

'What I'd really like to do,' said Fry, 'is take you back to when it happened, to jog your memory. I want you to try again, Maggie.'

'Why should I?'

'For Jenny Weston's sake. And to help us stop him from killing any more. Maggie – you can't refuse.'

Maggie blinked, and hesitated. 'Your colleagues always used a different approach. They tried to be sympathetic, to put me at my ease – all that sort of thing. I hated it.'

'I don't care about that. I've got a job to do. I need you to help me.'

Maggie stared at her. 'Coffee?' she said, and reached for the cafetiere.

Fry nodded. Her clenched fingers began to relax. She looked around the room while Maggie poured. The place really wasn't welcoming at all, even with a comfortable chair and the smell of fresh coffee. What would bring Maggie's memories out into the light again? When you had suffered that sort of trauma, you needed some kind of closure. It was possible that her memories wouldn't be fully released until they had her attacker behind bars.

On the other hand, there might be something deeper inside that was keeping Maggie's mind shut down. She had to find a trigger that would release those memories.

Fry had a twin-deck tape recorder set up. She had fully expected Maggie to refuse to be taped, but she had agreed readily; in fact, she had seemed almost relieved. Perhaps the tape machine could be a compromise, an impersonal middle ground. She probably thought a tape couldn't bring back memories, only capture the ones you already had. But Fry wasn't sure about that. Today, she meant to take Maggie further.

For a few minutes, they sat comfortably over their coffee. They even made a bit of small talk about the weather and Maggie's neighbours, just as if Fry were a friend paying a social call. Who knew – there might even be chocolate biscuits with the coffee.

'I feel as though I'm getting unfit sitting here all day,' said Maggie. 'Before I know it, I'll be putting weight on.'

No chocolate biscuits, then. Fry unwrapped two fresh tapes and inserted them in the machine.

'*You* don't look as though you have any trouble with your weight, Diane,' said Maggie.

'I don't have time to put weight on.' It was the answer she always gave when people asked her. She tested the tape machine, and both tapes began to turn. 'Ready?'

'There's something I want to tell you first.'

'Yes?'

'I've decided to go back to work,' said Maggie.

'Is that wise?' said Fry, immediately thinking of the dangers to Maggie rather than of the psychological advantages of getting her back into the outside world.

'I've got to get out of this apartment some time.'

'You must take precautions for your own safety. We'll send someone to your office to check out the security arrangements.'

Maggie sighed. 'If you insist.'

'If you're going back to work, I'll have to make an appointment, I suppose. Solicitors' time is expensive, isn't it?'

Maggie smiled at the comment. Fry liked to see her smile. It almost gave her an appearance of normality. But there was still a pain haunting her eyes, and still a strange physical vulnerability in the glimpse of pink gum.

'I'll pencil you in for Friday,' said Maggie. 'Two o'clock, at our offices in Mill Street.'

Fry made a show of getting out her diary and writing it down. 'Fine. At least it will take your mind off things. Do you find your work interesting?'

'Interesting?' Maggie considered the word. 'I suppose some people might think so. But in fact it's ninety per cent drudgery. Wading through mountains of paperwork until your eyes are sore, filling in reports and applications. Sitting in endless meetings.'

'Join the club.'

'And there are the most objectionable of people to deal with. Their concerns are unbelievable. It's all jealousy and selfishness and greed. Husbands and wives, children and parents, colleagues and business partners – all desperate to know about what someone else is up to. The times they have asked me to employ enquiry agents to look into their sordid little affairs. And not just the clients, either. My partners are just as bad.'

'You don't get on with your partners?'

'We work together satisfactorily. But they're all the same – complacent, self-centred and obsessed. They're so single-minded that their lives are empty shells. They'll discover it one day, but it will be too late.'

Fry nodded. The description Maggie had just given of her partners echoed her own file. Maggie Crew's history was one of professional achievements, and little else. Maggie talked of empty lives. But it only took a glance round the room to see whose life was the emptiest of all.

Fry watched the way Maggie drank her coffee without turning fully to the desk, then spun her chair back towards the window.

'Ready now?'

Maggie nodded and closed her eyes.

'Tell me what happened that day, Maggie.'

Maggie didn't need to ask what day she meant. 'I've been over it so many times before. I can't remember.'

'What would you normally have done that day? It was a Sunday, wasn't it?'

'All right, then. On a Sunday, I would have got up later than usual, had a leisurely breakfast. Toast and marmalade and two cups of coffee, probably. I need coffee to get myself ready for the day. I would have switched on the TV to get the morning news. Maybe I looked out of the window and I saw what a nice day it was.'

Fry watched Maggie gradually becoming less tense. She was starting to relax as she focused on the world outside herself. The best way was to ask few questions. Encourage the interviewee to close their eyes and picture the scene, down to even the tiniest details; let them recall smells, noises, their feelings at the time. Officers were no longer trained to take control of an interview. Too many courts had accepted the contention of defendants and lawyers that the police had suggested the answers themselves.

Eventually, this process might be conducted by machine entirely. Two tape decks to record the answers, and a third to repeat the necessary phrases: 'Now, just close your eyes …'

'Is that what made you decide to go to Ringham Moor? That it was a nice day?'

'I really don't know,' said Maggie.

'It's OK.'

'Ringham Moor is not too far away. I've walked there lots of times. I used to go there before I became a partner. Afterwards, there never seemed to be time.'

'All right. Move forward a bit. To when you reached Ringham –'

Maggie was silent. Fry tried to detect from the expression on just one side of her face whether she was remembering any more. But it was impossible to tell. Finally, Maggie's eyes came fully open, and her body tensed again.

'Does it tell you in my file that I'm unable to form relationships?'

Fry could only nod. The moment was lost. No point in trying to recreate it now.

'Yes, it would. But I was like that before, you know,' said Maggie. 'Too busy for relationships. And it's too late now.'

'Not necessarily.'

'Please don't try to patronize me on the subject. I'm learning to be a realist. People won't accept me now. But people have never really accepted me in my entire life.'

Fry frowned. If there was anything in the file to support this perception, she had missed it. Maggie Crew had received a perfectly normal education and upbringing. Her father had been a regional manager for British Rail, and the family had lived in Wingerworth, near Chesterfield. Mrs Crew had died some years ago of cancer, and a sister, Catherine, had married and lived in Ireland. Maggie's father was still alive, though, and living not so far away.

The two girls, Fry noted, had attended a well-known Catholic girls school in Chesterfield, and both had gone on to university. Maggie had studied for her Law degree in Nottingham. She had been successful in her career, yet had never married or had children.

'Do you see much of your father?' asked Fry.

'He's rather elderly now,' said Maggie.

'Yes?'

'And ... well, we were never a very close family, really.'

'Does the same apply to your sister?'

'Cath? She has her own family. A husband and four children. Why would she bother about me? She's as content as an old cat in her little town in Ireland.'

'And did you never want to do the same, Maggie?'

But Maggie smiled. Fry was beginning to recognize that smile as one that signalled a subject she didn't want to discuss.

'What about you, Diane?' said Maggie. 'Married?'

'No.'

'Children?'

'No.'

'Ah. It would interfere with the career, perhaps? No crèche at the police station? No husband at home, no mother-in-law to look after them during the day? It's so difficult for some women, I know. We see them in the legal profession, carrying their babies invisibly on their backs in court, disposable nappies spilling out of their briefcases, baby sick on their clothes, yawning from lack of sleep on the night before an important case. You can't help but feel sorry for them.'

'It happens in the police, too.'

'No broody feelings for you either, Diane? No ticking biological clock?'

'I don't believe so.'

'You're lucky, then. I find the idea pretty horrific, to be perfectly honest. Awful, puking things, aren't they? I can understand women who have abortions. It's a horrible business, but there must be times when it seems vastly preferable to the alternative.'

Fry was conscious of Maggie's gentle probing. It was well done, the sign of a skilful interviewer. The fact that Fry had allowed herself to be interviewed had encouraged Maggie, of course. At this point, she either went along with the game and told Maggie what she wanted to know, or she closed it down and risked losing the fragile intimacy she had built up.

'I had an abortion once,' she said.

Maggie's voice dropped a shade, sliding a sympathetic note into her next words.

'They tell me you always wonder what the baby would have been like, what sex it was. You think about what name you would have given it, if it had been allowed to live. Even an abortion doesn't mean a clean ending, it seems to me.'

'Yes, you're right.'

A small silence developed between them. Fry held on to it, valuing the suggestion of understanding. At the same time, she was calculating how she could use it. The time was almost right.

'But there's more, isn't there?' said Maggie quietly. 'Something else that you can't forget.'

'Yes,' said Fry. 'There is.' She told herself it was for the best. She could work it out of her system later.

Maggie seemed to decide not to push for details.

'Sometimes there are things you need to remember, no matter how much it hurts,' she said.

'A necessary pain?'

'Maybe. But that necessary pain … does it always have to be a pain that you inflict on yourself? Because that sort of pain hurts all the more, don't you find?'

Fry put her finger on the 'play' and 'record' buttons, and looked at Maggie.

'Shall we try again?'

Maggie closed her eyes. The tapes whirred quietly.

'Think about when you reached Ringham …'

Maggie breathed quietly. 'I remember the leaves under my feet,' she said. 'There were deep piles of them. They crunched when I trod in them. Thousands of dead leaves.

I kicked some of them up in the air, like I used to do when I was child. A great heap of them, all brown and gold.'

Fry thought she had stopped there. She waited for a moment, listening to the click of the tape decks. She had just opened her mouth to nudge Maggie with a question, when she began again.

'The wind blew the leaves about, and I grabbed at them, trying to catch them in my hands. Some of them landed on me; they were on my arms and in my face, touching my skin. They felt cold and clammy, not what I expected at all. They smelled of damp and rottenness. I tried to brush them off my face. There were leaves in my hair as well, sticking there like bats. Then I didn't think it was funny any more. I brushed at the leaves harder. I had my head down, to get them off.'

The sound of Maggie's voice had changed. It had a childish intonation that Fry had not heard before. It was slightly shocking coming from the mouth of this woman. It was as if she were recalling a childhood incident, not a trauma from a few weeks ago.

This time the pause was even longer. Fry squeezed her fingers together to stop herself breaking the silence and interrupting. She looked at the tapes to make sure they were both still running. But the silence went on too long.

'Is there anyone else around?' asked Fry as gently as she could, though her urge was to push Maggie harder as they reached a critical stage.

'Anyone else? No, she's not there.'

Fry shook her head, thinking she had misheard. 'Who?'

Now Maggie looked confused too, as if two different memories were mingling together.

'I had my head down, looking at the ground,' she repeated. 'I was looking at the ground, where the leaves were. That's why I didn't see him.'

Maggie's voice had become bleak. Her pitch had risen slightly as people's voices did when they were close to that crack in the facade that let through the tears.

'If I hadn't kicked at the leaves, I would have heard him coming. I could have got away.'

'When did you first become aware of another person, Maggie?'

'He was already close then.'

'How did you know? Did you hear him?'

'The leaves were rustling. They were too loud. I wasn't paying attention.'

'All right. You didn't hear him. Did you smell him, Maggie?'

'Smell him?' Maggie frowned. Her nostrils flared as if she was drawing in remembered odours.

Fry knew that smells were powerful aids to memory. If Maggie could recall a single whiff of something – a distinctive deodorant, body odour, cigarette smoke – it would be something to add to the picture.

'I can't smell him,' said Maggie. 'Only the leaves.'

'Can you hear him now?' asked Fry, switching to the present tense that Maggie herself had started using.

Maggie's eyes were distant. Was she listening? Fry was sure that Maggie could hear something. Some sound was replaying in her mind, but Fry was powerless to know what it was until she felt able to share it.

'A rustling noise,' said Maggie hesitantly, at last.

'The leaves again? He was walking through the leaves. You heard his feet in the leaves.'

'Yes, there was that too. But something else. A plastic rustling. No, not plastic – nylon. He was wearing a nylon cagoule or anorak.'

Fry felt a little surge of excitement. 'That's very good, Maggie. Think carefully now. Can you see it, this cagoule? What colour is it?'

Maggie shook her head. 'I don't know. Black. Maybe blue.'

'That's good. Can you describe it? Does it have buttons or a zip? Has it got a hood?'

'I can't tell.'

'Why not?'

Maggie paused. 'It's dark.'

Fry opened her mouth and shut it again. She looked at the tape machine, wondering whether it had heard the same thing that she had. Then she stared at Maggie Crew, resisting an urge to grab the woman by the shoulders and shake her, to force her to answer the biggest question of all.

'Maggie,' she said, '*what were you doing on the moor in the dark?*'

But Maggie was silent now. Fry thought she had lost her completely, that she had slipped away into sleep or some other world. But if she had, it was a world where there were only nightmares. Maggie's body was rigid, her face strained and frightened. Her eyes were screwed tightly shut. She shook her head abruptly, like someone throwing off brambles tangled in her hair. Fry caught a glimpse of red, puckered tissue, glistening as if freshly burned.

Then Maggie put her hands to her face, covering her right eye, her fingers pressed tightly to her forehead for protection. There was only the sound of her breathing in the room, a ragged hiss through her nose that the tapes would fail to catch, though they kept on turning. And there was a high, distant noise, like the wheeze in the chest of an asthmatic, or the faint whimper of a small creature dying at the side of the road.

'I can't remember,' said Maggie. 'I can't remember.'

Chapter Nineteen

'GOLDEN VIRGINIA,' SAID Owen Fox. 'It's their favourite.'

Owen had a six-pack of lager in one hand, a tin of tobacco in the other. Ben Cooper followed him uncertainly. He had paid for the lager and tobacco, and he knew perfectly well that he wasn't going to be able to claim them back on expenses.

'Are you sure it will work?' said Cooper. 'It seems a bit like bribing the natives with glass beads.'

'It's the only way to get close to these spiritual types,' said Owen. 'You've got to appeal to their materialism.'

'Still –'

'Trust me, Ben. I'm a Ranger.'

But Cooper was still doubtful. It was because he knew he shouldn't be there at all. This wasn't an official visit – there had been no action form issued for him to conduct another interview with Calvin Lawrence and

Simon Bevington. But he needed to talk to them on his own. There were things he couldn't concentrate on properly with Diane Fry and a bunch of uniformed officers crowding round the van.

Cooper could smell cigarette smoke on Owen's jacket. He guessed he had been to see Cal and Stride quite recently, and his red fleece had absorbed the scent of their roll-ups. Owen walked up to the van and stood by the cab. He gestured to Cooper to stand out of sight, and knocked on the side door. It was an unusual knock, a series of short and long raps. After half a minute, the door slid partly open.

'Cal,' said Owen. 'We come in peace.'

'Bloody hell, it's Red Rum. What's up? Got no tourists to piss off?'

'Yes, but pissing you off is more fun.'

Cal stuck his head out of the door and spotted Cooper. 'What's *he* want?'

'A bit of your friendly conversation. No hassle. He's all right, Cal.'

The youth stared at Cooper, then back at Owen. 'You saying he's all right? He's a copper. Coppers is bastards, period.'

'He's all right.'

Cal nodded. 'Give us the cans then, you mean sod.'

Owen winked at Cooper, and they clambered into the back of the VW. Cooper's senses sprang instantly alive, awakened by the powerful mixture of scents and sensations contained in the van. Cal and Stride had been smoking roll-ups for months in the enclosed space, and their aroma had ingrained itself into the panels of the van and soaked into the blankets and cushions and sleeping bags that lay on the floor. There was the pungent smell of unwashed bodies and dirty clothes. And, overlying it, the odour of cooked food, including a lingering trace of the chicken curry they had eaten at least two days before. There was also a slightly worrying whiff of gas from the two-ring camping stove behind the driver's seat.

Cooper hesitated when he saw Stride. He was sitting in the back corner, barely visible in the gloom.

'Don't worry about Stride,' said Cal. 'He's just doing an auric egg.'

'OK. That's fine.'

Cooper eyed Stride cautiously. He didn't seem to be doing much of anything, really, let alone laying an egg. He was very still, sitting upright, with his eyes closed and his hands in his lap. The expression on his face was concentrated, but calm. Cooper wondered if Stride genuinely hadn't noticed there was anyone else in the van. It seemed unlikely. It must just be a bit of acting talent, mustn't it?

'It's to protect himself against negative mind energies,' said Cal.

'Right.'

'He puts a shell round his aura.'

'No problem.'

Owen settled himself on a pillow to one side of an old chest of drawers. Cooper followed suit on the other side.

He felt something hard pressing into his hip. He looked down to find the biscuit tin packed with small mementoes that Stride had searched in for his NUS card.

The boy's entire previous life was crammed into that tin. Maybe he very rarely opened it, but at least he had brought it with him into his new life. It was useless for him to pretend that memories of his past life held no value for him. The evidence said differently.

'So what are you doing here on your own?' said Cal. 'Where's the heavy mob?'

'I just wanted to talk. I thought I might be able to help.'

Cal snorted. 'Bullshit. Since when did the cops help the likes of us? You're employed by middle-class, middle-aged folk with their property and comfortable lives to protect.'

'People like your parents, you mean?'

'Yes, people like them.'

'Well, we're here to protect everybody.'

'Stuff that. *I* don't pay your wages. I don't pay any taxes. So why should you bother about me?'

Cooper hesitated while he considered the answer. Everything depended on saying the right thing.

'Hey,' said Owen. 'I've just realized – that means you don't pay *my* wages either. Well, what a revelation.' He started to get up, brushing down his jacket. 'That's that, then. I'll be off. I can't be wasting my time with a couple of dirty, idle gypsies. I've got nice, clean middle-class people to look after.'

'Yeah. Fuck off, then,' said Cal, popping the ring-pull off a can of lager.

Owen stood over him. He didn't say anything. Cal looked at Cooper. 'I hate this bastard in the red jacket,' he said. 'He thinks he's my dad or something.'

'We all know you never had a father, Calvin,' said Owen.

'And if you call me Calvin again, I'll set fire to your fuckin' beard.'

'Get the matches out then, Calvin.'

Cal's eyes glittered. He offered a can to Cooper, who shook his head. Then he held it up above his head, and the Ranger took it.

'We both came for the solstice,' said Cal. 'That's how we ended up in this quarry. There were loads of people parked down here then. It was like a real community. But the van broke down, and I had no dosh to get it repaired. It's something to do with the drive shaft, they reckon. Coming down that slope knackered it.'

'And you've stayed ever since.'

'Everybody else drifted off and left us.'

'Did you and Stride come together?'

'No, we didn't know each other until then. He'd been camping over the valley there – the place they call Robin Hood's Stride. There's a cave there, some kind of hermit's place or something, where he was sheltering. He didn't know anything about the Nine Virgins, but he wandered over to see what was happening. That's how we met up, and that's why we called him Stride. We just seemed to hit it off. He had nowhere else to go, you see.'

Cooper realized he was being watched. He had forgotten Stride for a moment. He had been so still and quiet he could have been camouflaged by an entire forest of trees instead of sitting there in full view a few inches away. His eyes were open now and he was looking at Cooper.

'Nowhere else to go,' he said.

Stride's paleness was worrying. Cooper wondered what medical attention the two youths had access to. None, he supposed. In an earlier age, Stride would have been described as sickly and consumptive. Cooper would have liked to find out how he came to be camping in a hermit's cave in the Peak District in the first place. But it seemed too big a question to ask.

'You went to university, didn't you?' he said.

Stride nodded. Cal passed him the tobacco and the Rizlas, and he began to roll a cigarette.

'What degree did you get?'

Stride smiled. 'Did I say I got a degree?'

'It's usually the reason for going to university.'

'Only if you finish the course. Otherwise they get a bit stuffy about giving it to you.'

'I see. You dropped out.'

Now Stride laughed. 'You might call it that.'

'So what were you studying?'

Stride stared at him, a sudden gleam in his eye, his hand fluttering to his mouth in that curious gesture. Energy seemed to visibly flow through him. From an almost catatonic state he was transformed into a ball of vitality.

'You really want to know?' he said. 'Come with me.'

'What?'

He was excited now, tugging at Cooper's sleeve like a puppy wanting him to come out and play. Cooper looked at Owen, who just smiled and nodded affectionately at Stride.

'Go on,' he said. 'You might learn something.'

They jumped out of the van, and Cooper scrambled up the path after Stride to reach the top of the quarry. The chimes were moving slowly in the birch, jingling gently. One of them turned and caught the sunlight, and Cooper could almost make out the words scrawled on the silver foil in felt-tipped pen.

Stride turned to him at the top of the quarry face and held his hand to his ear, like a bad actor miming his reaction to a knock at the door.

'Can you hear it? We're right on the edge.'

'The edge?'

Cooper listened. All he could hear was the wind which caught at him now they were on the plateau. It carried a whispering in the bracken and the jingle of the chimes. He listened more carefully. He heard several types of bird call – finches twittering nearby, a robin singing in the birches, the jackdaws in Top Quarry; and something else further away, possibly rooks and a blackbird. There was nothing more. Cooper looked up. There was a kestrel hovering over the rough grass on the edge of the quarry, but it was absolutely silent.

'Do you hear it?' said Stride. 'That's great.'

'The edge of what?'

'The reality zone. From here on, all that stuff down there disappears.' He waved vaguely in the direction of Matlock and the A6.

'Not for me, it doesn't.'

Suddenly, Stride threw himself full-length into the damp bracken. For a moment, he disappeared completely as the brown leaves closed over him. Only his laugh could be heard from somewhere in the dripping depths.

'Look at this!' he said. His head appeared. He wiped a bracken leaf across his face, smearing the rain water on his skin and licking the moisture off his lips, closing his eyes in ecstasy. Bits of foliage and fragments of dead heather were clinging to his hair and shoulders; the sleeves of his jacket were soaked.

'I suppose you think this is just a weed. Farmers tear it up and burn it, because it's a pest. But bracken is a miracle. All ferns are a miracle. Look, look.' He stroked a tiny, furled leaf. It would probably never open now – it was too late in the year. 'Each of these produces hundreds of spores. They're spread around by the wind or animals. I'm doing it now. Look!' He rolled over on the ground, laughing breathlessly. 'I'm part of the process! I'm part of nature!'

Stride plucked a larger leaf and held it in front of Cooper's face. 'Every spore that lands grows into a little disc. And do you know what? It has both male and female sexual organs. It's a bisexual. Humans will tell you that isn't natural. But it is!'

He thrust the leaf into Cooper's hands. It smelled damp and green and broken. Cooper held it lightly, not sure what to do with it, reluctant just to walk away, too intrigued by the performance to stop it.

'The male organs release sperm. Oh, yes. We know about sperm, don't we? But ferns … their sperm use the rain water. See? The leaves are always damp up here, in the autumn, so the sperm can travel through the moisture to reach the female organs and fertilize the eggs. And then a new plant grows. A new fern. More bracken. More and more of it. And you know what else? Ferns have been doing that for three hundred million years.'

Stride stared at Cooper wildly. 'Pre-historic tree ferns grew to over a hundred feet. They're way down there now, under the ground, still there. Fossilized tree ferns. We call them coal.' He snatched the leaf back from Cooper as if he wasn't worthy to hold it. 'So which is the most successful species? The cleverest? The most efficient? The most useful? Humans?' He laughed. 'I studied botany. They tried to tell me it was a science; they tried to make me study mycology and phytopathology. They wanted me to look at diagrams of a monocotyledon or analyse the process of hydrotropism. They wanted me to see pistils and radicles and calyxes. But all I saw were miracles everywhere. Miracles of life.'

He stepped out of the bracken and bent down to the ground near the path. He picked up a small piece of quartz. He held it with gentleness, handling it as if it were a living thing, sensitive to his touch.

'Look at the earth. She looks so attractive, you could stroke her. Her fur is like velvet. But she's a wild creature, she can never be tamed. A huge beast, sleeping. Or maybe only pretending to be asleep. This is her body.'

Cooper was silent, feeling foolish and embarrassed, like a man who had wandered into the wrong church service and didn't know what to do when everyone else prayed.

'The dancers know all about it,' said Stride. 'The dancers became part of her body.'

A suggestion of movement on the moor made Cooper look up. For a moment, he thought there were people standing in the trees at the scene of Jenny Weston's murder – grey shapes that passed each other slowly, leaning to whisper to one another across the sandy earth of the clearing. Then he realized that he was seeing the Nine Virgins themselves, the stones momentarily transformed by the intensity of Stride's conviction.

'I can understand why our ancestors worshipped trees,' said Stride. 'Can't you? When you hear a chainsaw in the woods, when you see a JCB and smell new tarmac, don't you feel it? Don't you feel, deep inside your head, the cry of "murder"? Do you understand?'

Cooper frowned, wanting to see what he meant. 'I understand that you've found some sort of truth for yourself.'

'Believe those who are seeking the truth,' said Stride. 'But doubt those who say they've found it.'

WHEN THEY GOT back to the van, Stride seemed rapidly to become exhausted. He collapsed on the cushions, stretched out full-length, limp and breathing raggedly. After a few minutes, he spoke, though his voice was barely loud enough for them to hear.

'I can still see her face,' he said.

Stride's own face was hidden by the shadows of the candle, expressionless, moving with the flickering light in unnatural ways. Cooper felt too warm in the claustrophobic interior of the van. He was uncomfortably hemmed in by the rugs and blankets and the smell of unwashed bodies, too tightly embraced by the metal walls. He longed for escape.

'Whose face?' he said.

But Stride seemed to have departed. Though his body still sprawled against the cushions, his mind had left, perhaps to drift over the moor with the kestrel. He had sunk into a state of exhaustion, and when he spoke again it was no more than a whisper, addressed only to himself.

'I can still see her face.'

Owen and Cal seemed at ease with each other. Cooper wondered what they had talked about while he was away, whether they had simply exchanged comfortable insults as they drank their beer. Owen drained his can and they all went outside, leaving Stride alone. Cal was still looking at Cooper suspiciously.

'Do you really not have a life to go back to, Cal?' said Cooper.

'Oh, yeah. If I wanted to. There are the aged parents, if I want to spend the rest of my life being lectured at. There was a girlfriend as well. But, well … sometimes you're better off on your own, you know?'

'But you're not on your own now.'

'Me and Stride? Stride says it was karma, us meeting like that. You know, the idea of fate repaying you for what you've done in a previous life?'

'He seems to be quite knowledgeable about esoteric practices.'

'He knows sod all about it,' said Cal.

'Oh?'

'He's picked up a few phrases from books here and there, that's all. But it keeps him content in himself. That's what religion is for, isn't it? Whatever he believes in, it works for him.'

'Like the auric egg.'

'Yeah, well. If he actually believes it keeps negative mind energies away, then it probably does.'

Cooper considered this. It seemed as useful as any advice a psychiatrist could have given.

'How well do you really know Stride?'

'He's my brother.'

'You met him only a few months ago, at the summer solstice.'

'That doesn't make any difference. He's my brother.'

'I bet you don't know anything about him. Where is he from?'

'What does it matter? Who cares what he did or where he came from in another life? This is our life. This is what matters now.'

'Do you go up on the moor sometimes?' asked Cooper.

'Of course.'

'To the stone circle?'

'Stride likes to talk to the Virgins. Nothing wrong with that. He's not doing any harm.'

'Do you go with him? Or does he go on his own?'

Cal clamped his mouth shut. 'I think I've talked to you enough.'

'Does he go out on his own at night?'

'You're like all the others really, aren't you? You sneak your way into the van, thinking you'll get something on us. Well, just leave off Stride. He doesn't do anyone any harm, not now.'

'Not now?' said Cooper gently.

But Cal turned on his heel with a scowl and walked back to the van. Cooper looked at his watch. He had spent too long at Ringham Moor already. He had an appointment with another set of stones, and there would be trouble if he was late.

LIKE MOST THINGS in Edendale, the cemetery was built halfway up a hill. Over the bottom wall, beech trees ran down Mill Bank to an estate of new housing off Meadow Road, where white semis clustered round the back of the council highways depot. A squirrel foraged among the leaves and dead branches on the floor beneath the beeches.

Sergeant Joe Cooper was buried in the new part of the cemetery, brought into use four or five years ago, when the old one became full. In the new cemetery, there were no visible graves, only rows of headstones, with the grass mowed smooth right up to them. The dead were no longer allowed to be untidy. These headstones would never loosen and tilt and grow moss with age. They were orderly, almost regimented, a picture of civic perfection. Sergeant Cooper was far tidier now than he had been at the moment of his dying, when his blood had run out on to the stone setts in Clappergate, leaving a stain that had taken council workmen weeks to remove. His killing had darkened the reputation of the town for months afterwards. No wonder they wanted to tidy him away.

Occasionally, a jam-jar full of spring flowers or petunias appeared in front of the headstone. The Coopers never knew who they were from.

The brothers had said nothing to each other as they drove to the cemetery. By the time they were out of the car and back in the open air, Ben was beginning to feel uncomfortable with the silence between them.

'We went to see Warren Leach again yesterday,' he said as they followed the path towards their father's grave. 'I just wondered if you found anything out …'

Matt didn't answer. His shoulders stiffened a bit, and his stride quickened.

'There must be somebody who knows him, Matt.'

'I dare say.'

But Matt sounded so dismissive that Ben knew not to press it. The silence had grown even deeper by the time they reached the right spot. On every occasion they came, the row of graves had extended a little further, as if their father was somehow physically receding into the past.

Ben and Matt left their flowers and found a bench under the hawthorn hedge, where they could see the headstone. The cemetery grass had been raked clear of leaves. It glittered an unnaturally bright green against the browns and oranges of the hillside behind it, and the grey of the stone houses piled on top of each other on the outskirts of the town.

For a while, the brothers sat and watched each other's breath drifting in small clouds, cold and formless, vanishing before it had even moved out of reach.

'Two years, and it doesn't seem a day,' said Matt.

His words couldn't help but sound trite, but Ben was sure they were sincere. 'I know what you mean,' he said.

'I still keep expecting him to appear. I think he's going to come round the corner and tell me to stop idling around. It's as if he's just been on night shift for a while. Remember when we didn't used to see him for a few days, then he would appear again, looking so tired? He always said it was short turn that was the real killer.'

'He was already too old for night shifts by then.'

'But he wouldn't stop doing it. He always did his stint.'

There was a new National Police Memorial being created in Staffordshire, with a commemorative avenue of trees known as 'The Beat' and a daily roll of honour showing details of the officers who had died on duty. The work would take several years to complete, and Ben Cooper had offered to help.

Here in the cemetery, Sergeant Joe Cooper's name was carved in stone. Eventually, it would be worn away by the rain driven down the Eden Valley, and the February frosts would crumble the surfaces. But now, just two years from his death, the letters were still crisp and clear, with sharply chiselled edges, cold and precise. Life might be brief and transient, scrawled in the sand. But death was written in a much harder alphabet.

Ben had the names of the group of youths who had killed his father imprinted on his mind. Now and then, they cropped up in other enquiries, or in court cases he read about in the *Eden Valley Times*. Two of them were still serving ten-year sentences for manslaughter, but those who were free seemed to be following predictable careers. It wouldn't be long before they, too, had a taste of prison. The thought gave Cooper no satisfaction. It would solve nothing.

As always on these occasions, he found his brain spilling out memories like sour wine from an uncorked bottle; deeply stored images of his father that were preserved as if in vinegar. There were glimpses of a tall, strong man with wide shoulders and huge hands tossing bales of hay with a pitchfork, his face flushed and laughing. At other times he was frowning and angry, a terrifying figure in a dark uniform, opening his mouth to bring down the wrath of God on his sons. But among Ben's memories was also a picture of his father lying dead and bleeding on the stone setts of Clappergate. It was a sight Ben hadn't even seen, yet it was etched on his mind like a nail embedded in a tree – it was long grown over, but still there, hard and sharp, splitting the flesh that pressed too tightly around it.

But Ben had to close the stopper tight on his thoughts. He couldn't bear to taste those memories. The pain of them was too thick for him to swallow.

'He always expected great things of you,' said Matt.

'He didn't just expect great things – he demanded them.'

'He demanded a lot, that's true. But he was very proud of you. And you did exactly what he hoped for, always.'

Ben looked at his brother. 'Matt, he gave me an appalling time. He drove me like a maniac. Nothing I ever did was good enough for him. I always had to do better, to work a bit harder. But you were different. You were the favoured son.'

'Rubbish.'

'He never drove you like he did me. He left you alone to do whatever you wanted.'

'Exactly,' said Matt.

'What do you mean?'

'It shows that it was you that he cared about, Ben. He cared about you more than anything.'

'It didn't feel like it at the time.'

'It was obvious to everybody else. Obvious to me, anyway. It didn't matter to him what I did. It didn't matter how hard I worked, how successful I was at what I chose to do. It meant nothing to him. He would just say, "That's fine," and he'd turn away to ask how your training was going, or how you'd dealt with an incident, and what your feelings were about it. Every last detail about you was important to him. But me, I could just do what I liked. I might as well not have been there.'

Ben thought he and Matt had little in common physically, except perhaps a look of their father around the eyes and nose. Their mother was blue-eyed, but the eyes of both her sons were brown, their hair dark where she was fair. Though Cooper was five foot eleven, it was Matt who had inherited their father's size, the wide shoulders, the enormous hands and the uncertain temper.

'Matt, you're the one who's like him. Everyone says that. People always told me I took after Mum. But Dad and me, we were like chalk and cheese. It infuriated him every time he saw me reading a book. He nearly threw me out of the house when I got interested in music and joined the choir. For Heaven's sake, I barely came up to his shoulder. I was a pigmy in his eyes.'

Matt stood up. When he towered over him, with that exasperated frown, Matt looked more than ever like Sergeant Joe Cooper come back to life.

'Maybe you never saw the similarity, Ben,' he said. 'But everybody else did. I can see him in you now, over this case you're involved in, this woman who was killed on Ringham Moor.'

'What on earth has that got to do with it?'

'You stand here by his grave, today of all days, and you start asking me about this bloody Warren Leach. As if I cared about all that. But Dad would be proud of you, all right. Your head's full of the same big ideas that his was, like justice and truth. You think you have to put the world right on your own. Just like him. You're *exactly* like him.'

Before his brother could reply, Matt walked away to stand over the grave, leaving Ben on the bench. Matt rearranged the flowers at the foot of the headstone and re-read the inscription.

Ben stood up. 'I'm sorry, Matt,' he said.

Matt half-turned his head. His eyes glistened, and he wiped the heel of his hand across his face. 'You can't help it, Ben,' he said. 'Neither of us can help it.'

They walked in silence back through the cemetery, passing a workman sweeping up leaves. When they reached the car, Matt paused and looked back at the cemetery. Their father's grave was no longer discernible from here. It had merged into anonymous rows of headstones, swallowed up among centuries of Edendale dead.

'Ben ... this Warren Leach,' said Matt.

'What about him?'

'They say his farm is in big trouble. Creditors are calling the debts in, the usual story. He's very close to bankruptcy, they reckon, but he won't admit it. Leach is the type who'll try to pretend it's not happening until it's much too late. It'll only take one small thing to be the last straw.'

Cooper thought back to the two occasions he had met the farmer. 'He isn't exactly a barrel of laughs. But it can't be much of a life up there.'

'Those hill farmers are proud men. They think they don't need anyone else; they want to believe they're self-reliant, like their ancestors always were. It's hard for men like that to admit any sort of weakness. Losing the farm would be the end of the world for Warren Leach. He must be close to the edge.'

'I understand.'

'Do you, Ben? I'm not sure.'

'What do you mean?'

'I mean I'd watch out for Warren Leach, if I were you. When a man is driven close to the edge, he might do anything. And, unlike you, Ben, some men can completely lose sight of what's right and what's wrong.'

Chapter Twenty

EACH TIME DIANE Fry emerged from Maggie Crew's apartment, the rest of the world looked garish and unreal. It was like coming out of the cinema after a horror matinee. One minute it was all nightmare figures leaping out of the dark and blood splattering against the camera lens, and suddenly you found yourself standing at the traffic lights outside Mothercare with the sun in your eyes and an ice-cream van playing 'Greensleeves'.

Today, Matlock looked like a badly designed Disney-World set. There were the mock turrets of Riber Castle on one side of the valley and the Heights of Abraham and Gulliver's Kingdom on the other, with the River Derwent in the bottom and the old locomotives getting up steam at Matlock Bridge station. But in between, the design had gone wrong, with crowds wandering about searching in vain for Mickey Mouse and Pluto, and endless traffic choking the central square, where there ought to have been fountains and open-air restaurants, and children demanding Big Macs. And this was one of the quietest times of the year. During the summer, the chaos was mindless. Where were they all going? What were they looking for? What were they trying to escape?

Fry had yet to understand what made twenty-five million people a year visit the Peak District. There were no shopping centres, no big sports arenas, no exhibition centres or concert halls, not even a decent football ground. All these people did was cause problems and pollution, going nowhere and doing nothing. So pointless.

Today, though, Fry was glad of the crowds. Their aimless swarming was an antidote to the obsessive isolation of the apartment at Derwent Court. Maggie's solitary martyrdom was too reminiscent of periods of her own life – so painful and bitter, yet somehow horribly alluring, like the temptation to give yourself up to drowning when you were too exhausted to swim any more.

Fry knew how easy it was to reach that stage. She knew you could find yourself in a situation where a greeting from a stranger was a torture, and the words 'good morning' from the postman were as welcome as the plague. When somebody rang the door bell, you not only refused to answer it, you wanted to hide in another room, in case they saw you through the window and knew you were there.

Once you allowed yourself to become a recluse, then the world began to seem a long way off, beyond your reach. It became a place where you would be an alien, if you ever found yourself there. And you knew the people from that world would see you as an alien, too. You were not like them. You were different. Disfigured.

Fry supported herself against the side of her car and shuddered. Memory was such a physical thing. It was more physical than her own skin, than the clothes she wore, or the ground she stood on. A terrible, physical thing. And some memories never seemed to lose their power to hurt. They never weakened with age, nor dimmed as the years went by. They simply slipped behind a cloud of everyday concerns and trivial preoccupations, waiting until the right moment to emerge, more powerful than ever. And memories still hit hardest when they were most unexpected.

There was no doubt Maggie Crew was a damaged woman. Fry had begun to dread going to see her. While she was there, in Maggie's house, she felt somehow at home. Yet afterwards, within a few minutes of leaving, when she was sitting in the car with her hand on the ignition key, she would suddenly begin to shake. She realized now that she was sweating, her hands were trembling, and her legs felt weak, as if she hadn't eaten for days. She had to wind down the window and let in the cold air to shock herself back into alertness.

She wasn't used to feeling so drained of energy as she was now. She was usually able to direct energy into her body at a moment's notice. She had trained for years to feel it flow and channel it where it was needed. But an hour with Maggie Crew had sapped that vitality. So what was going wrong?

There were things for her to do back at HQ, but nothing urgent – she had been given a free hand to spend as long as she needed to with Maggie. That meant she had time to call at her own flat in Edendale on the way. She decided a shower would help wash away the cold stickiness that was clinging to her skin.

Yet Fry drove round town for a while, turning through the steep streets aimlessly, unwilling to arrive home until her energy had returned and her mood had dissipated.

Of course, there was a physical reason for her frame of mind, too. Her body craved action, something to focus the pent-up tension, some target to hit out at. Her old *shotokan* master in Warley had taught her to recognize the feeling and use it. Very soon, she would have to find time to visit her new *dojo* in Sheffield to get that release, or the dark well of anger would boil over and the wrong target would be in the way.

For Fry, each time she found herself back with Maggie Crew in that soulless apartment now it was like leaving the light to enter a tunnel. She recalled the tunnel on the High Peak Trail, with its dripping water and landslides of rock barely held back by the wooden roof. But she had been with Ben Cooper then, and that made a difference.

Gradually, she felt her normal equilibrium coming back, and she turned the wheel towards Edendale. Her flat in Grosvenor Avenue was depressing enough, but in a tangible sort of way. It was simply dismal and uncomfortable, not laden with painful emotions. That was what she had liked about the place when she had rented it – it held no memories, no associations, not even any significant possessions from her old life. She had thrown them all away, given them to charity shops or dumped them in recycling bins – books, clothes, the lot. So the flat was empty of feeling. A cold kind of comfort.

Fry waited outside the flat until she was sure that the mood had gone. But even then, when she got inside and stared with glad contempt at the filthy walls, there was a niggle at the back of her mind, a lingering suspicion that she had brought something of Maggie Crew with her into the room. She cursed. She had learned to recognize emotional entanglement the moment it began to infect her. The first twinge of it indicated a lowering of her defences, a weakness in her immune system that had to be tackled. A course of antibiotics was what she needed, a period of isolation, perhaps.

She looked at her diary. She had made an appointment with Maggie Crew for Friday. She would phone to cancel it in the morning. She took out her pen and put a thick, black line through the date. She immediately felt better.

STRIDE HAD STARTED *measuring the days. When each one arrived, it was shorter than the last. And the moor was changing as he watched; it was dying slowly on itself, folding and shrivelling, transforming like a chameleon to adapt itself to the new season. As the days shortened, the green chlorophyll broke down in the leaves. Its gradual ebbing away revealed the underlying colours – the yellows, oranges and reds that had been masked all summer. Toxic waste products excreted into the dying leaves made the trees shrink away from their own foliage. They were rejecting parts of themselves as superfluous, recoiling as if from something alien and repulsive, so that their stems dried and loosened on the branch and the wind carried the unwanted leaves away.*

But Stride knew this wasn't really death he was seeing. It wasn't an ending, only the preparation for another beginning. The leaves that drifted to the ground in their millions would slowly decay and disintegrate, returning nutrients to the soil and into the tree roots, ready for growth to begin again next spring. The great recycling system had started up. Millions of organic systems would break down and be renewed on a scale far beyond anything that Derbyshire Dales District Council could dream of.

In some places, though, he had found the foliage of the mountain ash and of more exotic, imported species, like the Russian vines that climbed the walls of roadside cottages. These leaves were red. And they made Stride think of death – of real death. He tried to avoid them, drawing back the toes of his Doc Martens as if touching the dead leaves would contaminate him. He hated the way they spread in soft, wet layers on the ground. He hated their colour and their slithery consistency. They looked to him like ever-widening pools of congealing blood.

Chapter Twenty-One

By Thursday, four days after Jenny Weston's body had been found, the enquiry team were starting to dissipate their energies fruitlessly, like men urinating into a strong wind. There were no answers to be obtained any more. The morning briefing seemed to consist entirely of questions.

'This young woman, Ros Daniels. Are there no indications to her whereabouts at all?' said DCI Tailby.

'We've got a decent description, but matching it to missing persons is hoping for a lot,' said DI Hitchens. 'Most of these young people who leave home are never reported missing in the first place. But Cheshire Police are still working on it. And we do have a couple of lorry drivers who saw a girl hitch-hiking out of Macclesfield towards Buxton on the A537.'

'That's the Macclesfield Forest road,' said Ben Cooper. 'It's a bit isolated up there. She was taking a risk hitching, a girl like that on her own.'

'That's why the truckers remember her particularly, Cooper. But one of them said she looked as though she wouldn't be frightened of much. He said she looked like Tank Girl.'

'I don't know who Tank Girl is,' said Tailby, 'but I dare say I can imagine it.'

Hitchens smiled. 'It was the combat trousers and the hairstyle, I suppose. And a certain aggressiveness of manner, too. Sounds like our girl, all right. In any case, she was staying at Jenny Weston's house, at least up to six weeks before Jenny was killed. Forensics found plenty of traces in the house that didn't belong to Weston.'

'There are other possibilities. What about Warren Leach, sir?' asked Cooper.

'He was certainly in the area,' said Hitchens. 'He has to be eliminated. And he has a connection to Maggie Crew – his wife was the finder on that one.'

'Mmm. I don't like coincidences,' said Tailby. 'And is there some significance in the way that the victim's body was arranged? Anybody had any ideas on that?'

No one answered. Cooper wondered whether they had all shared the same thought when they saw the position of Jenny Weston's body. He had put his own reaction down to another burst of imagination, the idea that Jenny had been made to dance at the moment of her death. It was certainly too strange a thought to be contributed to the morning briefing.

'And how do we find out more about Leach?' said Tailby, almost to himself.

Then suddenly there were voices chiming in from all round the room.

'Talk to his neighbours?' suggested someone.

'He hasn't *got* any neighbours,' said another officer.

'Friends, then.'

'Like who?'

'There's Keith Teasdale. The rat man.'

'Is he a friend?'

'The nearest thing he's got, probably.'

Tailby raised a hand, half-heartedly.

'OK, we'll talk to Teasdale again. Is there anything else?'

Cooper took a breath. 'Yes,' he said.

There was something about the way he said it that quietened the laughter.

'Cooper?'

'I checked the firearms register for Warren Leach.'

'Firearms?' said Tailby. Heads were raised, and ears pricked up. 'Leach has a shotgun, I suppose? Most farmers have them.'

'Yes, there's a shotgun. But when I was there the other day with Owen Fox, Leach also had a captive bolt pistol.'

'A what?'

'A humane killer. It's used for putting animals down. It fires a steel bolt directly into the brain.'

'Do you need an FAC for that, Cooper?'

'Well, not if you're a licensed slaughterman. But Warren Leach has no licence. Farmers can get them, if they can show that they need one. But there's no record of Leach ever even applying for one.'

'So he's in illegal possession,' said Tailby. 'OK, let's interview him again. Teasdale first, then Leach. Let's do it.'

Somebody patted Cooper on the shoulder. And Tailby hurried to close the meeting before anybody asked any more questions.

DI HITCHENS WALKED over to Ben Cooper. 'I want Diane Fry to go to the cattle market with you, not Todd Weenink,' he said. 'You're too close to some of these people. That's your problem, Ben. Diane sees things that you don't.'

Across the room, Fry was watching him already. Cooper couldn't read the expression in her eyes, but then he never had been able to read her. Maybe she did see things he didn't – but from the look on her face these days, they were things that he didn't *want* to see.

THE TWO FARMERS had been just about to leave the cattle market. The sale was over for the day, and most of the vehicles had left the car parks, but for a few transporters still waiting to load. The men were dressed in overalls and flat caps and smelled as though they had spent some of their money in the bar before setting off home.

'You couldn't buy a pint of beer for those prices I got,' said one of them.

'Bastards,' said the other. 'All pissing in the same pot, these dealers.'

Ben Cooper nodded sympathetically. 'I know what you mean. The farmer has to put up with lower prices all the time when meat is still selling for the same amount in the supermarkets.'

'Bloody right. There's no justice to it. What will they do when every farmer in the country has gone to the wall? That's what I want to know.'

Cooper was waiting for Diane Fry to finish taking a call on the radio in the car. He was the sort of person that people always chose to talk to, especially when they had problems. Maybe there was something about his face that encouraged them.

'They'll buy all their bloody meat from abroad, that's what,' said the second farmer. 'They don't need us any more. They can get anything they want cheaper somewhere else. These prices are just a way of killing us off one by one.' He spat into a drainage channel. 'Bastards.'

'If we had another war like the last one, they'd be buggered.'

'Aye, good and proper.'

Finally, Fry came back from the car and stood listening to their conversation in amazement. 'Have you finished writing the script for *Farming Today*? If so, I wonder if any of you know where Keith Teasdale is?'

The first farmer opened his mouth as if he might say something, then closed it firmly.

'You'll have to ask Abel Pilkington,' said the other man. 'He's inside somewhere. What's Slasher Teasdale done, then?'

'Slasher?'

The farmer said: 'It's a nickname.'

'What does it mean?'

'Ah. You'll have to ask *him* that.'

Cooper and Fry had parked at the back of the cattle market, close to where a double-decker transporter was reversed up to the loading area, its tailgate lowered on to the concrete apron. They scrambled up on to the concrete, but could see no one among the rows of steel pens. They crossed an iron platform that moved underfoot, and found themselves looking at the face of an enormous weighing scale. It recorded their combined weight at just over twenty-three stone.

'You've put a bit of weight on,' said Cooper.

'What?'

'Well, it isn't me. I'm thirteen stone and always have been. I never change.'

Fry stared doubtfully at the scale. Cooper wondered whether she knew he was joking. She looked genuinely worried. 'I shouldn't bother about it too much,' he said. 'They sell 'em by the kilo here, anyway. The more you weigh on the hoof, the more money you fetch in the ring.'

Fry wasn't amused. 'Tell you what,' she said. 'You hold on here and talk to yourself about the price of beef while I find this Pilkington character.'

'If you say so.'

Cooper waited by the transporter while Fry crossed the concrete and stood on the vehicle's steel ramp. Inside the market, the silence of the building was strange after the bellowing cacophony of Tuesday. The starlings gathered on the ledges were whistling plaintively and darting in and out of the gaps in the roof. All traces of blood and urine and the soft, green faeces of frightened animals had been hosed away into the gutters behind the pens. Here and there the floor was still wet, drying very slowly in dark, glistening patches.

'Where is everyone?' asked Fry, hushing her voice automatically at the first bounce of the echo from the breeze-block walls.

'In the back, probably,' said Cooper. 'Near the sale rings.'

'OK.'

She set off down the passageway opposite the ramp, walking between the steel pens.

'Are you sure you want me to wait here, Diane?'

'Yes. Just keep an eye out.'

'I might be able to show you the way,' called Cooper, his voice getting louder and more insistent, echoing in the roof space.

'For God's sake,' she snapped. 'I can find my way through an empty building without your assistance.'

FRY HAD HARDLY got halfway down the passage when a gate clanged open somewhere. She heard Cooper call something else to her, a single word that sounded like an insult. She couldn't quite hear what he said because of the noise, a crashing of gates and the thudding of hooves on concrete. But she reacted angrily to the sound of the word, and turned to answer him.

'Did you say "bollocks"?' she yelled.

Cooper began to shake his head and opened his mouth to shout at her again. But Fry was distracted by a vibration in the ground, the impression of an earthquake approaching from behind. She turned and saw double doors open and a great bellowing rush of animals burst through the gap into the passage where she was standing. The heaving beasts filled the entire width of the passageway as they barrelled towards her.

Fry spun to her left and found a section of brick wall and a six-foot wide pen that had long since lost its gate. She dodged into the pen as the cattle reached her, but found one of the animals following her blindly, barged aside by the rush of its companions. It was frightened and angry, and it swung its head from side to side, catching her clothes with the sharp points of its horns. She backed against the wall, braced herself and lashed out with a kick, which landed on the animal's heavily muscled shoulder. It hardly seemed to notice.

Now the beast was confused. It slipped and lurched around the pen, making Fry jump to keep her feet out of the way of its hooves. She smacked it twice on the nose with her fist. It shook its head, and backed off. She took the opportunity to leap out of the way over the nearest gate and into the next pen, where she slipped on the damp floor, twisted her ankle and fell flat on her back.

She became aware of Ben Cooper standing over her. She was infuriated to see a smile playing across his face as he looked down at her.

'Actually, I shouted "bullocks",' he said.

THE DRIVER OF the transporter had appeared and joined Cooper on the loading bay as the cattle thundered up the ramp into the wagon. He watched in amazement as Fry clambered from pen to pen.

'You could hurt yourself doing that,' he said.

Looking around for someone to blame, Fry saw a dark-haired youth in a pair of green wellingtons coming towards her.

'I nearly got trampled by those animals then,' she said. 'Aren't there any precautions?'

The youth merely chortled, flapping uneven teeth at her as he passed. Behind him, Abel Pilkington himself glowered from the wall of the sale ring, hooking his thumbs through the braces of his overalls.

'Any fool knows not to stand in the passages when cattle's being moved. How did you get in?' he said.

'Through the loading bay.'

'Well, you've no right. There's signs, you know. Authorized persons only past this point, they say.'

The dark-haired youth had connected a thick hose to a tap. A high-pressure jet began to hit the ground where the cattle had passed, and water cascaded down the passageway. Fry had to raise her voice above the noise, but Pilkington seemed used to it.

'We're looking for Keith Teasdale,' she said.

'Why didn't you say so? He's not here. Once we finish the sale, he goes off to his other job. Down at Lowbridge.'

'Do you mean the abattoir?' said Cooper.

'That's it. That's where you'll find Slasher Teasdale.'

'Why Slasher?' said Fry.

'It's a nickname. If you ask him nicely, happen he'll demonstrate.'

Pilkington continued to glower at them, and didn't bother saying goodbye as they walked back towards the loading bay. By the time they reached the car, Fry was limping slightly.

'Have you hurt your leg?' said Cooper.

'I slipped, that's all. The floor's wet in some of those pens.'

'Diane, you've, er, got your shoes a bit messy, too. It looks like cow shit.'

Fry looked down at her feet. 'Bullocks',' she said.

LOWBRIDGE WAS CALLED a village, but the spread of development along the valley bottom from Edendale meant there was no distinction any more between the two places – no green fields or farms to separate them, only a road sign indicating the point where one house was in Edendale and the one next door was in Lowbridge.

The abattoir was off the Castleton Road. Unlike the cattle market, it was modern and clean, all stainless steel and white tiles, like a vast urinal, its surfaces washed constantly. The air smelled of disinfectant, and the men moving around inside sloshed about in plastic aprons and thigh boots, with white caps covering their hair. The atmosphere reminded Fry of a hospital operating theatre.

'Ben,' she said, 'I know Teasdale claims to have a legitimate reason to be in the Ringham area when Jenny Weston was killed …'

'But you're sceptical. Maybe you're thinking about this nickname, Slasher. But it would be a bit of a give-away, don't you think? Like a burglar wearing a striped sweater and carrying a bag marked "swag".'

'Look at this place he works. Don't you think he might have some expertise with a knife – *and* access to a nice, sharp blade of his choice?' She got irritated when he didn't respond. 'Too obvious for you, is it? I suppose you prefer to look for the inner meaning of things?'

'Not necessarily. But I find keeping an open mind allows a bit of fresh air in.'

'Don't talk to me about an open mind. *Your* mind is so rustic it should be in a woolly coat with a sheepdog behind it.'

'Thanks.'

Fry took a deep breath. 'Let's have a word with Teasdale's employer before we speak to the man himself.'

She took a cautious peek round the wall into the building, and was relieved to see no dead animals, and no blood.

'TEASDALE?' SAID THE manager when they found him in his office. 'Keith Teasdale? Yes, he's on the books.'

The office was like any other – a computer in the corner and a desk littered with paperwork. From the extent of it, it looked as though an abattoir manager might actually have more paperwork to deal with than a police officer, though it was hard to believe. The manager had his work clothes in a kind of ante-room with a washbasin.

'Well, you can talk to Teasdale if you really want to. He's around the place somewhere.'

'How long has he been with you?' asked Fry.

'Oh, a year or two. I'm not sure exactly without looking it up. He's not one of the full-time staff, you know.'

'But experienced, though?'

'Experienced? Well ... In what way?'

'Experienced in the use of a knife? For bleeding animals. Gutting, and so on. Whatever it is you do here.'

'Teasdale?' The manager stared at Fry. 'We are talking about *Keith* Teasdale?'

'I believe so, sir.'

The manager began to laugh. 'Expertise with a knife.' He laughed some more. Cooper and Fry looked at each other.

'Could we share the joke?' asked Fry.

The manager pulled a tissue from a box on the desk. They expected him to wipe the tears of laughter from his eyes. But instead he began to wipe his hands, rubbing between the fingers as if to dry a sudden outbreak of sweat.

'Keith Teasdale does not use a knife in his work.' He began to snigger again. 'As far as I know, anyway.'

'So what does he do exactly, sir?'

'Keith Teasdale. Old Keith, eh? Expertise with a knife? Expertise with a yard brush, more like. Teasdale is a cleaner. He shoves a wet mop about the place. Not much of a lethal weapon, surely?'

'I see.'

'Unless you can be charged with being in possession of an offensive mop bucket.'

'But they call him Slasher at the market,' protested Fry.

'We call him that here too,' said the manager. 'Ah, I see. What's in a name? Is that evidence against him, then?'

Now another tissue had to be used. And this one did go to the face to mop up the tears. 'Do you want me to tell you how he got the nickname "Slasher"?'

A man appeared in the doorway of the ante-room, hesitated when he saw the visitors and began to go away again with an apologetic nod.

'Hey, Chris,' called the manager. 'This is the police. They want to know why we call Keith Teasdale "Slasher"!'

The other man began to laugh too. 'Are you going to tell them?'

'Of course. The truth, the whole truth, and nothing but –!'

'Poor old Keith.'

They both laughed for a while. Fry was beginning to go pink with anger.

'Basically, Keith Teasdale has a bladder problem,' said the manager.

'Sorry, didn't I explain? We're police officers, not doctors.'

'No, but that's why he got his nickname, you see. He's always having a slash somewhere. Round the back of the building. In the lorry park. Over by the hedge there. It got to be a joke that any time you went round a corner, there was Keith having a slash. One day the ministry inspectors were here, and they saw him at it. He got a real ticking off then. Head office wanted me to sack him. But he's harmless really. Since then, he's had to put up with everyone calling him Slasher, though. It's become quite a joke, I can tell you.'

'I'm positively splitting my sides, as you can see, sir.'

The manager looked at her. 'Well, you have to be a part of it to appreciate it, I suppose. You develop a peculiar sort of sense of humour working here.'

'So I gather.'

When they finally located Keith Teasdale, he was digging a solidified mass of dead leaves out of a drain cover behind the abattoir. There was a curious smell on this side of the building, more reminiscent of a butcher's shop than a hospital. But the brush Teasdale clutched in one hand looked particularly unthreatening.

'I've already told you I've been up to Warren Leach's place,' he said.

'Known him for long?' asked Cooper.

'Yes, years. How old is his eldest lad, Will? Eleven? I remember when he was just a nipper. He wanted to help me with the rats once, because he took a liking to the terriers. But his dad stopped him coming near me. He always was a bit of a sour bugger, Warren.'

'Would you say you know him well?'

'No one knows Warren well. It doesn't do to get too close to him. Nasty temper, he has.'

Teasdale folded his hands over the end of his brush. His fingers that had turned brown and creased and faintly shiny, matching his corduroy trousers.

'But you're still doing work for him. You were at Ringham Edge Farm on Sunday,' pointed out Cooper.

'I was. But Warren sent me packing, like I said. No money to pay for rodent control, he said. Can you believe it? That's no good on a farm, no good at all. You can't have rats round a milking parlour. It should be clean, like this place is.'

'When was the last time you went before that?'

Teasdale rolled his eyes and chewed the tips of his moustache. 'Can't remember exactly. It'd be a month or two, anyway. Is it important, then? Am I a witness?'

'Have you noticed anything unusual going on at the farm?' asked Fry.

'Unusual? There's nothing much usual about Warren Leach.'

'What about Mrs Leach? Do you know her?'

'Her you never see. Well, maybe just a passing glimpse now and then. But she never speaks, never wants to say hello. She's unsociable. But then, she *is* married to Warren, so you can't blame her, I reckon.'

Teasdale seemed to get bored with the conversation suddenly and tossed his clump of leaves into a wheelbarrow, where they landed with a wet thud.

'Did they tell you in there what they call me?' he said, watching the leaves shift and settle in the barrow.

'Yes, they did,' said Cooper.

Teasdale nodded. 'They love it. They think it's a great laugh here, and at the mart. They usually tell people to ask me to demonstrate. Did they tell you that?'

'Yes,' said Cooper. 'But don't bother.'

On the way to Ringham Edge, they had to slow down as they came up behind a tractor towing a trailer stacked high with bales of straw. Golden flakes spiralled off the load and drifted across the windscreen of the car.

'When we get to the farm, I think we should make a point of trying to see all the Leach family,' said Cooper.

'What's the purpose of that?'

'There's something wrong there.'

'We've had no reports of anything wrong.'

Cooper glanced at her face, thinking again how thin she was becoming. It made her look gaunt and haunted rather than tough and angular, as she had been when she arrived a few months ago from West Midlands. Fry's hair was shorter, too, as if she had taken scissors to it and hacked off a couple of inches in a bored moment.

There was one other thing that Cooper noticed about Diane Fry, though. She never mentioned his father now, not since that first time they had met. Sergeant Joe Cooper meant nothing to her.

He wondered what Fry did these days when she went off duty. He wondered what she would be doing tonight, after work. But, for once, Cooper found that his imagination failed him completely.

He had already agreed to go out for a drink with Todd Weenink that night. Weenink called it 'a session', which meant he intended to drink a lot of beer. Cooper wasn't really looking forward to it. He would miss a rehearsal for the police male voice choir, and it was getting to their busiest time of year, when they performed at community halls and old people's homes in the area. Besides, he had seen how morose and aggressive his colleague could become under the influence of alcohol.

But they were partners, and Cooper understood that these occasions were necessary, a kind of bonding. He thought Weenink had no one else to talk to since his marriage had ended. His relationships with women were probably not noted for their conversation. 'A session', he sensed, was code for Weenink needing someone to talk to, an admission that he was feeling lonely. That was why Cooper couldn't refuse.

IN THE CREW yard at Ringham Edge Farm, Warren Leach spoke to his sons in a voice thick with suppressed anger.

'Bring that beast down here,' he said.

The boys stood open-mouthed; Dougie was close to tears. They both knew about the death of animals. They had both seen the huge pit that the excavator had dug behind the barn a while ago, and had heard the shots as the ewes were dispatched one by one. Afterwards, they had crept out of the house to stand in horrified fascination on the edge of the newly turned earth. They had tried to imagine the lifeless bodies of the sheep below their feet; they had pictured them lying on their backs with their eyes blank and their thin legs stiff and pointing upwards, and the wet soil thick in their fleeces and in their mouths.

'No. Please, Dad,' said Will.

Leach lost his temper at the pleading tone, driven beyond patience.

'Am I talking to that wall? Now shift your arses and get that beast down here! Do as I say! If I have to say it again, I'll be saying it with this belt.'

Will pulled Dougie's arm and dragged him reluctantly away. Leach dug into an old canvas satchel and checked the captive bolt pistol that Keith Teasdale had given him. The steel casing of the gun was heavy and solid in his hand.

'Bloody animal,' he muttered to the gun. 'Draining money from me like water. Not any more.'

There was no one in the yard to hear him. He was thinking of the day they had bought the calf at Edendale cattle market. It had been Yvonne herself who had picked it out, and it had been her idea to buy it for the boys. It had been a fine young animal, too, and would have made a handsome heifer. But for weeks, Leach had found he couldn't bear to see the calf. Its eyes rolled at him accusingly, like the eyes of another bloody martyr; its coat gleamed with the gloss of an extravagance that he couldn't afford.

Now he couldn't even stand the thought that the animal was on the premises. He couldn't concentrate on any of the pressing problems that were piling up on him because of the time he spent dwelling on the calf. It had to be disposed of before he could work out how to get the farm and his life out of the mess they were in. It had to go. It was standing in his way.

'We'll sort this out once and for all,' he said, and snapped a cartridge into the gun.

Finally, the boys dragged the calf, protesting, on a rope halter into the yard.

'Dad –'

'Just shut up. Just bloody shut up!'

He snatched the halter from Will's hand and led the calf a few feet away. The boys stood fixed to the spot, unable to take their eyes away. Dougie winced and put his hand to his mouth to stifle a cry as his father lashed out with a boot to take the calf's front legs from underneath it. The animal folded up on to its knees in the dirt with a frightened gasp. As it struggled to regain its feet, Leach stood astride its neck to pin it down and grasped its halter firmly in his left hand. Then he pulled the gun from his pocket and centred the barrel against the top of the calf's skull, in the centre of its forehead. He worked the barrel through the hair and adjusted the angle between the horn buds. He needed a clear path for the bolt to penetrate the layer of bone and enter the brain.

The calf, sensing the uselessness of its struggles, suddenly relaxed in his grasp, resigned to an inexplicable end.

'It has to be done,' said Leach. 'It can't go on like this any longer. You've got to understand these things. It's part of your education.'

Leach looked up at the boys. But he barely saw their faces. Instead, he saw a small cloud of dust behind their heads. It was drifting above the stone wall that bordered the lane. Then he became aware of the noise of an engine, and a second later a red Toyota bounced through the pothole by the gate and entered the yard. Leach kept the barrel pressed to the calf's head, fingering the trigger. He smiled at the thought of the look that would be on his visitors' faces, when he pulled the trigger in front of them.

Then he recognized Ben Cooper at the wheel of the Toyota and saw Diane Fry get out of the passenger seat as the car slid to a halt. She had a clipboard in her hand, and she didn't seem to notice the boys or the calf as she walked up to Leach.

Surprised, the farmer let go of the animal. It scrambled away, leaving him standing straddle-legged, with the bolt pistol still in his hand.

'Mr Warren Leach?' said Fry.

Leach stared at her, making a tiny, abrupt movement of his head that she could take for a nod.

'Acting Detective Sergeant Fry, Edendale Police. According to our records, you do not have the required licence entitling you to possess that captive bolt pistol.'

Leach looked at the gun, baffled.

'I must have forgotten to get one.'

'We have to apply the rules, I'm afraid, sir.'

'What does that mean?'

'You're in possession of an unlicensed weapon.' She held out her hand. 'You'll be given a receipt. Then you can reclaim the weapon if and when you obtain the appropriate licence.'

'I don't believe this. Do you think I'm going to give my gun to you just like that?'

Fry raised her eyebrows at him. 'Are you refusing to surrender an unlicensed weapon, sir?'

Ben Cooper got out of the car and ambled towards them. He nodded at the farmer. 'Give it up, Mr Leach. Be sensible.'

The three of them looked at each other for a minute. Fry was beginning to get impatient. Cooper could see her muscles tense. He turned to the boys waiting to one side with wide eyes.

'Better clear off, lads,' he said. 'You really don't want to see this.'

'No,' said Leach. He turned the pistol round and gave it to Cooper. Fry began to fill in a receipt.

'Now, if you've quite finished,' said Leach, 'I've got work to do.'

Chapter Twenty-Two

OUT OF TRADITION, Ben Cooper and Todd Weenink started their evening at the Wheatsheaf. There were three pubs that stood close together around the market place, and three or four more down the side streets that they could take in without walking more than a few yards. But the Wheatsheaf had a whole range of guest beers on the bar, strong ales with names like Derbyshire Black and Old Sheep Dip. Weenink was the one drinking harder and faster, and he soon reached the stage where he wanted to share his personal insights.

'There's just no excitement in the job any more,' he said. 'Every day you come into work and they tell you to go and detect a burglary or something.'

'Several burglaries,' said Cooper.

'Six burglaries and four car break-ins. Every morning.'

'And a criminal damage or two, as well.'

'That's it. The same day after day. It's mind numbing. We don't even get a good ram-raid now. Not for ages.'

Weenink had spilled some beer on his leather jacket, and his sleeve stuck to the table when he moved his arm. Cooper was struggling to keep up with his consumption. He hadn't seen Weenink drink quite so hard since his marriage had broken up after less than two years. Weenink's wife had said she hadn't realized what she was tying herself to. And she hadn't just meant Todd. She had meant the police service.

'Ram-raiding has pretty well been designed out in the town centre,' said Cooper.

'Well, it's a shame. They were a bit more exciting than the other crap. All you get now is shoplifting. Where's the fun in that, Ben?'

THEY MOVED ON to the Red Lion, a comfortable pub with somebody's choice of seventies pop music piped discreetly into the bar, and a row of computer games. The landlord knew them both, and they got the first round on the house. It disappeared too quickly for Cooper's peace of mind.

'The CCTV cameras have cut out a lot of the other stuff, too,' he said.

'Bloody cameras. It's a bit too much like Big Brother, if you ask me.'

Cooper was impressed by Weenink's literary knowledge. He wouldn't have put him down as a George Orwell fan. *1984* was one of Cooper's favourite novels, along with *Lord of the Flies.*

Then he frowned. 'We *are* talking about George Orwell, aren't we?'

'Never heard of either of him,' said Weenink, and belched. 'Is he from another division? I suppose you've met him at Police Federation meetings, or something.'

Cooper took another sip of beer. So Todd Weenink only read the TV pages in the *Eden Valley Times*, after all.

THE THIRD PUB was the Station Hotel. They were heading downmarket now. There was no piped music here, no TV screens or bar meals – only a pool table and salt-and-vinegar crisps, and a jukebox full of heavy metal CDs. The customers all seemed to be wearing old Iron Maiden T-shirts. A woman walked past towards the bar in a pair of leather trousers.

'Eat my pants, look at the arse on that,' said Weenink.

'Don't say that. It's disgusting.'

Over the next beer, Weenink studied Cooper with exaggerated care.

'You're a fucking poofter, you are, Ben. Do you know that? A fucking poofter. But I love you. You're my mate.'

They nodded at each other, bleary-eyed. There was no need for words, really. The beer fumes drew them together in a warm, sentimental embrace.

Weenink took out a packet of cigarettes and offered Cooper one. Cooper took it. He hadn't smoked since he was sixteen years old. He looked at it for a minute. Weenink tried to give him a light, but Cooper shook his head and laid the cigarette carefully on his beer mat, lining it up alongside his glass. This particular mat had a picture of a female pop singer on it. Cooper laughed and laughed. It looked as though she had a cigarette up her nose.

'You know, Ben,' said Weenink after sufficient silence. 'You and me, we won't take any shit from *any*body.'

'Right.'

'Am I right?'

'You're right, Todd.'

Weenink watched the woman with the leather trousers walk back across the room and took a drag of his cigarette. 'What was I saying?'

'Let's go somewhere else, shall we?'

Cooper and Weenink walked out of the pub, across the street and through Market Square, staggering slightly as their feet slithered on the cobbles.

'Here, we can play leapfrog on these,' said Weenink, swinging on the black cast-iron street furniture, not noticing when he banged his shin on the metal. His voice sounded unnaturally loud in the square. A middle-aged couple getting into their car turned to look at them. Cooper could almost hear them tutting. For once, there were no noisy groups of youths in the square to distract attention.

'Come on,' he said.

Weenink allowed himself to be led away from the square, down the passage by the Somerfield supermarket. They came out on the riverside walk under the nineteenth-century bridge across the River Eden.

'Not much life down here,' said Weenink. 'Isn't there a night club open or something?'

'Night club? On a Thursday?'

'I need another drink.'

'It's closing time.'

'But we've missed some pubs out.'

Weenink slowed down and stared at the river. Dark shadows lurked just below the surface of the slow-moving water. They were only stones, though. The water was too shallow here for them to be anything else. You could walk across and barely get your feet wet.

'Those ducks are asleep,' said Weenink. 'Let's wake them up.'

'What for?'

'It's too quiet.'

Weenink picked up a handful of gravel and began to throw it at the mallards resting in the reeds with their beaks under their wings. His actions were totally uncoordinated, and the stones fell harmlessly into the water with small plops.

'I need something bigger.'

Cooper looked round, a vague anxiety creeping through the haze of alcohol. There was little traffic passing over the bridge. The only lights were those that burned in the supermarket. There were probably staff on the night shift in there, stacking shelves and taking deliveries. At any moment, one of them might come outside for a fag break.

'Let's move on a bit,' he said.

'What for?'

'We have to get home.'

'I thought we were going to a night club.'

'No.'

'That's what we want. Have another drink, a bit of dancing. Let's go to Sheffield. We could go to a casino.'

'You can go on your own.'

'Oh, Ben.'

Cooper wasn't impressed by the sudden wheedling tone. But he knew that he wouldn't be able to leave Todd to go anywhere on his own, all the same. Weenink sat down suddenly on a bench. The wooden slats creaked under his weight.

'God, I'm knackered,' he said. 'Totally knackered. I could just go to sleep right here, Ben.'

'Come on, Todd. We've got to keep going.'

'Sit down, Ben.'

Cooper sat reluctantly. He was cold, and he could feel the first spots of rain. The insulating alcohol was wearing off already.

'Ben,' said Weenink in a suddenly different voice. 'I've done something really stupid.'

Cooper's heart sank. Not now, please, he thought. Any time except now. He was tired. He had to get home.

'Really, really stupid,' said Weenink. 'And I think I'm going to be found out.'

On the way out of her house in Grosvenor Avenue that night, Fry caught a glimpse of a figure lurking in the shadows under the overgrown hedges near the street-light across the road. It wasn't unusual. The female students and nurses staying in her own house and the ones on either side attracted a motley selection of boyfriends, some of whom wouldn't look out of place in a cell in Derby Prison.

Fry studied the figure carefully. If she hadn't been alert on a professional level, she wouldn't have seen him. He was wearing dark clothes, and standing quite still, so that his movement didn't give him away. Nine out of ten people would have passed by without noticing him at all. Fry shrugged. It was nothing to do with her. When she was off duty, she didn't feel any obligation to concern herself about the dangerous private lives of her fellow flat-dwellers. She had plenty of concerns of her own to think about.

She fetched her car from behind the house and drove out of Edendale and through Grindleford to get on the A625 into Sheffield. She tried to keep her eyes closed to the scenery until she was into the built-up area near Ecclesall. She might live on the back of the moon, but she didn't have to admire it. She was a city girl, and always would be.

Fry began to curse Ben Cooper. She cursed him for being the one who had revived memories she had been trying to put behind her. There was only the one reason she had chosen Derbyshire to transfer to, when she ought to have gone south, to London. They always needed officers in the Met; it would have suited her much better in a big anonymous city, where nobody cared who you were or what you did with your life. By now, she would have been well established, instead of dickering about in this tinpot rural force. She had made the decision for her own reasons, and for months now she had been pretending that those reasons didn't exist. She had tried to let the job take over, and had hoped it would become her number one priority. No – her *only* priority. But it hadn't worked. The time for pretending was over.

A COUPLE OF hours later, she returned from Sheffield tired and frustrated. Pain was shooting up her leg, and she could feel her ankle had swollen to twice its size where she had twisted it at the cattle market. She had walked the streets of the city centre, hunting out the dark corners and following the sounds of the uneasy silences that lay beyond the bright lights around the pubs and night clubs. She had explored all the subways, lit and unlit, walking in areas most women would have avoided after six o'clock in the evening. She had visited a shelter for the homeless she had located north of the university.

But Sheffield was a big place. She might even have to widen her search to Rotherham and Doncaster. Fry knew it could go on for months or years, without success. But once she'd started, she would never be able to give it up.

When she reached Grosvenor Avenue, she noticed that the same figure was opposite the house again. He seemed to be watching a lighted window on the first floor. A peeping tom, no doubt about it. It was time to give him a nasty surprise.

Fry unlocked the front door and went into the hallway. She waited a minute, then switched off the hall light and took the bulb out of the fitting, in case one of the students came downstairs. Then she walked straight through the house and stepped out of the back door. She clambered over the garden fence and moved silently down the alley between the houses until she could emerge on to the road again.

She could see the man's back now. His shoulders were hunched in a black or dark blue jacket, his hands in his pockets. He was totally unsuspecting. A pushover.

When she touched him, he jumped like a startled rabbit and tried to turn round.

'What the –!'

But she already had him in a wrist hold, with her other hand above his elbow and his arm held straight out. From this position, she could force him easily to his knees, cuff him, do what she liked with him. The thought gave her a surge of satisfaction.

'What's *your* business?' she said.

He kept very still. Now she was close to him, Fry could see he wasn't a big man, though he was well wrapped up and wore a peaked cap. He said nothing, but kept his mouth tight shut and rolled his eyes towards her. She applied a bit more pressure to her grip.

'Whatever it is, I suggest you go and do it somewhere else, mate.'

He was so still that she knew he was going to try to take her by surprise and break free. If she had too firm a grip on him when he tried it, one of them would get hurt – and she knew which of them it would be. Fry didn't want to find herself responsible for a suspect with a broken arm at this time of night; maybe ending up on the wrong end of an ABH charge in the morning when the suspect got to talk to a lawyer.

She increased the distance between them slightly and relaxed her grip just enough so that he would notice. Suddenly, he jerked his arm free, put his head down and legged it as hard as he could for the corner of the road. Probably he had a car parked somewhere out of sight.

Fry let him go. There was no point in chasing him, even if her leg hadn't been hurting. She had definitely given him a scare, though. That was one weirdo who would think twice about following women in the future.

Ben Cooper managed to get Weenink moving again and they turned left at the top of the path and emerged on to Bargate. There was still some traffic passing across the lights a few yards away, where the pedestrianized area began.

'Uh-oh, got to have a piss,' said Weenink.

'You'll have to hold on.'

'Can't.'

Weenink began to unzip and stumbled into the doorway of Boots the Chemists.

'Oh, Jesus.' Cooper stood with his back to the doorway, watching the cars cross the end of Bargate, praying that none of them would turn down the street. The sound of a trickle turned into a steady stream, and a pool of urine began to run past his feet on to the pavement.

'Hurry up.'

Weenink just grunted. Cooper swore under his breath as a patrol car appeared at the lights and stopped on the red signal. The car had the distinctive green and yellow checkerboard pattern on the side that indicated it belonged to Traffic division. Cooper wasn't even likely to know the crew. Not that knowing them would help in the least.

He recalled travelling on the M1 one day with his father, back at the time of the year-long miners' strike – 1984, it must have been. Ben had been fourteen years old, and he had gone with his father and Matt to a football match. Derby County had been playing Aston Villa at Birmingham in the FA Cup. He remembered the match well. But he remembered the incident on the motorway, too.

On the way back, they had come up at the rear of a long convoy of coaches, one behind the other, travelling in the inside lane of the motorway. They all carried the name of a coach operator in London and they were packed with men, like some factory outing. When the Coopers' car was close behind the last vehicle, every man on the coach stood up on the seats and dropped his trousers. There was a sudden blooming of white buttocks like exotic lilies in a pond as the men mooned through the windows at passing motorists.

Ben and Matt had laughed, until their father became angry, then pulled out and began to overtake the coach. Maybe he had intended to pull the driver over, Ben wasn't sure. But Sergeant Cooper was off duty, and they weren't even in Derbyshire. This had been Nottinghamshire, somewhere south of Junction 27.

At some point, Ben had sensed his father change his mind. His foot had slipped off the accelerator. He had fallen back momentarily, then accelerated again and passed the convoy as quickly as possible. The boys said nothing. As they passed, they could see the uniforms. They could see the stickers in the front window of every coach. Ten coaches there were – they counted them as they passed. 'Metropolitan Police', the stickers said. They realized that the men were reinforcements arriving to help control the mass pickets of Yorkshire miners then threatening Nottinghamshire pits. Law and order was on the road.

The lights changed and the patrol car had moved on by the time Weenink reappeared.

'Have you got any beer back at your place?' he asked.

'What is it you've done, Todd?'

Weenink's mood was changing again, the cold air sharpening his tone. 'It happens all the time, Ben. You're not so innocent as you make out. You must know. I bet you've done it yourself.'

'I don't know what you're talking about.'

'I'm talking about a little bit of evidence being improved here and there. It happens. Everybody knows that it happens. Where's the harm? As long as you don't get caught.'

'But –' Ben Cooper struggled to capture all the reasons that ran through his mind why this was inconceivable. He thought of words like justice and integrity, like responsibility and honour. He thought of concepts like loyalty to your service, like honesty and truth. And self-respect. And he looked at Todd Weenink and knew that it wasn't worth mentioning even one of them.

'I can't believe that you're telling me this.'

'I'm telling you because you asked me. And because I know you won't shop me.'

'How do you know I won't?'

Weenink winked at him. 'Because you're so loyal and principled. You won't betray me, will you, Ben? No, I know you won't. It's against your morality. It's not what they tell you in the Bible of Bullshit, is it?'

'I'm surprised you've even read it.'

Cooper hadn't read the Police Training Manual much recently, either. Who did, when you had been on the job a while and had learned the realities of the situation? Todd Weenink had certainly been doing the job far too long for that. The Bible of Bullshit was read only by wet trainees and senior managers.

'You know what'll happen, Todd. In the public's eyes, you'll get lumped in with the worst there are. A copper gone wrong is never forgiven.'

'But all I did –'

'I don't want to know.'

'You just asked.'

'I've changed my mind.'

'Fuck you, then.'

Cooper watched Weenink weave away for a few yards along Bargate, then stumble and put out a hand to support himself on a lamp post. He was beyond hope, of course. Breaking the rules was one thing, but breaking the law was another. There was no way that Cooper or anyone else could help Weenink. It didn't matter how much you owed a colleague out of loyalty, or how close you knew other people were to being in the same situation – or even how close you had come to it yourself, at times. Weenink had made his mistake, and he would have to be abandoned to his fate. The wolves would be circling soon enough.

With a sigh, Cooper propped Weenink up and let him drape his arm round his shoulder. Despite the weight, he managed to make it to the lights at the corner of Bargate. Then he began to look for a taxi to get them out of there. The night threatened to stretch out endlessly ahead of him.

BY EIGHT O'CLOCK the next morning, it was already obvious from the sky that it was going to be a good day for a walk on the moors.

The two women had a second cup of coffee together, leaning their elbows comfortably on the kitchen table among the toast crumbs and the cereal bowls. Karen Tavisker's husband Nick had already gone off to work and left them in their housecoats, still chatting, so absorbed in each other's company that they had barely noticed him go.

'We'd better get ready, if we're going,' said Karen.

'Of course. But not for a minute yet.'

'This is so decadent.'

'I don't care,' said Marilyn.

'Nor me.'

Marilyn Robb and Karen Tavisker had been friends for years. Twelve months previously, Marilyn and her husband had moved away to Herefordshire when Alan had been transferred to a new financial services centre at Ludlow. Now Marilyn was back for a visit with her old friend at Karen's home in Mickleover – and the first thing she wanted to do was go for a walk in the Peak District, as they always had done before she moved away.

'Where shall we go?'

'Have you still got the OS maps?'

'Of course. They're right here. Dark Peak or White Peak?'

'Hmm. Normally I might be feeling a bit dark. But today …'

She looked out of the kitchen window. A brisk wind was tossing the dead leaves of the sycamores around the garden.

'Yes, you're right,' said Karen. 'It'll be pretty wild up there today. Best to play safe.'

It might seem bright and breezy now, here in the leafy streets of Mickleover, but by the time they reached Buxton they would have climbed fifteen hundred feet and the climate would be totally different. On the tops, anything could be waiting for unwary walkers. In November, the hills of the Dark Peak could be merciless, with wind, rain and sleet ripping furiously across the shelterless stretches. Both women shivered as they contemplated it.

'Somewhere in the White Peak then. It's nearer, anyway.'

'Why don't we just set off and see where the car takes us?'

'Why not? We're ladies of leisure, after all.'

'And a nice pub for lunch.'

'Perfect.'

Like everyone else, Karen had heard of the women attacked on Ringham Moor. The Jenny Weston case had been in the papers for a few days, but other stories had replaced it now. There were always other, more newsworthy murders taking place somewhere around the country. Karen knew the police had been warning lone women to stay off the moor. But time had passed, and it had begun to feel safe again. And two women together? Surely they would be all right.

By the time they were dressed and had collected their boots and anoraks, they were becoming quite silly, like two schoolgirls on an outing. They found an old Bruce Springsteen tape at the back of the glove compartment in Karen's car, and they sang along to the familiar tunes from fifteen years before, when they had been much younger and had enjoyed life together. They deafened each other with the chorus of 'Dancing in the Dark'.

Marilyn began to talk about the people they had both known, years ago. Karen laughed, her spirits lifted by the company of her friend. She hadn't decided consciously where they would go. But when they reached Ashbourne, she indicated left and turned on to the A515 towards Ringham Moor.

Chapter Twenty-Three

DIANE FRY HAPPENED to be at Divisional Headquarters in West Street when the call came in. As soon as DI Hitchens appeared in the door of the CID room, she knew that something had happened. There was no mistaking that air of excitement that came when there had at last been a breakthrough in a frustrating case.

'What is it?' she said.

'Another woman attacked,' said Hitchens. 'Near Ringham.'

Fry stood up, ready to go. 'Dead?'

'Oh no,' said Hitchens, with the first hint of a smile. 'This one's very much alive. And shouting the place down.'

E DIVISION'S PROBLEM had suddenly become a hot potato that nobody wanted. For the meeting later that morning, Detective Superintendent Prince made an appearance, looking like a man who had been reminded by the Assistant Chief Constable that he was supposed to be in charge.

Ben Cooper saw that even Owen Fox and Mark Roper were there. Owen looked uncomfortable in the stifling atmosphere. The heating had been turned up for the winter, but there were too many people in the room and there was no air conditioning. Away from the open air, Owen seemed out of his element. He was a slow, quietly-spoken middle-aged man among a crowd of younger people who were much noisier, more self-confident and aggressive. His untidy hair and beard made him look his age.

Also, Cooper now realized that it was only Owen's fleece jacket that was red. The jacket was so distinctive that he hadn't really noticed the rest of the Ranger's uniform before. Apart from the red fleece, everything else that he wore was grey – the shirt, the trousers, the sweater. Without the jacket, the Ranger would be a grey man.

'WELL, IF THIS was our assailant again, he made a big mistake,' said Tailby, with more than a trace of satisfaction. 'This time the woman he chose turned out not to be alone. If this lady, Karen Tavisker, had not walked on ahead when her friend stopped to rest, he would have realized there were two of them. I believe he would have left them alone and gone elsewhere. We have the lack of fitness of a thirty-five-year-old woman to thank for this breakthrough.'

Tailby pointed to the map of the Ringham area showing the sites of the previous attacks. He indicated a path above the village of Ringham Lees, which disappeared into a patch of green representing woodland before emerging among grey angular shapes that meant rocks.

'Karen Tavisker wanted to reach the top of Ringham Edge,' he said. 'But the path was too steep for her friend, Marilyn Robb. She stopped to rest about here while Tavisker went on. We believe our man was waiting in the trees. He must have thought Tavisker was alone, but he got a shock. Robb was only a few yards away. Everything went wrong for him at that point.'

'Did they both see him?' asked Cooper.

'Robb came running when her friend screamed. Unfortunately, the assailant was wearing a mask. But, yes, we now have two new witnesses.' Tailby beamed proudly, as if he had just created the witnesses himself out of a washing-up liquid bottle and a few bits of string.

'We've traced his approach route and we have some tyre tracks, plus reported sightings of a red Renault in the vicinity. Progress. It's progress at last.'

Tailby indicated a photograph of Karen Tavisker, and they all looked at it as if she were their latest pin-up.

'The other point is that Karen Tavisker lives out of the area and was on a passing visit. There seems little doubt that, in this case at least, the victim was chosen at random. Now DI Hitchens has a bit of news to share with you that may or may not be related.'

'This morning we've heard from Greater Manchester Police,' said Hitchens. 'They inform us that they are seeking a suspect who could be in our area. His name's Darren Howsley. They badly want to interview him about a series of attacks on women in the Oldham area. They say he has family connections in Derbyshire, having lived with an aunt at Chelmorton for a few years as a teenager. We've had his photo and details faxed over, and they'll be in your files shortly.'

'Is this particularly relevant?' asked someone.

'It is if you look at the nature of the incidents. These women were attacked while walking in the hills outside Oldham. The Saddleworth area.'

'Just like our man.'

'Right.'

'The other thing is that he seems to have been missing from their patch for at least three weeks.'

'Great.'

'Apart from that little tidbit, it's a question of going over old ground again, I'm afraid,' said Tailby. 'Roadside stops, questionnaires, appeals in the media. We need to involve the community. We're getting serious pressure now. So we have to put pressure on in return, let people see we're doing something. We revisit everyone who hasn't been eliminated. If they were in the area and can't account for their movements, then coincidence is abolished as far as I'm concerned.'

'I can think straight away of two who won't have alibis, except for each other,' said Hitchens.

'You mean the travellers in the quarry, Paul.'

'It's time we did something about them. Bring them both in. Their initial statements are useless. We should make them go through everything again and let HOLMES sniff out some inconsistencies.'

'What's the relationship between those two?' asked Tailby. 'Is there a sexual liaison?'

'Possibly, sir. There's certainly something not quite right there,' said Fry.

'No,' said Cooper.

'Ah? Why do you sound so sure, Cooper?'

'It isn't in their philosophy. They have different beliefs to us.'

'Well, that sounds interesting, Cooper. Could you explain what these beliefs are? Might they just have some bearing on the enquiry, by any chance?'

'I don't think so, sir.'

'It doesn't do to be too credulous, Cooper. For a start, are we supposed to believe they live just on the benefits claimed by Calvin Lawrence?'

'They hardly have an extravagant lifestyle.'

Hitchens interrupted. 'I can show you fifteen or sixteen reports of stuff being nicked from cars parked on the roadsides around Ringham Moor. Radios, cameras – you name it. Somebody's cleaning up from the tourists round there.'

'You think it's Cal and Stride? But what would they do with that sort of stuff?'

'Well – sell it, right? That's the usual idea, as far as I understand it.'

'Sell it to who?' said Cooper, starting to get agitated. 'These aren't your average local yobbos who can flog it in the pub. If these two had stuff they wanted to sell, they'd have to take it on the bus with them to Bakewell or Edendale. Or hitch with it by the roadside. Can you see that? And neither of them is local anyway, so who is there they would know? We'd have picked them up straight off if they'd been trying that. And Stride never leaves the van anyway, except to go on the moor.'

'Do we have sufficient grounds to turn over the van?' asked Fry.

Tailby looked around. 'Not unless someone can give me any evidence that puts them under suspicion of a crime. Something that would justify a warrant.'

'Unfortunately, we can't even move them on, unless the quarry owners get their injunction,' said Hitchens.

'We'd need a tow truck to get the van out, anyway.'

'More than that. The van hasn't moved for months. We'd have to winch it on to a flatbed.'

'Mmm.' Tailby looked round at the officers. 'Nobody's offering me anything.'

'Drugs,' said Hitchens.

'Grounds for suspicion?'

'Strange behaviour – they're uncoordinated, incoherent. I say we take a dog down and we sniff 'em out.'

'I've been in the van,' said Cooper.

'What?' Hitchens stared at him. 'What the hell did you think you were doing? Any defence lawyer will have a field day.'

'I was invited.'

'Oh, did they throw a party? Sorry I missed it. I mustn't have got my invitation.'

'I was with Mr Fox.'

Some officers looked around, unfamiliar with the name. Attention settled on the Ranger, whose face went a shade of pink that clashed horribly with his jacket.

'Mr Fox?' said Tailby.

'I've known Cal and Stride since they arrived,' said Owen. 'They talk to me.'

'What's your view on this drugs issue? Are they users?'

'No, I'm sure they're not.'

'Cooper?'

'I agree. There was no evidence that I saw. And there aren't many places to hide the stuff. They stick to beer and tobacco, I think. Addictive, but legal.'

Tailby looked unimpressed. 'Check up on the progress of Peakstone's injunction, Paul. It would be ironic if they got moved on before we've finished with them.'

Cooper raised his hand tentatively. He could feel that Todd Weenink was staring at him. More than that, he was using his famous glower. He managed to avoid Weenink's eye.

'Yes, Cooper?'

'There's Warren Leach as well,' he said. 'He *does* have a link to Maggie Crew. We shouldn't forget that.'

'We could put that surveillance on him for a while, I suppose,' said Tailby. 'We can spare the resources.'

'How do we put surveillance on that farm?' asked Fry. 'There's nowhere we can position somebody where he won't see them.'

Tailby considered it. 'It doesn't matter. In fact, it might be better if they do show out. It'll put some pressure on him. Fry, Cooper – you know the ground.'

'But surveillance? Are you sure? There's nothing to see up there, except cows.'

'In that case,' said Tailby, 'watch every cow that moves.'

'Meanwhile, we've got Wayne Sugden coming in again,' said Hitchens. 'In fact, he should be downstairs now.'

'Why?'

'That burglary at the Westons' cottage. It isn't so simple. When we looked at the files, it turned out that the officers dealing with the incident report called out a key-holder, because the Westons themselves were away in Cyprus. And the key-holder wasn't their neighbour. It was Jenny Weston.'

WAYNE SUGDEN WAS working himself to a peak of outraged innocence. He had been easily prompted to it by the first questions about the burglary. It had turned on a tap, the flow gradually becoming hotter until the steam began to rise.

'That tart, why did she say all those things? She said I nicked jewellery and all sorts of stuff. She said I pissed on her carpet and chucked some kind of sauce at her walls. Why would I want to do that?'

DI Hitchens explained patiently: 'It was done by whoever burgled her parents' house, Wayne. The court said that was you.'

'It's rubbish. I wasn't even there.'

'Come on, Wayne. There was enough evidence to convict you.'

'I don't care. It was all crap.'

Hitchens sighed. 'We can't help you if you're so stubborn.'

'That bitch got me sent down. The things she said, they were wrong. She turned the magistrates against me, otherwise I could have got off with probation or something. Pissing on the carpet – I mean. That's not me.'

'How well do you remember Jenny Weston? Did you see her in court?'

Sugden's face went pale.

'She got done, didn't she? I saw it on the telly.'

'Yes, she got done.'

'You're never going to try and fit me up for that! You're bloody not!' Sugden peered nervously at Hitchens. 'No, you're not. I can see you're not. Even you lot, you know better than that.'

Hitchens looked at Ben Cooper, inviting him to change tack. 'Wayne, how did you feel when young Gavin was killed on that school trip?'

Now Sugden really did look confused. 'What?'

'You remember the accident to your nephew?'

''Course I do.'

'They had to turn his life-support machine off. How did you feel about that?'

'I was upset. Obviously. We were all upset. Gavin was a good lad. But –'

'Who did you blame for his death?'

Sugden closed his mouth. His eyes flickered. He looked at the tapes.

'Wayne? It would be normal to blame somebody for what happened. To hold somebody responsible. Maybe even to want revenge on them,' said Cooper.

'Look, don't mess about with me,' said Sugden. 'I know it was Weston who was in charge when Gavin got hurt.'

'Do you still say you didn't burgle the Westons' cottage?' asked Cooper.

'And do you still say you don't know anything about their daughter?' added Hitchens.

'Yeah,' said Sugden. 'I do say that. Still.'

SUGDEN'S INSISTENCE WORRIED Cooper. If the man lurking around Jenny Weston's house wasn't Martin Stafford or some boyfriend, it had to be Sugden. The description was vague, but it did fit him. And he had a motive for wanting to do Jenny harm. But Cooper trusted his own ability to judge when somebody was lying and when they were telling the truth, even if he could never prove it.

Of course, Sugden might have dwelt on the idea of revenge long enough while in prison, with no one to contradict him, for it to have festered in his mind. Cooper could even imagine the conversations with other prisoners that would have taken place, full of mutual self-pity and recriminations against those on the outside. Sugden had alibis for the day Jenny was killed. But might he have made some jail-cell pact? It seemed unlikely, though the things that went on in the minds of men in prison were far worse than that.

As he walked out of the station towards his car, Ben Cooper became aware that he was being followed. He thought at first it was Diane Fry coming after him, determined to open some new argument. But then he recognized the jacket, and he saw that it was Mark Roper.

Cooper stopped. 'All right, Mark? Still here? Do you want a lift or something?'

'I came with Owen, but he's stayed to have a word with the inspector. They want us to put on more patrols round Ringham.'

'I know.'

'There's something I wanted to tell you. I didn't like to say anything in the meeting.'

Cooper leaned against his Toyota, noting how ill at ease the young Ranger was. Mark took a radio handset from his pocket, fingered the buttons, flexed the aerial, and put it back without seeming to realize what he was doing.

'Tell me about it,' said Cooper.

'It's Warren Leach. We see him often at Ringham Edge. He doesn't know we're there – he never bothers to look up at the hills these days, only down at his boots.' Mark paused. 'For a while now, I've thought there was something going on in the big shed at the back of the farmhouse. The new one, with the steel roof. It's always locked, and Leach doesn't go near it during the day. I've seen Yvonne Leach go out there and try the doors sometimes, when Warren is out of the way. She wants to know what's in there, too.'

'And at night?'

'People come. Vans, four-wheel drives. They all park by the shed. But only when it's dark.'

'Mark, you're not normally on patrol at night, are you?'

'Of course not. But I've been up there in my own time a couple of nights. I want to know what's going on. It's my patch, you see. Owen told me it's my patch now, up there.' Mark hesitated and looked sideways at Cooper. 'Owen doesn't know I go up on the moor at night.'

'All right, Mark.'

'Leach is going through a really bad time. You've been to see him, haven't you?'

'We took a captive bolt pistol off him the other day. It was unlicensed.'

Mark frowned. 'Why do you think Leach would have a captive bolt pistol?'

'To use on his own animals, I suppose. There must be some he has to put down.'

'Farmers are supposed to have their fallen stock removed by a proper slaughterman. There are regulations these days.'

'Even so . . .'

'Would he risk getting into trouble just for that?'

Cooper waited for him to say more, but Mark looked round at the door to see if Owen had emerged. He began to edge towards the Ranger Land Rover a few places away from Cooper's car.

'Have there been any people coming to the farm that you recognized, Mark?' asked Cooper.

'Oh, one or two vehicles that were probably local. Most of them I don't recognize.'

'What about a white van?'

The young Ranger nodded. 'Ford Transit? Almost ready for the scrapyard? Front bumper held on with baling twine?'

'Yes, that sort of van.'

'I know him, all right. That's the rat man.'

'You've seen him down at the farm?'

'Several times. He gets around a bit.'

Owen Fox came out of the station. He was chatting to a uniformed officer, and they paused on the steps. When Owen saw Mark, a faint shadow slipped across his face.

'Thanks for sharing that with me, Mark,' said Cooper.

Mark put out a hand to hold him back for a second. 'I'd rather that nobody found out who passed that on to you,' he said.

'Why?'

'I have to live and work round here. If people think I'm spying for the police, it won't make any difference to them whether what they're doing is right or wrong. No difference at all.'

DIANE FRY HAD a phone call she wanted to make before she got involved in anything else. It was to Maggie Crew's sister. Her name was Catherine Dyson, and her phone number was in the file – a number in the Cork area, in the south of Ireland.

'Yes, I know Maggie is having major problems bringing back the memories,' said Catherine when Fry got through to her. 'If you're asking my opinion, the more you press her to remember, the more she'll bury the memories. I think it's automatic with her now. It's her instinct to push things away, not to dwell on the past.'

'She is suffering partial amnesia from the assault,' said Fry. 'The doctors say she may never recover memory for the period several hours either side of the incident.'

'Well, if they say so. But Mags was always frightened of memories coming back out of the past. She's built up a whole system of defences. Her memories are locked up more securely than Fort Knox. Sometimes I think she barely remembers *me*.'

Catherine's voice was very like her sister's, but softer and more comfortable. There was even a faint hint of an Irish accent creeping into the vowels – more, anyway, than might be expected for a woman from Chesterfield. Fry conjured a picture of a white-painted cottage reflecting the sunlight on a hillside over an Atlantic fishing port, and Catherine Dyson in an armchair with a cat on her knee as she gazed out of the window. She pictured a large woman, her body allowed to run to fat after four children, her time taken up with washing and ironing, baking and tending the garden. A woman nothing like Maggie Crew. A woman who was happy.

'Are you thinking of any particular memories from your sister's past?' asked Fry. 'Apart from the assault, I mean?'

'Yes, of course,' said Catherine. 'I was thinking of her daughter.'

Chapter Twenty-Four

THAT MORNING, THE dowser was working his way backwards and forwards across the edge of the birch wood, treading carefully as if he was walking an imaginary white line, his eyes fixed on a forked twig held in front of him. He held it strangely, with his palms turned upwards. Every now and then, the twig twitched, and the dowser would stop and scuff at the ground with the toe of his boot. Then he would move on. He looked cold and disconsolate.

Diane Fry had a copy of the latest *Eden Valley Times*. The attack on Karen Tavisker had come too late for the newspaper's deadline, though it was already appearing on the local radio news bulletins. The *Times* did have three pages covering a public meeting and protests outside the hall, with all the old material about Jenny Weston and Maggie Crew rehashed into one big mess that somebody had to take the blame for. The guilty faces of Jepson and Tailby stared out from a crowd waving banners that said 'We demand action'.

There was a highly speculative piece headed 'The Sabbath Slayer?' It attempted to make a link between the legend of the Nine Virgins, who had been turned to stone for dancing on the Sabbath, and the fact that the attacks on Crew and Weston had both taken place on Sundays, when the women had been out walking or cycling on the moor. The conclusion was that a religious maniac could be punishing women for enjoying themselves on the Lord's Day. As a theory, it held plenty of tabloid drama, but little substance. Yet it had already been murmured by officers on the enquiry team, in their more desperate moments.

There was also an interesting secondary story on the third page. A reporter and photographer had found two young men living in an old VW van in an abandoned quarry at Ringham Moor, and they had scented a different angle.

'Have you seen this photograph? Calvin Lawrence looks a mass murderer if ever I saw one,' said Fry.

'But they've made Stride look like a half-wit.'

'That youth needs psychiatric help. Have you seen their background reports? He dropped out of university during one of his recurring periods of acute depression.'

'That doesn't make him a half-wit,' said Cooper.

'Simon Bevington tried to kill himself twice. It might mean that he shouldn't be out and about unsupervised. The bloke's a nutter.'

'He isn't a danger to anybody but himself. Besides, I think he *is* supervised. Cal takes care of him. I reckon Stride's better looked after where he is than he would be in any hostel. That's real care in the community. He's found someone who actually cares about him, no strings attached.'

'Oh, lucky him.'

'He isn't dangerous,' insisted Cooper. 'He just sees the world in a different way from most people. Different, that's what he is.'

'Yeah, yeah. Different like the Yorkshire Ripper was different. He's a nutter, Ben.'

'He's strange, that's all. My mother would say he was a bit fey.'

Fry snorted. 'You're a bloody strange copper, Ben. Do you really think there are people in this world who are complete angels?'

'Well ...' said Cooper. 'I suppose he *is* a bit like that. In a way.'

'*What*?'

'Innocent, you know. Detached from the real world. Ethereal.'

Fry stared at him. 'Hey, you don't have to look too far for nutters round these parts, do you?' she said. 'The real loonies can be right there in front of your eyes.'

Cooper read the newspaper article over her shoulder. 'They quote Stride as saying the wind chimes and tree sculptures will keep away the vengeful spirits of the moor.'

'Why do they print that crap?'

'It gives them a chance for a funny headline: "Tate for tat? Quarry dwellers' art is more than just rock and roll-ups".'

'Very clever. At least they don't mention Simon Bevington's history.'

'No,' said Cooper. 'But I think they might have done enough.'

'All the attention might persuade them to leave the quarry. That would be no loss, in my opinion.'

'They're all right. They're the sort of people we should be protecting.'

'*What* are you talking about?'

'You remember. That oath we took. "I do solemnly and sincerely declare and affirm …"'

'Yeah, yeah.'

'"… and prevent all offences against the person and properties of Her Majesty's subjects."'

'Ben, do you realize you're the only copper in the country who can still quote his oath more than two minutes after his swearing in?'

'Maybe I happened to check on it the other day.'

'What the hell has that got to do with those two van people, anyway?'

'I think they're at risk. Just like the others.'

'What others?'

'Well, like Jenny Weston and Maggie Crew. Like Will Leach and his brother, little Dougie. Their mother as well. Even their father, in a way. And, well … others. They're our responsibility.'

'Ben, it's a big mistake to think you've been recruited as one of the Knights of the Round Table. They don't issue shining armour these days. And your name isn't Sir Galahad.'

Cooper shook his head. 'Maybe I'm a bit old-fashioned and quaint. The fact is, I wouldn't be able to live with myself if I didn't try to do something for the people who need protecting. What a joke, eh?'

And he began to walk off, scuffing the loose stones, so that they left white marks on the toes of his shoes.

BEN COOPER REMEMBERED very well reading and rereading the oath on the back of his father's warrant card as a small boy. Whenever he had seen his father in his uniform, he had asked to read it again. He must have been a terrible pest. But, at the time, it had seemed the most noble and meaningful sentence in the world, a hero's vow of honour. He had regarded it with the superstitious awe and respect that only an over-imaginative child can produce. Though his hero had faded, and finally died a futile death, the power of the words had left a lasting impression. What was he here for, except to protect the innocent?

A potential for violence seemed to hang around the moor like low clouds. Cooper had been dwelling too long on the fate of Jenny Weston, on the question of why death had picked her out and flung her lifeless among the stones. It was as if she had been just one more bit of dead foliage among the masses scattered on the moor – her veins full of toxins, her living tissue turned brown and useless. But there was one difference. Leaves were sacrificed for the sake of a new beginning, the start of new life. The death of Jenny Weston had no such justification.

Cooper wondered about himself, too. Had he really joined the police because of his father? Was everything he did aimed at outdoing the memory of the Hero of Edendale? Or were people like Jenny Weston also part of his motivation? He hoped so. But it was hard to be sure.

COOPER WASN'T SURPRISED that his reception in the quarry was twenty degrees cooler than the last time. Cal and Stride had become a centre of attention since then – they had met the press, the police, and no doubt some of the less sympathetic elements of the public. It was surely enough to make them shut themselves off from the world.

Only Cal appeared in answer to Cooper's knock. This time, there was only a crack in the door for him to peer through.

'You. What?'

'Just a word of advice, sir.'

'Oh, wow. Surprise me, man.'

'Those things up there … those sculptures, or whatever you call them. The phallus farm.'

'Yeah?'

'I don't think they're very wise, just at the moment. Best to remove them. Put them out of sight somewhere.'

'They're a tribute to Gaia. We're using her space, so we say thank you. We make her gifts with our own hands. We wish her fertility.'

'Yes, fine. I'm not interested in all that. It's the appearance of the things that's the issue. People might get the wrong idea. They might be considered provocative.'

'Provocative?'

'There are lots of folk around here with different views to your own. They don't understand. Think about it.'

'OK, OK. We'll think about it.'

'It's in your own interests. For your own safety.'

'Our own safety! Cool.'

'You should seriously –'

Cooper found himself staring at the panel of the closed door. Directly level with his eyes, there were scratches in the paintwork, a few letters gouged right into the metal. They spelled: 'Perverts'.

WHEN SHE WAS back in the car, Diane Fry remembered Catherine Dyson's sigh at the other end of the phone line in Ireland, just after she had let slip the fact of Maggie Crew having a daughter.

'She'll know it came from me,' she'd said. 'But it doesn't matter. She's barely speaking to me anyway these days.'

'Did you say a daughter?'

'Yes. Maggie had a little girl. It was about twenty years ago now. It wasn't intended, far from it. Mags was a law student then. She didn't believe in abortion – a relic of our Catholic upbringing, I'm afraid. So she had the child adopted – there was no way she could have raised her. It would have interfered too much with her plans for her career.'

Fry recalled Maggie's comments about female police officers, and realized that she had probably been talking about her own situation.

'And Mags never even achieved what she wanted. She reached a plateau. She ended up in a small town, instead of becoming a partner in a big city firm. And it was a small town no more than ten miles from where we were raised. She is never going to get any further away now. There's some strange tie that she has to the area, though she would never admit it. She always thought I was the one who would stay around, and I would have agreed with her at one time. But when you reach a certain age you learn things about yourself – you learn that you're not quite what other people always told you.'

'Do you think your sister resents not getting further in her career?'

'Well, I certainly think she started to realize she'd reached that plateau. Of course she did. And she resented the fact that I'd escaped, as she saw it. That I'd left her to look after Mum and Dad. She couldn't move away then, you see – not without adding to her feelings of guilt.'

'She doesn't strike me as someone who feels guilty,' said Fry.

'Oh, she's good at blaming other people. She blames everyone but herself for her lack of real success – her teachers, her colleagues, our parents, me. And any friends she might have left. She was always a difficult person to like, but she became so prickly that people began to leave her well alone.'

'And the child? Do you think she feels guilty about the child?'

'Well, what do you think?' said Catherine brightly. And in that one sentence, Fry was able to fill in the background around her picture of Maggie's sister – the background was full of children hanging on to her skirt and bringing her their latest treasures to look at. All the children would be little copies of Catherine. Fry nodded at the clarity of the image. The arrival of each child must have been like salt in the wound to Maggie. What was it she had said at Derwent Court the other day? 'Perhaps I'll wake up one day and discover I have a maternal instinct after all.'

'I think, you know,' said Catherine, 'that Mags must have been wondering a great deal about the child. Wondering what she would be like now, and where she is. Wondering if she ever thought about her real mother.'

'And wondering what it would be like now to have a daughter of her own, instead of being so alone?' said Fry.

'Exactly,' said Catherine. 'And there's no one else she can blame for that, is there? No one but herself.'

Fry took a moment to readjust her assessment of Maggie Crew. She was seeing a different person, sensing a greater tragedy taking place in the darkened rooms of the apartment at Derwent Court than she had imagined until now.

Catherine Dyson must have wondered about the silence at the other end of the line. It was her turn to ask a question, and the astuteness of it took Diane Fry by surprise.

'Have you been going to see my sister often?' she asked.

'Well, yes,' said Fry. 'You know the circumstances, don't you?'

'Of course. You're doing your job, I see that. But ...'

'Yes?'

'I can't tell over the phone,' said Catherine, 'but may I ask how old you are?'

'What on earth difference does that make?' said Fry.

'Oh, never mind,' said Catherine hastily. 'I'm sure it makes no difference at all.'

THE OFFICES OF Quigley, Coleman & Crew were on Peveril Street. Diane Fry entered a reception area fronted by smoked plate glass. A blonde receptionist with a fake tan took her name without showing any interest in her warrant card, and took her time looking at a diary on her desk.

'I'm sorry, Ms Crew is not available.'

'What?' Fry was brought up hard. She had thought of cancelling, true. But she had never got round to it. 'What do you mean? I've got an appointment.'

The receptionist pretended to look at the diary. 'I'm sorry, she's cancelled it. Something came up. You know.'

The girl could hardly be bothered concealing her contempt for someone whose appointment had been cancelled at the last minute without telling her. She was obviously somebody of no importance.

'Did she say why?' asked Fry.

'No. I'm sorry.'

'Where is she now?'

'I can't tell you that.'

'Then give Ms Crew a message. You can do that, can't you?'

'I suppose so.'

Fry leaned closer over the desk. 'Tell her one thing. Tell her: "What if Jenny wasn't enough for him either?"'

The girl looked nervous. 'I don't understand that.'

'You don't have to. Just write it down and give it to your boss.'

'I think you ought to leave.'

'You haven't written it down yet.'

The girl wrote the eight words on a memo pad, her hand shaking slightly. 'There. I'll give it to Ms Crew when she's in the office.'

'Right. And then you can tell her to damn well phone me.'

'I think I'll really have to ask you to leave now.'

'You know I'm a police officer?'

'Yes. But that doesn't mean I have to put up with harassment.'

'You don't know what harassment is. Not yet.'

FRY DROVE STRAIGHT to Derwent Court. She was not surprised to get no answer from Maggie's apartment. But even here there should be a next-door neighbour with an interest in what went on. They were useful people. She tried the next apartment and introduced herself to a lady called Mrs Dean, who seemed quite happy to talk about Maggie Crew.

'I don't know where she is today,' she said. 'I thought she'd started going back into her office to work.'

'Yes, she had,' said Fry.

'I am glad. It's for the best, really. It'll help take her mind off things.'

'But she's not in the office today.'

'Isn't she? She went out at her usual time.'

'In her car?'

'I imagine so. I don't know.'

'On her own?'

'She's always on her own these days.'

'Was there a time when she wasn't?' asked Fry.

'Well, none of us has been in Derwent Court more than a year or two, just since the place was converted. I don't know anything about her life before that.'

Fry looked at Mrs Dean's apartment. It looked completely different from Maggie Crew's, though the layout must have been identical. Instead of being cold and unwelcoming, this one was full of deep-pile carpets and light and mirrors, and a hundred little personal items.

'She has no family who come to see her, has she?' said Fry. 'Any children?'

'No, no children. She has never married, as far as I know. But there's a sister.'

'Of course, yes. Does she come?'

'Not recently. Some people just can't deal with it – with physical disfigurement, I mean. They're frightened they're going to say the wrong thing, or that they won't be able to avoid staring. I'd like to think I wouldn't be that way, if it happened to one of my friends. I'd want to support them, wouldn't you?'

Fry searched her heart and wasn't sure. Mrs Dean seemed to pick up on her hesitation.

'Mind you, it *is* pretty awful to have to look at, isn't it? I can see that it might put you off if you were invited round for tea. Are you sure you won't sit down?' said Mrs Dean.

'No, thank you.'

'Still. You'd think the sister would make an effort to get here. It's at times like these that you need your family most, not just in the good times. Don't you agree?'

'Of course,' said Fry, though she was hardly in a position to know. 'So you haven't seen Miss Crew since this morning?'

'I heard her go out about ten o'clock,' said Mrs Dean.

'You didn't actually see her?'

'No. But I could tell it was her. You get to recognize the noises when you live so close together. You can identify all the familiar sounds. I know the way she closes her door, and the way her footsteps sound in the corridor.'

'And unfamiliar ones?'

'Sorry?'

'Any unfamiliar sounds. Any sounds of anybody visiting Miss Crew, anybody you didn't recognize?'

'I don't believe so. Not that I've been aware of.'

'Nobody hanging around the flats?'

'No.'

Fry looked at the window. She felt drawn to it in a way she hadn't in Maggie's apartment. The view was the same, but when she stood close to the window, she could see down into a paved courtyard that had been turned into a car park for residents.

'She leads a quiet life then, Miss Crew. Would you say so?' she asked.

'Oh, very quiet,' said Mrs Dean. 'Very quiet indeed. These days.'

THE TWO PCs had been deployed on a routine patrol in the Ringham Moor area. They were cruising as a visible symbol of positive police action, designed to make the area safe for law-abiding members of the community. And they were bored out of their minds.

On Hanger Hill, though, they found a little bit of excitement. A Renault coming down the hill too fast had braked on the sharp corner and skidded sideways in a scum of wet leaves. A stone wall had made a serious mess of its near-side front wing, and fragments of glass from a shattered headlamp littered the road. The officers stopped, and got out to help. The female half of the team went to talk to the driver.

'Had a bit of trouble, sir?'

The driver looked dazed rather than injured. He was trying to straighten out the wheel arch where it had crumpled against the wall and been pushed on to his wheel.

'Are you a member of the AA or RAC? If not, we can organize a garage to send someone out.'

'Oh, thanks. It's not too serious, but …'

'It needs to be made safe, sir.'

'Of course.'

The second PC had done a spell in Traffic. Since then, he had automatically looked at things like tyres and number plates. The thing that drew his attention to the rear plate of the Renault was the fact that it was white. He knew that front plates were white, but rear plates were supposed to be yellow. Car owners themselves often failed to notice this.

He looked a bit closer. He saw that there was a thin strip of clean paintwork showing around the edge of the number plate. He concluded that it had recently replaced a previous plate that had been slightly larger.

'I think I'll do a check on the number,' he said to his partner. They looked at each other, and the first officer walked over to engage the motorist in conversation again. They had worked together before, and they knew how to communicate.

Ten minutes later, they had obtained the motorist's documents and he was in the back of the police car waiting to accompany them to the station in Edendale, once some support had arrived to secure the Renault. The two officers were grinning with suppressed excitement. They had just arrested Greater Manchester's wanted man, Darren Howsley.

Chapter Twenty-Five

WHEN BEN COOPER got back to West Street, the change in the atmosphere was immediately obvious. DCI Tailby strode by along the corridor and was almost smiling. DI Hitchens was handing out peppermints.

'What's happening?' asked Cooper.

'Him,' said Diane Fry, pointing at a file. 'That's what's happening. He's the happening man, all right.'

Cooper read the first page. 'Darren Howsley. Aged thirty-two. That's the bloke Manchester are looking for.'

'Two uniforms brought him in last night. He'd run his car into a wall on Hanger Hill. A bit of bad luck, you might say. Or then, you might not. Depending on your point of view. Just a patch of wet leaves in the wrong place, and he was a bit hasty on the brake for the conditions. It could have happened to anyone.'

Fry started laughing. Cooper smiled tolerantly. He knew there had to be more.

'And the bobbies were efficient for once. Thank God they weren't on their way for a tea break or going off shift, or they'd just have banged a sticker on his car and given him a lift to the bus station.'

'Any evidence on him?'

'A mask and a carving knife in the glove compartment. Will that do? Don't say it too loudly, Ben, but it looks like we've got him.'

'He has family in this area, doesn't he?'

'He was staying with his aunt at Chelmorton. It seems the old dear was terrified of him. She knew what he was like, but she was scared of telling anybody about him. Howsley had been at her house for two or three days when he turned up with the Renault. She knew it was stolen. I don't think he bothered to hide anything from her. Also, the carving knife is the one missing from her kitchen. It's just what we needed – he made a mistake.'

THE NEXT CALL came through directly to the CID room, because the caller had asked specifically for Diane Fry.

'I thought you might want to talk to me again, Diane.'

Fry stiffened, surprised by the strength of her own reaction to the voice. 'Maggie? Is that you?'

'Yes. I hear from the news that there's been another attack.'

'That's right.'

'Tell me about it, Diane.'

Fry noted the 'it'. Maggie didn't really want to know about the woman who had been attacked; she wasn't interested in who she was. She wanted to know what had happened, to hear the physical details of the attack. She wanted to know if it was the same as what had happened to her. For reassurance? Or simply for the purpose of inflicting yet more pain on herself?

Fry could have gone through the litany, as she had done with Jenny Weston. She could have told Maggie all the details she knew about Karen Tavisker. But she kept her mouth shut, waiting to hear the voice at the other end of the line, listening for meaning in it that she knew was never communicated by phone, but only by the expression in the face and the subtleties of body language.

'Tell me. I want to know,' said Maggie petulantly into the silence.

'It's not something I can discuss with you,' said Fry. 'We've made an arrest.'

'An arrest? Who is he? Tell me about him. Does he have a connection to Jenny Weston – the one with the mountain bike and an interest in history and astrology?'

Fry felt her heart lift for a moment. It was five days since she had told Maggie about Jenny Weston, but Maggie had remembered Jenny's interest in history and perhaps the idea that she might have visited Hammond Hall. It meant Jenny had become real to her.

But Fry thought of Darren Howsley, with the mask and the knife in his stolen car, and the independent, credible witness they had to identify him. She thought of the sweat she had shed over Maggie Crew and the strain on her own emotions, and of how little she had achieved. She had not even known that Maggie had a daughter adopted until her sister had mentioned it. And Fry worried about the question that Catherine had asked her – 'how old are you?' What did she mean by that?

She thought of Maggie's attitude, of how she had cancelled her appointment, stood her up and humiliated her in front of the secretary. There was no way she was going through all that again.

'There's no point, Maggie,' she said. 'Because I don't need you. You're no use to me any more.'

DARREN HOWSLEY WAS an innocuous-looking man. When processed through the detention suite, he measured in at five foot nine inches and ten stone eight pounds. His hair was recorded as 'light brown'. He had a small moustache, hazel eyes and a discreet tattoo of a tiger on his left forearm.

He spoke quietly, sometimes hardly at all, his hands clasped apologetically together in his lap. But he had been questioned by Greater Manchester Police on suspicion of multiple stabbings, in which three middle-aged women had died and a seven-year-old girl had lost an eye. Howsley was currently on bail for an assault on a taxi driver who'd had the temerity to demand his fare.

He was questioned intensively for several hours, allowing for the statutory rest and meals breaks prescribed by the Police and Criminal Evidence Act. The details of his movements at the times of the attacks on the three local women were gone over again and again, until all involved became tired of hearing the same questions and the same answers, or the lack of them.

Only when the last dregs of hope had been exhausted and an exercise in futility was staring them in the face did the interviewers falter. They took a break. They consulted with each other, they took advice from upstairs. Then they went back in again.

'Mr Howsley, you've told us that on Sunday 2nd November you were at a pub in Matlock. Which pub was it again?'

'The White Bull.'

'And what time did you arrive?'

'I've told you.'

'What time did you leave?'

'I've told you.'

'How many drinks did you have? Who were you with? Who did you speak to? Where did you go when you left?'

But Howsley's answers didn't vary, no matter how often they asked him. He had clear memories of what he was doing on the days that Jenny Weston and Maggie Crew were attacked, and his statements were consistent. He had been a long way from the area, on his home patch in Greater Manchester.

Only when told about sightings of the stolen car did he seem less confident. He couldn't be sure where he was when Karen Tavisker was attacked, he said. The interview team had an advantage on this one. The Renault driven by Darren Howsley had been sighted in the Ringham area, and they had two reliable witnesses – the Rangers, Owen Fox and Mark Roper, who had recorded the make, model, colour and false licence plate, as they had been doing with any unfamiliar vehicle near the moor. It was then Howsley asked for his solicitor.

'I think he wasn't able to resist falling back into old habits when he read about our two assaults,' said DCI Tailby afterwards.

'A copycat,' said DI Hitchens.

'In a way. Tavisker was lucky, anyway.'

'Aren't we going to try for an identification?' asked Fry.

'I don't think it's worthwhile. Greater Manchester are keen to get him back. I think we'll let them have him.'

OWEN FOX HAD completed the first course of stones and had begun sliding the big throughs back into the wall. The throughs would hold the whole structure firmly together. With these and the topping stones in place, the wall would stand for another hundred years or so.

'Why would a man do that? Attack all those women?' asked Mark Roper. 'What would he be thinking of?'

Owen didn't pause in his work. 'I don't suppose thinking came into it,' he said.

'What then?'

'I think it would be a physical thing. An instinct that the mind has no control over.'

Mark considered this, and nodded. 'I know what you mean.'

It seemed to Mark Roper that Owen was like a stone wall himself, solid and reliable, calm and controlled. He never raised his voice. But then, Mark's father had never raised his voice, either. He had never smacked, or even criticized – not that Mark could remember. Instead, he had joked all the time, and talked about all sorts of subjects. His father had loved to make things. He collected useful bits of wood which he would never get round to doing anything with. He used to drive his mother mad by stopping the car to pick up a broken piece of pipe or a sheet of corrugated Perspex from the side of the road, or a wooden crate fallen from a lorry.

But his temper had changed after Rick had died. And Mark's parents had drifted apart instead of supporting each other, until his father had moved out. And then there had been the new man.

Mark could see the stones in the completed length of wall were bonded like brickwork, laid across the joints in the course below. Every stone touched all its neighbours, allowing no room for movement. They were wedged in tight, each with its own role and no possibility of shifting without a danger of bringing down the entire structure. In this part of the world, there were whole villages made like that, thought Mark – not just the houses, but the people too. You weren't allowed to wander out of line. There was no room for movement, no shifting from your allotted role. Wedged in tight.

Clumsily, Mark tried to express this thought to Owen. The Area Ranger listened to him for a few moments, then rubbed a hand through his beard.

'You haven't come across a suicide yet, have you, Mark?' he said, as if picking up the thread of an entirely different conversation.

'No.'

'You will, in this job. I think suicides are the saddest deaths of all. It means someone has decided that life has no part for them to play any more.'

Mark knew what that meant. There were people who had tried to shift from their place in the wall, and whose foundations had collapsed. Mark tilted his head to listen more closely to what Owen was saying. It didn't sound reassuring. But he always learned things from Owen, and he had to listen in case he missed something.

'There's a spot where a lot of people go to do away with themselves,' said Owen. 'The car park at the top of the Eden Valley, where you can see Mam Tor. They call it Suicide Corner.'

'Yes, I know it,' said Mark.

'They always seem to go to that one spot. They park up in their cars to enjoy the view for one last time, then write their notes and drink their whisky and connect a hose up to the exhaust. Sometimes they use pills, sometimes a knife or razor blade across the wrists. Occasionally, they change their minds when they see what they've done, when the blood begins to flow and the pain they've only imagined becomes real.'

Mark nodded. But he wasn't sure if the Ranger was just talking generally, or whether he was communicating some personal message.

'There's a story about a student,' said Owen. 'I don't know if it's true or not. They say he drove from Suicide Corner to the hospital in Edendale with blood pouring from both his wrists where he had hacked his arteries open with a pair of dressmaker's scissors. The car was warm, and the blood flowed pretty well from the cuts he made before he panicked. It had run down his arms and on to his trouser legs, soaked into his lap and pooled on the rubber mat. They say the car looked like a slaughterhouse. But it's over five miles to drive into Edendale, and the student said afterwards that he had stopped at three red lights in the centre of town, waiting for the traffic to pass. By the time he arrived at Accident and Emergency, he was almost unconscious. He sat in the car outside the hospital entrance for ten minutes before an ambulance crew found him. His hands were glued to the steering wheel with congealed blood. The nurses had to prise him free.'

'It isn't right,' said Mark. But he didn't think Owen had heard him. His eyes were on his hands, though they were hidden by his gloves. He rubbed the palms together, as if irritated by some persistent itch.

'On balance,' said Owen, 'I think carbon monoxide is probably the best. It takes only a few minutes. I've seen men still sitting in the driving seats of their cars after the exhaust has done its job. They seem just to have fallen asleep. A paramedic once told me that your blood turns cherry-red from the carbon monoxide, when it works properly,' said Owen. 'Your brain swells, and so does your liver and kidneys and spleen. Even the tiny blood vessels in your eyes haemorrhage. But that's internal damage, the things you can't see. At Suicide Corner, you always think they're asleep at first. Until you notice the smell of the urine soaked into the cloth of the driving seat.'

Mark shifted his feet uneasily. Now he wanted Owen to stop talking.

'This paramedic said the carbon monoxide replaces the oxygen in your blood,' said Owen. 'You die of oxygen starvation, a sort of internal suffocation. You can't smell or taste or see the gas; all that happens is that you begin to feel drowsy. You get a slight headache and a shortness of breath. Then your movements slow down, there's some nausea and chest pain, perhaps a few hallucinations. We've all had hangovers worse than that. But this is the sort of hangover you don't wake up from.'

'Owen –'

'You wouldn't believe the mistakes that some of them make, though. They don't seem to plan their own deaths properly. They come with lengths of hosepipe that are too short to reach through the car window. Or they arrive with nothing to seal the gap where they have to lower the window to get the pipe through. At Suicide Corner, they can sit for a long time with the wind howling through the gap in the window and blowing away the carbon monoxide as fast as it trickles into the car.'

Mark thought for a moment of the woman, Jenny Weston, who had died with her own blood choking her heart. Her death had been sudden; she had been given no time to consider, no time to reflect on what she had done with her life, for good or for evil.

'None of it is right,' said Mark. At least Owen lifted his head now and met his eye. Owen's face looked tired and drawn. The wind up here was making his eyes water. There was rain coming from the east – fat clouds were bouncing over the hills, and all the weight seemed to be in the sky.

'Owen ...'

'Yes, they seem just to have fallen asleep,' said Owen. 'But it's not a sleep that has any comfort in it. Only nightmares.'

Mark peered at his face, seeking to understand more clearly what he was hearing in the Ranger's words.

'We'll not let that happen, Owen,' he said.

Owen just stared at him. And then he said something that made Mark wonder whether he had understood any of it at all.

'Let me tell you, Mark,' he said. 'It's always your body that lets you down, in the end.'

Chapter Twenty-Six

DIANE FRY STRAPPED on the scabbard for her extendable baton. Police officers called the baton an ASP, after the name of the manufacturer, Armament Systems and Procedures of Wisconsin, USA. It extended to sixteen inches when fully racked, and the handbook claimed it offered unparalleled psychological deterrence. Even closed, it consisted of six inches of heavy-duty steel. Most CID officers simply carried the weapon in their pocket, but on Fry's build the bulge of the closed ASP was still noticeable. So she had bought a back pocket scabbard with a Velcro flap which stopped the baton falling out when she ran. On the other hip was the holder for her kwik-cuffs. When she put on her jacket, their outline was barely visible.

She considered her protective vest. But it was heavy and uncomfortable to wear for any length of time, and it gave her pains in the muscles in her back. She put it back in her locker.

Ben Cooper had said that they were supposed to protect people like Calvin Lawrence and Simon Bevington. But it was difficult for Fry to understand why. The two travellers weren't part of the society that she served; they paid no taxes to help meet her wages. They were never likely to become members of the police liaison committee. Still, there was something about them that she didn't understand, all the same. Against her own judgement, she was curious what it was that Cooper saw in them. His mind was a puzzle and frustration to her – she never understood what perverse instinct it was that made him believe so strongly in things that she couldn't even see. Yet the need to understand him was like an irritating itch on her skin, a rash that she had to scratch. In this case, he was way off target. Lawrence and Bevington were on the wrong side of the law. Well, they *were* – weren't they?

WHEN SHE ARRIVED at the quarry, Fry found a bored constable sitting in his car with half an ear on the radio, a chocolate bar in his mouth and his eyes on a fishing magazine. The windows of his car were streaked with rain on the outside, and steamed up on the inside.

'Anything happening?'

'Nope. Quiet as the grave,' he said.

'What's your name?'

'Taylor.'

The rain was getting heavier as Fry banged on the door of the van. The curtain behind the cab was pulled aside and light spilled out on to her face. Then the door slid open, and Cal stood on the step.

'What do you want?'

'Just a few words.'

'Oh, yeah?'

'There's something I want to know. I thought you and your friend might be able to help me.'

Cal eyed her suspiciously. 'Leave us alone. We'll be out of here by Monday morning. What's the point of hassling us now?'

'No hassle. Just a question.'

'One question? OK, go ahead.'

Fry turned her jacket collar up against the water trickling on to her neck. 'It's wet out here,' she said.

'Yeah. It's the rain that does it.'

'Can I come in?'

'Is that the question? 'Cos the answer's "no".'

'I can't hear you, because of the rain in my ears.'

A voice came from inside the van, lazy and amused. 'Hey, let her in, Cal. She sounds fun.'

Cal hesitated, but pulled open the door. Inside the van, Fry squeezed into a space next to the chest of drawers, sitting on a cushion that smelled of Indian spices. Stride watched her through the blonde hair that had fallen over his face. He smiled, like an Arab prince welcoming her to his tent.

'Our last visitor. I hope you bring us luck.'

'Yes, they'll have you out of this quarry tomorrow.'

'We know.'

'If it were me, I'd be glad to leave. There's nothing here. What sort of life can it be?'

'You want to know what we do all day? Is *that* the question?'

'Not really.'

'We talk. We think about things. You could try it. It doesn't hurt.'

'You're young. You should be out in the world enjoying life,' said Fry. 'This place is so empty and bleak.'

'No. All you see is a landscape of rocks and heather,' said Stride. 'But the moor is a living thing. It has moods; it has desires.' He grinned at Fry, and his voice hushed. 'It has *secrets*.'

'Stride's right,' said Cal. 'The moor was here long before us. The Fiddler will still be playing long after we've gone.'

'The who?'

'The Fiddler. Don't you know the story?'

'I've no idea what you're talking about.'

'Have you seen the stones?' said Stride. 'Don't you know what they are? Nine virgins, turned to stone for dancing on a Sunday. Punished for their sin. They desecrated the Sabbath with their dancing. But that single stone, outside the circle ... They say that's the Fiddler, who played the tune for the dancers. He was turned to stone, too. But he wasn't dancing. Do you think the Fiddler got justice?'

'What nonsense.'

'Is it? Don't underestimate the power of nature. The spirits don't forget.'

Fry was concentrating on the manner of the two travellers as much as on their words. She already knew she was never going to be able to ask the right questions, no matter how long she stayed here. There was something rehearsed about their performance that only reinforced her scepticism.

'But what do you *believe* in?' she said, voicing the real question that was on her mind.

'Stride talks to the Fiddler at nights, sometimes,' said Cal. 'He tells him about things like that. The Fiddler knows the truth.'

'The truth? And what truth is it you're looking for?'

Stride only smiled. The smile became wider, and turned into a laugh that filled the van. He leaned forward, and laid a hand on Fry's knee. She flinched, but was unable to pull back from his touch in the confined space. Stride's hand lay still and steady, as if he were trying to calm her thoughts, to transfer some of his own contentment by direct contact.

'How can you know the truth until you find it?' he said.

For a moment he stared directly into her eyes, as if seeking a shred of understanding, willing her to share a bit of enlightenment. But she kept her face expressionless, resisting. Even Stride finally realized the futility, repulsed by the rigidity of her muscles beneath his hand.

Then Cal stepped in. 'Stride believes there may be a vengeful spirit of the moors, driving intruders away.'

'And what the hell does that mean?' said Fry angrily.

Cal didn't even seem to have heard. He looked at Stride, who was still staring at Fry and seemed to be attempting to drive his thoughts into her head by willpower.

'Well, if you find this vengeful spirit has a physical body and a face, let us know,' she said.

Stride looked unperturbed. 'It's the Fiddler himself,' he said. 'It's obvious, isn't it? It's the Fiddler who makes the women dance.'

BEN COOPER TURNED right at the Fina petrol station and dropped the Toyota down a gear to go up the steep street. He wasn't familiar with this estate on the southern edge of Edendale. It was a fairly recent one, with cheap housing built to provide somewhere that local people could afford to live without having to move out of town. The houses were small stone semis, with narrow alleyways and car ports.

The homes on Calver Crescent looked like all the others, and the only thing that distinguished number 17 was a slightly neglected air. The paintwork on the front door was starting to peel, and part of the car port's Perspex roof had come loose and split, leaving a gap plugged by a sheet of polythene that flapped and rattled in the rain.

Mark Roper was waiting outside, under the light of a bare bulb. He ran down the short drive and climbed into Cooper's car. He was wearing jeans and a denim jacket, and Cooper hardly recognized him.

'Can we go somewhere?' asked Mark.

'Sure. Anywhere in particular? A pub?'

'No, somewhere quiet, where we can talk. I'll show you where.'

'OK.'

Mark told him to drive westwards out of Edendale until they left the street lamps behind and there was only the reflection of the Toyota's headlights from the Catseyes in the road and from the rain that drifted across the bonnet. Two miles out of town they turned and headed uphill until they were rising through the dark, dripping fringes of Eden Forest. They saw few cars on the road and passed even fewer houses – just the occasional farmstead wrapped in its own little bowl of protective light.

'Where are we going?' asked Cooper.

'Not far now.'

After a few more minutes, Mark directed him off the road. Cooper found they were in a gravel car park with litter bins and a map in a glass case pointing out the major features of the view that must lie somewhere out there in the darkness. He turned the Toyota round so that it was pointing back towards the road.

'Well?'

Mark hesitated. Cooper knew better than to try to push him. It was better to let him take his time, now that they had come all this way. Gradually, his eyes started adjusting to the darkness. There were faint strings of light floating in mid-air in front of him, marking a hamlet or a village on a hillside across the valley. Then the hills themselves began to come into focus, black humps against the sky. Directly ahead, he had the sensation of a steep drop into a vast hole in the darkness.

Eventually, Mark felt the moment was right.

'You know I told you this morning about something going on at Ringham Edge Farm.'

'The big shed,' said Cooper. 'Vehicles arriving at night.'

'That's right.'

'We haven't had a chance to look into it, Mark. We've all had a lot of other things on our minds. You'll just have to wait. Give us time.'

'I know, I know.'

'It will probably turn out to be nothing, anyway.'

Mark chewed his lip. The rain was beginning to obscure the Toyota's windscreen. Cooper turned on the wipers to clear it, so that they could see the car park. There were no other vehicles, not even passing on the road. He almost turned the ignition on to drive back to Edendale, disappointed in what Mark had brought him out here to say. But something held him back.

'There's more to it than that,' said Mark. 'Things I haven't told you.'

Suddenly, Cooper felt that old surge of excitement rising through his chest, leaving him short of breath. 'Mark? What are you talking about?'

'Dogs,' said Mark.

'What?'

'I think it might be dog-fighting.'

'You're joking. Does that still go on?'

'Oh, dog-fights take place every week, somewhere. And it's on the increase. The RSPCA have made a few prosecutions, and a few fights are broken up now and again. The thing that's most difficult for these people to find is a safe venue. There's money in dog-fighting – a lot of cash changes hands in bets on the dogs. Just by renting his shed and keeping his mouth shut, Leach could have been doing quite well out of it, whether he joined in or not. The winning dogs are worth something, too. But the losers – sometimes the losers just die from their injuries.'

'How do you know about this sort of thing, Mark?'

'There's a Rangers' liaison group with the RSPCA. They showed us a video once that had been seized by their Special Operations Unit. It was sickening. These people film the fights so that they can show off the success of their dogs to buyers, you see. This one had been filmed in the attic of a house somewhere, with armchairs and an awful blue carpet and a colour TV in the corner. They normally use pit bull terriers. Those things are bred for fighting, and nothing else.'

'It's illegal to breed pit bulls,' said Cooper. 'Since the Dangerous Dogs Act, they all have to be neutered. The breed should be dying out by now.'

'Oh, sure. And is cancer dying out, too? How much time have your people got to go round the Devonshire Estate checking whether anybody's breeding pit bulls in the kitchen or out the back in the garden shed?'

'Not a lot.'

'And the police in Sheffield and Manchester have even less time, I suppose.'

'So you think they're using Ringham Edge for dog-fights? Are these local people involved?'

'They come from all over the place. A lot from the Manchester area, I think. If Warren Leach has a dog-fighting pit in there, he'll be mixing with some pretty unpleasant people. And they won't take kindly to anyone sticking their nose into what's going on.'

A Peak Park Ranger's Land Rover pulled into the car park for a few minutes. Mark looked at the driver, but didn't seem to recognize him. The thin red stripe on the silver side of the vehicle could have been a streak of drying blood, caught in Cooper's headlights.

'It was the captive bolt pistol that made me think I was right,' said Mark.

'What do you mean?'

'The point is, those dogs will fight and fight until they're half-dead. You can't take them to a vet, because – like you say – they're illegal. And you don't put an animal like that out of its misery by wringing its neck. You need to have somebody there with a gun, or preferably a captive bolt pistol, if you can get hold of one. They're a lot safer than having a free bullet flying around inside a shed somewhere. Dangerous, that is.'

'I can see that.'

'Very dangerous,' said Mark. 'That way, somebody could get themselves killed.'

The Land Rover drove off again. Maybe the Ranger had just stopped to use his radio or to have a drink of tea from his flask. Maybe he was checking on the Toyota. Everybody was suspect these days. Cooper watched the vehicle's lights heading further west, following the tight bends until they disappeared into a dark band of conifers.

Out of the corner of his eye, he noticed a sudden flicker of movement, and saw a stoat run across in front of his bonnet into a clump of gorse.

'I know this spot,' he said. 'It's the place they call Suicide Corner.'

'That's right. It's where all the suicides come.' Mark pointed up the valley towards Castleton and Mam Tor. 'Owen says the view sometimes makes them change their minds.'

The unstable slopes of Mam Tor looked like a melted chocolate cake in the darkness. Erosion of the soft shale underneath its gritstone bands meant that its sides were in continual movement, long cascades of stone sliding and slithering into the valley, where the landslips had closed the A625 many years before. Now cars struggled over Winnats Pass to where the River Eden and the River Hope sprang up on the bleak moorlands of the Dark Peak. The locals called Mam Tor the 'Shivering Mountain'. Its vast, soft outline dominated the head of the valley. And on the very summit, the defensive ramparts of a Bronze Age hillfort could clearly be seen against the sky, even from this distance.

'I don't want to see Owen here,' said Mark. 'He might not change his mind.'

'Mark ...?'

'I think Owen's involved. He must be.'

'But why?'

'He's worked in that area a long time. He must have noticed what I noticed. But he's never said anything to me about it. He always talks about Warren Leach as if they hate each other, but I'm not sure about that.'

'There seemed to be no love lost between them when I was there,' said Cooper.

'I know. But I'm almost certain that Owen goes down to the farm on his own sometimes, when he should be somewhere else. I think that might have been where he was when I found the woman on Ringham Moor. It was the TIP that made contact with him in the end, you know. I couldn't get through to him. I think he was away from his radio.'

'I can't see it. Not Owen.'

Mark looked at him. 'I knew you wouldn't believe me. You want to defend him, like everyone else. You think Owen's a good bloke. They all say that – Owen Fox is a good bloke. Well, he is. But I think he's got mixed up in something he shouldn't have done, and now he's frightened and he can't see any way out. I don't like the way he's been talking these last few days. He *is* a good bloke. And he's done a lot for me. I want to save him.'

'And how exactly are you going to do that?' asked Cooper.

The young Ranger wound the window down a few inches, just enough to let the cool wind in and blow away the fug they had built up in the car.

'I want you to arrest him,' said Mark, 'before he ends up here. I want you to keep Owen away from Suicide Corner.'

DIANE FRY JUMPED up from the cushion, banging her head on the metal roof as a burst of flame lit up the quarry. A small explosion rocked the van and the blast echoed backwards and forwards off the rock walls.

'What the hell was that?'

She pulled the sheet aside to look through the cab. Black smoke poured into the sky, and the air was filled with an acrid smell and the sound of sizzling, like a huge barbecue. The blaze was clearly petrol-assisted, and it flared dramatically for a few moments before dying to a hiss.

In the light from the flames, she saw something begin to creep over the quarry edge. Whatever it was, it slid in a slow liquid movement. Fry turned on her torch and shone it through the windscreen. She saw a series of small rivulets running free, breaking apart, then slowing and congealing, until they had stopped, frozen on the rock. More rivulets followed, their bright colours twisting and mingling until the quarry face looked like psychedelic curtains picked out by the light of her torch. She remembered the phallus farm that Cal and Stride had created on the cliff edge, and she realized that she was seeing the multi-coloured wax melting in the flames.

'I've never seen anything like it.'

There was a thump on the back of the van, and the vehicle jerked as if it had been hit by a heavy object.

'Oh Jesus,' said Cal.

Stride folded his head into his arms and began to mutter unintelligibly, repeating a phrase over and over again.

Fry peered cautiously out through the windows of the cab, but could see nothing in the surrounding darkness.

She went to the door and pulled it open a few inches. A cold gust of rain blew in. All she could see through the blackness was the faint glow of the interior light in the patrol car, where PC Taylor was reading about skimmers and wagglers, or more likely had fallen fast asleep and was only now wondering what on earth had woken him up.

In a narrow path between the van and the car, Fry could see the rain hurtling past. The ground was glistening alarmingly as the sand began to turn to mud.

Then she saw vague shapes moving in the darkness.

'Taylor!' she called. But she got no response.

'What's going on?' asked Cal from behind her.

'Stay in the van. Shut the door. Lock it.'

'It won't lock.'

'For God's sake.' She struggled desperately with the door as she felt it slip off its bottom runner and jam two feet short of the frame. 'Try to get it shut. Stay inside.'

'But –'

Fry stepped outside and was immediately drenched by the rain. She slid on the ground as she set off towards the patrol car.

'Taylor!'

The noise of the downpour in the quarry drowned her voice. She tried to set off at a run, but her feet slipped and slithered. She turned to look back at the van, and saw figures surrounding it. They were dark, shapeless forms – human, but only just. The van began to sway. Glass smashed as a window was shattered.

At last a beacon flashed as PC Taylor woke up to what was going on and revved the engine of his car at the incline. Near the top, his wheels began to spin in the mud, and the bonnet slid sideways towards the drop, its headlights swaying drunkenly across the quarry.

Then Fry found herself suddenly in the midst of a crowd. They gathered close around her, silent but for the sound of their breath and the damp rustling of their clothes. All she could see were their eyes.

'I'm a police officer. Stand clear.'

She was grabbed from behind and dragged further from the van. She felt a weight on her back, and arms clutched round her chest. She was aware of the other figures all around her, none of them speaking. Fry struck backwards with her right hand to grasp her assailant's testicles, and missed. Twisting, she found herself facing him, though barely a glint of the white of an eye was visible through the holes in the mask he wore. She hesitated as she felt a *frisson* of familiarity.

And that hesitation was her mistake. Pain shot through her leg as a blow landed on her right knee. Her leg gave way and she slid to the ground, still hanging on to the man's coat. Then she saw something swinging towards her again from the side, a shape like a baseball bat. She put her hand out to ward it off as she threw herself to one side, gasping from the agony in her leg.

Fry rolled over in the mud, glimpsing feet around her and covering her head in anticipation of boots coming in. She fetched up hard against a rock and pushed herself into a crouch ready to jump up, but realized that her leg was not going to support her. Only one dark figure still stood in front of her, watching her for a moment, before it turned and ran off to join the others around the van.

Now the noises came to her through the night. She could hear the van being trashed. She could hear other sounds, too. Shouts and curses, and thumps.

Taylor had switched on the siren in his stranded patrol car. But the noise didn't help at all when the scream came. It was so high-pitched that it ought to have been female. But Fry knew that it wasn't.

Chapter Twenty-Seven

'THERE HAS TO be *something* in the damn computer, Stewart,' said Chief Superintendent Jepson. 'That's what it's there for, to come up with the right answers. You've got a multi-million pound guaranteed *Mastermind* winner. All you need is Bamber Gascoigne to ask it the right questions.'

Normally, Jepson loved to be kept up to date on the progress of a major enquiry. It made him feel involved, instead of just a man sitting in an office with a lot of brass on his uniform. And sometimes Tailby found that talking a case through with him could put it in a different light. But not this morning. This Sunday morning there was no light to be found of any kind, not even from a phallus-shaped candle. The reports of the incident in the quarry the night before made painful and depressing reading. Three people had been injured, one of them a police officer. And the perpetrators had come and gone like a flurry of dead leaves in the wind, vanishing back on to the moor before PC Taylor could dig himself out of the mud.

'Bamber Gascoigne was never on *Mastermind*,' said Tailby wearily. 'In fact, *Mastermind* hasn't been on TV for years.'

'So? Pick some other quiz. It doesn't matter.'

'These days contestants get to phone a friend or ask the audience.'

'Well, we can't ask *our* audience,' said Jepson. 'If we admit that we know sod all, they'd be down on us like vultures.'

'And we haven't got any friends either, have we?'

Jepson sighed deeply. 'That's true.'

Tailby stared at the files on Jenny Weston and Maggie Crew. He didn't need to read them again. He knew them practically by heart. But he turned over the pages anyway.

In the Weston file was the report from the officer who had first responded to the call from the Rangers. The call had come from the Rangers' TIP at Bradwell, not directly from Mark Roper, nor from Owen Fox at the Ranger centre at Partridge Cross. Maybe this was standard procedure – it was worth checking. There was a detailed witness statement from Roper himself, as well as further statements from the cycle hire centre manager, Don Marsden, and the farmworker, Victor McCauley, who seemed to have been the last people to see Jenny Weston alive. No one had come forward to say they had seen her once she had reached the moor.

The vast amount of forensic material that had been collected was confusing rather than helpful. Even Jenny's pants and cycling shorts, found in the quarry by a SOCO who had been lowered down the rock face, had yielded no positive traces. The only item still missing was the pouch she had normally worn round her waist when cycling.

'The injury to Bevington suggests punishment for a sexual assault,' said Jepson. 'But there was no such assault on Jenny Weston.'

'There was no evidence of sexual intercourse, no body fluids or traces of DNA. But the profilers talk about a "disorganized" killer, and for that type the killing is a sexual act in itself. On the evidence, the profile was definitely that of the disorganized type, with a sudden attack, and no attempt being made to hide the body – on the contrary, it seems to have been put out on display. That might also explain the stripping of the lower half of the body. A symbolic sex act.'

'That's rather academic for the average vigilante to figure out, Stewart.'

Tailby sighed. 'I know.'

'Bevington does have a history, though. Can he be linked to Weston?'

'It must have been Bevington who wrote his name on the ground in the stone circle. But that could have been days earlier. It means nothing.'

'And what about Ros Daniels?'

'Oh, she's long gone from the area. That kind of person – she could be anywhere. Using a different name by now, probably.'

'Do you think so?'

'Certainly,' said Tailby. 'Remember, the last time she was seen anywhere in the area was six weeks before Jenny Weston was killed.'

'Yet an unknown man was seen hanging around Weston's house and workplace. Someone made a phone call to her, claiming to be a police officer.'

'We've ruled out the ex-husband, Martin Stafford. All the old boyfriends in Jenny's address book have been eliminated. If there was a more recent one, she didn't bother to put his number in the book. It would have been unlike her, though. She was well organized in other ways. And there's the note we took from her house. "Buy some fruit-flavoured ones," it said. That had to be a boyfriend, surely.'

'Perhaps the man the neighbours saw wasn't looking for Jenny Weston, but for Ros Daniels,' said Jepson. 'She had already disappeared by then.'

'Whoever the killer was, he was very audacious,' said Tailby. 'And very lucky.'

There had been a number of public appeals during the past week. But no one had come forward to say they had seen a man on the moor at the right time.

'We have a partial footprint and a smear of sweat on the bike frame. We have the shape of a knife blade. But it's really nothing at all. Nothing – without evidence to place a suspect at the scene.'

Tailby paused, as if unsure how his next statement would be received. Jepson noticed the hesitation and fixed the DCI with his sharp blue eyes.

'Yes, Stewart? What are you going to say? Is it something I don't want to hear?'

'Could be.'

Jepson sighed again. 'I didn't really think things could be worse. But go on.'

'If you don't mind,' said Tailby, 'I'd like to wait for Paul Hitchens and Diane Fry to join us at this stage.'

DIANE FRY LIMPED up the stairs towards the incident room. Earlier, she had been writing up her report on the attack on Calvin Lawrence and Simon Bevington the previous night, and her mind was still full of images from the moments immediately after the mob had scattered in the quarry. She saw the scene that PC Taylor's headlights had illuminated. She saw the rain glittering like knives in the twin beams; she saw the bright, jagged holes in the windows of the VW van, and the walls of the quarry black outside the range of the lights. And she saw Stride sprawled half-naked in the mud on his face, with the broom handle still bloodily protruding, his body writhing like a worm cut into pieces.

She had been finding the task of reliving the night's events painful and humiliating. She was in physical pain, too, from the bruises on her leg. But she wasn't about to make that an excuse for anything. And then she had to run into Ben Cooper hovering near the top of the stairs. He was the last person she wanted to see; it was entirely because of Cooper and his stupid ideas that she had been in the quarry in the first place, listening to the ravings of those two travellers. But she couldn't avoid him. He moved straight in on her, thrusting himself into her personal space.

'You did your best, Diane,' he said, with that infuriating habit of reading her mind.

'Oh, sure I did.'

She turned away from him too suddenly. Her injured knee gave way and her foot slid off a step. Cooper grabbed her jacket to stop her falling back down the stairs and yanked her towards him. Fry found herself nose to nose with him. She felt his breath on her face and saw his eyes, big and brown and concerned, like the eyes of one of Warren Leach's Jersey cows.

'What the hell do you think you're doing, Cooper? Get your hands off me.'

'Look, I know how you feel,' he said.

'No, you bloody don't.'

'Diane – even you couldn't fight them all.'

'They neutralized me in seconds,' she said. 'I hardly tried.'

Fry kept remembering that she hadn't even drawn her ASP. It had been in her scabbard, readily to hand. But she had not used it.

Cooper held on to her for a moment longer than he needed to, steadying her with a hand on her back. She could feel his fingers against her spine through the cloth. He was pressing gently but insistently on her vertebrae, triggering a small nerve that sent sensations running down into her abdomen. For a second, it even seemed to ease the pain in her leg.

Then Fry yanked herself free and straightened her jacket. 'Isn't this supposed to be your rest day?'

'Yes.'

'Then what the hell are you doing in the station? Haven't you got anything better to do?'

She watched Cooper's face crumple and the flush start to creep up his neck. He was the only detective she knew who blushed when he was spoken to sharply.

'As a matter of fact, I have,' said Cooper.

'Enjoy your day then. I've got a meeting with Mr Tailby and the Super.'

CHIEF SUPERINTENDENT JEPSON laid his hands flat on the desk and looked from one officer to the other. 'OK, who's going to start? Put me out of my misery. Let me know what this is all about.'

As Diane Fry expected, it was DI Hitchens who took the bull by the horns.

'Chief, in the Weston case, the fact is that there is only one person we can place anywhere near the scene at the time.'

'Ah, the old story,' said Jepson. 'The first person that comes under suspicion is always the finder. Is that it?'

Diane Fry leaned forward. 'Mark Roper,' she said. 'But he *was* there.'

Fry felt her superiors watching her closely. The pain in her leg drove her on like a spur.

'He had plenty of time to kill Jenny Weston and do whatever he wanted to do before he reported that he had found her body. And he had scouted the area first, quite legitimately, so he had no worries about being observed.'

'Obviously,' said Jepson. 'But what would his motive be?'

'Well, there's nothing obvious that we can see,' admitted Fry. 'But we've had some discreet enquiries made into his family background.'

Jepson raised an eyebrow. 'Have we indeed?' He looked at Hitchens, then at Tailby, but Fry was determined to keep his attention.

'Three years ago, Mark's older brother died and his father went off the rails. He started drinking and became depressed and lost his job. Frank Roper eventually walked out of the family home when he found out that his wife was having an affair. According to the neighbours, he hasn't been seen in the area since. Mrs Roper promptly moved the boyfriend into the house, and Mark still lives with them. But he was very close to his father.'

'This is a story no different from a thousand others, Fry. What are you trying to tell me? That Mark Roper has a grudge against women?'

'We've heard much more incredible motives,' put in Hitchens. 'But this is simply background on Roper for now.'

'OK. Weapon, then? What would he have done with the knife?'

Fry shook her head. 'We don't know. But he's very friendly with the other Ranger, Owen Fox. He's got a bit of a surrogate father there, from all accounts. Fox could be covering up for him. They could have concocted their story together.'

The Chief Superintendent was looking more and more unhappy. 'We have an excellent relationship with the Ranger Service. Excellent.'

'I don't like it myself,' said Tailby. 'But we can't ignore it. We need to look at elimination.'

'All right, all right,' said Jepson. 'Could Roper have been the man Jenny Weston's neighbours reported? How would he know where she lived?'

'Oh, that's the easy part,' said Fry. 'Weston's details are recorded in the book at the cycle hire centre. The Rangers are in and out of there all the time. Either one of them would have had no trouble getting her address.'

'All right.'

'Not to mention the correlations the computer has thrown up. If it was anyone else –'

'Yes, I know.'

'If we could show some inconsistencies in the stories of the two Rangers, it could be just the opening we need.'

Jepson said gently: 'Don't you think you're getting a bit carried away here, Fry? What about Maggie Crew? Are you forgetting her? Besides, the Rangers have been helping us. Suddenly you're suggesting they're public enemy number one.'

'But Roper *was* there. If only there was something ...'

'Stewart, have you spoken to Alistair Prince recently?'

'Yes, sir,' said Tailby. 'He suggested a re-enactment.'

'But there was nobody there. You have no witnesses. The place was deserted.'

'Superintendent Prince says it works very well in central Derby.'

Jepson chewed his lip. 'So that's it. You think we're going to have to admit defeat on this one otherwise, Stewart?'

'To be honest, I'm not very hopeful, sir. We thought we had a stroke of luck with Darren Howsley. But that was a poisoned chalice.'

Jepson folded his fingers together and stared at the ceiling for a while. The others waited expectantly. Fry knew only too well that what they were suggesting was a difficult thing, a politically sensitive issue. 'Somebody had better talk to DI Armstrong, then,' said Jepson.

Fry blinked and looked at Hitchens, who shrugged. It wasn't what *he* had expected either.

'Why?' he said. 'Kim Armstrong is engaged on the paedophile enquiry. They're about ready to make some arrests, aren't they?'

While they waited for more, the Chief Superintendent tapped his pen on the desk and looked at the broken end of it sadly, like a man contemplating something particularly unpleasant.

'Go and talk to her,' he said. 'And tell her I said it's a need-to-know situation.'

Ben Cooper particularly liked the narrow lanes and arcades in the oldest part of Edendale, between Eyre Street and Market Square. There were shops that sold decorated wooden elephants and pencil boxes, pine furniture, chocolates and malt whisky; there was an Italian restaurant and several coffee shops. And halfway up Nick i'th Tor, the steep alley off Market Square, was the window of Larkin's, a traditional bakery. During the day the window was full of pastries and cheeses – apricot white stilton, homity pies, pasties, and enormous high-baked pork pies. Cooper came down to Larkin's as often as he could at lunchtimes if he was in town. He was happy to queue with the tourists and listen to the assistants explaining one more time that Bakewell tarts should be called Bakewell puddings.

But today the window of Larkin's was completely empty. It might as well have been selling picture frames, like the shop next door. All the shops here had been cleaned and painted up, and the stone setts had been relaid into the footpaths, while new arcades had been created in what had once been warehouse yards. Now the coffee shops sold exotic coffees – Jamaican Blue Mountain, Monsoon Malabar Mysore and Yemeni Mocha Ismaili.

In the Market Square itself was Ferris's, a butcher's that was also a licensed game seller. Normally, a few brace of pheasant dangled their tails in front of the window, their necks stretched and tied with string. Often there would be a pair of pigeons or a mountain hare. Tourists had been known to take exception to this – to burst into the shop with allegations of animal cruelty and obscenity.

Ben Cooper had seized the chance of his leave day to take Helen Milner for lunch. Helen had been quiet during the meal. She was concerned about the progress his mother was making, and she always asked about Matt and Kate and the girls. But he couldn't help being aware that she was interested in almost everything except him. She didn't ask what he was doing at work at the moment. She didn't want to know. Not today.

Cooper sat through lunch hardly eating. He watched Helen's hair as she talked, remembering when he had been enchanted by the coppery sheen of it in the summer sun and had begun to hope that its glow symbolized a bit of light entering his life. It had been just when he needed it, too, when everything else had seemed to be going wrong – when his mother's descent into schizophrenia had seemed unstoppable, and when Diane Fry had appeared on the scene to complicate his life like a tangle of briars that he couldn't shake off. Helen had seemed to be the answer to all that.

But now August seemed a long way off. The leaves of the trees in the Eden Forest had taken on the colours of copper and gold, and the yellow of sunlight, too. And then they had died.

AFTER LUNCH, THEY walked towards the river. In the side streets, the houses huddled together, like little groups of people gossiping. They stared into each other's windows, and knew each other's business. On the paved steps that ran down to the River Eden the rain had brought out all the colours in the Yorkshire stone, the browns and reds and greens. The steps were uneven, and some of them were slippery with wet leaves. At the bottom, leaves had collected in a drain, and dirty water had flooded the path.

Helen had been talking about school, telling Cooper about the children in her class. Cooper had been content to listen to her talk. He had come intending to make amends for standing her up at the rugby club the previous Sunday. He knew he had been neglecting her. Yet the lack of necessity for a response allowed his thoughts to drift occasionally. His mind kept returning to the reports of the attack on Cal and Stride in the quarry the previous night. The details had been shocking in themselves; but his imagination was able to provide much worse. Cal and Stride were the typical victims – a pair of innocents who had found themselves in the wrong place at the wrong time. He had seen what they were, and he had been unable to do anything to protect them.

And now Cooper had something else on his mind. He had to decide what to do about Mark Roper and Owen Fox. Mark's suspicions were insubstantial, yet Cooper would have to report them. Perversely, he felt he would have liked to be able to discuss the subject with Diane Fry. He would also have liked to have been part of the team that was trying to identify the vigilante group which had attacked her. They had the reports from Fry and PC Taylor, and Cal and Stride themselves were being interviewed. But the scene was a mess – the rain had left it a quagmire. An assault on a police officer had to be treated seriously, but all that had been achieved so far was to spread the division's resources even thinner. It was enough to make Cooper feel guilty about taking time off. But there was no more money in the budget for overtime.

Helen dipped into her shoulder bag and produced a packet of photos. Cooper looked at them, puzzled.

'The pictures of the children,' she said.

'Oh, right.'

On Sundays, the riverside was always busy with families feeding the ducks. From the river walk, the water seemed to be full of movement. Mallards and coot clustered anxiously round the bankside, darting for the tidbits. Flocks of black-headed gulls wheeled and screamed over the surface, landing and taking off again, noisy and bad-tempered.

They sat down on a bench next to an elderly couple. The photos were all badly composed and had a strange cast over them, a combination of artificial light and direct flash.

'This is my little favourite, Carly,' said Helen, pointing to a little girl of about six, with fair hair cut raggedly across her forehead and a selection of teeth and gaps like a half-demolished wall.

'She's really sweet. She likes to draw, and she insists on giving me her drawings as presents. Look at this.'

The picture she showed Cooper was crayoned with great care, but little subtlety. There were small children with stick arms and clothes of various colours, and there was a figure with a white beard and a red coat patting them on the head and offering them brightly coloured gifts. It was captioned 'Fathr Chistmass.'

'A bit early to be doing Christmas, aren't you? It's only just gone Bonfire Night.'

Helen laughed. 'Yes, they do get confused sometimes.'

But somehow it didn't look quite right. There was something wrong about Father Christmas's costume. He looked like one of those cut-price Santas in the shops in Edendale at Christmas, with home-made suits and cotton-wool beards that never fit. Most of them would scare the kids to death, if they got too close. But these days, there was no touching allowed, not even by Santa. No 'come and sit on my knee, little girl.'

Cooper thought of Warren Leach's boys, their air of guarded distance, an instinctive wariness of strangers. There had seemed little innocence about the Leach place. He wondered what the two boys had seen or experienced in their lives that made them nervous of visitors.

He looked again at the drawing in his hands. It wasn't the red jacket that made it look wrong. It was the trousers. Every child knew that Santa's trousers were red, the same as his jacket. But Carly had changed crayons halfway through drawing her picture of Father Christmas and his presents. She had selected her new colour carefully – and it wasn't a colour that a child of six would normally choose. It wasn't bright or dramatic enough; it was too dull and adult somehow.

Yes, everyone knew Santas were dressed all in red. But this Santa had grey trousers.

THE HOUSE WAS set deep into the hillside, below the level of the road. Its front door was at the foot of a steep, narrow flight of stone steps lined with wooden tubs and pots of wilted sweet peas, enclosed by a well of sheer walls and blocked-up windows. The remains of dead plants trailed down to the door, leaving patches of dark mould and slime on the steps, treacherous patches that would send an unwary postman hurtling to the bottom. Yet on the window ledge of the room above the road there was a single pelargonium in bloom, its red flowers gleaming against the grey curtain.

When Owen Fox answered the door, he appeared to be standing at the bottom of a deep hole. He looked as though he had been dozing; he was sleepy-eyed and half-dressed, and his beard and hair were tangled. When he saw Diane Fry standing on the steps above him, he pulled his dressing gown around his chest.

'Do you want some help?' he said. 'I suppose you need my local knowledge again?'

Owen began to ease the door closed behind him, trying to shut himself out on the step with the police, as if distancing himself from his own life. He looked faintly ridiculous in his T-shirt, dressing gown and slippers.

'Is it about Cal and Stride?' he said. 'Give me a minute, then I'll be with you. No problem.'

Then Owen looked up and saw DI Hitchens standing on the roadside, and he read something in his expression. He stared at Hitchens like a man contemplating the final ascent of Mount Everest and knowing he would never make it, because the effort was too great. Owen Fox had become a small man at the bottom of a dark pit. He stood out of the light, away from the world, desolate and alone. The sun that reached his pot plants fell short of crossing his doorstep.

'Don't bother shutting the door,' said Hitchens. 'We've got a search warrant.'

Chapter Twenty-Eight

'THAT WAS THE *river, this is the sea.*'

Ben Cooper turned up the volume on his stereo and opened the cover of his Waterboys CD. He was amazed to find it dated from 1985. In fact, most of the music he possessed was the stuff he had liked twelve or fifteen years ago as a teenager. Somehow, his tastes hadn't changed during the time since he had joined the police service – or maybe he just hadn't had time to discover any new kinds of music.

Cooper looked at his books. The copy of *Captain Corelli's Mandolin* he had been trying to read was written in 1994. It was about the most recent thing on his shelves, and somebody had given him that. Apart from the job, it seemed his time had been spent drinking beer with other police officers, taking part in individual sports or walking in the countryside. At least he had some friends outside the service. He made a mental note to get in touch with Oscar and Rakki. It had been months since they had gone anywhere together.

One of the CDs in the rack was of a concert by the Derbyshire Constabulary Choir, recorded six years ago. There was a photo of the choir on the cover, and on the back row with the tenors was Ben Cooper himself, then a uniformed PC. Cooper compared the picture with his reflection in the mirror in the wardrobe door. His hair was a bit shorter at the back now, his face a bit fuller. But he looked much the same, didn't he? So why did he feel so different inside? Was it the police service that had done that to him?

Suddenly, he felt weary. He replaced the CD and lay down on his bed, letting the sound of Mike Scott's voice roll over him. *'Once you were tethered, now you are free. That was the river, this is the sea.'*

Cooper had begun to drowse when there was a knock on the door and his sister-in-law Kate's voice called: 'Ben? Phone.'

He turned down the music and went out on to the landing, where there was a telephone extension.

'Yes?' he said.

'It's Diane Fry.'

'Oh.'

'Don't sound so disappointed. I'll try not to hog the phone line too long if you're expecting one of your girlfriends to ring.'

'Did you want something, Diane? As you pointed out before, it's my rest day.'

'Sorry, were you doing something important? I don't know why, but I pictured you sitting in your bedroom on your own like a sulky teenager, with some awful music turned up too loud.'

Cooper felt certain she could tell that he was going red, even at the other end of the line. 'If you've rung up just to take the piss, I'm going to put the phone down.'

'Oh well, I thought you might be interested in the news, that's all.'

'What news?'

'We've just pulled in your friend. Owen Fox.'

Cooper stared at the wallpaper. Its green swirls seemed to run together in a blur. He became aware of movements behind the door of his mother's room, faint sounds like the stirring of an animal emerging from its nest.

'You've got to be joking,' he said.

SHORTLY INTO THE meeting, DI Hitchens began to find himself on the defensive. He looked sideways at Tailby, as if wondering why the DCI had let him take the lead.

'Cooper, the fact is that HOLMES was already showing up a link,' said Hitchens.

'But that's just one of those things.'

'With only one correlation, it wouldn't be worth mentioning. But his name also came up in the earlier case. Look at this. There were plenty of vehicles seen in the area at the time Maggie Crew was attacked. But three witnesses reported seeing a silver Land Rover. Two of them were specific that it belonged to the Peak Park Ranger

Service. We checked with the PPRS and identified the vehicle. It was the one that Owen Fox drives.'

'It means nothing.'

'It couldn't be ignored when his name also cropped up in the paedophile enquiry.'

Ben Cooper had checked the action forms for the last few days. The allocator hadn't followed up the Owen Fox link from HOLMES. So he must have taken the same view – that it was just like a police officer's name cropping up more than once in an enquiry. It was inevitable; it meant nothing. Owen Fox was right there, on the spot, and he was bound to appear in the system.

'We had to bring him in,' repeated Hitchens. 'We have to let people see us doing something.'

'What about Roper?' asked Tailby.

'We'll have him here in a few minutes.'

'And have we let the Ranger Service know what's happening?' said Tailby.

'Of course. Fox is suspended from duty, as from this morning. They're arranging a solicitor for him.'

'That job is his life,' said Cooper.

'If the allegations are true, he's abused his position,' pointed out Diane Fry.

'Owen Fox and Mark Roper were in the area at the time Jenny Weston was killed,' said Tailby. 'They were *there*.'

'Fox knows the area better than anybody,' said Hitchens.

'Yes, everyone would expect to see him around. They might even be glad to see him. They would trust a Ranger, wouldn't they?' said Fry.

'And Jenny Weston was killed by someone who got close to her. We said from the start it was someone she knew or trusted.' Hitchens looked as though he felt he had made his point sufficiently. 'Fox has a suspended sentence for an assault on a woman ten years ago. If it hadn't been for his address turning up in the intelligence gathered by DI Armstrong's enquiry, his background would never have been checked out. It's unbelievable. The sort of thing that trips us up every time.'

'He's very highly regarded,' said Cooper. 'Very highly.'

'He's never been married,' said Hitchens. 'He's a loner.'

'He seems to get on well enough with his colleagues.'

'With other men, you mean.'

'For Christ's sake!'

'That's enough, Cooper,' said Tailby. 'Let's calm down.'

Cooper flushed. 'But Owen Fox …'

Tailby sighed. 'Yes, Cooper?'

'Well …' Cooper struggled for the words with the eyes of the DCI on him. 'It's just that I always thought … he's on our side, sir.'

But Cooper was remembering the drawing that Helen Milner had shown him, the one by little Carly. Fathr Chistmass. But a Father Christmas who had grey trousers.

Tailby looked at him with a mixture of contempt and bewilderment. 'On our side?' he said. 'Cooper, there's no such thing.'

Ben Cooper was seething as they walked back down the corridor.

'It's crap, Diane,' he said. 'It stinks. It's scapegoat time.'

'Oh God, here we go. Stand by for a lecture on righteousness.'

Cooper felt his face glowing red. His hands trembled in the way they always did when he felt that surge of anger and outrage. He knew his feelings had no place at all in the rigid procedures laid down by computer packages like HOLMES.

'It isn't right.'

'It doesn't suit *you*, obviously,' said Fry. 'Did you know about Fox's conviction for assault? No, of course you didn't. Well, face the facts, Ben. You chose the wrong friend again.'

'Not Owen Fox.'

'Have you got a better idea?'

Cooper stared at Fry, started to speak, but closed his mouth. He felt his face flushing even more.

'Ben,' she said, 'you look as guilty as hell. What are you up to?'

'I think all of you are wrong,' he said. 'This time you've picked the wrong scapegoat.'

OWEN FOX'S HOUSE was cluttered and warm. There was a stunning view out of the back window, casting light into the back rooms. But the rooms at the front of the house, below street-level, must have been permanently dark.

There were a couple of cats somewhere – black, elusive shapes that slunk out of the way when the police appeared. They darted in and out of a cat flap on the back door and peered malevolently through the windows from outside. Maybe they just wanted feeding, but it was a job they would have to delegate to the neighbours.

Between thick walls, the rooms were crammed with old furniture. A lot of the pieces might have been items Owen had inherited from his parents, or even his grandparents. They looked to be full of history, an integral part of their surroundings. A solid-fuel Raeburn stove stood in the kitchen, the plaster above it covered in a layer of red dust.

'It's weird,' said Hitchens. 'The computer looks really out of place.'

'Computer?'

'In there.'

The computer stood among heaps of books, with a used coffee mug on the mouse mat and Friday's *Buxton Advertiser* draped over the printer. One of the detectives working with DI Armstrong's team had arrived and booted it up. He already had a Microsoft Windows image on screen.

On a small shelf behind the desk there was a framed photograph of Owen. He was standing against the side of a Land Rover in his Ranger uniform. The photo was a few years old, but Owen's hair and beard were already grey.

'Apparently the kids call him Father Christmas,' said the detective cheerfully.

'So I'm told.'

'Plug the printer in for me, mate. I'm going to print some log files out.'

Cooper looked for the leads, found a whole tangle of them at the back of the table, and tried to trace the power and data leads for the printer.

'What's this one?'

'That's the phone connection.'

'I can't see a modem here.'

'It's an internal.'

'He's got access to the Internet?'

'Oh, yes,' said the detective. 'I can't wait to see what Santa's got on his hard drive.'

COOPER WENT UPSTAIRS to look at the bedrooms. The rooms smelled musty, and it was obvious Owen didn't do much cleaning, or even open the windows very often. One room contained a double bed. Cooper remembered that Owen had looked after his mother until she died, aged ninety. Her room was still as it must have been just after her death – the sympathy cards still on the window ledge, the tea tray next to the bed, even the bed itself unmade, as if the old lady had only just got up. The smells of this room were familiar to Cooper. They were redolent of the worst periods of his own mother's illness, the schizophrenia that had thrown the Coopers' lives into chaos in the past two years.

He drew the curtain back a few inches, loosening a shower of dust. He was startled by a small explosion and a burst of coloured light above the neighbouring houses. Then he remembered it was the weekend for official village bonfires. He had passed the site of the Cargreave bonfire on his way into the village. The mere sight of the enormous heap of branches and old doors had brought back to him all the familiar smells of the Guy Fawkes nights of his youth – the black stink of the gunpowder and scorched fireworks cases, the stab of woodsmoke on the back of the throat, the scent of trampled grass, the hotdog stands and baked potato stalls. His mouth had begun to water at imaginary wafts of fried onions and melted cheese mingling with the sharpness of a November frost.

Presumably there would be plenty more fireworks later on. But there would be no stuffed Guy Fawkes on the bonfire this year. No one considered it acceptable to burn Catholics in effigy these days, not even in Derbyshire.

Cooper looked in the smaller bedroom, but found it was jammed full with old furniture and boxes of books. The frame of a single bed was hidden under there somewhere, but there was no way of getting to it. He looked along the landing. There was only a bathroom and a small airing cupboard left.

He went back to the first bedroom again. It was dark and stuffy, like a sick room. Cooper wanted to yank back the curtains and let the light in, but he imagined the whole thing would wither and crumble to dust when the sunlight touched it. He had just realized why the bed was unmade. Owen had been sleeping in it himself.

THOUGH THE DETECTIVE was still downstairs and a constable was on the door, the forensic team had already moved on from the cottage in Cargreave. They had left to search the Ranger centre at Partridge Cross, where Owen Fox spent so much of his time. Later, they would carry away papers from his desk, along with a spare pair of boots, a rucksack, and a waste-paper bin.

'What sort of cigarettes do you smoke?' DCI Tailby asked the Ranger in the interview room.

'I don't,' said Owen.

'Just a crafty one now and then, is it? Maybe you're not supposed to smoke in the briefing centre?'

'I don't smoke.'

'Really? Do you know your jacket smells of smoke?'

'No.'

'Well, it does.'

Owen looked pained. 'I don't smoke.'

'We know about your record, Owen,' said Tailby. 'You've got a bit of a temper, haven't you? You take it out on women sometimes. No doubt cigarettes help you to keep calm.'

'I don't smoke.'

'We'll see.'

'I don't know what you mean.'

'Which of your colleagues smoke? The other Rangers?'

'None that I know of. They like to stay fit. It's no good being short of breath if you have to walk up hills.'

'What about visitors? Do you let them smoke in the centre?'

'No, it's a no-smoking zone.'

Tailby let the tapes run for a few seconds and glanced at Diane Fry across the table.

'So how do you explain the cigarette ash in the bin in your office?' she said.

Owen looked baffled. 'I've no idea.'

'I mean the waste-paper bin.'

'I've still no idea.'

'Do you recognize this rucksack?' Tailby produced the item in a sealed plastic bag. It was a blue Berghaus with green webbing shoulder straps.

'Yes, it's one of mine,' said Owen.

'This rucksack was recovered from the briefing centre. Can you explain the ash and the cigarette end we found at the bottom of it?'

Tailby saw the Ranger hesitate. The DCI kept his face composed, careful not to make the Ranger aware of the importance of the question. He set the reaction aside to come back to later.

'No, I can't,' said Owen.

'As well as the waste-paper bin, and the rucksack, our forensics people found cigarette ends at the scene of Jenny Weston's murder. All the same make of cigarettes. That's a lot of evidence of smoking, Mr Fox. For someone who doesn't smoke.'

Owen shook his head. 'I can't help you.'

'I suppose,' said Tailby, after a pause, 'there must be a lot of stress in your job now and then.'

'Oh yes.'

'Is there anything that's stressed you out particularly that you can think of?'

Owen seemed to turn inwards, his eyes becoming distant. 'You mean like Cargreave Festival Day,' he said. 'Do you know about that? I think about Festival Day all the time.'

'Tell us,' said Tailby.

'It was in all the papers. Pages and pages of it.'

'Tell us anyway.'

Owen stroked his beard nervously. He looked like a man who ought to be pale and afraid of the light. And perhaps he would have been, too, if it weren't for the job; it kept him out of doors, up on the hills, exposed to the weather. For most of the time.

'I think one of the worst things was the crowd. All these people just stood there watching as the bodies fell and broke on the rocks. Three of them, one after another.'

Tailby glanced at the triple tape decks as the Ranger's voice faded, wondering whether they would pick up the words that had become almost a whisper. But Fox rallied again as he looked at the detectives.

'There was counselling by then, of course. But it depends what kind of person you are, how you deal with that sort of thing. Sometimes, you can't deal with it at all.'

Tailby leaned forward. 'All right. I understand. And the woman you were convicted of attacking, Owen? Was that something else you just couldn't deal with?'

Owen gazed at Tailby directly for the first time in the past ten minutes.

'That was different,' he said. 'That was about sex.'

Back in Cargreave, the detective from DI Armstrong's team had accessed the temporary internet files downloaded on to Owen's PC to track the sites that he had visited. It had never occurred to Owen to delete any of the files. So it didn't take the detective long to find the child porn.

Chapter Twenty-Nine

Mark Roper wasn't under arrest. But he had heard that Owen was, and the thought was making him nervous. He assumed that Ben Cooper had acted on what he had told him about the dog-fighting. But gradually he was realizing that the questions were about something else. And when he got nervous, he got angry. He had never learned to keep a cool head, like Owen.

'It's the women who are the worst,' said Mark.

'Who told you that?' asked DI Hitchens.

'Owen did.'

Mark glanced at the tapes, as if feeling guilty at mentioning Owen's name.

'They're so absorbed in themselves that they don't notice what they're doing. They don't notice what's going on around them,' he said.

'It upsets you when people litter the countryside, doesn't it, Mark?'

'Yes,' he said. 'They're destroying the environment. They don't understand the damage they're doing with their rubbish. Their drinks cans and plastic bags kill animals and birds and all sorts of small creatures. I've seen them. I know.'

'And you think it's part of your job to clean up after people?'

'It's part of the job of a Ranger to care for the environment.'

'Perhaps you sometimes take it too far, though, Mark?'

Mark looked sulky. 'Someone has to care.'

'Did you see Jenny Weston leave any rubbish?'

'I didn't see her at all. I mean, I didn't see her until she was dead.'

'No, of course. What about anybody else? Did you see anybody else that day on Ringham Moor?'

Mark shook his head.

'Say it aloud for the tape, please,' said Hitchens.

'No, I didn't see anybody on the moor. There was nobody.'

'Ah, but you're wrong there, Mark. If Jenny was already dead when you saw her, then obviously there was somebody.'

'Yes, all right. There must have been. But I didn't see them.'

'I expect you're quite good at following the signs, though, aren't you, Mark?'

'The signs?'

'Signs that anybody has been around. Tracks, damage to plants, the rubbish they leave. You must have learned to see that someone has been past that way.'

Mark shrugged. 'It's obvious, sometimes.'

'And that day?' said Hitchens. 'Could you tell someone had been on the moor?'

'I could see the bike tracks,' said Mark. 'A mountain bike. But they were *hers*, weren't they?'

'Yes, we think so.'

'She'd been out to the tower and back across to the Virgins. That was obvious. I picked some rubbish up at the tower. I don't know if it was hers or not.'

'Did it annoy you that she was there?'

'It's private land,' said Mark. 'There's an access agreement, but there shouldn't be mountain bikes up there. It's against the by-laws.'

'Would you have told Jenny Weston that? If you had seen her alive, I mean.'

'Of course I would. Some people think they can just go anywhere they like, and they can't.'

'Isn't there a Right to Roam Act or something now?'

Mark snorted. 'Right to roam! Responsibilities go with rights. But some of them have no sense of responsibility. They think they just have rights. And the women are the worst.'

Now Mark looked confused. He watched the tapes going round. So many people seemed to do that in the interview rooms, as if somehow they could will their words to erase themselves from the recording.

'Owen again?' said Hitchens.

Mark looked stubborn. 'He talks to me a lot. He's joking most of the time.'

Hitchens nodded. 'But can you tell when he's not?'

'Sometimes,' said Mark. 'Have you talked to Warren Leach? Was I right about the dog-fighting? Is Owen involved?'

Nobody answered him. Hitchens produced an evidence bag made of clear plastic, bearing a yellow label. He showed it to Mark. 'We found these in a locker at Partridge Cross,' he said. 'We think they're yours.'

Inside the bag was a plastic wallet full of newspaper cuttings and photocopies. Some of them were ageing and yellow. They referred to incidents that had taken place over a period of several years – rescues and accidents, the recovery of dead bodies from the moors, searches for missing children.

'They're not important,' said Mark.

'We checked them out with your headquarters at Bakewell. The newspaper reports don't say so, but it seems all these incidents have one thing in common – they all involved Peak Park Rangers, and in every case one of the Rangers was Owen Fox.'

'Yes. That's right.'

'A bit of a hero to you, is he, Mark? It might be advisable to choose your heroes more carefully in future.'

'Look at that one,' said Mark. He pointed at a front page from an old *Eden Valley Times*. One story took up the whole of the page, with several photographs of the scene of the incident and some of the people involved. There were head-and-shoulders pictures of three young men, and one of a team of exhausted Rangers with rescue equipment. The three young men had died when they had climbed a fence on Castle Hill, Cargreave, to chase their ball towards a slope. It was a steep, convex slope, but you couldn't tell until it was too late, when you couldn't go back and could no longer stand upright on the grass. The three boys had plunged into the rocky gorge below Castle Hill in front of tourists queuing for admission to the show cave.

'We know Owen Fox was one of the Rangers who recovered the bodies from the gorge,' said Hitchens.

'Yes. But you see those lads that were killed,' said Mark. 'One of them was my brother.'

WHEN OWEN FOX frowned, his eyebrows looked worn and ragged. They tended to spread across his forehead like well-used brushes. He took his hands away from his face and studied them. He had fingers that were thick and shabby, and his palms were creased like an antiquarian map of the Peak, all narrow valleys and hills.

'I thought you brought me here to ask about the photographs,' he said.

'Not really,' said Tailby. 'Is that what you'd rather talk about?'

'I didn't know what I was doing.'

'That's what they all say.'

Owen seemed to rally for a moment. 'In my case,' he said, 'it's true.'

He told them that he had bought the computer after his mother had died, using the money she left him. He needed a distraction to take his mind off his memories of her. For so many years, she had been all that he had, apart from his job. Other memories had begun to come back to him, too – more memories of death.

At first, Owen said, his only idea was to learn about computers because they were coming into the Ranger Service and he didn't want to be left behind by the young ones. He was terrified of having to retire early. What would he retire to? So he bought the computer to teach himself at home, where no one would see his ignorance.

He had heard of the internet, he said, but had never thought of using it. It had come as a surprise that the PC he ordered came complete with an internal modem and pre-loaded with software to get free internet access. Naturally, he had tried it out.

At first, Owen had joined innocent newsgroups on national parks and non-league football. He had found a website for the Dry Stone Walling Association. But then he had begun to notice spam messages on the newsgroups, and out of curiosity he had visited the sites they were promoting. He had been absolutely amazed at what he had found. Amazed and guiltily fascinated. There had never been anything like that in the house at Cargreave, certainly not when Mum was alive.

'If a TV programme got a bit saucy, we had to switch it off,' he said.

Then Owen learned how to download images on to his hard drive. He had found that he was spending more and more time on the net, surfing from site to site. He realized he was becoming addicted, but he couldn't stop. He had missed parish council meetings for the first time, and people in Cargreave had thought he must be ill. He had been spending entire evenings on the internet, forgetting to eat, staying up into the early hours of the morning.

DCI Tailby nodded at that. The police team had found Owen's latest phone bill – it showed three hundred hours of calls to an 0845 number.

Owen said he had given his address several times when asked to register for free access to new sites. Then he had suddenly found that he was in contact with other people around the world, people he had never heard of, who sent him e-mail messages. He was delighted that they addressed him as if he were an old friend. They seemed to regard him as someone with the same interests. He had become part of their community.

WHEN MARK ROPER had been sent home and Owen Fox had been allowed a break, Diane Fry found DI Hitchens already in the DCI's office. They watched her warily when she produced a report sheet from the folder she carried.

'Yes, Fry? What have you got there?'

'This is the latest surveillance report on Ringham Edge Farm.'

'Have we still got that surveillance on?'

'We have. This is the report from last night.'

'Riveting stuff, is it?' said Hitchens.

'Well, judge for yourself. On Friday, the two boys left for school at the usual time in the morning. Their father saw them off. After that, Warren Leach went about his normal work on the farm, as far as could be ascertained by the officers on surveillance duty. Their reports are a bit lacking in technical detail, but some of Leach's observed activities did involve cows and a tractor, so I suppose we have to take it on trust.'

Tailby didn't seem interested. 'We could get Ben Cooper to de-brief them, I suppose. He might spot some anomalies, if you think it's worthwhile.'

'Maybe. The report goes on to say that the only visitors to the farm were the postman and the milk tanker driver, both early in the morning. That was it until the boys came home from school, when they were dropped at the bottom of the lane by the school bus. There was nobody at all for seven hours, apart from Leach. Not even a feed sales rep. It must be a pretty quiet life at Ringham Edge.'

'It sounds idyllic to me at this moment.'

'I'd call it downright tedious,' said Hitchens.

'Saturday was even worse. The tanker driver came as usual, but not the postman. There was no school for the boys.'

'We can't justify continuing surveillance on the basis of that sort of report. Call the team off, Paul.'

'There *is* one thing, though,' said Fry.

'Yes?'

'DC Gardner was the last officer on surveillance duty. She has added a note on the report at the end of her shift yesterday.'

'What did she see?'

'It's more a question of what she didn't see.'

Tailby began to get irritated. 'Don't play Sherlock Holmes with me, Fry. That's my role.'

'Sorry, sir. Gardner says that she understood there were two adults and two children resident at Ringham Edge. She observed the movements of the boys and their father, but not their mother. She never saw any sign of the mother at all, on either of her shifts. DC Gardner queries the whereabouts of Mrs Yvonne Leach.'

Tailby sat up straight. 'Damn.'

'Do you think it might be important?' said Hitchens.

'It's something we've overlooked. Check the rest of the surveillance reports, Paul. But I'm pretty sure that you'll find she was never mentioned. Not in any of them. But nobody thought that was in the least remarkable, did they? Not until Toni Gardner.'

'The others probably assumed Mrs Leach was slaving over the kitchen sink or something,' said Fry.

'Idiots.'

'If she was there, she would have seen the boys off to school in the morning, at least. In fact, she would probably have walked them down the lane to the bus. There's a killer about somewhere, after all. Any mother would do that. If she was there.'

'Yes, you're right, Fry. Let's establish when she was last seen. We've all been going up and down that lane for a week, right past the gate. Somebody must have seen her.'

'Can I take Ben Cooper with me?' asked Fry.

Tailby nodded. 'Good idea. Keep his head down and his mind focused.' He looked at Hitchens. 'I've got a bad feeling, Paul.'

'There's probably an innocent explanation. She may have gone away to stay with a relative or something for a while. She may be ill in bed. There's a bit of flu about, they reckon.'

'I've still got a bad feeling. *Everything* about this case gives me a bad feeling.'

When they finally let Mark Roper leave, he knew exactly where he had to go. Though Owen had said the local farmers were important, and that Rangers had a good relationship with them, Ringham Edge was one farm where Mark could see it wasn't true. Warren Leach reminded him of the man his mother lived with, his so-called stepfather – a man who needed everyone to be submissive to his will to be at ease with himself.

Leach regarded the Ranger with unconcealed hostility when Mark found him in the tractor shed.

'Well, if it isn't Ranger Junior. What do you want?'

Mark tried to recall Owen's advice about dealing with aggressive reactions. Sometimes you had to turn the other cheek, he said, to ignore rudeness and provocation. He had called it diplomacy.

'I want to talk to you about Owen Fox, Mr Leach.'

'Him? I heard he got a bit of a shock. Found out what he's been up to, have they?'

'Do you know anything about it?'

'I know I'm not likely to shed any tears over him,' said Leach. 'I've got my sons to think of.'

Mark frowned. It wasn't the response he had expected. 'What about your sons?'

'What about them?' Leach looked suddenly even less friendly. 'I hope you're not interested in my lads, Ranger Junior. What's your mate been teaching you?'

'I don't know what you mean.'

'Some folk took it out on those two youths in the quarry. But personally, I would have trusted those youths a damn sight more with my boys than I'd ever trust that friend of yours.'

Now Mark was confused. The conversation seemed to have drifted away from him to some other subject. 'Who are you talking about?'

'Who do you think?' Leach laughed, without any humour. 'I'm talking about the Lone Ranger. God in a red jacket. Your mate, Owen Fox. Do you know the kids round here call him Father Christmas? When he goes in the schools, they think Santa has arrived. I bet he likes to get the little boys on his knee and give them a nice present, all right.'

For a moment, Mark didn't understand what the farmer was saying.

'What's up?' said Leach. 'Bounced you on his lap a time or two as well, has he? I'd have thought you were too old for him. I reckon he likes them a bit younger, the dirty bastard.'

Mark felt the anger rushing up through his body before he even understood the reason for it. It was a physical response, visceral and frightening, a great flood of rage burning through his veins and overwhelming his judgement. Before he knew what was happening, he had hurled himself at the farmer, lashing out wildly with his fists.

Leach spread his shoulders, drew back a meaty hand and punched Mark in the mouth, knocking him down. The farmer laughed, thrilled at the chance to hit somebody. Mark got back up, flushed and furious, but his blows were uncontrolled and fell harmlessly against

Leach's chest and shoulders. The farmer knocked him to the floor twice more with blows to the face, until the Ranger was bloodied and crying.

Mark wiped the blood from his mouth and touched a loose tooth. He knew he was helpless. But the only thing he could think of was that he wanted to tell Leach that he wasn't crying because of the pain.

Then Leach noticed his sons watching, wide-eyed, from the corner of the shippon. He looked at Mark on the floor and saw that he was only a boy, too, beaten and humiliated.

'Go on, clear off,' he said.

As soon as the Ranger had gone, Warren Leach felt a black depression descend on him. The boys had vanished somewhere. They didn't even have the excuse of the calf needing attention now. The animal had brought in a bit of money at market. Not much, but enough to pay a fraction of the bills. They had food on the table for a day or two, and a cupboard full of bottles of whisky, which was one of the necessities these days, Leach was discovering.

The boys had gone somewhere they didn't think he would find them. They didn't want to be near their father any more, he realized that. Why should his own sons avoid him? He was sure it was because of their mother. After all these years, she seemed to have become his enemy. He was convinced she was in touch with the boys somehow, turning them against him. He didn't know how she was doing it, but she was poisoning their brains. They had always been such good lads before.

Leach was aware he hadn't always been a perfect father. And he shouldn't have let Will and Dougie see him hitting the young Ranger. At first, he had thought they would admire him, see him as the strong father he used to be, a man who was afraid of no one. But the feeling didn't last long. It became mingled with a sense of shame. The boy he had beaten could just as easily have been one of his own sons, in a few years' time.

When Leach tried to think about what had happened in his life over the last couple of months, his mind shied and balked at the enormity of it. It was a problem so huge that he couldn't contemplate it, couldn't even begin to consider how to cope with it. He could only follow helplessly the little trickles of thought that ran this way and that in his brain, seeking a way out of the nightmare.

And finally, Warren Leach faced the possibility that he might not be around to see his sons reach Mark Roper's age.

Chapter Thirty

WHEN BEN COOPER and Diane Fry drove into the yard at Ringham Edge Farm early next morning, they had to swerve to avoid the front bumper of a milk tanker. When they got out, they could hear Warren Leach yelling at the driver.

'What good is that to me?' he was shouting. 'How am I supposed to survive?'

'It's not my fault, mate. Your cell count is way up. You know the way it works as well as I do.'

'They're robbing me blind. I need that milk cheque to live on.'

Cooper saw Leach and the driver facing each other. They had their hands on their hips, and both looked angry and stubborn. Leach had been loading a stack of heavy fencing posts into a trailer attached to the back of his tractor.

'I can't help you,' said the driver. 'It's nothing to do with me. Do you want me to take this milk or not?'

'What's the bloody point?'

The driver finally lost patience. 'Suit yourself then. I can't hang around any longer.'

He got back in his cab and the diesel engine rumbled. Leach grabbed a fencing post and hurled it like a javelin. It bounced off the back of the tanker, leaving a small dent in the paintwork above the rear number plate.

'I wouldn't do that, Mr Leach,' said Cooper.

'Piss off,' said Leach.

'Some trouble with your cell count, is it? That can be tricky to sort out. Not mastitis, I hope.'

'They reckon I'm not cleaning the equipment properly. Not changing the filters. So they've docked my milk cheque. Now they're threatening not to take my milk at all. Bastards.'

'That would be pretty serious, I suppose.'

'Serious?' Leach went goggle-eyed with amazement at the understatement. 'My cows give better milk than any in Derbyshire. What the hell did you want, anyway?'

'We're hoping to speak to Mrs Leach.'

'You can hope, then.'

'Where is she?'

'She's gone, that's where.'

'Left?'

'Aye. So why don't the rest of you bugger off and leave me alone as well? I've had enough.'

'Can you tell me where she is, Mr Leach?'

'No, I can't.'

'We'd like to speak to her.'

'Well, you can do what I have to do – speak to her solicitor. That's what the letter says that I got. If I want to communicate with her in the future, I have to do it through her solicitor. And I'm her husband! I didn't even know she had a bloody solicitor.'

'Perhaps you could give us the name of your wife's solicitor then.'

'Bloody hell. Will you go away and leave me alone, if I do?'

'For the time being, sir.'

Leach turned and marched towards the house. They began to follow him, gradually closing the distance.

'Stay here,' snapped Leach, and slammed the door behind him.

They had no option but to wait until Leach came back. A ginger tom cat strolled across the yard and stared at them. The cat was scrawny, its ears bitten. But it was a farm cat, used to fending for itself and finding its own food in the dark corners of the buildings, used to fighting its own battles against rats, dogs and other cats. Cooper clicked his tongue at it and held out his hand in a friendly gesture. But the cat ignored him.

Fry walked over to look at the house. She found some black plastic bin liners by the back door that were split and bursting with rubbish. She looked at Cooper and screwed up her nose. There was a lace curtain across the window which prevented her from seeing in.

When Leach returned, he had a letter which he pushed in front of Cooper's face.

'Yes, divorce proceedings,' said Leach. 'What do you think of that?'

Fry found herself behind Leach, near the open door of the farmhouse. Out of the corner of his eye, Cooper saw her stand on the step and push the door open a bit more so that she could see inside, being careful not to enter.

Cooper wrote down the name and address of Mrs Leach's solicitor in his notebook.

'I'm sorry to hear that, Mr Leach. What about the boys? It's always tough on the children.'

Leach stared at him suspiciously, but said nothing.

'That's all I need for now, sir, thank you,' said Cooper.

Leach turned suddenly, moving quickly for a big man, and saw Fry standing in his doorway. The expression on her face seemed to infuriate him.

'Bitch!'

Leach hurled himself across the few yards that separated him from Fry. He was like a charging bull, and looked likely to flatten her against the wall. Cooper reacted too slowly, reached out and tried to grab his belt, but missed. He saw Fry step away from the door, giving herself a bit of clear space, flexing her leg to test the strength of her injured knee. She put out her left hand, her palm facing out towards Leach like a traffic officer. It looked like an appeal, a feeble defensive gesture, but Cooper knew it was her weak hand that she was offering as she adjusted the balance of her body.

Leach threw a vicious punch. His fist whistled past Fry's shoulder as she blocked his elbow with her right forearm. She jabbed her heel into the back of his knee and he hit the ground heavily, rolling on to his face in the muck left by the cows.

'Ouch,' said Fry, as she stumbled, rubbing her ankle. 'That damn cattle market has something to answer for.'

Cooper finally caught up. He put his knee in the flat of Leach's back and grabbed for one of his wrists with the intention of getting the kwik-cuffs on. But he hesitated. All the fight had gone out of the farmer suddenly. His body was slack and unresisting.

'Going to be sensible, Mr Leach?'

The farmer grunted. The grunt didn't seem to communicate much, but Cooper let go of his wrist and didn't bother with the cuffs.

'What are you doing, Ben?' asked Fry.

'It's all right.'

Cooper checked Leach's breathing, his pulse and his heart. The farmer still didn't resist. In fact, with small movements of his arms and legs, he seemed to be trying to dig himself deeper into the mud. An indistinguishable mumble came from his mouth. Cooper turned the man's head and looked at his face. Suddenly, he got up and dusted off his trousers. Leach still didn't move, except to turn his face back into the muck as Fry came across to stand over him, limping slightly.

'Is he all right?'

'Let's go,' said Cooper.

'Hold on. He might need medical attention. Let me take a look.'

'No. Leave him.'

'Ben?'

'Let's leave it. No harm done.'

Fry shrugged. 'He didn't touch me, anyway.'

'I know he didn't. No point in making a charge, is there?'

'He's not worth the paperwork. You sure he's all right?'

'He's all right, Diane. Trust me.'

'OK. Let's go.' She hobbled back towards the car.

'As right as he'll ever be,' said Cooper, quietly.

As they drove away, Cooper glanced in his rear-view mirror. Warren Leach had got up from the ground. He sat slumped against the tailgate of his trailer with his head in his hands. He had only the ginger cat for company now. And even the cat was looking at him with something like pity.

AFTER A PHONE call to his client by the solicitor, Cooper and Fry were given an address near Bakewell. They found it was a small B & B, its rooms empty now for the winter. Yvonne Leach had a first-floor room, overlooking a similar row of Victorian semi-detached houses with dark brick porches and dormer windows.

'I got too frightened of him,' she said. 'I stood it as long as I could, really I did.'

'Are you saying you suffered physical abuse, Mrs Leach?' asked Fry. Cooper could see her trying to relax the woman, who was plainly intimidated by having the two detectives standing in the room. Mrs Leach looked round at the cheap dresser and the washbasin in the corner and shrugged, as if accepting things were out of her control now.

'Not really,' she said. 'He never hit me, I mean. I'm not making a complaint about that.'

She rubbed her hands together and felt the radiator under the bay window. The room was chilly and miserable. She pulled her cardigan around her shoulders and stared out of the window.

'The Ranger was the only one I could ever talk to. Owen. He used to come to the house sometimes to see if I was all right. But only when Warren wasn't around. Warren wouldn't have him near the farm, if he could help it.'

Cooper sighed with relief. That sounded much more like the Owen Fox that he knew. How could Mark Roper have got it so wrong about the reason for Owen's visits?

'Do you think I should go back?' said Yvonne.

They stared at her. 'Mrs Leach, there must have been something that frightened you enough to make you leave,' said Fry.

Yvonne Leach nodded. She made them sit down on the bed. Then she told them how her husband used to threaten her when she wouldn't have sex, how he had broken the lock of the door when she had gone to sleep in another room.

'He's a highly sexed man. He always has been. It's one of the things that attracted me to him, once.'

She told them how much worse her husband had been since the farm had got into financial trouble. She knew that things were bad. She didn't know what the debts were – Warren never told her things like that – but she knew it was very bad. She could understand why Warren drank. It was very hard on him, the way things had gone.

But it made his temper even worse, and he always took it out on her. She seemed to provoke him simply by being there. She had left, she said, because she didn't want the boys to see it any more. She thought, if she was out of the way, he would have less to provoke him and wouldn't drink so much.

'It was the most difficult decision I ever made,' she said.

Cooper realized Yvonne Leach was one of those women who had to feel they were needed, that they had a role to perform to give meaning to their lives. Some women were afraid of stepping out of their place and finding that the gap they left had closed up behind them straight away. He imagined Yvonne's fear was that everyone would forget about her in a single moment and carry on with their lives as if nothing had happened, as if she had never been there. And then she would know that her life had never had any meaning at all.

'Because I love him, you see,' said Yvonne.

THE LANDLADY KNOCKED on the door and brought in a tray of tea for the visitors, looking at them curiously, with the air of being prepared to welcome them as long as they didn't put their shoes on the bed and steal the soap.

Cooper tried his tea and found it weak and insipid. 'Mrs Leach, did your husband have many visitors?'

She hesitated. Her face set into a stubborn line that reminded him for a moment of her husband's expression. There must have been a time when they had something in common.

'You've wondered yourself what happens in the big shed, haven't you?' he said.

Yvonne nodded, and she looked as though she might cry at the softness of his tone.

'It was awful. The men started coming at night, after the boys had gone to bed. Warren warned me to stay in the house. But I heard the dogs, the snarling and the howling. I could imagine what was going on. He told me it was the only way to make some money to pay off the debts. But with people like that, something was bound to go wrong. He isn't a very clever man. I knew they would take advantage of him.'

'And what did go wrong, Mrs Leach?'

'I don't know. But one morning, after they had been, he was in a terrible temper. He was frightened, too. But angry.'

'You don't know what had happened?'

'No, he never told me.'

'How long ago was this?'

'Oh, six weeks or so. I remember, because the men haven't been back since then. They used to come every week. Every Sunday night.'

'Why do you think they stopped coming?'

'I always thought it was because of the Ranger,' she said.

'Owen Fox? Are you saying he was involved in this?' asked Fry.

'No, no,' said Mrs Leach. 'But he knew. I think he knows everything that goes on in the area. He came to the farm and asked me to use my influence to persuade

Warren to stop it happening. My influence! He didn't understand the way it was, of course.'

'But why did he do that? He could just have reported it,' said Fry.

'He said he didn't want to get Warren in trouble. He was worried it would be the last straw for Warren. The Ranger understood that.'

'And did your husband take any notice?'

'Not of me. Nor of the Ranger.'

'But something made them stop,' said Fry.

'Yes.'

Fry looked at Cooper. He shook his head, and she frowned.

'What about women?' she asked.

'They were all men, I think,' said Yvonne. 'But, of course, I never saw them.'

'I mean other women your husband may have met.'

Yvonne Leach put down her teacup. She hadn't drunk any of it. But then neither had the two detectives.

'I thought you might mean that.'

'You said he was highly sexed. Do you think it's possible that he might have looked elsewhere?'

Yvonne smiled and shook her head. 'You don't understand the life of a small farmer. Warren wouldn't have the time or the opportunity for an affair. Where would he meet women? He spends every hour working on the farm.'

'Are you sure?'

'Oh, I've seen him looking at the hikers sometimes. You know, the women who come past on the track up to the moor. Sometimes, when I didn't know where he was, I thought he might have gone up there to look at them. In the middle of summer, you can see them all gathered round the stone circle, the Nine Virgins, all the young ones. But he would never do anything except look, I'm sure.'

She must have seen the sceptical look on Fry's face. 'Warren is a good man, really,' she added. 'Things just haven't gone right for him.'

'What about the boys, Mrs Leach?' asked Cooper.

'I wanted to bring them away with me, of course. But how could I?' She gestured at her surroundings. 'I had to come here, because I've got no family to go to. But I can get a job, can't I? I've been looking. I can earn some money and I'll get somewhere bigger that I can take the boys to.'

'But in the meantime … are you quite sure they're safe?'

She shook her head vehemently. 'Oh, Warren won't do anything to harm the boys. He thinks the world of them. They're his whole life, but for the farm. He wouldn't do a thing to harm them.'

'IT *WAS* LEACH you had in mind, Ben?' said Diane Fry as they drove back to Edendale.

'How do you mean?'

'You said your friend Fox was being made a scapegoat. If so, he has to be a scapegoat for somebody else. Who did you have in mind? It must have been Leach. But if it was, you seemed a bit soft on him earlier on.'

'He won't take pushing any further,' said Cooper.

Fry slapped the steering wheel in irritation. Then her shoulders slumped, and she sighed. 'I don't understand you,' she said.

'Shall I call in?' he said.

'Go ahead.'

Cooper reported in to the incident room. His head lifted as he listened to the latest news. Fry turned impatiently.

'What is it?'

'Information from the RSPCA special investigations officer dealing with the Ringham Edge Farm enquiry.'

'Yes? Have they got any firm evidence? Enough to act on?'

'They've passed on the name of one of their informants. They don't usually do that, because they have to protect their identities. But this one happens to be dead.'

'Dead?'

'Yes. One of their informants was Jenny Weston.'

WILL LEACH HAD already seen the shotgun standing against the wall, where it had been taken out of its steel cabinet. He knew this was wrong, that a shotgun should never be left out. His father had always said so. The police might call at the farmhouse at any time and see it, and then his father would lose his shotgun licence. But he didn't seem to care about that at all now.

Will hated it when his father shouted and swore. But he hated it more when he fell into a long silence. At those times, his eyes seemed to be looking far away and his body quivered, like the strands of wire in the electric fence in the top field. Will had known what his father was thinking when he had looked at Doll and had been so silent. And now Doll had gone. Will had tried to guess what his father was thinking when he had looked at their mother and was silent, too. And now their mother was gone as well.

It was the first day of half-term, and this morning Will had listened very carefully. His sense of hearing was trained to pick up the sound of his father's footsteps in the yard or the clink of a glass against a bottle in the front room. His father had been more silent this morning than he could ever remember. And this time, Will thought he knew what his father was thinking.

WARREN LEACH HAD never really known the meaning of shame. He had heard people talk about it, but had never understood, and had just thought them weak. Now it was an emotion that came upon him suddenly, devastatingly, roaring over the hill and scything him down like ripe corn under the blade of the combine.

His cheeks had burned under the policewoman's stare. This woman looked at him differently from the others. It was more than antagonism, it was contempt. She had seen what had become of his life, and she thought it was his own fault. She saw the squalor and had no hesitation in blaming him for it. And, of course, she was right.

His world took a sudden shift and became vivid and clear, as if somebody had shaken it to bring the picture into proper focus. Now he saw the colours of his life distinctly, and they were all dark. The revelation coalesced in one great lump all the burdens that had been piling up on him in the last few weeks. He knew now that they had drained his strength and his will, and had been the cause of all those strange, crippling aches in his belly that he hadn't been able to explain.

For the first time, Leach faced the impossible magnitude of his problems; the disastrous hole that he had fallen into loomed way over his head like the walls of a deep well. And he had no energy left to climb any more.

'But I never hurt the boys,' he said to himself. Then louder: 'Dougie, I never hurt you, did I?' He reached out to take his youngest son by the shoulders. Dougie wriggled to get away, but his father gripped him harder, making him cry out.

Leach knew he had to make his decision. He was sure the police would come for him anyway because of what had happened with the young Ranger. The boys would be taken away from him. They would end up in one of those homes. But he had already thought about this moment, and he knew what he had to do. He let Dougie go, and the boy ran towards his brother, pale and shaking with the fear of the unknown. The boys clung to each other, watching their father as they would have watched a wild animal prowling through the house, afraid to move a muscle in case they attracted its attention.

Leach fingered the barrels of the shotgun, feeling the certainty and solidity of the heavy steel. His hand itched to grip the stock. He reached out to it like a man greeting an old friend. Then he drew back, and looked at the boys as if he had just remembered they were there. He had made careful plans, but he had nearly forgotten them. That was what his brain was like now. Soft as sponge. As rotten and stinking as the stuff he scraped out of the hoof of a cow with foot-rot.

'Will ...'

'Yes, Dad.'

'You know where your Auntie Maureen lives, don't you?'

'Yes, Dad.'

'You catch the bus into Edendale and walk to the bus station. Get a Hulley's number 26. It stops at the corner of Bank Street, near the old library. You know your way from there. There's enough money for the fare for you and Dougie in an envelope on the table.' Will said nothing. 'Can you remember that?'

'Yes.'

'There's a letter for your auntie in there, too. Don't open it, Will. It's for Auntie Maureen to read. And there's two chocolate bars I saved for you. One each. They're the ones you said you liked. Crisp and crunchy.' Leach tried a smile, but swallowed it as his throat constricted in a spasm. 'And Will ... make sure young Dougie is all right, won't you? Promise?' said Leach.

'Promise,' said Will.

'That's a good boy.'

Leach found his eyes drifting towards the shotgun again. Not much time now. Not much left to say.

'All the things I did, I did because I was trying to save the farm for you. For your future? Do you understand?' he said.

The boys nodded, because it was what he expected of them. But Leach could see from their faces that they understood nothing. Probably they never would. By the time they were old enough, their mother would have talked a different story into their heads, one where their father was a weak fool, a drunkard, a bully, a criminal. But that wasn't right. All he was, really, was a man who had failed. But probably the boys would never understand that, either. If they were lucky.

'Dad?' said Will.

'Yes?'

'When have we got to go?'

'Best go now, son,' said Leach. 'Before it goes dark.'

He stared at the boys, wondering what else he should do. There were things which Yvonne had always done, which he had no idea of. He was vaguely aware that Will had taken charge of some of these things himself – somehow young Dougie always seemed to be washed and his hair was clean. But there ought to be something that a father did to look after his sons, some little thing that showed he cared. Especially when he was saying goodbye.

He saw that Dougie's jacket collar had been turned over by the strap of his rucksack, exposing the lining underneath. It looked untidy. He reached out a dirt-stained hand to straighten the collar, his fingers passing close to Dougie's cheek, so that he felt the warmth from the boy's skin. Dougie was trembling, and his eyes looked puzzled and afraid.

Leach turned to Will, but the older boy flinched away, and Leach let his hand fall back to his side. He felt a small flicker of anger and hurt, but it died as quickly as it had come, leaving him cold. Cold, and ready.

'Off you go, then.'

He watched them walk across the yard and down the lane without looking back. He glanced at the cows, whose heads showed over the wall of the barn. They were unsettled because they had been brought inside when there was still grass to be eaten in the fields. But they would be all right.

Leach went back into the kitchen and stared out of the window. The rain had left dirty streaks on the panes, and the world outside looked blurred and distant. The moor had retreated into low cloud. He could just make out the car parked in the trees at the top of the track, but even that held no meaning any more.

In contrast, the objects immediately around him seemed alive and weighted with unbearable significance. The colours of the boys' clothes draped over the rail of the cold Aga were bright and painful, and the smell of the wet earth from his boots on the tiles bit so hard into the back of his nose that it made his eyes water. The clutter that pressed around him seemed to be composed of living things, like an army of rodents gathering to gnaw at his body. If he left it any longer, the vermin would start to eat him alive. But he wouldn't give them the chance.

THE NUMBER 26 to Edendale was late. It had been held up by roadworks and temporary traffic lights in Bakewell, and by an old lady who had slipped on the platform as she fumbled for her bus pass. The driver spent several minutes fussing over her to make sure that she was all right. It wasn't because he was worried about a claim against his employers for negligence. It was because the old woman's daughter knew his wife, and because all the other people on the bus were watching him, and a lot of *them* knew him, too.

Will and Dougie Leach were standing at the bus stop, carrying the rucksacks they took to school in the mornings. They had their clothes in them for tomorrow, their pajamas and toothbrushes. The driver wasn't surprised to see the boys on their own. He had done the school run at one time, and he remembered them. When the Leach boys had first started getting on the bus, they had been accompanied to the stop by their mother, or sometimes by their bad-tempered father, who never seemed to have a good word to say to anybody. The driver thought Will was bit of a moody child, and expected he would probably turn out just like his dad in a few years' time. He felt sorry for Dougie, though. He always looked unhappy; even more so today.

The driver took the boys' money and watched them for a moment while they found seats. Then he released the brake and let in the clutch, and forgot about them as he accelerated towards the bend and the descent from the moor towards the A515.

Will's face was frozen. But he saw the tears start in Dougie's eyes. Just as the bus turned the bend, Will grabbed his brother roughly by the shoulder and pushed his own chocolate bar into Dougie's hands.

'Here, have mine,' he said. 'I don't really like them anyway.'

The bus was only a few yards away from the stop when they heard the shotgun blast. The boys looked back towards the farm. Above the juddering of the diesel engine and the grinding of the bus's gears as it approached the hill, they could hear the rooks that roosted in the beech trees behind the farmhouse erupt into the air, complaining raucously; they could hear the old farm dog, Molly, begin to bark hysterically in the yard.

And then they heard the silence that followed. And the silence was the loudest sound of all.

Chapter Thirty-One

MARK ROPER STOPPED on the path to Ringham Moor and touched his face gingerly where Leach had hit him. His lip was split, and a tooth was loose. If it was true about Owen, he knew he ought to feel the outrage that had been expressed by his fellow Rangers. But Owen's arrest the day before had confused him. Mark knew that Owen would have been up here to check on his wall, if he could have done. Instead, Mark was doing it for him.

When he got near the top of the path above Ringham Edge Farm that afternoon, Mark saw a woman in a yellow jacket climbing towards the Hammond Tower. It was the first time he had seen a woman walking on her own for over a week. There had been plenty of warnings about the dangers for lone women. But some of them couldn't stay away. There was something that drew them, like the women who were attracted to form relationships with convicted murderers and rapists.

He had brought a rucksack from home, because the one he usually used for patrols had been in the briefing centre, which had been closed by the police. But at least this rucksack held a pair of binoculars. He focused them on the woman, following her movements through the high bracken until she reached a clear spot. She paused, and looked around. And then Mark saw her face. He recognized the long, red scar and the disfigured cheek, the twisted eye. He had seen her photograph in the incident room at Edendale, during the briefing three days before. Even if he hadn't recognized her, he would have had to do something. Women weren't safe alone on Ringham Moor any more.

Mark called in. 'Peakland Partridge Three. Put me through to the police incident room.'

Then he leaned on the wall and looked down on Ringham Edge Farm. And he saw that the police were already there.

WARREN LEACH HADN'T bothered to move out of the kitchen after the boys had left the house. The blast of the shotgun had shredded the back of his skull, and his body had been thrown off the chair and on to the floor, where it lay among the debris of dropped food and unwashed clothes. A dog chained near the back door was barking ferociously, driven into a frenzy by the arrival of so many strangers. No one dared go near it. Someone had called for the dog warden and a vet.

When Ben Cooper had first arrived, a middle-aged man wearing jeans and a tweed jacket had been standing in the yard next to a red pick-up, talking to Todd Weenink. He turned out to be a farmer from across the valley, and Leach had rung to ask him to milk the cows that afternoon.

'He's taken that way out, has he?' said the farmer. 'I can't say it's a surprise. He isn't the first, and he won't be the last. Some prefer to finish it cleanly, like.'

When Cooper looked at the state of the farm's kitchen, he realized clean wasn't the word for what Warren Leach had done. He stood in the doorway of the room, careful not to go too near. He could see a white envelope on the cluttered kitchen table. It was an official-looking envelope, with the address neatly typed. Unlike some of the others, which were obviously bills and unopened, Leach had slit the top of this envelope open with a knife, leaving a greasy butter stain on the edge of the flap. Cooper didn't need to look at the letter inside. He guessed it was a notification to Mr Warren Leach that a prosecution was being considered under the Firearms Act 1986.

Cooper wondered whether there was anything else they could have done. They had contacted Social Services after their visit to Yvonne Leach, but that had been out of concern for the children, Will and Dougie. Who had been concerned about the fate of their father? Warren Leach had needed help, if anyone had. The evidence was there to be seen on the floor and walls.

A few minutes later, Cooper was very glad of the call that took him and Weenink away from the farm and up the hill to meet the young Ranger, Mark Roper.

Mark seemed even younger today. It wasn't just the fact that his face was bruised and swollen. In between the bruises, he looked pale and lost, like a boy waiting for somebody to tell him what to do.

'Are you sure it's her?' asked Cooper.

'I'm sure.'

Cooper felt certain Mark was observant enough to be right. This was a situation where Diane Fry would have to be involved.

It was late afternoon by the time Diane Fry arrived at Ringham, and she was in a bad mood. She drove up the track past the farmhouse to where she could see other vehicles parked on the hill.

'Where is she?' she asked when she saw Cooper and Weenink under the trees. Cooper bent down to her car window.

'She's up there.' He gestured vaguely, irritating her still further.

'On the moor?'

Fry got out of the car and flexed her leg. She could feel her knee starting to swell up. She ought to be at home with a bag of frozen peas on it – if only she had any frozen peas in the freezer compartment of her fridge. She struggled up the rocky slope to look towards the plateau. She was no more than half a mile from Top Quarry.

'Where is she *exactly*?'

'Near the Cat Stones, where she was attacked,' said Cooper. 'It was Mark Roper who reported sighting her earlier this afternoon. She refuses to come down. We were just discussing taking her into custody for her own safety.'

'What?'

'She can't stay up there. She's not safe. What if she runs into our killer? That would be just great, wouldn't it?'

'It's not very likely.'

Cooper shook his head in exasperation as she pulled on her black jacket. 'OK, I'll come with you.'

'Don't bother,' she said.

Fry began to walk away, tugging her jacket around her as she strode towards the path, brushing past a PC talking on his personal radio. Cooper and Weenink watched her go. Weenink's expression was puzzled as he leaned towards his partner.

'Ben?'

'Fetch the car,' said Cooper.

'Where are we going?'

'To see Mark Roper again.'

'Why?'

'Because I feel like something to cheer me up.'

'But –'

Cooper gritted his teeth. 'Will you just *fetch the car*?'

'Jesus,' said Weenink. 'I thought it was only women who had a wrong time of the month.'

Mark was sitting on the ground in his red fleece jacket, with Owen's walling hammer in his hand. Occasionally, he dug the cutting edge of the hammer hard into the soil and studied the shape of the gouge he had made.

'So is the wall finished?' asked Cooper.

'I thought it was,' said Mark. 'But look at that.'

He pointed down the length of the newly-rebuilt stretch. The stones had bulged and bellied outwards, and the coping stones had slipped from their places, exposing the filling, which trickled from the interior of the wall like grain from a split sack.

'What did that?'

'A rotten stone,' said Mark. 'One single rotten stone that crumbled with the weight and let down everything above it. Owen must not have spotted it when he put it in place. He says every stone has to play its part. You can't have weaknesses, or the whole thing comes down.'

'That's a shame.' Cooper looked at the young Ranger more closely. 'Mark, how did you come by those bruises?'

Mark touched his face again. 'Oh, I slipped and landed face first on some rocks. I'll survive.'

'You sure?'

'Of course.'

'Mark, has Owen ever said anything to you about children?'

The Ranger looked away. 'Not much. He always says: "Kids? I love 'em. But I couldn't eat a whole one."'

Cooper nodded, listening for something beyond the old joke. 'I suppose you have to do school visits as a Ranger.'

'It's part of the job these days. They say if we educate youngsters about what Rangers do, they'll respect the Peak Park and what goes on in it. That's the theory, anyway. But Owen says a school visit just gives the kids a chance to take the piss out of you all at once instead of one at a time.'

'Yeah, I know what he means. But Owen has no children, has he?'

'He's a good bloke, Owen,' said Mark.

Todd Weenink was getting impatient at the turn of the conversation. He kicked at the wall and watched as more filling spilled out from between the stones.

DIANE FRY COULD see Maggie Crew from a distance, her yellow jacket marking her out like a beacon. She was standing a little way from the tower, on the edge of the escarpment where the gritstone plateau fell away into the valley. Maggie was a few yards short of the contorted rock formations that Ben Cooper called the Cat Stones. She was standing quite still, as if afraid to go any closer. Beyond the rocks was the Hammond Tower, which ought to have represented the hand of humanity on the landscape of the moor, but failed to suggest any hint of civilization to Fry's eye.

The wind coming down the valley was cold, carrying the first suggestion of November storms. But Maggie made no attempt to shelter behind the rocks. She seemed happy to expose herself to the full blast of the weather.

She didn't look round when Fry limped up behind her. But Fry felt as if Maggie had been waiting for her to arrive.

'Maggie, come on. It's time to go back home.'

'Give me a few minutes, then I'll go.'

'All right. I'll stay with you, then.'

'If you like.'

Maggie didn't move for a moment. She hesitated as if she wasn't sure which way to go. Fry had automatically walked up to her left side, understanding Maggie's vulnerability. Now she watched Maggie's face, looking for clues about her thoughts in the set of her mouth and squint of her eye.

'I want to remember more,' said Maggie. 'I know that's what you need from me, Diane. I want to be able to tell you that I remember.'

'Maggie, it doesn't matter. We can do it another way.'

'You said you didn't have enough information. Insufficient evidence. You needed me to make an identification.'

'There are other leads we can follow.'

Maggie shook her head. 'No. You're lying to me now.'

As if on a signal, they walked in step towards the Cat Stones. Maggie's footsteps became slower as they reached them. Imperceptibly, she seemed to have moved nearer to Fry, until their elbows were touching, making contact for mutual reassurance.

'I would have brought you here, Maggie,' said Fry.

'You don't understand. I wanted to do it on my own.'

Fry nodded. 'Yes, I suppose I can see that.'

'Can you? You wanted me to share everything with you, all my memories. But there are things I can't share.' Her eyes went distant again. 'Tell me,' she said. They were the words that Fry feared to hear from her. 'Tell me, why did you have an abortion?'

'Because I didn't want the baby,' said Fry. 'Obviously.'

They stopped by the Cat Stones. They were lumbering great rocks, precariously balanced on smaller, softer slabs of gritstone that had been worn away by the weather and shaped like the back-jointed rear legs of an animal. The rocks crouched like leaping cats – or so local folklore said. Maybe they were leaping at the tower, determined to knock it from its perch.

'But there's more to it than that, isn't there?'

Maggie touched one of the stones gently, as if she hoped to make it move with the lightest brush of her fingers. 'Was it rape?' she said.

'Yes.'

'But you never talk about it, do you?'

'Of course not.'

'Bottled up. Is that the best way?'

'I don't talk about it,' said Fry firmly.

'But it's a denial,' said Maggie. 'A sort of lie that you're living.'

They were in the right spot. This was the place they had identified as the location of the assault on Maggie Crew – the brief, horrific attack that had left her disfigured. They had found little forensic evidence, nothing that could have led them to the identity of an assailant. There were no witnesses except Maggie herself. And no trace of a motive.

'You can't live your life by lies,' said Maggie.

Then Maggie Crew began to laugh. Fry was mortified that her confession should be treated with hilarity. Then she began to get angry.

'What's so funny?'

Maggie put her hand on Fry's arm to support herself. Her laughter bounced off the Cat Stones and seemed to drift off down the valley towards Matlock.

'It doesn't matter, Diane,' she said. 'Don't worry about it.'

She looked to be about to start chuckling again. Fry pulled away abruptly.

'You're getting a bit hysterical. Let's go down. It was a mistake to come up here.'

'Perhaps it was,' agreed Maggie.

'You're doing yourself no good.' Fry shivered. 'Besides, I'm getting cold.'

Maggie smiled and shook her head. 'Diane, there are things I remember.'

'That's good, Maggie,' said Fry automatically.

'I remember him running. He was on me so suddenly, before I knew what was happening. I remember him breathing heavily, like a runner, or ...' Maggie hesitated. 'I think he was frightened.'

'Frightened, Maggie?'

'Yes. I don't believe he meant to attack me. I was in the wrong place.'

'What do you mean?'

'Diane – I think I was just in the way.'

There was a faint scuffling, and a sheep peered at them from around a rock. Its black face and staring eyes looked ludicrous. Fry noticed there were hundreds of small black pellets scattered on the bare ground around the Cat Stones, drying in the wind. The sheep gazed at them for a few seconds, seemed to register that they were living creatures, and scuttled away down the slope.

'Maggie, you told me the other day there were leaves. You remembered kicking the leaves, just before you were attacked.'

'Yes.'

Fry gestured at the rock face, the tumbled boulders, the bare earth. 'There are no leaves here. There are no trees.'

'But I remember it.'

'All right,' said Fry. 'So perhaps you're mistaken about where it happened.'

'I don't think so.'

'Some of these boulders look very much alike to me. What about a bit further up?' Fry pointed towards the tower. Maggie didn't move. 'Maggie?'

'All right.'

They walked a few yards to the north. As they rounded the central boulder of the Cat Stones, a view of the valley came into sight. Traffic could be seen moving on the A6 at Darley Dale, with the houses of Two Dales climbing the hill behind to the forest plantations on Matlock Moor and Black Hill. Nearer to the tower, the beeches began to cluster together, mixed with the occasional oak. Now there were plenty of leaves underfoot.

'What about here?' said Fry. 'Surely this is more likely?'

'It could have been, I suppose.'

'But it's important, you see. If we've got the scene of the attack wrong, then we ought to have the SOCOs up here again, to see if there's anything that might still be left. Though it's so long now …'

'Yes, it's so long,' said Maggie. 'Too long. It can't matter that much.'

'You never know,' said Fry. She began to cast her eyes about the area, worried now about where she and Maggie were treading. They could be contaminating the scene. There could be a vital piece of forensic evidence waiting to be found, the one piece of evidence that would link the attack definitely with a suspect. Just one bit of evidence. If only it hadn't blown away, or been trampled into the ground. Or eaten by a sheep.

'You shouldn't have come out here, Maggie. You're still alone out here, you know. Just as much as you were when you were at home.'

Maggie shrugged. Fry watched her carefully. They were close enough by now for her to gauge Maggie's reactions without being completely misled.

'Maggie, I know about your daughter,' said Fry. She saw Maggie lift an eyebrow a fraction. It was her left eyebrow that moved, while the right one merely twitched like a facial tic and settled into its bed of red scar tissue again. 'I know you had your daughter adopted.'

'I don't know what you're talking about,' said Maggie. 'I'm afraid you've lost me.'

'Your sister told me,' said Fry. 'But it was a long time ago, wasn't it?'

Maggie walked a few yards further on, hunching her shoulders and turning up her collar when the wind cutting between the boulders caught her in the face, on her damaged side.

'Do you have memories of your daughter?' asked Fry. 'It might help to let the memories come.'

'You might be right,' said Maggie quietly. 'It *could* have happened about here.'

'You shouldn't just bury it, Maggie.'

'I still don't remember exactly. It's a wonderful view. You can see forever from here. Right down the valley. Right across the hills to Chatsworth.'

'Maggie –'

Maggie sighed. 'Do you blame me?' she said.

'No. But does that make it any better?'

Then Maggie touched her. It was the first time they had touched each other since they had met. A week ago, that was. A lifetime away.

Maggie put her hand on Fry's sleeve and gently drew her towards the edge of the rock at the base of the tower. They stood close to the drop, with the wind whipping round their ears and stirring their hair. They were elbow to elbow, with Fry standing, as always, on Maggie's left side.

Fry's injured leg was throbbing from climbing up the rocky slope. She knew she had done too much, pushed herself too far. Her heart and lungs were struggling with the effort of breathing in the face of the wind. She waited to hear what Maggie had to say, not knowing what she hoped for.

'There's the train, look,' said Maggie.

A trail of steam was emerging from the trees towards Rowsley, as the Peak Rail train ran along the far bank of the Derwent near Churchtown and the houses on Dale Road.

'It's the last train of the day. They'll be shedding the engines at Darley Dale station. They don't run as far as Matlock in November.'

Fry realized Maggie was directing her attention away – well away, towards the centre of Matlock and her own home. The smell of smoke was strong; it seemed to reach her all the way from down in the valley.

BEN COOPER'S NECK was starting to get stiff from staring up at the moor. The overcast sky made the slopes look dark and ominous. But it was like that in the Peak – the landscape could change its mood from one moment to the next as the weather shifted and the clouds blew over the tops.

'It's a pretty bleak place to die, really,' he said. 'I never saw it like that before.'

'It wouldn't be my choice, either,' said Weenink. 'I reckon I'd like to die in bed, preferably on the job with a blonde with big tits. That'd be the way to go.'

'It would suit Jenny Weston, though,' said Cooper, as if Weenink hadn't spoken. 'From what her father says, it sounds as though she had a pretty difficult life. It would be no wonder that she was depressed.'

'Is that them?' said Weenink.

Diane Fry and Maggie Crew were halfway down the path, walking close together as if supporting each other. Weenink did a double-take when Maggie Crew got close enough for him to see her face.

'Shit.'

'I know it's a bit nasty,' said Cooper. 'But you've seen worse things than that, surely? Don't let her see how you react.'

'OK, don't tell me. I'll fetch the car.'

Cooper shrugged. 'If you like.'

Fry put Maggie straight into her car. Maggie kept her head down, like a defendant being led into court. She looked as though she ought to have been wearing a blanket over her head. Except that Maggie Crew was the victim, not the accused.

'Ben, I'm not sure we have the right location for the assault on Maggie,' said Fry.

'Oh?'

'Her statement doesn't tally with the memories she's getting now. She told me the other day that she remembered piles of leaves underfoot. But there are no leaves at the Cat Stones. I know it sounds like a small thing, but if we've missed examining the proper scene ...'

'I'll take a look,' said Cooper.

'We ought to get Forensics –'

'I'll take a look first, and see if I can narrow down the possibilities before we do that.'

'Of course, her memories may be distorted. They seem to be coming back, but who can say whether they're accurate or not?'

'It would take a psychiatrist to do that. If her evidence ever comes to court, we'll need to back it up with expert opinion.'

Fry sighed. 'She's really going to love that.'

'If only we could produce a case without her. But we can't.'

'Another thing. She says she thinks she was just in the way.'

'What does that mean?'

'That she wasn't the intended victim, I think. She says her attacker was breathless and running, not lying in wait for her.'

'That doesn't make sense.'

'I'm not responsible for whether it makes sense,' said Fry. 'I'm just sharing information, right?'

'Fine.'

Cooper watched them drive off, then waited for Weenink to come back with their own car.

'Where to now, Ben?' he said.

'Up there.'

'What? Ben, do you know it's Monday? I'll be missing drinking time soon.'

'Are you coming, or what?'

Weenink locked the car again. 'Yes. But only because you're not safe on your own.'

When they reached the Cat Stones, Cooper instinctively followed Diane Fry's footsteps to the place where the attack on Maggie Crew was supposed to have taken place. He could see straight away what she meant about the leaves. No trees grew on the exposed gritstone edge.

'Why shouldn't it be here?' said Weenink. 'She might have been walking through the leaves earlier. She could have gone through them on the way up.'

'Possibly.'

Weenink began to get impatient. 'Ben, there are things to do.'

'Let's try this way a bit.'

'But bloody hell –'

Cooper turned angrily. 'Todd – just keep out of it!' His face felt flushed. It was only a moment's loss of control, but nagging doubts had made him irritable, and exasperation with himself was eating at him.

He worked his way north, as Fry had done. Weenink sat on a rock and watched him, like a tolerant parent. After a minute or two, Cooper reached the spot where the rocks parted, and he could see down to Rowsley and the railway line. The last train had gone, but he could see where the line ran. Which way had Maggie's attacker come from? Not from the other side of the rocks, that was sure – not unless he was Spiderman. The slope behind him was steep, too, and covered in loose stones that would be noisy and difficult to negotiate. If you were going to run at someone at speed and take them by surprise, there was only one way to do it – downhill. People had known that ever since violence had been invented. That was why Iron Age forts were built on the summits of steep hills.

There was more dead foliage on the ground near the Hammond Tower, certainly. But how much would there have been seven weeks ago?

Then, in front of the tower, Cooper suddenly stepped into a hidden hollow filled with wet drifts of leaves. They lay in layers, where they had collected over the years. Below the surface, the older material was black and slimy and decaying into mould. You could wade through this lot, if you wanted to, and be very vulnerable to someone approaching from above.

Skirting the edge of the hollow to reach the base of the tower, he wrinkled his nose as a trace of something acrid and familiar reached his nostrils. Could he be mistaken? Were his senses playing tricks on him again? No, the smell was quite distinct and recognizable. Cal and

Stride's van had smelled of chicken curry. Yet the Hammond Tower smelled of petrol.

From the tower, a steep track ran down to a ledge below the Cat Stones. Cooper scrambled down the track, puzzled at the origin of the petrol smell. But as he moved away from the tower, the smell dissipated. It was lingering around the wall of the tower itself.

He looked at the outcrop of rocks above him. They formed one of the biggest of the cat shapes – a pile of wind-sculpted blocks of gritstone perched on a softer layer that had been worn almost completely away by wind and water. A yawning gap had been left underneath on this side – a great empty gash that made you wonder how the cat-shaped blocks stayed hanging in that precarious position. One day, the cat's legs would give way under the weight of rock and it would topple into the dale, forfeiting all of its nine lives in one go.

Cooper peered under the overhang. The cavity went deep under the rocks, six feet in, the height getting less as it receded to the back, a very shallow cave formed by the weathering of the stone. On the outer edge lay a handful of damp, grey feathers, where some predator had stopped long enough to dismember a wood pigeon. Cooper's nose twitched. There was something else here. Not petrol now, but something that smelled stale and unpleasant.

He crouched and ducked his head below the rock, then waited for his eyes to adjust to the darkness. The smell was more powerful and unmistakable. At these moments, he always remembered his first shift sergeant telling him to learn to breathe through his mouth at a death scene. If you were going to deal with dead bodies often, he said, it helped if you had a sinus problem, or chronic nasal congestion.

Cooper saw a hand, then an arm. Where the body touched the rock, the surface was stained dark with leaking fluids. The muscles and tissues had shrunk inwards away from the skin, leaving it hanging loose, like the flesh of an old, old woman. On one edge of the forearm, the skin had burst open, exposing the layers of muscle and fat underneath. Next, he noticed the dark snakes of hair that lay around the head. Although the ledge was dry, enough moisture had been supplied by the body's own fluids to support the process of putrefaction. By now, decomposition was well advanced, despite the cool air of the White Peak autumn. The body had been lying here a few weeks.

Cooper knew exactly what to do. It was as if the past few days had drawn him inexorably to this point, as if he had reached an inevitable conclusion without knowing any of the steps he had taken along the way.

He looked at the decomposed arm for a while, without surprise. There didn't seem to be any hurry to do the next thing. In a dying landscape, one more death seemed completely natural.

Chapter Thirty-Two

WITH THE FORENSICS team already fully occupied at Ringham Edge Farm, the news of another body mouldering away among the rocks just over the hill set up a howl of complaint about the shortage of resources. Little could be done until the next morning. By then, the lock on the big shed at the farm had been cut and the doors had finally been opened to let in the light. Leach's chaotic kitchen was being sifted through, and it looked like a long job.

Ben Cooper was helping the SOCOs to reconstruct the dog-fighting pit. They had found a heavily bloodstained area of floor and were placing straw bales from a stack in the shed around it on the assumption the bales might have been used for spectators' seating. They discovered that some of the straw was itself splashed with animal blood. And the trousers of the people who had sat on it must have been marked, too – here and there, you could make out the outline of their legs against the straw. It was obvious that efforts had been made to clean the place up, but the distinctive smell of blood still filled the shed, undisguised by the disinfectant.

'It's positively medieval,' said Diane Fry, appearing in the doorway behind him.

'It's fairly nasty,' said Cooper.

'The RSPCA have drawn us up a list of names – suspects they think may have been involved in this dog-fighting business. There could be some action at last.'

'Fine. But what about Ros Daniels? Did she come here before she died?'

A few yards away from the shed, police tape had been used to cordon off the burnt-out pick-up. Traces of petrol found on the decomposed hands of the corpse under the Cat Stones suggested one possible connection to the farm, at least. But with the scenes of crime staff already at full stretch, it was anybody's guess when they would get round to examining the vehicle and making comparisons.

Even the identification of the body was only tentative. The victim was the right age and the right general appearance to be Ros Daniels, though the injuries to the head and the process of decomposition made it difficult to be precise about facial features. She had been dressed all in black – jeans and a sweater, with a nylon cap lying nearby. And she had been wearing a silver disc on a chain round her neck, like a military dog-tag, with a stylized symbol engraved on it of an animal behind prison bars. The body also bore tattoos that would help identification, and the dreadlocked hairstyle was unusual.

There had once been debris under her fingernails, which might have been traces from an attacker. But as the skin of her fingers had shrunk away from her nails, the debris had loosened and fallen away. Although it reacted to tests for human blood, the sample was too small to hold any prospect of obtaining a grouping or DNA profile.

To Cooper, it seemed that the investigation constantly took one step forward and another one back. They had already been looking for anything that might connect Warren Leach directly with Jenny Weston, or with Maggie Crew. Now they were faced with the task of establishing what had happened to Daniels, and when. Because there was one thing that was obvious even from a cursory examination of the body that Cooper had found. Ros Daniels had been dead for weeks.

'What is it with you people in this area?' said Fry. 'Don't you know how to adapt to civilization? I mean, dog-fighting, for God's sake. Hasn't the world moved on from the Middle Ages? What do people like Warren Leach get out of it?'

'Maybe we should be asking what drove him to it,' said Cooper. 'Maybe it was people like you.'

DIANE FRY WALKED across the yard towards DCI Tailby and DI Hitchens. They were sitting on an upturned piece of agricultural machinery, a red steel object with vast prongs that dug into the ground.

'Well, it's very unsatisfactory,' said Tailby. 'I mean, Warren Leach being dead. It makes it look as though everything we've done has been too slow. Too late.'

'There was no obvious sequence,' said Hitchens. 'The pieces didn't fit. If we just react to pressure, that's when mistakes are made.'

'Leach may still be a mistake,' said Tailby.

'Jenny Weston used to go up on the moor regularly,' pointed out Fry. 'She must have passed by Ringham Edge Farm many times. And she was a great animal lover.'

'So she might actually have faced up to Leach and his friends and told them she was going to report what was going on?'

'Some people feel very strongly about these things.'

'It would be a really stupid thing for her to have done,' said Hitchens.

'But she did tell the RSPCA that she had some incriminating photographs,' said Fry.

'So where's her camera?'

'It wasn't in her house. There were plenty of photographs – scenic views, historic houses, that sort of thing. But no camera. It wasn't in her car either.'

'Her parents say they bought her an expensive autofocus job for her birthday last year to replace her old camera, but there's no sign of it,' said Hitchens. 'We've put the details out.'

'It would be very useful if it turned up somewhere. Especially with a film still in it, eh?'

'I wish,' said Hitchens. 'But if Jenny Weston had photos, why on earth didn't she tell us about them?'

'Didn't trust her friendly neighbourhood bobby, perhaps? Some people don't.'

'There's the question of Ros Daniels,' said Tailby. 'We need to clarify the relationship between them.'

'Cheshire Police think they've traced Daniels' home address to Wilmslow. Her parents are away at the moment, but the neighbours confirm the description. They didn't seem too impressed with her, apparently. But it's an upmarket area – more tennis club than Tank Girl. We'll just have to wait for the parents to come back from holiday.'

'Could it have been a lesbian relationship that went wrong?' said Tailby.

Fry frowned. 'We've no evidence of that.'

'But why was she staying with Weston? Why did she come to this area? And how did she get herself killed? After all, Daniels must have been the first victim, not Weston.'

'You're not suggesting Jenny Weston killed her?'

'If Mrs Van Doon confirms that Daniels died about the same time Maggie Crew was assaulted, as seems to be the case, then we do at least have Crew's fragmentary memories to go on.'

'A big man in a blue or black anorak or cagoule,' said Tailby, quoting from Fry's report of her interview with Maggie Crew. 'Well, I suppose Leach fitted the description. We could have put him into a parade.'

'But we didn't get the chance,' said Fry.

Tailby sighed. 'I suppose all the junior officers are blaming me,' he said.

'They don't understand the position you're in as senior investigating officer,' said Hitchens.

'And you, Paul?' said Tailby. 'Do you understand? Or do you blame me as well?'

Fry watched Hitchens stiffen awkwardly, and she knew he was seeking a way to avoid the direct answer. 'I'm sure you'll find all the team very supportive, sir,' he said.

LATER THAT MORNING, in the West Street canteen, Todd Weenink was watching a workman in blue overalls measuring the width of the room and checking for load-bearing walls. Weenink looked cheerful, as if the canteen was being redesigned entirely for his benefit. He had loosened his tie and unbuttoned his collar, and his shoulders bulged under his shirt as he leaned forward to bite into a Danish pastry.

'Well, Tailby really screwed up big this time,' he said. 'Another body, and a potential suspect topped himself before we could lay hands on him. Doesn't look good, does it? They'll be saying he hesitated too long.'

'It's not his fault,' said Ben Cooper.

'Let's face it, Tailby's lost it. Wasn't there some talk about him going for an admin job?'

The workman made a few notes on the back of an envelope and then started to put away his tape measure. The woman behind the counter followed every movement he made as if she were prepared to repel him with boiling hot tea if he came any closer.

'Looks like we could be seeing the last of Teabag Tracy there as well,' said Weenink.

'Probably.'

Weenink turned to look at Cooper. 'What's up with you, then? I can't get more than one word out of you. And you've got that look on your face again – the one like a constipated camel.'

'I'm worried about Wayne Sugden.'

'Come off it! Sugden? That is definitely a bloke whose parents were wading in the shallow end of the gene pool.'

HALF AN HOUR later, DI Hitchens burst through Tailby's door and found him staring morosely at the ceiling, an unlit pipe in his mouth.

'Forensics report,' said Hitchens breathlessly. 'We've got a result.'

'Already? The Leach house?'

Hitchens shook his head vigorously. 'No,' he said. 'Owen Fox.'

THE DI SET a new batch of tapes running when they brought the Area Ranger back to the interview room.

'Tell me again what sort of cigarettes you smoke.'

'I don't,' said Owen. He looked tired, his beard tangled from constantly running his fingers through it.

'When did you give up?'

'I've never smoked,' said Owen. 'You've asked me this before. What's the point of this?'

'All right. Do you recognize these cigarette stubs?'

'Of course not. You're joking, aren't you?'

'Do they look pretty much the same to you?'

'Of course they do.'

'You're right, they are. Identical. The same brand, the same batch, smoked in just the same way. Look at how exactly the same amount has been left before the filter, how they've been pinched between the fingers in precisely the same way. They could almost have come from the same packet, Owen. Except for their age. Do you agree?'

'I suppose so.'

'We found one in the bin at your briefing centre.'

'I've told you, I don't smoke. If you found it there, I don't know how it got there.'

Hitchens nodded. 'Do you want to know where we found the other one?'

Owen didn't respond.

'I'll tell you anyway,' said Hitchens. 'It was under Rosalind Daniels' body.'

BEN COOPER LOOKED at the stack of interview reports on his desk. His eyes were going blurred from staring at descriptions and dates, and his mind was starting to drift.

Cooper could see all the people he would have liked to protect becoming victims one after another – Cal and Stride, the Leaches, Owen Fox. Even Todd Weenink was his colleague and was owed some loyalty. So was Cooper himself the Jonah, the curse they had in common?

He searched his heart and instincts for the source of the problem. He knew it must be within himself. Was it a weakness to see people like Warren Leach as victims, just as much as the Jenny Westons and Ros Daniels and Maggie Crews were? And Owen Fox? And Calvin Lawrence and Simon Bevington? Or had he just not realized who it was he should be protecting these people against? But then Diane Fry had tried, too.

He knew Fry didn't see things the way he did. There was a clearer perception of black and white in the way she saw the world. It must be a huge advantage not to have the complication of always seeing both sides of the story. But then Fry had tried, too. She had tried to protect Cal and Stride against the vigilantes, and she had failed.

Cooper paused, and went over that again. There was something wrong with his thought processes. He got to the end of the thought, and realized what it was. Diane Fry – failed? This was the woman who didn't know what failure was. No matter what the circumstances of her life, she had risen above them, consumed by a determination to succeed. And succeed was exactly what she had done, so far. This woman was a fourth dan black belt, as tough as they came, and as ruthless. Surely she was capable of tackling more than one assailant, even in the dark. She could certainly have deterred an untrained and probably thoroughly scared group of amateurs. So would Fry really have failed to prevent the worst of the assault on the two travellers?

He turned over some more reports. Then he put his head in his hands, staring at a photo of Wayne Sugden.

Cooper knew it was his father who had made him try too hard. And he was still doing it, from the grave; Cooper was forever trying to live up to his expectations, and he would be doing it long after everyone else had forgotten him.

But things had changed since his father's day. These days, things weren't so clear cut. There no longer seemed to be the villains and the innocent members of the public, the black and the white, the good and the evil, with the police protecting the one against the other. These days there were only shades of grey, when everyone was classed as a victim, and evil no longer officially existed. As often as not, the law seemed to be a weapon to be used against the police, not by them. Was there still something called justice out there? Was it something that Sergeant Joe Cooper would recognize? Would he think that his son was doing his best to pursue justice? Or would he have growled: 'Do better, lad.'

Cooper heard the door open and a step approached his desk. There was a familiar exasperated sigh close to his left ear.

'Still tilting at windmills, Sir Galahad?'

'Don Quixote,' muttered Cooper without looking up.

'You read too much,' said Fry. 'It's addled your brains.'

Cooper sat back and looked at her. She seemed as tired as he felt himself. Her face was drawn, and there were blue patches under her eyes.

'How's it going down there?' he said.

'With your friend the Ranger? Badly. They've bailed him.'

'Really? I thought there was some forensic evidence. Cigarette ends –'

'Unfortunately, there are no traces of Fox. The saliva samples from the cigarettes don't match. And Fox's colleagues confirm he has never smoked. They weren't his fag ends.'

Cooper tried not to show how relieved he was. But he suspected Fry knew his thoughts anyway.

'Anything on Leach?' he said.

Fry shook her head. 'Not yet. Maybe it'll all come down to you and your instincts, and we'll find that Ben Cooper is right and everybody else is wrong. Because you seem to take the opposite view every time these days. You even want to defend Warren Leach, for God's sake. How can you do that?'

'You have to look at what makes people do things. Their actions don't exist in isolation.'

'You should have been a social worker, not a copper.'

'You've got more against social workers than most people do, haven't you?'

Cooper looked up and noticed the expression on her face. Too late, he knew he shouldn't have said that about social workers. He knew perfectly well that Fry and her sister had been taken into care after allegations of sexual abuse by their parents, and the sister had run away and become a heroin addict. Why Fry had shared those things with him, Cooper didn't know. There was so much about her that he didn't understand.

Now, he waited in shame and embarrassment for her to rip into him. But she didn't do that. Her brief spasm of rage was brought under control.

'Do you care nothing about your own career any more, Ben? Because the way you're heading, you're risking everything. Do you know that?' She didn't wait for him to answer. 'That's what it's all about, isn't it? You're never going to forgive or forget that I got the promotion. You thought you had a divine right to it, just because you've been in the area for ever and your balls are made of limestone or something. And now you're going to sacrifice yourself for some self-righteous idea that you'll probably call justice, just to prove that you don't care about the job, that you never really had any ambition after all. Well, go on, then – enjoy your martyrdom.'

After she had slammed the door behind her, Cooper read a few of the memos that were in his tray, but without taking in what they said. He made some notes on an assault case that was waiting to go to court. He looked through his drawers and found a half-eaten packet of Polo mints. He ate a mint. Then he ate another. And then he began to wonder what Owen Fox was doing now, back at Cargreave.

Owen was a man whose life and background had not stood up to close investigation. Whose life could? He had heard Owen described as a good man; but what did that mean? Was it a person who had never made a mistake? The papers would call Owen a sex beast, if they got the chance. But he wasn't an animal, just a man whose circumstances had left him with a weakness. His fallibility had contributed to an evil in the world, it was true. But there were so many evils – too many to count, even in Edendale. And being weak didn't make Owen Fox a monster; it only made him human.

Cooper knew that he had failed to help Cal and Stride, and he had failed to prevent the tragedy that had destroyed the Leach family. Maybe it wasn't too late for him to help Owen Fox. But there would be a price to pay, if he tried.

He was aware that he was walking a fine line already; his loyalties were under question, and not just by Diane Fry. It was vital that he stayed away from Owen Fox. There would be plenty of people ready to throw stones after all this, and it would be madness for Ben Cooper to put himself deliberately in the line of fire. Absolute madness.

Chapter Thirty-Three

There was no answer at the cottage in Cargreave. Ben Cooper stood on the bottom step, his feet crunching shards of broken clay pot and lumps of soil tangled with roots. All the plant pots on the steps had been smashed and the plants uprooted. Now they lay in a wet mess of soil. The bottom step had also been used as a toilet, almost as if the entire village had stood and urinated on to the doorstep. Urinated and worse. The smell was appalling.

All the curtains were drawn on this side of the house. Cooper walked a few yards along the road until he found a ginnel that ran between the cottages, with steep steps at the bottom where gates led into adjacent gardens. He clambered over a wall into the field and walked along it until he reached the back garden of Owen Fox's cottage and forced his way through an overgrown hawthorn hedge. A woman stared at him from a first-floor window next door, then turned away.

Cooper peered through the windows, remembering the gloom of the little room at the front of the house where Owen's computer had stood among the old newspapers and magazines. He banged on the back door, knocked on the windows, watching for a hint of movement inside. Nothing. Feeling foolish, he shouted Owen's name. There was no reply. So where else could he be? They had taken the Land Rover off him when he was suspended, and Owen wasn't the type to be drowning his sorrows in the pub. He would want to be somewhere quiet, where he could think about things.

Cooper found himself looking up at the bedroom window. The line of bereavement cards still stood there, mostly white and silver, fading in the sun. They were decorated with all the symbols of religion – crosses and stained glass windows depicting the Virgin Mary. They were the usual things on bereavement cards, often meaning nothing. But, of course, Mrs Fox had believed in religion. Owen had said so himself. He had taken her to the village church until she became bedridden. And the old lady could see the tower of the church from her bedroom window.

THE GRAVEYARD AT Cargreave parish church was full of local names – Gregory, Twigg and Woodward; Pidcock, Rowland and Marsden. There were lots of Shimwells and Bradleys here, and someone called Cornelius Roper – an ancestor of Mark's, perhaps? One of the most recent headstones was down at the bottom of the graveyard, in one of the last available plots. Annie Fox, aged ninety, beloved mother of Owen.

Even in the dusk and from the far side of the churchyard, Ben Cooper could see the red of the Ranger's jacket in the porch. He walked up the path. Inside the porch, Owen Fox was dwarfed by a slate slab, eight feet tall, bearing the Ten Commandments. Cooper sat down next to him on a narrow stone seat.

'It's locked, Ben,' said Owen. 'The church is locked.'

'Too much trouble with thieves and vandals, I suppose.'

'After she was gone, I didn't think I needed the church any more,' said Owen.

'Your mother?'

'We always used to come on a Sunday when she was well enough. After she died, I didn't think I needed it any more. Then suddenly today I thought I did, after all. But it's locked.'

Dozens of starlings were flocking in the churchyard, chattering to each other as they rustled from one yew tree to the next, deciding on a place to roost for the night.

'Look, it might be a good idea if you stayed at home for a while, Owen,' said Cooper. 'Watch the telly, read a book, mow the lawn, feed the cats. Anything. Go home.'

'I can't.' Owen scowled across the churchyard at the valley and the opposite hill. 'Not knowing your lot have been through the house and pawed over my life. It doesn't feel like my home any more. It's a place where I'm a pervert, a sicko, the lowest of the low. But not outside the house. Outside, I'm someone else entirely.'

Cooper looked at the notices pinned to a board inside a glass case next to the slate slab.

'According to this, you can get the key from the churchwarden at 2 Rectory Lane. The white house across the churchyard, it says.'

'Yes, I know,' said Owen.

'It's just over there, look.'

'Yes, I know.'

Cooper looked at the house, studying its curtained windows and tall chimneys. There was smoke coming from one of the chimneys, and it looked as though there was somebody at home.

'In this village, the churchwarden is also the chairman of the parish council,' said Owen. 'Councillor Salt. She knows me well enough.'

Then Owen changed the subject. It might have been the subject that had been running through his mind all along, whatever the words he had been speaking. It all spilled out as if Cooper had suddenly tuned in halfway through a conversation.

'I looked after Mum for so many years, you know,' said Owen. 'We were more than mother and son. We were a team. Do you know what I mean? It was like a marriage, in a way. I looked after her, and she looked after me – or she liked to think she did. She used to drag herself out of bed to get a meal ready for me when I came home. I would find her sitting on the kitchen floor, with the cutlery tipped out of the drawer and a pile of unwashed potatoes. And she would be apologizing for dinner being late.'

Owen's voice cracked. Cooper looked away, over his head, to avoid seeing his expression, waiting while he recovered. He felt like a voyeur suddenly faced with something far more personal and intimate than he had expected.

'Her mind was fine, but her body was long past being able to keep up with her,' said Owen. 'I think that's the saddest thing of all, don't you? It meant she knew exactly what was happening to her. It was a long drawn-out torture.'

'How long did you live together, just the two of you?'

'Thirty years.'

'Thirty years? Owen, you must have been –?'

'Since I was twenty-three.'

'Well, you're right about a marriage. Except that not many couples stay together so long these days.'

Owen nodded. 'We depended on each other. That's the difference, isn't it? You stay together when you need each other. Most of the couples I see, they don't really need each other – not after the sex thing is done with and the kids have grown up. Sixteen years at most, and the reasons for their marriage have gone. There's no real tie to keep them from drifting apart. No ties like there are with a parent. Real blood ties.'

'But never to have your own life, Owen ...'

'You still don't really understand. Mum *was* my life. Oh, I had the job. I've always loved being a Ranger, and I wouldn't have done anything else. But I've never really had friends – plenty of acquaintances, but no friends. And I was never going anywhere else, because I was needed right here, in Cargreave. I had a purpose. Until she died.'

'That must have left a big hole in your life,' said Cooper, aware of how inadequate the words were. He had an inkling of what it must have meant to Owen – not just to lose a part of your life, but to lose its entire purpose. It made him think of Warren Leach, who had come to the same point himself, in his own way, but had chosen a different method of dealing with it. Owen had followed a different path – less violent, perhaps, but just as destructive.

Cooper ran his eye over the ornate writing on the stone slab. The old-fashioned letters were difficult to read, full of curlicues and elegant swirls, not like the nice, plain print of a newspaper headline. The effects of the weather and the rubbing of many hands had worn the inscriptions down so much over the centuries that they had almost been lost entirely. The Commandments were so difficult to see that they were easy to ignore, too empty of significance to draw meaning from any more. Cooper traced the wording of number nine, taking his time, almost reluctant to get to the end of the sentence.

'"Thou shalt not bear false witness against thy neighbour,"' he said.

The Ranger stared at him, puzzled. 'Just because I had that stuff on the computer, it doesn't mean I'd do anything to children, you know. I want to tell people that, but they won't listen. On the way here, I passed a man that I've known all my life. He came to Mum's funeral. Today, he crossed the road to avoid me; when I got past, he spat on the pavement.'

The flock of starlings in the yew trees fell suddenly quiet. Cooper glanced nervously at the churchyard. For the third time in a week, he found himself worrying that someone might see him where he shouldn't be. There were several routes he could take to get into big trouble, and he was following them all simultaneously.

He couldn't help wondering what his father would have done. Would he have followed the path he thought to be right, and tried to achieve justice? Or would he have stuck to the rules? Cooper wished he could get a message from him somehow. But he was in the wrong place for that – Joe Cooper had never believed in a God bigger than himself.

'That woman you were accused of assaulting ten years ago …'

'It was different,' said Owen. 'Totally different.'

'You can see why it might look similar.'

'Not at all. That woman pursued me constantly. It was well known in the village that she wasn't right in the head. She would never leave me alone. It was terrible. Despite everything I could do to avoid her, she managed to get me on my own one day at home. All I did was push her away to make her leave. But she fell on the steps outside the house and banged her head. That was it. That was all that happened. Of course, her version was quite different. The things she said afterwards …'

Owen rubbed his fingers through his beard, so that the grey hair stuck out in odd directions. He tried to wipe away a trickle of sweat from his temple and left a dark smear instead.

'Do people here in the village know about your conviction?' asked Cooper. 'You've lived here all your life, after all.'

'Yes, they know. They knew all about it at the time, and they don't forget.'

'Yet nobody has said anything to us. Of all the calls that have come in to the incident room, no one from Cargreave has pointed out your history. If it hadn't been for your name cropping up in the paedophile enquiry, it would never have come to light.'

Owen nodded. 'It's because I belong here. Those other people, on the internet, I meant nothing to them. I had no place there. And now look what I've done to my life in Cargreave. I've been on the parish council for fifteen years. But the chairman left a message on my answerphone last night and said the most appalling things. Mary Salt used to be one of Mum's patients. Mum delivered both her children. I can never look Mary Salt in the eye again. I've just put my resignation through her letter box.'

Cooper began to feel as if he were standing at the front door of someone's house, searching fruitlessly for the right words to break the bad news when a family had lost a loved one – a father killed in a car crash, a teenager dead of an ecstasy overdose, a young girl snatched and dumped dead by the roadside. After a while, you learned there *were* no right words. You just did it, got it over with, and tried to keep up the barriers against the emotions you were bombarded with.

People wanted you to play God. They wanted you to bring the husband or daughter back to life somehow. In training, you were told how relatives might react, but not how you were going to react yourself. You weren't trained in dealing with your own feelings. And those emotions didn't come from a bottomless well. Every time you drained the emotional reserves, it took a bit longer to refill. Cooper had started to worry that eventually it wouldn't refill at all. One day that well might prove to be dry, and instead of normal feelings, all he would touch would be a dry, cracked surface, barren and stinking, like the sides of Ladybower Reservoir after a hot summer.

'I don't understand, Owen. Did you never have a girlfriend?' said Cooper.

The Ranger shook his head. 'It's old fashioned, I suppose.'

Old fashioned? Cooper didn't comment on the understatement. Most people these days would find it incomprehensible. Perversely, he knew, this would be another thing that Owen would find held against him.

'I was always awkward and shy as a teenager,' said Owen. 'I never developed the knack of forming relationships.'

'And when there was just you and your mother? Surely it wasn't too late?'

For answer, Owen stared at the Ten Commandments. Cooper tried to follow the direction of his gaze. Which commandment riveted his attention, and what thoughts had his question provoked that made Owen look so amazed and appalled at the way his life had turned out?

Cooper looked down the list, until he arrived at the right line. Owen was right to be amazed, if that was what he was thinking. He was looking at number seven: 'Thou shalt not commit adultery.'

'I had to do everything for her, in the later stages,' said Owen. 'I had to get her up, wash her and dress her, take her to the toilet, wipe her, feed her, clean her teeth, then undress her and put her to bed again. What marriage involves that kind of intimacy between a man and a woman?'

Owen had begun to cry; the tears crawled over his skin like tiny slugs, slow and painful. 'I'm sorry,' he said. 'I'm just glad she isn't here now.'

Cooper looked away. He looked at the headstones in the graveyard, the yew trees and leaf-covered paths; he studied the village street, where a delivery van was parked outside the butcher's shop, and he looked at the shadowed windows of the white house on the corner.

'Owen?' he said. 'Shall I fetch that key for you?'

THE INTERIOR OF the church smelled of stone flagged floors that had recently been mopped clean. The light came from high in the walls, fragmented by the stained glass windows in a way that reminded Cooper of the cattle market at Edendale. The wooden pews were lined up just like narrow holding pens for worshippers waiting to be herded into the afterlife. He half-expected to see Abel Pilkington up there in the pulpit in his black suit, shouting out the prices, knocking down lost souls to the highest bidder.

'You have to appreciate they're treating this child pornography enquiry very seriously,' said Cooper. 'There was a little girl who ended up dead at the hands of two of these men. There may have been more we don't know about.'

Owen nodded. 'Of course, I regret what I've done. Somehow, I didn't think of it as involving anyone else. I was still in my own private world, where it had always been just me and Mum, but now it was just me. And somehow – it was strange …' Owen screwed his face up in an effort to explain the inexplicable. 'But sometimes those little girls, Ben … I thought of them as if they were my mother. My own mother, as a child.'

Cooper lowered his eyes. There was nothing he could say, no platitudes that slipped into his mouth to meet the situation. His mind balked at being drawn into the dangerous, aberrant ideas that had appeared suddenly in front of him, like treacherous bogs across his path.

He felt guilty for stopping Owen. Being able to talk to someone would help him. But Cooper shouldn't be talking to him about it at all. At any moment, Owen might make some damaging admission, and they would both be in an impossible position.

'The cigarette stubs,' said Cooper.

'They've already asked me about those. Why do they matter?'

'They matter because one was found under the body of Ros Daniels, as well as near where Jenny Weston was killed. You know that. We think the killer smoked those cigarettes and dropped them – the one careless thing he did. And the one they found in the bin at Partridge Cross was identical.'

Cooper paused. He wished he could still see the Commandments for inspiration. His lips moved silently. He had been about to ask Owen if he had noticed the cigarette stub in the bin before the police search. If nobody smoked at the Ranger centre, it was something he ought to have noticed.

'Where did the cigarette in the bin come from, Owen? The bin had been emptied, but the ash was stuck to the bottom. Who uses that bin for their rubbish?'

'Anybody could.'

'And the rucksack. I know it's yours, Owen. But could anybody else have used that rucksack?'

Owen said nothing. He stared at the high windows, as if wondering why the birds perched in the branches of the yew were silent, why the stained glass saints said nothing, why the whole world was waiting for his reply. A realization had come over him like the passing of a cloud.

'Could anybody else use it?' repeated Cooper.

And then Owen said: 'Yes. Mark uses it.'

Owen Fox sat alone in one of the pews when Ben Cooper had gone. His head was down, his hands clenched together until the knuckles whitened. He had his eyes closed, like a man praying. But he wasn't praying – he was remembering. Remembering the little girl.

She had been about six years old, and she had been alive at first. He had pulled her out of the back seat of the wrecked car, with his lungs full of fumes from the petrol pouring out of the ruptured fuel tank, and his eyes averted from the bloody and shattered bodies of the little girl's parents, particularly the sight of her mother, with the branch of a tree skewering her cheek to the seat.

Owen had seen the car go out of control and hit the tree, and a second later he had heard screams that had died suddenly in the noise of the impact, lost in the crumpling thud of metal and the splintering of glass. He used his radio as he ran. But by the time he got to the road, he had no doubt the man and woman were dead.

The stench of the petrol panicked him when he saw the child still alive in the back seat. He barely knew what he was doing as he pulled her out, clumsily dragging her by her leg and a fistful of her blue dress, a thin summer dress that tore in his hand.

Then he had backed away to a safe distance and held the child in his arms while he waited for the ambulance to arrive. He seemed to be holding the girl for a long time, and he realized straight away that she was badly injured. He could feel the bones of her pelvis shift and bulge under his hand, and an unnatural swelling in her abdomen that seemed to grow and tighten under his fingers as he waited, not knowing what else to do. The child's body felt like a flimsy plastic bag that was no longer able to support the weight of its contents. At any moment it was in danger of splitting open and leaking its liquids, spilling soft, glistening objects on the ground.

Owen had held the child gently, willing her to survive, trying to pour his own life into her through his hands to help her fight the shock of her injuries. He found his fingers becoming extraordinarily sensitive, as all his attention concentrated on his sense of touch, on the close physical contact with another human being. He held a small, fragile life in his hands, and the sensations were like nothing he had ever known. He was aware of the faint beating of her heart, the pulsing of her blood, the slow lift and fall of her chest and the living warmth of her skin against his own.

Then Owen had become conscious of other feelings as he held the girl. He had noticed the soft flesh of her upper thighs where her dress was torn and pulled up to her waist. He noticed the white smoothness of her belly; and he saw the shape of her genitals, tiny and clear through the fabric of her knickers.

He stood frozen in confusion at his own reactions, frightened to move, praying for the ambulance to arrive soon and take his burden away. Yet a few minutes later he continued to hold on to the girl, oblivious to the sound of sirens and the voices that followed, clustering around him, asking questions. He held the girl desperately to his chest, feeling her softness in his hands, her weight pulling on his shoulders, conscious of his fingers staining her pale innocence.

Finally, the girl had opened her eyes and focused on his face. In a moment of consciousness, she had seen his red jacket and his Peak Park badge.

'Oh, you're a Ranger,' she said. And Owen remembered even now the rush of senseless, guilty pride he had felt that the girl could recognize who he was, and had felt secure in his arms.

Then the child's eyes had closed, and a trickle of blood escaped from the corner of her mouth. And a warm flood of urine seeped from her and ran down the front of his red jacket, as she died.

Chapter Thirty-Four

In the incident room, the faces of the officers were expectant. They were thinking that there had to be something at last. After all this, there had to be some good news.

Examination of Ros Daniels' body showed that she had died from serious head injuries, though there were other marks on her that awaited interpretation. The fibres of the victim's clothing were distinctive. Forensics were sure they would have been shed on her assailant's outer garments, if he had made contact. Vegetative traces and powdered gritstone taken from the scene might also have adhered. Cross-matching would provide proof of contact. Now all they needed was a firm suspect.

'Owen Fox has been bailed in regard to a separate matter,' said DCI Tailby. 'We have discounted any connection with our present enquiry.'

There were murmurs of speculation. But Ben Cooper wasn't surprised. The cigarette stubs they had found under Ros Daniels' body could never have belonged to Owen Fox. Cooper could think of three people directly connected with the enquiry who smoked cigarettes, and Owen wasn't one of them. Forensics had found traces of saliva remaining on the filters of the cigarettes, which had been prevented from drying out by the girl's body lying on top of them. There was a residue of moisture in the tobacco, too. The cigarettes had been smoked very shortly before Ros Daniels' death. And the DNA from the saliva would identify the person who had smoked them.

'And so far we have been unable to establish a direct link with Warren Leach,' said Tailby. 'Though he remains a suspect.'

Leach hadn't smoked, either. Not many farmers did, when they worked around hay and straw and agricultural fuel. Yet somebody had been smoking when Ros Daniels was attacked, and again when Jenny Weston was killed.

Tailby's head drooped slightly. His face was tired, and his eyes were sunk into dark sockets. 'We're still looking for leads,' he said. 'But where?'

He spoke for the whole room. How was it possible that they could have two bodies and a third, surviving, victim, yet after ten days be further away than ever from identifying a suspect? A police officer had been injured by vigilantes, and no one had been arrested yet. Questions were being asked all the way up the line. And the newspaper headlines said: 'How many more?'

Tailby hung his head. 'Let's think positively. Apart from the fact that Daniels stayed with Weston for a while, the only link we have between them is that they were both animal lovers. Paul?'

'OK,' said DI Hitchens. 'Examination of the shed at Ringham Edge Farm by ourselves and the RSPCA confirms the suspicion that it was being used for dog-fighting. We know that Jenny Weston saw what was going on there. She passed by there one evening when she had been late on the moor. She reported her information to the RSPCA, and she claimed to have photographic evidence. Whether she went any further than that, we don't know. Whether Daniels did the same, we don't know either. However, with the help of the RSPCA special investigations unit, we have drawn up a list of known or suspected participants in the dog-fighting ring. There are some pretty unsavoury characters among them, and one or two are known to us.'

'Is one of them Keith Teasdale?' said Cooper.

'Yes, his name is on the list. Today is Operation Muzzle. We're going to make some arrests.'

WHEN BEN COOPER walked back into the CID room, DS Dave Rennie was there, looking relaxed, like a man at home in front of the TV watching *Coronation Street*. He should have had his slippers on. Cooper saw that there was a stack of paper on Rennie's desk, forms filled with scrawled handwriting in ballpoint pen. Some of the writing looked almost illiterate.

'What's all that lot, Sarge? Witness statements?'

'Questionnaires,' said Rennie. 'I've got all these back already from the early and day shifts. I've just collected them from the box in the canteen.'

'Oh, the vending machines.' Cooper picked up a couple of sheets. 'What sort of things are they saying, then?'

'I haven't looked at them yet. But I dare say they'll go for it, generally. We gave them a multiple choice, look – hot food, sandwiches, snacks or drinks. All they had to do was choose which they'd use. It makes it look as though the vending machines are a foregone conclusion, but actually we're using their responses as evidence to push the idea through. Clever, isn't it?'

Cooper's eyes widened as he read one of the questionnaires. 'Amazing.'

Rennie nodded. 'It's surprising what management will come up with.'

'Sarge, the person who filled in this questionnaire here says they'd like hot food, but hot women would be even better.'

Rennie sniffed. 'Well, you know what it's like, Ben. There are always some who have to take the piss, no matter what.'

'And under "other suggestions" they've asked for condom machines and somewhere to dispose of their used hypodermic needles.'

'I might have to take one or two out before I show them to the DCI in Admin,' said Rennie.

'Who wrote this one, then?'

'They're all anonymous, Ben.'

'Is that wise?'

'You know as well as I do, if people have to give their names, you don't get anything from them. Coppers are dead suspicious of putting their names to something that looks official.'

Cooper looked at the questionnaire again. 'Look how this one's spelled "fruit-flavoured".'

'I can't believe they're so ignorant. What happened to the education system?'

'And the handwriting's appalling. A graphologist would have a field day with this. He'd probably say it was written by some homicidal psychopath.'

Rennie looked over Cooper's shoulder and frowned. Then he began desperately flicking through the other questionnaires. Some of them were written in garish purple ink, some had obscene drawings scribbled in the margins. One had an insulting cartoon of the Chief Superintendent. Another had letters cut from newspaper headlines pasted on to it to form a message. It read: 'You have ten minutes to evacuate the canteen before the steak and kidney pie explodes.'

'Psychopath would describe just about everybody in *this* station,' said Rennie sourly. 'There isn't a single one that's been filled out properly.'

Cooper didn't respond. He was staring at the questionnaire form in his hand. He was holding it so tightly that the paper crumpled and almost tore between his fingers.

'Er, Sarge?' he said. 'Can I keep this one?'

Rennie shrugged. 'Suit yourself. They're no use to me at all.'

TODD WEENINK WAS going to the cattle market, too. He wasn't making any preparations, though, except to eat a quick sandwich. Bits of tomato had slipped out of the bread and dropped on to his desk. Ben Cooper tapped him on the shoulder and signalled with his eyes. Neither of them spoke until they were in the corridor.

'What's up, Ben?'

'Come across the road. We're going for a coffee.'

'What if I don't want one?'

Weenink tried to slow down, but Cooper gripped his elbow and kept moving. 'You're coming anyway,' he said.

'Ben, you're getting a bit forceful all of a sudden. I'm not sure I like it, mate.'

'We've got some talking to do.'

'Oh, Christ. Do you never get sick of talking?'

May's Cafe was off West Street, in a lane running steeply downhill to the Clappergate shopping centre. It was comfortable, without being too appealing to the tourists. A sign in the window said 'Ristorante Italiano', but it was hand-painted in a bit of white gloss left over from when the kitchen walls were last redecorated, and it didn't look very convincing.

Cooper had been coming to May's for years. He remembered the sign in the window first being painted – it was just after May and her boyfriend, Frank, had come back from a fortnight's holiday in Rome. In that fortnight, May had discovered pasta. She arrived back in Edendale full of stories of the most wonderful fettuccine and funghini. A whole range of pasta dishes had made an appearance on the menu, scrawled in blue ballpoint that had faded with time. Now you could search for Italian influences and find only a word that might have been 'tagliatelle' written sideways in the margin next to the steak and chips. But if you wanted to be in May's good books, you could still ask for pasta.

There was only a middle-aged couple in the cafe, drinking tea silently at a table near the counter. The woman had plastic carrier bags full of groceries from Somerfield's; the man had a blank look, as if he wished he were far away. They stared briefly at the detectives, then looked away, embarrassed to be noticed.

Cooper ordered a couple of coffees – black and strong, the way May always made it.

'That bit of trouble of yours, Todd ...' he said.

'I'd prefer it if you'd just keep your mouth shut, mate,' said Weenink. 'It's an old story anyway. You've heard it all before.'

'Did you fit somebody up?'

'Just helped things along, Ben. Some would say it doesn't matter if the suspect is guilty. We can't have them getting away on some technicality, can we? You know what the courts are like – not to mention the bloody Criminal Preservation Society. You can see when a bloke is gearing up for a spell in Derby. So what's the problem?'

May herself was behind the counter. She was a big woman, well into her fifties, with a face permanently pink from the heat of the kitchen and large, widespread breasts like upturned soup tureens that had been pushed down the front of her blue apron. Her hair was dyed a pale strawy colour today that reminded Cooper of something.

'Todd, there are people round here who have it in for you. They'd take any chance ...'

Weenink threw out his arms. 'Oh, tell me about it. That's why you need your friends to stand by you. Of course, I'm relying on you to keep this to yourself, Ben. As long as we stick together, they haven't got anything.'

'But why do it, Todd?'

'Why? Can't you see they're all laughing at us? I even got bollocked for abusing a prisoner the other week. I called him a Scotch pillock and got my arse chewed off by the Super for racism. But he *was* a Scotch pillock, Ben.'

'I know it's difficult.'

'Difficult? Have you seen the guidelines for interviews? Confrontation and intimidation are out. Exaggerating the evidence, emphasizing the seriousness of the crime. All out. What a load of crap. What do they think we are? A bunch of nannies?'

'It's only being realistic. A confession obtained like that will get thrown out by the court.'

'Yeah, great. So we have to say, "Don't worry, it's nothing serious, and we've hardly got anything on you, anyway." That'll make them confess, all right. I can see them rolling over on their backs and spilling their guts to help me out, just because I'm a really nice man.'

'I think you're over-reacting.'

'No kidding? You were never one for over-reacting, were you, Ben? Take the shit and don't complain, eh? Well, that's a good boy. The management will love you.

Maybe you'll still be here putting in your thirty years for your pension when the rest of us have got out to start earning a clean living. Maybe you'll still be stacking up the paperwork and processing the same old scumbags in and out of the custody suite while we're all working as security guards in Woolworth's or as private enquiry agents for that Eden Valley firm, doing nice little divorce cases. That's if you last that long. But my bet is they'll get to *you* in the end, too. Even you, Ben.'

Cooper found himself staring at May's hair. She smiled, and flushed a deeper pink. Her boyfriend, Frank, stuck his head round the kitchen door and eyed her suspiciously. He was wiry and black-haired, with a moustache and a dark stubble. He looked typically Italian, but he was a scrap merchant from Macclesfield.

'I know which case it was,' said Cooper.

'OK,' said Weenink. 'So you figured it out. Go to the top of the class. Yes, it was the break-in at that little retirement cottage at Ashford. The Westons' place.'

'Wayne Sugden.'

'Sorting Sugden out was easy,' said Weenink. 'There were some cotton fibres from an armchair that were the clincher. I sat in the chair myself when I went round to the cottage, and I noticed how easy the fibres came off. I had an informant who agreed he might have seen Sugden – and bingo. And he had a handy little motive, too – that business of old Weston's with the nephew.'

Cooper could hear the tea hissing in the urn and the wet rattle of Frank clearing his throat in the kitchen. May was humming behind the counter, the same snatch of

'Nessun Dorma' over and over again. He looked at Todd Weenink, but Weenink stared out of the window, as if his attention had been taken by a passing lorry. Cooper knew that his colleagues weren't angels. Every one of them was human, prone to emotions and acts of folly. He had known officers driven to the most appalling stupidities by anger or fear, or by some desperation in their lives that undermined their self-control. But this was too cold, too calculated.

'If they're guilty, Ben,' said Weenink, 'what does it matter?'

Cooper knew why it mattered. It mattered because the likes of Wayne Sugden were likely to focus their grievances not on the police, but on the people who testified against them. In this case, Sugden's grievance had focused on the key-holder for that cottage at Ashford, who had listed the damage that Wayne said he had never done. If he needed a motive after the death of his nephew, Sugden's resentment would have had an obvious target.

'And Jenny Weston?' he said. 'How did she come into it?'

'The fact is, I fancied Jenny something rotten right from the start, as soon as I clapped eyes on her at that cottage. I thought I'd be all right there. But she seemed to need a bit of encouragement, you know. She was a bit uptight about the burglary, about what her parents would say when they got back. She kept on about it ruining their holiday, so I reckoned what she needed was reassurance. A quick arrest.' Weenink winked. 'A hero on a white horse. It works a treat.'

'How long did that last?'

'Last? It never lasts. We had a few nights, that was all. We used the cottage, so her neighbours at Totley didn't see me. It was a bit of fun. She wasn't interested in anything else.'

'In this day and age, don't you know any better?' said Cooper.

Weenink scowled. 'You're not going to lecture me about AIDS and all that stuff, are you? You only live once, mate, and you've to take it when you can get it. If I die young, so what? Nobody will exactly be breaking their hearts, and at least I'll have had a good time.'

'So you didn't see Jenny Weston after that?'

'No, I didn't. Like I said, it was just a quick in and out for her. Scratching an itch. She was quite honest about it. Besides … well, she wasn't entirely walking the line, you know.'

'What?'

'She wasn't a hundred per cent kosher. She had a leg either side of the fence. She swung both ways, Ben.'

'Todd, are you telling me Jenny Weston was bisexual?'

'That's what they call it when you've been to college, I guess.'

'Are you absolutely sure?'

Weenink stared at the muddy remains of his coffee. 'To tell the truth, I reckon she was bored with blokes already by then. Doing it with me, it was kind of a last try sort of thing. "Never done it with a copper before – it might be different." I was a bit surprised at first; I thought she was good for a few more nights. But then I realized why she had dumped me so quick – it was because she'd already got herself a girlfriend. That was a bit of a blow to the old pride for a while, I must admit.'

Cooper stared at Weenink. 'How do you know that?'

'Ben, I made it my business to know.'

'Do you mean to say that Ros Daniels was Jenny's lover after all?'

'I never heard Jenny mention her. But it's pretty damn certain, I reckon.'

'Todd, you've got to say something.'

'You must be joking. My mouth is shut tight.'

Weenink turned his stare on Cooper. But for once there was something missing in the stare; there was a shadow in his eyes, a doubt that dissipated the menace and exposed a naked appeal that contradicted the tone of his voice.

'And what about you, Ben?' he said. 'Going to throw me to the lions, or what?'

Cooper's eyes were drawn back to May. She straightened her dress and patted that strange, pale hair whose colour he couldn't name. Frank had emerged from the kitchen and was wiping a knife on his apron as he studied the two police officers. Cooper knew he would have to report what had been said. Surely Todd Weenink would understand that. But where did that leave the concept of loyalty to a colleague? Or the reluctance in his heart to see one more person destroyed?

In a flash of insight, he had the answer. May's hair was the colour of pasta.

BACK AT THE station, Ben Cooper managed to find Diane Fry in the CID room.

'Some proper arrests at last, then,' said Fry, rubbing her hands. 'We should have done it before.'

'Diane, have you looked at the file on the burglary at the Westons' cottage?'

'Of course. It was a fairly routine case.'

Cooper knew she was right. The crime report was adequate, nothing startling, though it had generated the usual morass of paperwork. It wasn't surprising that senior officers couldn't be bothered wading through it all. The important thing was that the enquiry had been successful, and a conviction had resulted. Wayne Sugden had a record of similar offences, and even the Edendale magistrates had finally lost patience and given him a twelve-month sentence. The difference was that Sugden had pleaded not guilty to this one.

'The evidence was fairly conclusive,' said Fry. 'Even the CPS were perfectly happy with the case. He had the video recorder in his possession at his flat. That was careless.'

'He claimed he'd bought it in a pub car park,' said Cooper, his memory of the details perfectly clear. 'He seemed to expect a receiving charge. He still insists he didn't nick the video himself.'

'Videos are among his favourite items, according to his PNC record. And cotton fibres found on his jacket matched the cover of an armchair in the cottage.'

Cooper noticed that Fry's recollection of the details was good, too, though it was much longer since she had seen the file.

'The video was on a stand next to one of the armchairs in the Weston house,' she said. 'The evidence indicated that Sugden had sat or kneeled on the chair, presumably while disconnecting the video from the telly.'

'But all the other stuff?' asked Cooper. 'The cash and jewellery that was taken. None of that was ever found. Sugden couldn't account for it. And then there's the damage. The broken furniture, the smashed pictures, the Tabasco sauce on the carpets. You'd think he'd have got some Tabasco on his shoes, at least.'

Fry shrugged. 'You can't have everything. He was a bit lucky. But the fibres were enough to establish his presence in the house.'

'Of course. But now Sugden has been out of prison for three weeks.'

'I know you think he might have had a grudge against Jenny Weston. But surely *she* should have a grudge against *him*, not the other way round?'

'Some of these people don't think logically. If he had a really bad time in prison, he might blame her for it, in his own way. We've known stranger things.'

'It's possible, I suppose.' But Fry sounded unconvinced. 'Wayne Sugden is a petty thief. He doesn't sound like a killer to me.'

'It depends what happened to him at Derby. It depends on who he's been mixing with. They go in as petty villains and they come out like Reggie Kray. It's called rehabilitation.'

Fry stared at the file in Cooper's hands as if she was hardly listening. 'Remind me – how did we manage to get a search warrant in the first place?'

'The investigating officer had a tip-off,' said Cooper. 'A reliable source who placed Sugden in the vicinity of the Weston house and acting suspiciously.'

'This was someone who knew Sugden by sight?'

'Apparently.'

'The usual, I suppose. Some pal he'd fallen out with, who decided to get his own back.'

'Why do we trust the information we get from these people?'

'Because they're often right,' said Fry. 'This one was. The search turned up the video recorder. He was guilty, Ben.'

Cooper put down the file, dispirited by the echo of Todd Weenink's words.

'I wanted to ask you about Maggie Crew,' he said.

Fry frowned. 'What about her?'

'How badly damaged is she? Psychologically, I mean.'

'It's not for me to say. The psychiatric reports say she's recoverable.'

'But what are the long-term effects of the trauma? Would she be able to make an identification if we produced a suspect?'

'That's what we're all hoping, isn't it?'

'You're getting to know her pretty well, aren't you?'

Fry pulled on her jacket. 'Not as well as I thought.'

'Why?' Cooper was surprised. 'What's the problem? Are there things she isn't telling you?'

'Aren't there always?'

'Something in particular?' he insisted.

Fry sighed. 'Well, I spoke to her sister in Ireland. The sister mentioned that Maggie had a child, when she was a law student. She had it adopted. But Maggie never told me that.'

'I see.'

'All that time I spent telling her about Jenny Weston. I tried to make Jenny real to her. And all the rest of it … well, I gave it my best shot. But Maggie was never giving me anything in return. Not really.'

Fry adjusted the scabbard for her ASP, sliding it further round the back of her belt, patting her jacket to make sure it wasn't too obtrusive. She never seemed to go anywhere without her baton any more.

Cooper watched her tighten her belt a notch over her hips to make it more secure. Fry had changed over the last couple of weeks. She had always been a woman with secrets, he knew that. But before, she had been all hard shell on the surface, rejecting any contact. Now, though, there was a faint whisper of a softening in her manner, as though a small breach had been opened up. Cooper didn't know how or why it had happened, but he prayed he was right, that he could get through to the sharp brain behind her barricades of hostility.

'Are you not coming to the cattle market this morning?' asked Fry.

'No. I've got an interview to do. Some youth called Gary Dawson, who's suddenly remembered that he was on Ringham Moor the day Jenny Weston was killed.

There's just an off-chance he might have seen something. Then I've got a couple of other things to do.'

Fry was already heading for the doorway when she stopped and turned. 'OK, Ben – what are you up to?'

'Nothing.'

'Do you realize I can see straight through you?'

Cooper shuffled uncomfortably.

'Who are you trying to protect now, Ben? What lost cause have you taken to your bleeding heart?'

'I don't know what you mean.'

She watched him suspiciously. 'Let me give you a word of advice. Be careful who you associate with, Ben. It could affect your future in a major way.'

'What are you talking about?'

Fry came closer. 'Your friend, Detective Constable Weenink, that's what.'

'Todd?'

'I've been picking up a few things, and from what I hear, Weenink could be in big trouble. And if you don't watch out, Ben, he's going to take *you* down with him.'

'He's all right, Todd, really.'

'All right? Are you kidding? We all know his brain drops into his testicles every time something female walks past, for a start.'

Cooper laughed. It was the wrong thing to do. Fry took him by the forearm. Her grip was painful, and very quickly his hand began to go numb.

'Are you involved in something with Weenink, Ben? Tell me.'

'Of course not.'

'You're lying. What's more, you're a pathetically bad liar. You're the worst bloody liar in the police service, and that's saying something. What have you done?'

'Nothing.'

'I see,' said Fry. Cooper tried not to give her the satisfaction of showing that she was hurting him. 'But there's something going on. I know there is. Maybe you haven't done anything yourself. But you're so bloody naive, you'll get yourself dragged in, and that'll be the end of you. Have you been covering up for him?'

Cooper said nothing.

'Oh yes, you're really one of the lads these days, aren't you, Ben? The loyal colleague.'

'If somebody needs support –'

Fry snarled at him. 'Support? You bloody idiot! For a prat like Weenink!'

Cooper's eyes were watering from the pain in his arm.

'If you're up to something, Ben,' said Fry, 'I'll have your balls for clothes pegs and string 'em up on the same line as your pal Weenink's. If you'll take my advice, you'll bury him. Good and deep.'

'OK, OK,' he said. But Fry kept her grip. 'But there's one thing, Diane.'

'What now?'

'Take a look at the Sugden file again. Do you remember who his defence solicitors were? Quigley, Coleman & Crew.'

Fry's grip tightened even more. 'You're suggesting that Maggie Crew was his solicitor?'

'No, it was one of the firm's juniors who represented him in court. But don't you think she might have met him? Don't you think she would be able to identify him? Do you think she might even have known who Jenny Weston was?'

'Rubbish.'

Cooper rubbed his arm as Fry stalked off. If he had been hesitating over what to do about Todd Weenink, now he had been pushed into a corner. Cooper could report what Weenink had told him. But now, if he did, it would be just one more victory for Diane Fry.

THE PREVIOUS NIGHT, *Cooper's sleep had been disturbed by a scene that played over and over through his mind like a clip from a horror video shot in poor light. There were figures moving slowly in a circle, leaning towards each other, slipping in and out of the mist that hung over Ringham Moor. The figures were dancing. They danced like the Nine Virgins themselves.*

First, he recognized Jenny Weston. She was naked from the waist down, kicking high with her legs, her skin ghostly white and bloodless, a red streak running down the front of her blue cycling vest. Behind her came Cal and Stride, stumbling blindly as they felt their way among the birches, their faces frightened and confused. Stride's trousers were round his ankles, and a bloodstained broom handle wagged like a tail as he shuffled after Cal.

Then there was Warren Leach. Cooper wished he could turn away from the sight of Leach's head, a red mass that made him almost unrecognizable. He was followed by Yvonne, her wide hips giving her a distinctive waddle, one hand rubbing at her mouth, her other hand trailing the two boys, Will and Dougie. Owen Fox was close behind them, stumbling after the boys with his red jacket flapping open. And then came Ros Daniels, all in black, her dreadlocks flying, a nose ring glittering, the skin of her arms and legs split and bursting, laid open to the air as she brought up the rear of the dance.

But no – Daniels wasn't at the rear at all. There was another figure, very dim, still shrouded in the mist so that Cooper couldn't make it out. There was a ninth victim. One more who had made a mistake.

And then Cooper had gradually become aware of the faint music they all danced to. And he knew that, somewhere in the thickening mist, was the Fiddler.

Chapter Thirty-Five

DESPITE THE APPEALS in the paper and on TV, the youth, Gary Dawson, had been pushed into coming forward by his mum. Only a second dead body had made a difference to the potential excitement of being a witness. As a result, Gary's evidence had been almost too late.

'Did you know we were looking into the death of Mr Warren Leach?' Ben Cooper asked him.

'I heard. Did himself in, didn't he?'

'You worked for him.'

'Used to. I walked out. I told him I wouldn't stand for it any more. He got to be such a foul-arsed bugger. But I told him. "I don't need to put up with this hassle and abuse all the time," I said. "I can soon get a job somewhere else."'

Gary was wearing a red woollen cap, even indoors. He had protruding ears that he had made look even bigger by pulling his cap down over them.

'And have you? Found another job?'

'Well, not yet. There's not much about.'

Cooper produced the photographs of the three women. 'Did you ever see any of these three near the farm?'

Gary pointed immediately at the picture of Maggie Crew. "That's the one Yvonne Leach found, isn't it? Warren went on and on about that for days. I saw her picture in the paper.'

'Were you there when Mrs Leach found this woman?'

'No.'

'Did you see her around the farm at all?'

'Not around the farm, no.'

'All right, Gary. What about the other two?'

He tipped his head on one side. 'I'm not sure,' he said. 'But that one, I think I saw her.'

'Yes?'

'She looked different from that picture, but I reckon it could have been her on the moor. Bird on a bike, is that right?'

'Gary,' said Cooper carefully, 'what day was this?'

'The day I walked out on Warren Leach. I wasn't hanging around to hear him ranting at me any more, so I walked out. Usually he gave me a lift home when I finished work, but I didn't wait for that. I walked back over the moor. I live at Pilhough, just the other side.'

'What day, Gary? Please be exact.'

'It was a Sunday,' said Gary. 'But not last Sunday.'

'The one before?'

'Yes, it must have been.'

'And on your way back over Ringham Moor, you saw this woman?'

'On a bike – it was her, all right. She gave me the evil eye, she did. She didn't want someone like me hanging around. There was no one else up there that day – no one else at all, except her and the other woman.'

'The other woman?'

'The one that was waiting for her.' Gary noticed the sudden silence and read the expression on Cooper's face for the first time. 'Well, she was going up there to meet someone, wasn't she?'

'Why do you say that, Gary?'

'She had that look about her. Like she was expecting to see someone, only it wasn't me. Do you know what I mean? In any case, I saw the other one a bit earlier. Up near the tower, she was.'

'The other one? Gary? Which other one?'

'That one, the one that Yvonne Leach found. I never saw her near the farm, but she was up near the tower that day. And you could see she was waiting. She was smoking cigarettes like there was no tomorrow.'

A HERD OF heifers was being sold in the cattle market. The mart men dodged and danced round them as they went through the ring. The heifers were being sent for breeding, to a suckler herd, where they would meet the bull for the first time. And the bull would be some giant Limousin or Charolais, weighing two tons and bulging with double layers of muscle so heavy and deep into his body that he could barely move, except to hoist himself into position for the thrust. It would come as a shock to them, these black and white virgins. Their white eyes showed they were already getting a suspicion of things that lay ahead.

From where they were parked, Diane Fry could see through the doors to the side of the auction ring, where farmers and buyers milled around, absorbed in their own conversations.

'Keith Teasdale is inside,' said DI Hitchens. 'His vehicle has been located in the car park.'

'When do we make a move?'

'We want to do it as discreetly as possible.'

'Wait for the auction to finish, then?'

'Yes. We take it easy, keep an eye on them and let the crowd disperse. It's too full of people in there at the moment.'

The radio crackled, and Fry answered it. 'I think we might have a problem, sir,' she said.

'What's up?'

'DC Weenink reports a group of women gathering in the car park. Fifteen or twenty of them, he says.'

'What the hell do they want?'

'It looks like some kind of protest.'

As HE ENTERED the hospital ward, Ben Cooper nodded to the nurse at the desk, who smiled at him. She looked a nice girl, but tired and preoccupied, too busy to engage in social intercourse. But for the colour of her uniform, she could have been in the police service.

There were twelve beds in the ward. Some of the patients were old men, stirring restlessly or sitting up in their striped pyjamas, staring at the unexpected visitor. It was outside normal visiting hours and there was little to occupy them until the next meal arrived.

At first Cooper thought it might have been a mixed ward, one of those relics of the NHS. But then he remembered who he had come to see. Stride lay on his side, a slight figure too slender and too mannered in his pose to be at home among the old men. He was running his pale hand through his long hair, pushing a strand away from his face.

As Cooper came nearer, he saw that Stride's eyes were distant and unfocused, like a man listening to a personal stereo or an audio tape of some absorbing thriller that had taken him away from the real world. But there were no headphones. Stride needed no artificial aids to distance himself from reality. That distancing must be a great talent.

'Visiting time, Simon,' he said.

The young man didn't stir. 'They call me Stride.'

There was a bottle of mineral water on the bedside cabinet and a glass. Stride seemed to be fascinated by the slow floating of the bubbles towards the surface.

Stride had told the police nothing so far – nothing useful either about the night he had been attacked, or about anyone he might have seen on Ringham Moor. But Cooper knew Stride spent more time on the moor than anyone else. He was there at night, too – to talk to the Virgins, according to Cal. Like Mark Roper, he probably saw more than was good for him.

But Stride's vagueness was more than just an absence of memory which might be brought back by the right triggers, like Maggie Crew. What sort of unimaginable triggers would release Stride's knowledge?

'I wanted to tell you something,' said Cooper. 'There was a youth on the moor that day – the day that Jenny Weston was killed. His name was Gary and he'd been working for Warren Leach at Ringham Edge, but they had a row and he walked off. He saw Jenny reach the top of the path, and he says she went towards the Hammond Tower. It was very helpful that Gary came forward. Eventually.'

'Yes?'

'*You* didn't come forward, though, Simon. You didn't tell us anything. All that stuff about the Fiddler. What was the point?'

'Leave me alone.'

'This youth, he saw Jenny Weston. Who else do you think he might have seen?'

'I could call for the nurse. You're not good for my condition.'

'I thought about you first. Were you there, Simon? And was your friend there too?'

Stride stayed on his side and stared straight ahead.

'He means a lot to you, doesn't he?' said Cooper.

'Nobody ever accepted me for what I am. But Cal did.'

'I understand,' said Cooper. 'But, Simon – did you see Jenny Weston?'

'Why do you ask that?'

'It was something you said once. You said: "I saw her face." Simon, I think you saw her after she was dead.'

'Oh.'

Stride shifted uncomfortably in the bed, his face pale.

'Do you need more painkillers?'

'No, don't worry.'

'It looks uncomfortable.'

'Yeah. Will you tell me something?'

'What?'

'Is this what anal sex is like?'

Cooper blinked. Stride laughed at his expression, and his fingers went to his mouth. Men in the other beds turned to look at them. They were already curious about Stride.

'No, you wouldn't know, would you? Anyway, it'd have to be a bloke with a cock as big as a broom handle. Not many of those about.'

'I'll ask around a bit,' said Cooper.

'Don't do that,' said Stride. 'For your own safety.'

'Cool.'

Stride looked around for the mineral water. Cooper poured it for him and passed him the glass, to save the young man having to stretch too far.

'Did you actually see her?' he said.

Stride looked dreamy again. But if the painkillers were wearing off, he couldn't blame the medication for his spiritual absence.

'Did you?' said Cooper. 'Did you see her? Jenny Weston?'

But Stride didn't answer.

'Or was it the other woman you saw?' said Cooper. 'The one with the scars on her face?'

Finally, Stride stirred. 'No, the first one. Jenny.'

'You won't be going very far, will you?' said Cooper. 'We'll want a statement from you.'

'I've already given one. I never saw them properly – it was too dark.'

'Not about that, Simon. About the murder of Jenny Weston.'

Stride could be sharp enough when he wanted to be. Yet his eyes were closing, and he looked about to drift off to whatever place it was he went to.

'I don't know who killed her,' said Stride. 'There's no point in asking me.'

'Maybe not. But it was you that found the body first, at least,' said Cooper. 'Nobody else would have arranged her like that, in the stone circle. I have to tell you that Jenny was no virgin, Simon. And it wasn't the Fiddler who made her dance. It was you.'

Stride closed his eyes tightly. His face was a ghastly white now, as pale as the underside of one of those obscene fungi that never saw the light.

'But I don't believe you killed her either,' said Cooper. 'Not you or Cal. Not in a million years. It was you that made Jenny dance, Simon. But you and I both know that it's someone else who has been playing the tune.'

DIANE FRY WATCHED Todd Weenink make his way round the edge of the building, looking for their car. DI Hitchens rolled down the window to speak to him.

'There's not much we can do,' said Hitchens, 'if the women don't seem to be committing any offence. They could just be here for the auction, like anybody else. They do let spectators in, apparently.'

'But they're not even trying to go inside,' said Weenink. 'The town centre PC has spoken to them, but they say they're just looking at the animals.'

Fry leaned across. 'What do you think their intentions are, sir?'

'No idea,' said Hitchens. 'All we can do is keep an eye on them.'

'They're going to be in the way,' said Weenink. 'Do you want to call it off?'

'Oh no,' said Hitchens. 'We can't do that. We need an arrest.'

'There is one thing,' said Weenink. He looked at Diane Fry in the passenger seat. 'One of the women is known to us.'

'You recognized her?'

Fry felt a cold sensation. There was an awful inevitability about what Weenink was going to say. He was looking at her when he spoke again, not at the DI.

'It's that woman who was attacked the first time. The one who had her face cut.'

'You mean Maggie,' said Fry.

'Yes, her,' said Weenink. 'Maggie Crew is with them.'

As Ben Cooper walked through the door of the CID room, the phone was already ringing. It was Cheshire Police at last.

'Your people are back,' said the DC in Wilmslow. 'Mr and Mrs Daniels. They had booked a midweek flight to Ringway, so that was lucky. They've been to Hawaii, had a great time and they've got wonderful suntans. It makes me sick.'

'When can they come to make an identification?'

'They're on their way. They'll be with you in a couple of hours.'

'Have they said anything?'

'Mainly "Aloha" and "Book him, Danno."'

The Cheshire DC sounded much too cheerful for Cooper's liking. Policing must be very different in the affluent towns on the plains between the Pennines and Wales to make him so happy in his work.

'What about their daughter? Did you ask them when they saw her last?'

'Yes, but it was months ago. They're upset about what's happened to her, but not too surprised, it seems to me. They never expected her to come back home when she left. Rosalind said as much to them, in fact. She said she had things she wanted to do with her life, which didn't involve them. She also said she was going off to find her real mother.'

Cooper frowned. He thought the DC was making another joke. 'Sorry? What was that?'

'She's not the Daniels' real daughter, apparently. They adopted Rosalind nineteen years ago. Brought her up as their own and all that. But they finally told her she was adopted when she came of age. And, far from showing any gratitude, she seemed to resent them for it, according to Mrs D. It seems Rosalind decided to opt out of the respectable life they had planned for her and got into bad company. She got involved in all sorts of causes, but animal rights was her latest big thing. She'd been in trouble a few times already for her part in some demos that went too far. Direct action, they call it. Trespass, criminal damage – you know the sort of thing. Like Mrs Daniels says herself, "Blood will out." I thought that was rather an unfortunate turn of phrase myself.'

'So Ros Daniels was looking for her real mother?'

'That's right. What do you think, mate? Do you reckon she ever found her? It would be something at least, before she got killed.'

THE WOMEN HAD gathered in the corner of the cattle market car park. They huddled together in a tight circle of anoraks, bending towards each other conspiratorially, with glances towards the buildings behind them and at the PC waiting by the offices.

For a few minutes, Maggie Crew stood to one side, a little outside the circle, hesitating, as if unsure whether she was part of the group or not. But then the women parted and let her in, and immediately she was absorbed and became one of their number. Under the cover of coats and shoulder bags, there was a surreptitious glint of steel. And Maggie found herself in possession of a knife.

DIANE FRY STOOD with Todd Weenink below the seating of the store ring, where they could see the group in the car park from the shadows. Fry took Maggie's presence as a personal insult. It was as if the woman were taunting her.

'It's her, all right,' she said.

'You can't make a mistake with a face like that,' said Weenink.

'What the hell is she up to?'

'Is she a member of this animal rights group?'

'Not that I know of. If she is, it's another thing she never told me.'

'Here comes Slasher, anyway,' said Weenink. 'The DI wants to do it now, before the women cause any complications. You know, like women do.'

Teasdale was herding a group of brown heifers from the outdoor pens towards the auction ring, swishing his stick from side to side as they clattered against the steel gates. Fry waited for Teasdale to look up. Then she saw him glance towards the women and see Maggie. He winced, half-closing his eyes at the sight of her scars, stared for a moment, then went back to his job. No recognition.

As Teasdale walked past them towards the ring, he twitched his stick against the haunches of a lumbering heifer. He grinned up at the police officers, showing a double gap in his teeth. Watching Fry, he gave the animal an extra slap between its back legs, and it broke into a frightened trot.

Fry looked at Maggie. She was frowning at the treatment of the animal, but showed no sign of recognizing Teasdale. DI Hitchens was already waiting for Fry near the ring, and she turned towards him to help make the arrest.

BEN COOPER RAN down to the control room. He needed to get the information through to DI Hitchens and Diane Fry as soon as possible. There were too many coincidences stacking up. How was it that Daniels had been killed at about the same time and in the same place that Maggie had been injured? And Jenny Weston, whom Daniels had lived with for a short while? Was it really Maggie who had been waiting to meet Jenny on the moor?

Before he could do anything, Cooper became aware that the control room sergeant was already taking an urgent call from Edendale cattle market.

SUDDENLY, THE GROUP of women had begun to surge forward. They surrounded a cattle transporter in which two large dogs were occupying the cab – an Alsatian and a Rottweiler. The dogs began to leap around on the seats, bouncing off the half-open windows and setting up a loud, furious barking as the women crowded round the lorry.

'Remember Ros Daniels!' one woman shouted.

'She didn't die for nothing!'

Weenink signalled to the PC and they moved towards the women to intercept them. But Diane Fry was watching Maggie, startled by the transformation in her manner. Maggie stood transfixed as the officers moved in. She had tilted her head to one side to listen to something, and her nostrils flared as if at a distinctive smell. Her whole body had changed; she straightened and stood to her full height. Her eyes widened in astonishment.

Just before the broad shoulders of DC Weenink moved in front of her, Fry saw Maggie's expression change again. Shock was followed by fear, then anger. Her mouth opened in a scream of rage.

Then there was a confused melee, a mass of suddenly struggling bodies, shouting and shrieking. Fry couldn't see what was happening, and she could tell that the women and the police officers didn't know what was going on either. There were just a lot of bodies near to each other, barging, stumbling and staggering, like cattle herded too close together.

Then a gap appeared and Maggie was standing in the middle of it, with a knife in her hand. A trickle of blood ran down the blade to the hilt and dripped on to her finger. But Maggie didn't notice it. She looked as though her mind was far away from the cattle market, maybe somewhere up on Ringham Moor on a night she had almost wiped from her memory. She seemed oblivious to the stunned crowd close around her, unaware of the noise of screaming women and barking dogs. Unaware of the body of DC Todd Weenink, lying on the concrete at her feet.

Chapter Thirty-Six

THE VOICE ON the radio was becoming incoherent as it called on Control for an ambulance and back-up. It requested officers with protective equipment, dog handlers, and a public order team for a violent person arrest.

Ben Cooper leaned in towards the control room sergeant.

'Who is it?' he said.

'Please confirm the identity of the female suspect,' said the sergeant.

'The woman's name is Maggie Crew.'

'OK, support is on its way.'

'The suspect is armed, Control. We need an ARV.'

'Understood.'

Cooper and the sergeant looked at each other. There was no Armed Response Vehicle anywhere in E Division. The nearest would be patrolling the M1 in the

Chesterfield area, nearly half an hour away. Cooper knew it could be too late.

'Sarge, remind the Duty Inspector that I'm an approved firearms officer,' he said.

DIANE FRY HAD followed Maggie Crew as far as a long, narrow passage between the two sale rings. On one side were rows of steel pens packed with nervous calves; on the other side, a breeze-block wall was lined with plastic barrels of some dark liquid, stored for a later sale.

Maggie stopped and stared at her. 'Well, you've done it in the end, Diane. Congratulations. You got under my skin, like a parasite I couldn't get rid of.'

'This is madness, Maggie. Put the knife down.'

Fry's voice faltered as Maggie's expression hit her like a bucket of freezing water. Though the sun that reached them through the high windows was weak and cold, its light was enough to change Maggie's face. It clearly picked out the ragged edges of the scar tissue that ran across her cheek and into her hairline. The scar had flared angrily, marking her face like a fresh brand. Suddenly, Fry realized she was trapped in the narrow passage. They were alone among the rusted iron gates and the nervous cattle.

The knife in Maggie's hand had a bright steel blade and a black hilt. Fry could see every detail of it – the markings on the handle, the narrow groove to channel the blood. Maggie held the knife out towards her, as if offering a treat for her to share.

'We were going to use them to slash their tyres,' she said. She smiled then – the first time that Fry had seen

Maggie smile properly. But the corner of her damaged eye puckered and twisted her smile into a dreadful, ironic wink. 'Ros would have been pleased.'

'Do you mean Ros Daniels?'

'Yes, Ros,' said Maggie. 'You knew about Jenny Weston too.'

Her grip tightened on the knife. Fry tensed, and her hand began to creep towards her scabbard, where the solid weight of her ASP sat, the foam grip protruding slightly, ready for her fingers to grasp.

'When I was talking about Jenny Weston, it was because I wanted to make her a real person to you,' she said. 'Not just another victim.'

'Oh, Jenny Weston *was* a real person to me,' said Maggie. 'But there was one thing you didn't tell me about her. Was she my daughter's lover?'

'Your daughter?'

'Yes – my daughter!'

Maggie's shout reverberated around the tightly packed pens. The calves shrieked and scattered, crushing each other against the furthest corners of their steel cages. Fry's hand slipped down to her scabbard. The handle of the ASP dropped into her palm and she flicked her wrist. With a hiss and a click of the ratchet, sixteen inches of steel baton suddenly shone in the artificial lights.

'Stay back.'

Maggie grew calm again immediately. 'Do you think you need that?' she said. 'You're the great unarmed combat expert, aren't you?'

'How do you know that?'

'Perhaps you're not the only one with a file. The details of a police officer's history are well recorded. Everything is available, if you have the right contacts.'

Maggie advanced, and Fry retreated, trying to keep more than an arm's length between them. Her instructors had always said the same thing – in a knife fight, you first had to accept that you might not avoid getting cut.

She backed up against a gate and turned too quickly to keep her balance. She felt her ankle twist and pain shoot up her leg. Her foot went numb, and for a moment she lost control of her right leg and had to drag it with her round the corner of the pen. Maggie kept advancing, walking steadily, until she had backed Fry beyond the occupied pens towards the empty fatstock ring, away from the noise and the crowd. Fry risked a glance over her shoulder and saw that she was reversing into the end of the passage. Behind her was the gate into the ring. She briefly considered taking a stand and relying on the chance of deflecting the knife with her baton. But realistically, she knew that her best hope was to gain time until support arrived.

In a ceremonial *kata*, with two opponents equally matched and wary, you had to watch for the opportunity, the first opening that would enable a strike. Movements became rhythmic and formal, just as they did now. But for Fry, the first opening she allowed could be her last. She had to watch the knife, refuse to be distracted by Maggie's eyes. She had to keep Maggie talking.

'Maggie, put the knife down.'

'You can't tell me anything about memories either, Diane,' said Maggie. 'I know what memories are. I know now that Ros is dead.'

'But how did she die, Maggie?'

Maggie lashed out suddenly with the knife, a casual sideways stroke without even looking where she was aiming. The blade sliced through the side of one of the plastic barrels as if it had been paper. A sweet, sickly smell filled the passage.

Fry glanced at the tear in the plastic for only a second before she recognized the attempt at distraction, and then she quickly met Maggie's eye again.

Fry remembered her 'CUT' technique. Create distance. Use cover. Transmit and ask for assistance. She had to watch her assailant's hands; stay alert, state red. Expect to get cut. She felt behind her with her left hand for the sliding handle of the door. She pulled it open quickly and slipped through the gap. Maggie feinted suddenly with the knife, and Fry jumped backwards, stumbled as her ankle sent another jolt of agony through her. Now they were in the auction ring itself. They moved from side to side, back and forth, manoeuvring for advantage, reluctant to get too close, their movements mirroring each other's. Fry began to imagine that Maggie was mimicking her, dragging one leg as she moved.

The first lights of approaching police vehicles flickered through the wooden slats in the walls, bouncing their colours against the ceiling lights and the pen sides. They distorted shapes in the auction ring and created dozens of new shadows that cascaded through the tiers of seats. It was almost as if there was an entire crowd up there, waving, stamping their feet, cheering, ready to give the thumbs down to the defeated.

Fry cursed herself silently. It was always the case that you weren't wearing your stab-proof vest when you needed it. The heavy vest hindered her movement, and she had left it off. Uniformed officers had a side-handled baton, a much better weapon against a knife attack. An ASP was more easily concealed, but it was an attacking weapon, not designed for defence against a knife. If Fry had been in uniform, she would have been better equipped. But now she was aware of the thinness of her jacket, a flimsy layer of fabric that provided no protection at all from a blade. She felt as though her chest and abdomen were exposed and vulnerable. She was also aware of her bare hands, the left held out, palm facing Maggie, the classic defensive gesture taught in the personal safety handbooks. She imagined her palm being cut, the tendons of her fingers severed.

'It's so ironic, Diane,' said Maggie. 'Because I think that you were looking for someone, too. The search can take you to some strange places, can't it?'

They stared at each other – Maggie cool, Fry becoming more angry.

'Who is she, Diane?' said Maggie. 'Who is the woman you're looking for?'

'None of your business.'

Fry lunged forward and struck with her ASP at Maggie's knife hand. But in that moment of anger, she had made her mistake – she had forgotten her injured leg.

Her knee threw her off balance, enough for Maggie to jerk her arm out of the way and let the baton hiss harmlessly past her wrist. Before she could right herself again, Fry glimpsed a flicker of steel as the knife came towards her. She closed her eyes just one second before the point of the blade carved open her skin.

BEN COOPER RAN along the auctioneer's walkway, distracted by the clanging gates and the movement of the cattle. He looked around, saw only rows of pens, inquisitive bovine faces, damp concrete and cold streaks of light from the broken roof. He could see no sign of Diane Fry. All he knew was that his slowness had put her in danger.

Outside, DI Hitchens would be organizing the troops as paramedics arrived to take over the task of battling for Todd Weenink's life. But for Cooper, there was no time for waiting.

A market attendant saw Cooper and pointed towards a passageway between the sale rings. At the end of the passage, a pool of something dark and sticky was trickling across the concrete into the drainage channel.

AT FIRST, DIANE Fry felt no pain, just a strange kind of exposed feeling to her face as the flesh parted under the knife and cold air struck the tissues underneath. As she backed away, the stinging pain started and the blood began to run down her face.

Maggie watched her. 'That was your fault,' she said. 'Now you'll be scarred, like me.'

Fry tried to wipe the blood away from her eye with her hand, but it trickled down her jawline and on to her neck. Mentally, she had been prepared for it. But physically, the sudden laying open of the skin still jolted her body, and caused a shock to the nervous system that twisted her stomach and drained the strength from her limbs.

Ben Cooper had reached the fatstock sale ring. He stopped at the end of the passageway, with the high steel bars of the ring between him and the two women.

'Armed police!' he shouted. 'Drop the knife!'

Both the women turned towards him, startled. Then Cooper saw Fry fall as her leg gave way. She hit the concrete, and her baton dropped out of her hand, rolling under the seats at the edge of the ring.

Diane Fry could hear the panic in Cooper's voice. Maggie looked towards Cooper and met his eye, defiant. It was then that Fry recognized something in Maggie's face. It was the most dangerous look of all – the look of somebody whose life was already over. If you had lost everything that you ever cared about, it didn't matter what else you did. It was all irrelevant. This was the way Maggie wanted it to go. She would not drop the knife – she wanted someone to shoot her.

'Armed police! Drop the knife! Now!'

With a great effort, Fry hoisted herself up on her left hand and kicked Maggie's feet from under her with her good leg. Their limbs tangled together, and they both went tumbling down the tiers of seats.

The two women lay in the sawdust, clutching each other like lovers. They sweated and gasped as they stared into each other's eyes. Now she was so close, Fry could smell the cigarette smoke in Maggie's hair, no longer masked by the perfume. She could picture the ashtray on Maggie's desk, alongside the telephone and the letter opener, the only objects that had been important enough to earn space on that pristine surface. And Maggie Crew never had visitors to her apartment – so whose was the cigarette ash? It was a question Fry had never thought to ask.

Other armed officers had joined Cooper outside the ring. They shouted more warnings. But they couldn't fire now. They had no clear target – the women were too closely entwined.

'This was how you felt, that night at the Cat Stones,' said Fry. 'I know you, Maggie.'

Their faces were pressed against each other, Fry's mouth touching Maggie's disfigured cheek. But now she didn't flinch away from the scars. Their breath mingled, and Fry felt their hearts beat hard against each other.

'You're going to have to give me the knife or kill me, Maggie.'

Maggie's hand moved, and Fry felt the touch of the steel blade, sharp and cold. Maggie's grip on her neck tightened.

It was a long moment, frightening yet exquisite, the feel of this person in her arms. Fry closed her eyes, unable to do anything to protect herself, or to prevent what might happen. She was waiting. Waiting for the knife to cut her again; waiting for it to enter her body.

Chapter Thirty-Seven

Derwent Court still had much of its original Victorian guttering. The increasingly blustery winds that battered around Matlock had swirled heaps of wet leaves into the iron channels and downspouts, and now the rain was spilling over and cascading down the front of the building. Ben Cooper had to dodge a waterfall near the front door, wondering whether this was part of the water treatment that the Victorians had once flocked to the hydro to enjoy.

When Cooper joined the team in Maggie Crew's apartment, they had already emptied her desk, and papers littered the surface. DI Hitchens was working his way through them, and when he saw Cooper he offered him a heap.

'We found a rucksack back there in one of the bedrooms with Ros Daniels' clothes and a few belongings in. She was travelling light, by the looks of it.'

Cooper began to look through some of the papers. Many of them were bills, bank statements, insurance policies, all carefully organized and filed. There were law books, a copy of Maggie's partnership agreement, an address book packed with names. Who were all the people in the address book if Maggie Crew had been so alone? He turned over some leaflets about Hammond Hall, and showed Hitchens what he found underneath.

'This looks like a diary of some kind,' he said. 'Or a journal.'

'Is it Crew's diary? We haven't found one yet.'

'No. It's just some times and places, almost an itinerary. It's from somebody called Eve. Who's Eve?'

'I don't know.'

Cooper stopped and stared at the page. 'Oh,' he said. 'Grosvenor Avenue, Edendale. But that's –'

'Mm?'

'So who's Eve?' repeated Cooper.

'No idea. A friend of hers?'

'There's a phone number, anyway. It's a local number.'

'Try it then,' said Hitchens.

Cooper looked uncertain. What he had read had thrown him. It wasn't what he had been expecting. 'What do I say?'

'You can think of something, Cooper. Just ask for Eve and play it by ear.'

Still he hesitated, reading and rereading the bit about Grosvenor Avenue. 'Shall I, sir?'

'Go ahead.'

Cooper dialled. 'I'll tell her I'm selling something. Nobody thinks there's anything unusual about that.'

'That's a good idea. So what are you selling?' said Hitchens as the phone began to ring.

'Soffits.'

'What the hell are soffits?'

'Exactly. Nobody knows. You can tell them any old rubbish.'

Then the ringing stopped, and a voice answered. But Cooper was speechless. He seemed to have forgotten he was a salesperson. His opening line had gone right out of his head.

'Sorry,' he said. 'Wrong number.' And he put the phone down.

'Was it?' said Hitchens.

'What?'

'A wrong number?'

'Not at all. Very much the right number, I think.'

'You didn't try to sell them any soffits.'

'No,' said Cooper. 'They didn't need any.'

MAGGIE CREW SEEMED almost at home in the interview room. Its sparseness suited her. She was able to live with her own thoughts, staring at a blank wall as she tried to recapture the elusive memories. Ben Cooper listened, fascinated, as she talked about the triggers that had achieved what nothing else could do.

'It was the sounds and the smells that suddenly brought it back to me,' she said. 'You could have sent people to talk to me endlessly and you would never have achieved that. The voices, the way the men smelled of animals. And there were dogs barking somewhere, but I couldn't see them ...' Maggie shuddered. 'And then somebody screamed. One of the animal rights women.'

'And you'd just had it confirmed that Rosalind Daniels was dead,' said DCI Tailby.

She nodded. 'It was like something physical hitting me. The memories poured over me. It was as if I was existing in two places at once, at two different moments. The sounds and the smells connected them. And I knew what had happened to Ros.'

Maggie put her hands on the table and looked at them. Her long fingers were very still, her nails blunt and pale.

'Ros had decided to trace me, you know,' she said. 'After all that time, my daughter decided to trace me. They allow adopted children to get access to information on their real parents, but not the other way round. It's one of the provisions of the Adoption Rules. I don't know what she hoped to achieve by it.' Maggie paused and let out her breath. 'Yes, I do. She wanted to get whatever she could from me. Money. A convenient place to stay.'

'When did she first contact you?'

'Around the middle of September. She said she was in the area, but she didn't tell me why or where she was living.'

'It seems she was staying with Jenny Weston at Totley during that time.'

'Yes, I found that out later. These animal rights groups have networks they communicate through. And when

Ros arrived with nowhere to live, Jenny Weston offered to help. She had a spare bedroom in her house.'

'You know a bit about Jenny Weston, after all,' said Cooper, recalling the efforts Diane Fry said she had made to bring Jenny alive in Maggie's mind.

But Maggie ignored the comment. 'Ros came on a mission – a mission against dog-fighting. She was following a link from the area she came from, somewhere in Cheshire. When one dog-fighting ring was closed down, some of the men began to travel to Derbyshire, to Ringham Edge Farm. Of course, the dog-fighting was much more important to Ros than finding her mother. I was just a side interest.'

'That's not what she told her adopted parents,' said Tailby.

Maggie shook her head. 'I expect she resented them, too. No – she came with a purpose in mind; I was merely a useful accessory.'

'But Jenny didn't agree with what Ros wanted to do, did she?'

'Apparently not. Ros was much more radical in her views than Jenny. She believed in direct action. In fact, she believed in violence.'

'And that's what led her into trouble in the end,' said Tailby.

Maggie dropped her head. 'I suppose it has to be my fault.'

'Does it? Why?'

'Because there's no doubt she would have been raised differently if I had kept her with me when she was a child.

Well, that's obvious,' said Maggie. 'She would never have reached that stage if I had brought her up myself.'

'There's no reason to believe that,' said Cooper.

Maggie just stared at them and didn't trouble to discuss it. 'Ros had an argument with Jenny Weston when she found out what Ros intended to do. There were angry words. And Ros walked out and came to me.'

'How did you feel about that?'

'At first I thought it was the moment I'd always dreamed of,' said Maggie. 'My daughter had come back to me. But it wasn't like that at all.' She looked from Tailby to Cooper. 'Nothing ever is how you hope it will be, is it? It's best not to expect anything. It's best not to hope for too much. Because the worst thing of all is when you have your hopes raised and then dashed again. That is very painful. That can be devastating.'

They gave her a moment to recover, while the tapes recorded the silence.

'What did Ros want exactly?' asked Tailby.

'My daughter saw that she might be able to make use of me.'

'But in what way?'

'She needed somewhere to stay, a handy base. That was the way she put it. And my home was much nearer to where she needed to be. Much nearer to Ringham Moor.'

'Did she tell you what she planned to do?'

'Oh, yes.'

'And what was your reaction to that?'

'Ironically, I think I probably reacted the same way that Jenny Weston did, but more so. I told Ros she was mad, that what she planned to do was criminal and dangerous. We argued terribly. Of course, I said all the wrong things. A lot of stupid things. I expect it's because I've never known how a mother is supposed to behave. I've never learned by my mistakes how to deal with a daughter – so I made all the mistakes at once, in one blazing row. I told her I wouldn't allow her to do it.'

'I expect she didn't like you telling her what to do.'

Maggie smiled. 'That's rather an understatement. It was obvious she was going to go to Ringham Moor, whatever I said. It became very personal, and all her bitterness poured out. Mine as well, I suppose. But Ros believed that I owed her a great deal. And I found I couldn't argue with her any more. Because she was right, you see. I owed her more than I could say, for having let her down.'

'So you allowed yourself to be persuaded …'

'Yes, from that moment, I was lost. I should have stuck to my guns, locked her in the flat … anything. I can see that now. But she told me that if I was a real mother I would understand what she was trying to do, that I would support her in the one thing that was most important in her life. That if I was a real mother, I would go with her. She said I was the only one who could help to keep her out of danger. That it was what a mother would do.'

'And so what did you do?'

'What *could* I do?' Maggie shrugged. 'I went with her, of course.'

Cooper looked at Tailby, but the DCI just nodded. He was a father himself. Cooper could only imagine how difficult it was to stand by and watch your child walk away from you into danger, when all your instincts were urging you to keep them by you and protect them. How much stronger must the feeling have been in Maggie, who had only just discovered it? She had finally found her child, only to face the prospect of losing her again. There was no way that she could have stood by and watched Ros walk off alone.

'Yes, I drove her up to Ringham,' said Maggie. 'We were both so angry that we didn't speak a word to each other in the car. I had driven right through Matlock before I even remembered to put the headlights on. When we got to Ringham, we parked above the village and walked up to the tower. Ros told me it was the meeting point, where I had to wait until she came back from the farm. I didn't want to just sit and wait. Waiting was the worst thing. On the other hand …'

'Yes?'

'Well, there are other instincts, too.'

'You couldn't bring yourself to be too closely involved in a criminal act?' said Tailby. 'Is that right?'

'All my training was against it, you see. All my beliefs. How could I? I was taking such a risk already.' Maggie's face betrayed a moment of appeal, a deep uncertainty. 'Do you understand?'

Cooper looked away from the appeal. That was the crucial issue, in the end. Maggie Crew had waited at the Hammond Tower, torn between fear for the safety of her daughter and her horror at what Ros was doing out there on the dark moor. She hadn't wanted to be there, but she couldn't leave. Two powerful instincts had been battling inside her, and no doubt she had paced backwards and forwards at the foot of the tower, staring helplessly into the darkness, smoking cigarette after cigarette. Cooper could picture the unfinished butts tossed away, still glowing as they flew into the night. How many might Maggie have smoked during that time? Many of the cigarette ends would have landed among the trees on the slope, in the deep undergrowth. But not all. Some of them had landed on the ledge below the tower.

'And what exactly was it Ros intended to do? Did she tell you?'

'Oh, she didn't just intend to do it. She actually did it,' said Maggie. 'She prepared her plan beforehand. She had two home-made petrol bombs hidden behind some loose stones in the wall of the tower. She had even collected some bits of rubbish and shoved them into the hole – empty drinks cans, chocolate wrappers, you know the sort of thing. She said nobody would bother to look in the hole when they saw the rubbish. I suppose she was right.'

'Well, almost,' said Cooper, thinking of Mark Roper and his preoccupation with clearing up after other people.

'That makes me an accomplice,' said Maggie. 'I knew what she intended to do, and I helped her to do it. Technically, I'm guilty of conspiracy to cause an explosion.'

Neither of the police officers said anything. At that moment, it seemed the least of her concerns.

'Ros had put petrol in two Evian water bottles. I don't know who taught her how to do that. But then, I don't know how she was brought up. I don't even know who her adopted parents were. I don't know anything about her at all, even though she was my daughter. I might have been able to put that right, in time. But *they* denied me the chance.'

'Who do you mean by "they"?'

'The men at the farm. The dog-fighting people. They killed Ros.'

'Are you sure? Did you see it happen?'

'I didn't see it. I heard it.'

'Tell us.'

'Something must have gone wrong at the farm. I heard the first fire bomb go off, then the second, though it wasn't as loud. But for some reason Ros didn't get away as quickly as she meant to. The men came out of the shed with their dogs and they chased her back up the hill towards the tower. She was coming back to meet me, and I was supposed to keep her safe. But she never stood a chance. Oh, she might have been able to outrun the men, to escape among the trees in the darkness. But there were the dogs.'

'If Ros never made it to the tower ...'

'I remember hearing the voices of the men shouting. And the dogs barking and snarling in the dark somewhere. I didn't know what was happening, and I couldn't see anything. Then there was a scream –' Maggie stumbled to a halt. 'The only other thing I remember is the man running at me out of the darkness, and then the knife and the pain ...' She looked at Tailby. 'What actually happened to her? Can you tell me?'

'Your daughter fell off Ringham Edge, very near the tower. She ran off the top of one of the Cat Stones trying to escape from the dogs.'

'I see,' said Maggie. She took a few seconds to digest the idea, as if trying to fit it in with her mental picture. 'It's ironic, isn't it? It was all because of the dogs. It was the dogs that she was trying to save.'

'I'm afraid those particular dogs were trained to kill,' said Tailby. 'We seized six pit bull terriers from various addresses when we made our arrests. Now they will have to be destroyed anyway.'

'So it was the fall that killed her.' Maggie took a deep breath. 'Will the CPS carry forward a prosecution on a murder charge? Or will the men plead guilty to manslaughter? I'm sorry, that's a lawyer speaking again.'

'Unfortunately,' said Tailby slowly, 'we believe the fall didn't kill her outright. Your daughter didn't die straight away. The pathologist thinks she was still alive for a while as she lay on that ledge. She had dragged herself a foot or two. The debris under her fingernails included gritstone sand from where she had been lying.'

Maggie's face went white, and the confidence in her eyes died. 'She was still alive, then. And I left her.'

'You weren't to know that,' said Cooper.

'I left her there to die.'

The DCI looked at Cooper sharply. But Cooper felt he understood Maggie at last. He knew there was nothing to stop you being consumed by guilt when you failed to protect someone who relied on you.

'There was nothing you could have done,' he said.

'I abandoned her again,' said Maggie. 'And this time she'll never come back, will she?'

THEY ALLOWED MAGGIE a rest period. They had plenty of time to keep her in custody before she had to appear in court. More evidence was needed yet, before they could decide how many murder charges she would face.

'Why did you associate yourself with the animal rights group?' Tailby asked her later.

'I wanted to find out where Ros had gone, why she hadn't got in touch. I couldn't remember clearly enough, and I thought the details had become distorted, as they do in a nightmare. Most of all, I couldn't believe that she was dead. I thought she had dropped me because I was no use to her any more. And with Jenny Weston dead, those other women were the only connection to Ros I had left. I'm afraid I pestered them until they let me join in their activities.'

'How did they react to you?'

'They felt sorry for me, I think. That made me angry. But I needed them – I needed the information I thought they had about Ros. On the other hand, some of them had heard that I was attacked near Ringham Edge Farm. They wondered whether I had been attacked by the dog-fighters. None of them ever dared to ask me outright, but I think it was that which earned me acceptance.'

'But they didn't know what had happened to Ros?'

'No. And if they knew what Ros had planned to do, they wouldn't have told anybody about it. They have their own loyalty, you see.'

'Perhaps they just thought she had moved on again somewhere else, to undertake some other mission. She seems to have seen herself as some kind of animal rights commando,' said Cooper.

'But they heard about the latest body, and they knew perfectly well who it was. It seems I was the only one in ignorance. I had gone along to the cattle market still hoping. I was so blind – but only because I didn't want to give up hoping.'

'Hoping that Ros would turn up?'

'I thought she might have appeared at the cattle market – it was her sort of thing, direct action. The plan was to slash the tyres on the vehicles of the people that had been targeted. That's why we were all given knives. They almost didn't let me have one, you know. It was a kind of sign of acceptance. Ros would have been pleased to see me there.'

'Even though you were actually committing a crime yourself this time, Maggie.'

She nodded. 'You see which instinct won? Besides, it was already too late for anything else by then. Too late for the old Maggie Crew. You can't go backwards. You can't get parts of your life back, once they're dead.'

KEITH TEASDALE AND five others had been arrested, despite the distractions at the cattle market. They were all believed to have been involved in the dog-fighting ring at Ringham Edge Farm. Under questioning, Teasdale told the story of the night Ros Daniels had staged her single-handed fire-bomb attack and the chaos that had followed as men and dogs spilled out on to the hill in a mad chase lit by flames from the burning pick-up.

Teasdale had admitted that he and Warren Leach had made a search of the area near the Hammond Tower at first light next morning and had found the body of the young woman on a ledge under the most northerly of the Cat Stones. They had moved it deeper into the cavity to conceal it, he said. At the same time, Yvonne Leach had stumbled across Maggie Crew, injured and incoherent from the hours she had spent on the moor. Ben Cooper wondered if Yvonne had guessed what had happened that night.

After that, Warren Leach had lived for the best part of two months with the fear and expectation that an injured woman's memories would return. He had tried to live a life under those circumstances, seeing every visitor as an enemy, recognizing the potential for betrayal even in his own wife. Perhaps especially in his own wife. Cooper knew that no one could live with that kind of uncertainty. No wonder Leach could see no point in carrying on.

Maggie Crew had been a serious threat to Leach, that was obvious. Yet there had been someone who had seen Jenny Weston as the main target. Had that been Leach? Or had that been Maggie herself?

'Teasdale will be charged with manslaughter and a few other things,' said DCI Tailby. 'They all admit the assault on Calvin Lawrence and Simon Bevington at the quarry. They made a good job of drawing our attention there. And, of course, there's the dog-fighting pit.'

'There must be more,' said Chief Superintendent Jepson.

'We're quite sure there are others involved. But these people have their own sense of loyalty, too. They won't implicate anyone else.'

'I don't mean more people. I mean Jenny Weston. Please tell me we can connect *somebody* to Jenny Weston, after all this …'

But Tailby shook his head.

'YES, I LAY in wait for Jenny that day,' Maggie had said. 'I waited at the tower, because she always came that way. I had met her before, two days earlier, and we had argued. I was angry with her – I didn't believe her when she said she had no idea where Ros had gone. She was my main hope, because I suspected then that there was more to their relationship. But of course I did it all wrong. I antagonized her.'

'We don't believe there was any relationship between them, other than a loose connection through the animal rights group. No sexual relationship. Jenny Weston and your daughter were not lovers.'

'That's what Jenny told me, too. As far as she was concerned, Ros was just a silly, hot-headed girl who had passed through her life and was soon forgotten.'

'But you didn't believe her.'

And Maggie hesitated. 'Actually, I suppose I did.'

'So why did you attack her? Why did you use the knife?'

'Did I do that? But yesterday, it felt as though I'd never held a knife in my life before. No, I don't believe I saw Jenny

Weston. Either she never came to the tower, or I was too late. I didn't see her. Not that day.'

'You expect us to believe that?'

'You'll have to,' she said. 'I think it's true.'

CHIEF SUPERINTENDENT JEPSON scowled angrily at his officers, his blue eyes glittering.

'Yes, I'm afraid it *is* true,' said DCI Tailby.

'Are we *sure*?'

'The shoe print over the bloodstain is much too big to be Maggie Crew's. Or Simon Bevington's either, for that matter.'

'Damn.'

'Also, some strength was needed to drag the victim into the stone circle,' said DI Hitchens. 'We doubt that either of them would be capable of it, or would even attempt it. Besides, there's the missing camera.'

Jepson frowned. 'The camera?'

'Well, Jenny Weston had reported the dog-fights to the RSPCA,' said Hitchens. 'We believe she'd taken some photographs, too. She carried an auto-focus camera with her when she was on the moor. Most likely, it was in her pouch.'

'Which was missing when the body was found.'

'Yes.'

'Suggesting that whoever killed her knew what was likely to be on the film. So it has to have been one of the dog-fighters.'

'Teasdale has told us that she took photographs of him and Warren Leach burying a pitbull terrier that had to be put down because of its injuries. They had taken it well away from the farm – close to the stone circle, in fact, in the trees there. But Jenny saw them. Teasdale says they stood no chance of catching her, because she was on a bike. But she knew they'd seen her.'

'And Leach was in a good position to spot Jenny when she came back to the moor again.'

'That's pretty much what we think. And we found a whole range of knives and other implements in his workshop. Not *the* knife, though.'

Jepson considered the evidence. 'So Warren Leach's associates plan on him taking the blame for Jenny Weston's murder. How convenient for them.'

'And clever. They've all got their story straight.'

'Well, let's face it,' said Hitchens. 'It's convenient all round.'

They all looked at Ben Cooper. But Cooper sat very still, his lips pressed together, saying nothing. Now was the time for saying nothing, if ever it had been the time. They were expecting a comment from him that would never come.

Soon, there would be another police funeral for him to attend, when Todd Weenink was buried with all the honours befitting an officer who had died in the course of duty. But for now there was nothing to be said. Nothing that Cooper could possibly hope to put into words.

NEXT DAY, THERE was a new notice pinned to the board in the corridor. Officers were gathered round to read it.

'Mr Tailby's being posted to Ripley,' one said. 'And the new DCI's been named.'

'Oh? Is it DI Hitchens?' Ben Cooper elbowed his way closer to the noticeboard. He was aware of an odd mood among the officers around him. A dark, cynical mood.

'No, mate,' said someone. 'We're getting a new Detective Superintendent from South Yorkshire, and a DCI is transferring from B Division. More foreigners on our patch.'

Cooper read through the praise of Tailby and some indecipherable details of his new headquarters role, then skimmed through the new appointments before reaching the final pay-off line: 'Detective Inspector K. Armstrong has been appointed Detective Chief Inspector, B Division, to succeed DCI Maddison.'

'Armstrong's done well for herself,' said someone.

'Right.'

'Her paedophile operation got a good press. Lots of arrests.'

'Well, what can you say?'

They looked over their shoulders, watchful for unfriendly ears, afraid of uttering a politically incorrect word.

'It's good news for some,' said Cooper.

'Yes, if you're one of the sisters.'

'Who do you mean?' It was DC Gardner, trying to force herself into the group. 'Acting DS Fry is it? Her and Armstrong? There's more to it than that, from what I've heard. Sisters is right.'

'You listen to the sound of your own voice too much, then,' said Cooper. Then he turned and saw Diane Fry herself, standing at the corner of the corridor. He wasn't sure how much she had heard. She was pale and drawn. The wound on her cheekbone was red and angry, the stitches stretching the flesh tight below her eye.

Before anyone else noticed her, she had slipped away, disappearing back into the shadows as if she hadn't been there at all.

HALF AN HOUR later, Diane Fry emerged from DI Armstrong's office knowing that she had burned her boats. It was a curiously satisfying feeling. Armstrong had not been pleased at her decision not to take the job with her team. But Fry knew it hadn't been right for her. Not now.

Sisters. It was that one word that had finally repulsed her. She had no sisters here. Not Kim Armstrong, nor any of her associates. Not Maggie Crew, nor any of the other women she was obliged to be polite to during the course of her job. They were not sisters, not even friends – merely acquaintances, or colleagues. It was the claim of sisterhood that she could not stomach, that made the bile rise in her throat.

Fry opened her bag and slipped the creased photograph out of her credit-card holder. She had only one sister, and this was her. This young woman would now be a stranger, as unrecognizable to Fry as the homeless druggies of Sheffield were. Their relationship was a dead thing, a fragment of the past, yet still remembered and treasured.

Carefully, Fry put the photo back. The things that people craved were so strange. The longing for what would do you no good at all was utterly incomprehensible.

Sisters? Like daughters, sisters were something special, not to be taken lightly. No, ma'am. You were not Diane Fry's sister, and you never would be.

Chapter Thirty-Eight

AT ONE TIME, there had been far more prehistoric remains on Ringham Moor than there were now. But local people hadn't always seen the value of their ancient monuments. Stones from the henges and burial chambers had disappeared over the years, to be built into the dry-stone walls that separated the moor from the fringes of the farmland. It was ironic, now, to see the vast heaps of unwanted stone that lay in the abandoned quarries.

Reaching the top of the slope, Ben Cooper turned and reached out a hand. Diane Fry hesitated, then took it, accepting his help over the last bit of the hill.

'Are you all right?'

'A bit stiff, but exercise is what I need,' she said.

'If you're sure.'

They had both needed the fresh air. Cooper had been shut up in the office for much too long, struggling to make sense of a mountain of paperwork, the grinding anticlimax that always followed the conclusion of an enquiry. He knew Fry had been imprisoned in her dismal flat, with only the walls to look at and her own thoughts for entertainment. Cooper had intended to arrange a day out walking with his friends, Oscar and Rakki. But instead he had found himself asking Diane Fry. No doubt it was another mistake. He hadn't done much that was right recently.

'Maggie Crew will get the appropriate psychiatric treatment,' he said. 'Appropriate to her condition.'

'That's good,' said Fry. 'I suppose.'

'She had lost the ability to relate to the world. It's just that there was nobody close enough to her to notice.'

They were two hundred yards from the Nine Virgins. Cooper could feel the first real chill of winter creeping across the moor, insinuating itself into his clothes and settling on his spirits. So many things had changed since the beginning of the month. Autumn had passed in a glance, the wind stripping the trees, baring their thin branches to the sky. The rain that had fallen in the last few days had turned the leaves underfoot into a black sludge, slippery and treacherous, full of worms and pale, wriggling insects.

'Bloody screwed-up women,' said Fry. And Cooper saw her smile, but he turned away quickly so that she wouldn't see him noticing.

Mist lay in the valley below Ringham, long tendrils fading the colours of the hillsides and the trees. As the sun rose on the valley, it reflected from the surface of the mist, creating a pale bowl of light, from which the tower of the church in Cargreave emerged like the battlements of a drowned castle.

Yesterday, Cooper had heard that Owen Fox had resigned from the Ranger Service. He had decided to make way for a younger man, it was said. Cargreave Parish Council was advertising a vacant seat, but there was no competition to fill it – a candidate favoured by Councillor Salt and her ruling group would be co-opted to make up the numbers. The house in Main Street, with its wonderful view from the kitchen window, had a 'For Sale' sign outside.

'What *is* that tower?' asked Fry, gazing across the dying bracken to Ringham Edge.

'They call it the Hammond Tower. It's named after some member of an aristocratic family, the people who owned Hammond Hall. The Duke built it so that everyone could see it for miles around. A symbol of his own power and importance, I suppose.'

'It's where Maggie's daughter was supposed to meet up with her on the day she was killed.'

'And it's where Maggie came back to. She hadn't given up hope that Ros would reappear, even long after she was dead.'

Cooper looked at Diane Fry. She was too thin, and the wound on her cheek had turned red and did nothing for her looks. She was arrogant and infuriating, too. But sometimes she seemed to know what was right.

'Maggie Crew left her cigarette ends there,' he said. 'But Mark Roper cleared them away.'

'Another obsessive.'

'All the time you spent with Maggie Crew, Diane. Did you not realize she smoked Marlboro?'

'No.'

They began to walk towards the stone circle. Their feet crunched through the leaves as if they were walking through three inches of fresh snow. Cooper walked slowly, to let Fry keep up. But at the edge of the clearing around the Virgins, he stopped.

'Diane –'

'Yes?'

'The transfer. It's all fallen through, has it?'

'Looks like it. But another job will come up.'

'Sure. Welcome back, anyway.'

'*What?*'

'I always thought you were one of the team, that's all.'

Fry shook her head in total disbelief. 'Ben, you are such a prat.'

That's what Helen Milner had said to him too, though in different words. There was an awful lot of work for him to do if he was to stand a chance of rescuing any of his relationships.

Cooper pulled a lump of fungus from the trunk of a birch. It was one of the white, obscenely shaped ones, but now it was starting to darken and decay, releasing tiny, soft spores into the air.

'Who was it you were looking for, Diane? In Sheffield?'

Fry jerked as if he had kicked her injured leg. 'How the hell do you know about that? Is my private life public knowledge now? Why do you have to pry into things that don't concern you?'

'It's my nature, I guess. I'm sorry.'

Fry sighed. 'If you must know, it was my sister,' she said.

'Your sister? The heroin addict? But I thought you hadn't seen her for years.'

'Sheffield was where her friends said she'd gone when she disappeared.'

'I didn't know that.'

'Why the hell do you think I came here? Did you think I *wanted* to live in sheep-shagger country? This was the closest posting I could get to Sheffield.'

Cooper nodded, not wanting to argue just now. 'And have you found her?'

Fry grimaced. 'I don't think Angie is there. I'm looking in the wrong places. Angie would never let herself get to the same state as those people I saw. She is my sister, after all.'

The clouds had closed down on the horizon and settled on the high tops to the north, where visibility would be pretty well zero, so close that you would be lucky to get a glimpse of your own boots in the heather. Cooper held the fungus gingerly towards Fry. She barely glanced at it, as if used to his peculiarities now. But she wrinkled her nose and turned her face away. Then he threw the fungus into the heather and wiped his fingers on a tissue. He was right – her sense of smell was perfectly good enough to detect cigarette smoke.

'Have you heard of Eden Valley Enquiries?' he said.

'A firm of second-rate enquiry agents? Divorces and process-serving, that sort of thing. I think they have an office in one of those small business centres on Meadow Road.'

'That's right. Discreet confidential enquiries. No questions asked. I rang them the other day.'

'Yeah? Looking for a new job, are you? Thinking of joining the private detective business?'

Cooper shook his head. 'No. I was thinking of trying to sell them some soffits.'

Fry stared at him. 'Ben, have you completely flipped?'

'It was something we found at Maggie Crew's place. It had the name "Eve" and a phone number. We thought it was some friend of hers. Only it wasn't Eve, a person; it was EVE, in capitals. It stands for Eden Valley Enquiries.'

'Yes? Is there a point?'

'Well, there were some other details, a sort of journal.'

They had almost reached the Nine Virgins. The tape had gone now, and the public had been allowed back into the stone circle. Someone had laid a bunch of flowers against the base of one of the stones, where Jenny Weston had died.

Cooper took his notebook from his pocket. 'Do you want to hear it?' he said.

'If it will make you feel better.'

'It says: "Left place of residence in Grosvenor Avenue 21.10, travelled by car to Sheffield. Parked in multistorey car park in The Moor and proceeded on foot to railway arches near junction of Shrewsbury Road and Dixon Street.' Cooper paused. 'There's a lot more. Do you want to hear it?'.

'No.'

'It goes into quite some detail, on two separate occasions. And it ends with an unfortunate incident involving a confrontation with one of their operatives.'

'So Maggie had me followed.'

'The name of the subject isn't actually mentioned,' Cooper pointed out.

'But why would she do that?'

Automatically, Cooper counted the stones. Some legends said that you could never count the Virgins, because they always moved before you got to the last one. But today there were definitely nine. Nine, plus the stone that stood away from the rest, on its own. The Fiddler.

'It was how she traced Jenny Weston,' he said. 'EVE located Jenny's home in Totley for her. Then they had an operative track Jenny's movements – he was seen by at least two of the neighbours. He followed her, and recorded her habits. Unfortunately, Jenny made the mistake of going to the same place too often.'

'Here. Ringham Moor.'

Cooper nodded. 'So Maggie knew exactly where she would be going that day, and she set off to meet her on the moor.'

'But surely it must have occurred to Eden Valley Enquiries after Jenny was killed –'

He shrugged. 'Discreet and confidential. No questions asked.'

'Jesus. I'd string them up and break every bone in their bodies.'

'You did a decent job on one of their operatives, by all accounts. For someone with an injured leg.'

DIANE FRY RECALLED the memories that Maggie Crew had eventually produced for her tape. She had thought at the time they seemed confused, a mingling of more than one memory dredged from the depths of her mind. Now it occurred to her that Maggie might have been producing them solely to please her interviewer. At the next meeting, perhaps, she would have reached the critical moment, a shared trauma that would have bonded them permanently. She would have told of the rape twenty years ago – the rape that had left her pregnant with a female child that she hadn't wanted. Unlike Fry, Maggie's beliefs hadn't allowed her to take the abortion option. But Fry hadn't let her reach that point. She hadn't needed Maggie Crew any more, or so she had thought.

'Diane,' said Cooper, 'what's the secret of keeping your memories buried?'

Fry looked up. 'Avoiding those triggers, I suppose. The ones that set off the memories. The only way is to avoid them.'

'Maybe.'

Fry studied at him carefully. 'Had you something particular in mind, Ben?'

'I'm going to move out of Bridge End Farm, I think.'

'Oh.'

'I need to get away from the place. There are too many reminders of the past for me to be comfortable there any more.'

'But your family are there.'

'I can visit them. But there comes a time when you have to be on your own. I think it's come rather late in my case. Anyway, I don't think Matt and Kate will be sorry to see me move out. They must think I'm in the way, but they're too polite to say so.'

'Where will you go?'

For a fleeting moment, Fry had a picture of Ben Cooper living in one of the little flats in the house on Grosvenor Avenue, a flat next to her own.

'Oh, I expect I'll find somewhere.'

Fry nodded. The vision had passed instantly. Cooper just wouldn't fit in among the peeling wallpaper and the grubby carpets.

AT PRESENT, THERE were no cattle in the fields at Ringham Edge Farm. The implement sheds had been emptied, the barns cleared, the milking parlour dismantled. Three days ago, the last traces of the work of generations had been laid out in the paddock behind the house and sold off at knock-down prices to the highest bidder. Farmers had come to pick over the pieces – not to buy anything, necessarily, but to see what fragments of a life were left when a man went the way that Warren Leach had gone, and to wonder whose turn it might be next. The two boys, Will and Dougie, had gone back to their mother, and Social Services had found them a new home in the suburbs of Derby. They might never live in the countryside again.

Ben Cooper sensed Fry's change of mood with some apprehension. He crouched to examine the flowers, which were covered in cellophane and had been tied to one of the stones with string. The writing on the card was faint, but he could see it was from Jenny Weston's parents. Fry stood outside the circle and watched him.

'So, Ben,' she said, 'if someone came along here after Maggie Crew and before Simon Bevington, who was it?'

'I don't know,' he said.

'We always thought it must have been someone Jenny trusted, didn't we?'

'Another woman seemed a possibility.'

'Or a Ranger.'

'Yes, Diane. But it wasn't a Ranger.'

'Are we quite sure? Jenny let somebody get too close to her. She would recognize the Ranger's jacket and feel secure. She would trust a Ranger.'

Cooper shook his head. 'No.'

Fry seemed to have something squeezed up inside her that was causing her discomfort and had to be released.

'You know when I was here,' she said, 'that night in the quarry with Calvin Lawrence and Simon Bevington? We'll never be able to prove who all of those people were.'

'Not a hope.'

'But one of them was familiar. The one who attacked me. For a moment, I thought I knew who that was. But unlike you, Ben, I don't believe in relying on feelings, only on hard evidence. It makes life a lot simpler, sometimes.'

'I don't know what you're trying to say,' said Cooper.

Fry hesitated. Then, uncharacteristically, she seemed to wander off at a tangent again 'The person who approached Jenny Weston might have been a Ranger, because she would trust him ...'

'But it wasn't a Ranger,' repeated Cooper.

'... and she would trust a police officer too,' said Fry.

Cooper stared at her. 'If the police officer was in uniform, of course,' he said. But as he said it, he knew it sounded more like a question than a statement.

Fry met his eye for a moment, and he held his breath. He had a sudden fear that he understood her. Was it possible that he and Diane Fry might be close to the same, inevitable conclusion? The thought made Cooper shiver at a premonition of disaster, at a vision of a dark, grinning cloud hovering over his horizon. He could hear the wind in the heather and the rumble of machinery in the limestone quarry outside Cargreave. The sound of the cows munching the grass in the fields below the Virgins seemed very loud.

Uneasily, he watched Fry square her shoulders and push the collar of her jacket further up around her ears. She was staring at the stone circle without seeing it at all – neither the cold reality of its lumps of gritstone, nor the martyred maidens of local folklore.

'The psychiatric reports said that Maggie Crew would probably never regain her memory for several hours either side of the assault, which is normal in trauma cases,' she said. 'Those files were readily available. If you knew that little detail, you might not worry too much about Maggie. Jenny Weston, on the other hand, knew all about Ringham Edge Farm and what went on there. It was Jenny who told the RSPCA what she had seen. Jenny had the photographs, too. She could identify people.'

'Right.'

'You'd think Jenny would have told the police, wouldn't you? Even if it was only to ask advice from an officer she was friendly with.'

'Maybe,' said Cooper.

'And yet there she was that afternoon, back on the moor, in the same vicinity. And she had those photographs with her – the ones she said she was going to hand over as evidence. Why did she have them with her, do you think?'

'For safety?'

'Safety? Or was she expecting to meet someone? Someone she could hand the photos to. And might that same someone have decided they couldn't leave her alive any longer?'

'But she was only ever a threat to the dog-fighting ring, no one else.'

'Right. And did you not wonder why they were never raided, Ben?'

'They stopped meeting at Ringham Edge,' said Cooper.

'Yes. Because they knew they were under observation. They knew exactly what was happening, all along.'

'Did Teasdale say all this, Diane?'

'Keith Teasdale is saying nothing more than necessary. The only person he's prepared to implicate is Warren Leach. But we knew Leach was involved, anyway.' She paused. 'And, besides, Leach is already dead.'

'So Teasdale is loyal, then,' said Cooper.

'Yes. But it's a misplaced loyalty.'

Cooper felt Fry's eyes on him, assessing him, seeing right through him to his innermost thoughts. Suddenly, there was contempt in her face, and her whole body seemed to draw away from him, as if she had seen something she could not bring herself to touch.

'You've always been very big on loyalty yourself, haven't you, Ben?' she said.

The accusation made him think of the day of the rugby match, when Todd Weenink had arrived for the match at the last minute. What was it that had made him late the day that Jenny Weston had died?

Then Cooper's mind slipped back to his room at Bridge End. In a drawer in that room was a vending machine questionnaire form, slipped under some large-scale OS maps and a Peak District caving guide that no one else would ever look at. Todd Weenink hadn't been able to keep his mouth shut about condoms. And he couldn't spell 'fruit-flavoured' either.

But Jenny Weston's killer was dead.

FROM SOUTH QUARRY, the old VW Transporter had finally been winched on to the back of the low loader and delivered to a scrapyard in Edendale, where its radiator, back doors and starter motor had already been removed for spares.

Calvin Lawrence had taken a job as a forecourt attendant at the Fina garage on the Buxton Road, taking people's money and handing out car-wash tokens. Simon Bevington had discharged himself from hospital and had not been heard of since. He had disappeared into the hills, blown away like a scrap of autumn debris, like another dead leaf hurled into the heather by the gales.

Yet a single wind chime still hung from the branches of the oak tree on the edge of the quarry. It had been left where it was because it was too high for anyone to reach. The chime was cracked and its edges were starting to fray. Its note was a strange, discordant clang. It no longer created peace and harmony. Instead, it tolled for the dead, the damaged, the destroyed and the defeated.

'Was any of it worth it?' said Cooper.

Fry laughed. 'You what?'

'Did we manage to protect anything that is important to us? Did we achieve justice?'

Fry gave him a cool look. It was the look of a woman who knew that she would forever have a weapon she could use against him, the look of a woman who held him in the palm of her hand.

'Bear the answer to that in mind when you make your decision, Ben,' she said.

Then she turned away. Her knowledge gave her power over him now, and there was nothing else she needed to say.

Cooper stroked the top of the nearest stone, drawing a peculiar comfort in the gritty texture, finding a surprising warmth beneath his hand, as if the stones might come back to life at any moment and resume their interrupted dance.

In the late afternoon light, the long shadows made the stones seem to tilt more than ever. They leaned inwards or outwards from the centre of the circle, dipping like a ring of dancers at the start of a barn dance or a Greek mazurka. They seemed to move slowly, almost imperceptibly, in time to the faint stirring of the hair grass and the continuous settling of the dead leaves.

Of course, it wasn't possible. The stones weren't moving at all. But if it wasn't the stones, then it must be the moor itself that was turning around him, wheeling slowly against the sky.

If you wanted to know about justice, you might as well ask the Virgins. The stones had seen it all. They were the only witnesses to the murder of Jenny Weston. So what would their view of justice have been after three and a half thousand years? Would they see it as an irrelevance, a minor casualty of that confusing, pain-filled thing called human life? Had they thought about it deep and hard over the millennia, and had they come to any conclusion?

Ben Cooper would have liked to ask the stones. He wanted to be able to get down on his knees and persuade them to whisper their secrets. He wanted to tell them all about the doubts that lay in the bottom of his heart like a pound of lead shot, like a pocketful of wet rocks.

He would have liked to tell them everything, but he knew they wouldn't answer. Because the Virgins had made their own mistake once. And now they were punished for ever.

Acknowledgements

I AM GRATEFUL to Derbyshire Constabulary and the Peak Park Ranger Service for their willing help in the writing of this book. However, the characters portrayed in its pages are entirely imaginary, and their activities bear no relation to those of any members of the real organizations. I know that many Derbyshire police officers and rangers are heroes in their own way.

So many people have made contributions to the story that this is a real team effort. But in particular I owe thanks to my agent, Teresa Chris, without whom none of it would have happened.

Author's Note

Lines from 'This is the Sea' by The Waterboys reproduced by permission of Mike Scott and Edel Music.

About the Author

Stephen Booth was born in the Lancashire mill town of Burnley and has remained rooted to the Pennines during his career as a newspaper journalist. He is well known as a breeder of Toggenburg goats and includes among his other interests folkore, the Internet, and walking in the hills of the Peak District, in which his crime novels are set. He lives with his wife, Lesley, in a former Georgian dower house in Nottinghamshire.

www.stephen-booth.com